The Spanish Bride

W9-CQM-979

By Walter O'Meara

The
Spanish Bride

by

WALTER O'MEARA

Friends of The Palace Press
Santa Fe, New Mexico

Grateful acknowledgment is made to Dr. Arthur
Leon Campa, and to the University of New Mexico
Press, for permission to quote from *Spanisk Folk
Poetry* in New Mexico by Dr. Campa.

New Material copyright © 1990 by Museum of New Mexico
    Foundation
All rights reserved
Published by the Friends of the Palace Press
Palace of the Governors
P.O. Box 9312
Santa Fe, New Mexico 87504-9312

First Printing

Library of Congress Cataloging in Publication Data

Library of Congress Catalog Card Number: 90-80521

O'Meara, Walter A.
    The Spanish Bride

    This is an unabridged reprint of the original 1954 editions, pub-
lished by G.P. Putnam's Sons, with new notes and foreword.

ISBN 0-941108-02-3

FOR
ELLEN AND DEIRDRE

FOREWORD

On the morning of August 13, 1720, an expedition of Spanish soldiers and Pueblo Indian auxiliaries was ambushed by a group of armed Frenchmen and their Pawnee and Oto Indian allies near the confluence of the Platte and Loup Rivers in present eastern Nebraska. The Spaniards, under the competent but inexperienced command of Lieutenant Governor Pedro de Villasur, had been ordered north to conduct a reconnaissance by New Mexico Governor Antonio Valverde y Cosio. Spain and France had gone to war in Europe, and Spain's viceroy in Mexico City feared a French attack on the Spanish American empire from the north. His concern resulted in Governor Valverde's order to send the group of forty-six Spaniards with some sixty Pueblo Indian auxiliaries onto the Great Plains in search of French intruders into what was then the Spanish Empire in North America. An ambush virtually annihilated the expedition. Only twelve of the Spaniards survived, as well as a proportionally small group of Pueblo Indian auxiliaries. The survivors returned to Santa Fe to recount the calamity.

Against the background of this story of intercontinental rivalry between Spain and France for the control of North America in the eighteenth century, a beautiful green-eyed woman, the fictional Josefina María del Carmen Torres, dances her way into fleeting fame in Spain, befriending herself along the way to the man who would one day become governor of New Mexico. Inevitably her startling beauty attracted the attention of an important and vindictive nobleman. Spurning his persistent advances, she was forced to flee Spain for Mexico City, eventually settling in Santa Fe, the capital of New Mexico, in the far northern frontier. She became the mistress of her friend, the newly appointed governor, and resided with him in the venerable Palace of the Governors, only recently recaptured from the Pueblo Indians who had taken it during the bloody Pueblo Indian Revolt of 1680-1693. (The Pueblo Revolt is the subject of the first volume in this series of historical fiction works on New Mexico: *The Royal City*, by Les Savage, Jr.)

Josefina's free spirit leads her astray from the governor when she became involved in local political intrigue and fell in love with the dashing Captain Pedro de Villasur, the lieutenant governor. The enraged governor took revenge by sending the offending officer on an apparent suicide mission onto the Plains into areas occupied by hostile Indians and possibly the current enemies of Spain, the French. Josefina, driven by her love for Villasur, concealed herself among the participants of the expedition. Was she among the casualities of the attack? Was she the mysterious and beautiful woman rescued by the

French and who later became the subject of many rumors in New Orleans? Did she end up married to a French nobleman in France? These are all questions that arise in Josefina's fascinating story.

As you read this historical saga, you will meet real-life historical figures such as Governor Valverde, who was blamed for the Villasur expedition's tragic consequences; Lieutenant Governor and Captain Pedro de Villasur, whose inexperience was brought to light in subsequent investigations; the Frenchman Jean l'Archévàue, who was one of the Sieur de La Salle's assassins; and the famous San Juan Pueblo Indian warrior and military scout, Joseph Naranjo. You will read no better description of what it must have been like to participate in an eighteenth century expedition into a dangerous and unexplored area, or, for that matter, to have suffered a pitched and disasterous battle.

As an historian and director of the state history museum, housed in the Palace of the Governors—the very building around which the story of this book is centered—I am anxious for the general public to have another chance to read this book since its original publication in 1954. Furthermore, among the collections of the Palace of the Governors museum are two paintings on bison hide known as the Segesser Hide Paintings. Recently purchased through public donations and an unprecedented legislative appropriation, one of the hide paintings is a contemporaneous depiction of the attack on the Villasur expedition, executed in such exacting detail that we feel it is the result of assistance from eyewitnesses to the debacle. As one studies the painting, the anguish, grim determination, and resignation described in this book are clearly visible.

The Spanish Bride follows *The Royal City* chronologically in terms of New Mexico history, and constitutes the second publication of the Friends of the Palace of the Governors. The proceeds of your purchase will go into the Palace's endowment. As you read this book for its enjoyment, the staff of the Palace of the Governors and the Friends of the Palace hope that your curiosity will be piqued sufficiently to make a personal visit to the almost four hundred-year-old adobe building and learn more about the remarkable history and cultures of New Mexico and Santa Fe.

It is indeed our pleasure and honor, threough the courtesy of the author, to present this timeless classic account of Spanish America for the benefit of readers everywhere.

Thomas E. Chávez, Ph.D.,Director
Palace of the Governors
Santa Fe, New Mexico

ABOUT THE AUTHOR

Walter O'Meara was born in Minneapolis on January 29, 1897. He studied at the University of Minnesota, and graduated from the University of Wisconsin in 1920. Upon graduation, he worked as a reporter, logger, government official and advertising executive. During World War II he helped organize the Office of Strategic Services working for General William "Wild Bill" Donovan. Upon leaving the OSS he became department head for the Information Department of the Office of Price Administration of the Federal Government. After the war, Mr. O'Meara entered advertising with the J. Walter Thompson Agency as group head, in Chicago and later creative director in New York. O'Meara served as publicity director for Adlai Stevenson's first presidential campaign.

In 1941 Mr. O'Meara began researching and writing about logging operations, principally in Minnesota between the year 1890 and 1910. He soon broadened his historical interest to the Southwest, spending some twenty years of his life in Arizona on the Mexican Border. Mr. O'Meara published fifteen books under the imprint of Knopf, Putnam, Harcourt-Brace, Houghton-Mifflin, Crown, Holt, the Minnesota Historical Society Press, and the University of Pittsburg Press; Two of his books *The Grand Portage* and *Minnesota Gothic*, were bestsellers in the 1950's.

Two years of intensive research supplied a solid historical base for *The Spanish Bride*, including a thorough search for primary and secondary sources in various archives and libraries in the United States, a month in Santa Fe for research and background, and two separate trips over the possible route of the Villasur expedition to the side of the massacre. The book was published in 1954 by Putnam, received glowing reviews, and was published in England, Italy, and in Spain under the title *La Dama de Nuevo Mexico*.

When contacted by the Friends of the Palace of the Governors, Mr. O'Meara graciously consented to the republishing of *The Spanish Bride*, penning the "Author's Note" that appear in this edition in August, 1989. Mr. O'Meara died at the home of his daughter Ellen O'Meara Woolf in Cohasset, Massachusetts, on September 29, 1989 at the age of 92 years. Mr. O'Meara's personal papers reflecting the many facets of his long life and career are preserved in the Minnesota Historical Society.

ABOUT THE ARTIST

The cover illustration, by Jose Cisneros, was commissioned by the Friends of the Palace of the Governors. Born in Ocampo, Durango, Mexico, Cisneros grew up in Dorado, Chihuahua. At the age of 15 his family moved to Cuidad Juarez, where he received some art education at the Lydia Patterson Institute in El Paso, Texas. He continued his studies at the Institute until 1928. By 1934 his illustrations were being accepted by Mexican publishers. Artist, Tom Lea, recognized the importance of Cisneros' work and introduced him to Carl Hertzog, a book publisher and designer-printer. Cisneros illustrated dozens of books for Hertzog including decorated and lettered maps. By 1972 he had also illustrated more than forty books for other publishers.

Jose Cisneros is known for his historically accurate drawings of figures from the different periods of Southwestern history and he has emerged as a leading authority on the subject. He has collected data in his personal library on historical events, and details of costumes, weapons, and trappings. Several exhibitions of his drawings have circulated throughout the United States. A sampling of his life's work has been featured in the acclaimed book *Riders Across the Centuries* published by the Texas Western Press. Jose Cisneros resides in El Paso, Texas.

IN APPRECIATION

The Friends of the Palace of the Governors are grateful to the Museum of New Mexico Foundation for financially supporting our efforts on behalf of the Palace of the Governors, Santa Fe, New Mexico.

We also wish to express our appreciation to the Museum of New Mexico Press for its valued contribution and assistance. Special thanks to Walter O'Meara's daughter, Ellen O'Meara Woolf, Cohasset, Massachusetts, and son, Wolfe O'Meara of Bisbee, Arizona, for their assistance. Thanks also to Riley and Betty Parker, Santa Fe, New Mexico who recommended *The Spanish Bride* for the Friends of the Palace of the Governors historical novel series. Finely, our thanks to Charles Bennett, Assistant Director, Palace of the Governors for his assistance in bringing *The Spanish Bride* once again to the public.

THEIR WORLD TODAY

Most of the towns, pueblos, roads, and geographical features familiar to the people of this eighteenth-century tale still exist under the same names, in the same places.

In some instances, however, names have changed, towns have shifted or been obliterated, and a battlefield has been forgotten.

For those who wish a guide to the scene of this story in terms of modern road maps, a gazetteer has been provided at the end of the book.

O'M.

AUTHOR'S NOTE

More than thirty years ago, Mr. Lon Tinkle, reviewing *The Spanish Bride* in *The Saturday Review of Literature*, wrote, "Obviously the author is in love not only with his subject, but with his heroine." And do you know, he may have been right!

For of all the fictitious creations who people my many stories, it is Josefina María del Carmen Torres who stands before me most vividly—still a figure of absolute reality, an object of almost true-life affection.

And so it is with a special kind of gratitude that I welcome Josefina's return, in this new edition of *The Spanish Bride*, to enchant a new generation of readers. And I find it wonderfully fitting and gratifying that this should be brought about by the Friends of the Palace of the Governors—the very Palace in which Josefina played out her beautiful albeit tragic destiny.

So to the Friends of the Palace, and to all others participating in the reprinting of my novel, I extend my very special thanks. And to Josefina—welcome back!

Walter O'Meara

Book One

Ella que quiera azul celeste, que le cueste.

She who wants the blue sky must pay for it.

1

OSEFINA sat at the end of the long table, under the high vigas of the Palace dining room, in that attitude of relaxed yet almost hieratic dignity which was natural to her; and she gazed at Don Antonio with her deep-green, heavily lashed and, at this moment, soberly contemplative eyes.

Like all Spaniards, Don Antonio was rather inordinately sensitive to the charm of beautiful eyes; and, like all Spaniards, he associated true loveliness in women not with dark eyes, or even blue, but with those of the subtle and indescribable pigmentation usually termed green.

Not only were Josefina's eyes of this classic color, but they were also definitely rasgados—wide and a trifle aslant—and extraordinarily large now in the shadows of their dark lashes.

She is still beautiful, Don Antonio decided.

She was almost more beautiful than when he had first seen her, a young girl with a troupe of roving players, floodbound like himself in a dreary mountain inn. That had been long ago and many leagues away; and it was the spring of 1720 now in the Villa of Santa Fé; and Josefina was eight years older. But Don Antonio, regarding her with a kind of pleasurable complacency, could find no serious reason to regret the bargain he had made with Josefina at that little inn.

Still beautiful, he repeated to himself, and eight years more a woman.

Don Antonio prided himself on exercising—even in the uncouth wastes of Spain's outermost frontier—a certain nicety of taste; and he said this with an inner smile, such as might accompany his comment on the gait of a blooded horse, or the slope of a mestiza girl's shoulders, or the bouquet of his own Bernalillo brandy.

But as he looked into Josefina's eyes, Don Antonio's rather pleasant reflections merged into emotions less agreeable. Something in the way she was looking at him gave rise to a sensation of discomfort. This was followed immediately by a sudden flare-up of anger—anger more with himself, however, than with Josefina.

3

That he, Don Antonio Valverde y Cosio, Governor and Captain-General of the Kingdom of New Mexico and Castellán of its Armed Forces and Presidio—that he should feel himself thus affected by the mere glance of a woman, and that woman his own mistress for so long, was somehow incompatible, he sensed vaguely, with his great, and even exalted, dignity. He pushed his silver goblet forward a few inches and a Navajo slave girl filled it.

Don Antonio's eyes followed the slender form of the girl as she left the room; he tasted the wine with a somewhat exaggerated air of virtuosity.

"It's coming along well," he said. "I'd match it against the best of Castile. What do you think, my dear?"

"I haven't your taste," she answered mechanically. "But I like it very much."

He sighed. "Ah, yes. It's only the dessert wines I miss. What wouldn't I give for a single bottle of good Malvasia!"

He had said this, or something like it, often; for with the accumulating years he had fallen into the common habit of repeating himself. But he said it now, not only from habit, but to provide a kind of refuge in talk from Josefina's disquieting gaze. Uncomfortable, a little annoyed with himself, he asked: What is in her mind tonight?

The answer to this question was nothing, however, that Don Antonio could ever have guessed. For what was in Josefina's mind, what she was thinking at that moment as she studied the slack, candlelit features of the Governor and Captain-General of the Kingdom of New Mexico, was: *Here, alas, is a man who is all but finished.*

A shadow of sadness, or regret—or perhaps some buried fear—disturbed for an instant the accustomed serenity of her expression.

Qué lástima! she whispered to herself. What a pity that this should happen to us! Then she corrected herself in her thoughts: But let us leave ourselves out of it, Josefina!

She heard Don Antonio saying: "Or even a little Málaga . . . in a thin crystal glass."

"That would be very pleasant," she replied absently.

"Very pleasant," Don Antonio repeated in a faintly ironic tone. "What are we having for the sweet, my dear?"

"A surprise, Antonio. Panchita has been three days preparing it."

"Ah, that Panchita!" Don Antonio exclaimed fondly. "How I have missed her piñonate!"

"I don't doubt you missed Panchita more than ever you did Josefina," she commented dryly. "Do you think of nothing but your stomach, Antonio?"

She looked at his satin waistcoat, which bulged out so that he had to sit back a little from the table. He had been away for almost three

4

months on a visit to El Paso del Norte. But even three months in the saddle had not been enough to stem his expanding girth.

"A man must eat," Don Antonio said. "It is one of the few pleasures left to a gentleman in this God-forgotten country. Fortunately, it is in some ways the most satisfying of pleasures. Have you ever, my dear, considered that only the enjoyment of food—and drink, of course—gratifies all five of the senses? Take, for example, Panchita's green corn tamales——"

She had heard that many times also, and always with Panchita's green corn tamales as the example; but she gave him a wifely attention and followed her own thoughts as she listened.

Don Antonio was at this time forty-nine years old. His balding head and heavy jowls gave his face a rather pear-shaped appearance which, in another man, might have created an effect of massiveness and perhaps strength, but in Don Antonio's case seemed to suggest only a degenerate softness.

He was rather surprisingly pale, and since he burned badly, protected himself carefully with large hats and parasols against the powerful New Mexican sun. This paleness accentuated a certain puffiness of his features and the pinkness of his rather small mouth. Only Don Antonio's eyes, in this somewhat untidy setting, retained a suggestion of what must once have been considerable force. They were small and pale, but hard and steady and faintly alight with an inborn Castilian arrogance. Don Antonio focused these eyes with a sudden, almost malevolent intentness on Josefina's face.

"Why do you stare at me so?" he demanded.

"You appear tired, señor," she said soothingly. "When will you learn not to undertake these long journeys? Why don't you send someone else?"

"In my place?" he asked with mocking incredulity. "Whom would you suggest, my dear?"

"Why don't you send Don Pedro?"

She was surprised, a little alarmed, to hear herself speak Don Pedro's name. Her words had the strange sound of a sentence spoken by someone else—by another woman sitting with them at the table.

What passes here, Josefina? she asked herself. Is this Don Pedro so much in your mind that his name slips from your tongue unbidden?

She smiled at the idea—then became serious. It was a habit of Josefina's to catechize herself thus about her own acts—even about her own thoughts and impulses; and now she was curious to know why this strange, sudden notion had come to her.

In reality, she told herself, it was but simple common sense. Don Pedro Villasur was young and vigorous, and yet he had already won a vast experience in war and politics. In Santa Bárbara, Chihuahua,

5

and the mines of Cosaguriachi he had served as alcalde. He had also acted as visitador of Rosario, and as lieutenant of the presidio at El Paso. Who, in fact, was better fitted than Don Pedro to spare Don Antonio the great fatigue of these long and arduous trips that a governor of New Mexico must make hither and yon?

Who indeed? Josefina repeated to herself ironically.

For she had never found it useful to deceive herself. And now, reflecting, she knew that neither logic nor common sense nor a concern for Don Antonio's health had anything to do, really, with her odd allusion to Captain Villasur. It was simply that her mind had been making certain comparisons—as her eyes might compare the hues of two ribbons, or her tongue the flavor of two sweets. . . .

Yesterday she had stood at the window of her apartment in the Palace, looking through the carved wooden grill across the Plaza de Armas where preparations were being made for a flogging. It was not a very important flogging, evidently; not important enough, at any rate, to be held on the main plaza in front of the Palace. So the culprit, a stout young mestizo, had been trussed up by the wrists to a stake set into the parade ground at the rear of the long, low government building.

"What has he done, Tichi?" Josefina asked her maid.

Tichi shrugged her plump shoulders. "The usual thing, señora," she said. "What they do too much of in this miserable pigsty they call a Villa. This one did it to the daughter of Jesús Garzía—the small one they call Chayo."

"How many lashes will he receive?"

"I don't know, señora. But not many, you may be sure. The offense is not considered very serious here. The punishment will be light, as usual."

It was being carried out, however, with a rigid Spanish regard for form that even the victim appeared to honor. He stood erect beside the post, his head bowed, his bare brown back curved inward at the waist. A squad of soldiers, stiffly at attention, stared past him with bored eyes. The sun made two rows of lavender glints on their leather helmets and the tips of their lances; it splashed the Plaza with its inky midday shadows. Around the square, under the long cool portales of the royal houses and barracks, a few idlers looked on and chewed piñon nuts. A fat soldier known as "El Gordo" walked with indolent importance across the Plaza with a coiled mule whip in his hand.

"What a low, stupid spectacle!" Josefina exclaimed suddenly. "We are no better than those vagabonds watching it. Come, Tichi, do up my hair."

As she was about to turn away, a horseman rode out of the

6

passageway from the Palace and reined his mount. Josefina, recognizing him as Captain Don Pedro Villasur and surprised that one of his rank should appear at such a time—to see a mere flogging, and an unimportant one at that—paused beside the window.

"Jesús María!" she said softly. "I guess I was mistaken, Tichi. This makes it a thing of consequence, no?"

But Don Pedro, it appeared, had no intention of letting himself become part of this affair. He remained discreetly in the passageway, invisible to those on the Plaza, yet able to view the proceedings there. Josefina watched him from her concealment, curiously and with the ancient fascination of the secret watcher.

There was dust on his blue military cloak, and his horse's withers were a little damp. He had come some distance, apparently, and had ridden hard to arrive in time. Yet, oddly, he appeared to have no more than a very detached interest, after all, in this flogging of a young mestizo for the rape of some poor Villeño's daughter.

"Your hair, señora?" Tichi asked.

"Never mind," Josefina said.

The roll of a drum echoed in confusion from the four sides of the Plaza, and a big voice shouted a series of unintelligible phrases. It was Sebastian Rodríguez, the Negro drummer, proclaiming the sentence.

"Forty lashes," Tichi said. "No more."

"Observe his face," Josefina said. "I mean Don Pedro's. It is like the face of a wooden image."

"But more handsome," Tichi said.

"Still wooden."

And there was no doubt that, at this moment, Don Pedro's bronzed and beardless features did strongly suggest a carving in dark and polished wood. His face at all times, it was true, had a rather somber impassivity that tended to impress men—and often irritated women. But now, it seemed to Josefina, it wore an expression of special gravity.

A succession of sharp, explosive sounds echoed from the Plaza. It was "El Gordo" testing his whip and showing off a little.

Don Pedro's horse reacted nervously to these sounds. His rider tightened the reins ever so slightly, the great Spanish bit exerted its cruel persuasion, and horse and man relapsed into immobility. Don Pedro tapped his thigh lightly with a plaited rawhide quirt; then even that small movement ceased.

"Es de Usted, señor!" the squad corporal said in clear, precise, formal tones: "He is yours, señor!"

There was an interval of silence—the length of an indrawn breath: then the sudden, shocking slashing sound of the lash: from somewhere under the watching portales a stifled scream.

"One," Tichi said complacently. "Thirty-nine to go."

7

Josefina glanced at her reproachfully. She had never relished floggings. Violence sickened her—and particularly violence in the form of beating. Even the common sight of a muleteer belaboring his poor pack-animal could fill her with a sudden and unaccountable revulsion.

But now, gripped by a perverse fascination, she stood fast and tried not to show her repugnance. She fastened her eyes on Don Pedro. She centered her attention desperately on his calm, dark face. . . .

And that is what she thought of now as, sitting beneath the high vigas of the Palace dining room, she looked down the long table at the Governor and Captain-General of the Kingdom of New Mexico and responded absently to his rambling talk of wines and sweets and heard Don Pedro's name fall from her own lips. She thought of Don Pedro's face as the blows fell on the naked back of the young mestizo—of the strong, somber calm of that soldier's face, reflecting no more emotion than a carved image; and of how it had filled her at first with a kind of awe, and then with a strange and foolish fury.

She thought also of another thing: of the plaited rawhide quirt in Don Pedro's hand; and of how, as the blows fell, that quirt had tapped Don Pedro's thigh—tap for blow—tap for blow—tap for blow . . . forty times, until she could have cried out to stop it.

"Why?" she had demanded of Tichi. "Why? Does he go to floggings as if to cockfights? Is this his amusement?"

"You are upset, señora. You should——"

"Look at him, Tichi. I think he is smiling."

"Perhaps for a reason, señora."

"So? What reason?"

"This is only my idea——"

"Ay, caramba! You drive me crazy, Tichi!"

"This little Chayo—she is a beautiful child, señora. She came often to Don Pedro's house. To visit Rosita, the señor's servant, who is said by all to be the best chocolate cook in the Villa——"

"And what have chocolate cooks to do with—with this?"

"Why nothing, of course, señora. This little Chayo, as I was saying, señora, came often to the señor captain's house to see Rosita. The señor became fond of her, no doubt. I myself have seen him carry her before him on his horse—like a little lady. The señor is a soldier, and has a reputation for sternness; but I think his heart softened for Chayo, no?"

"I see," Josefina said.

"And one can understand, then, why the señor captain might take a certain pleasure in—in this." She gestured toward the Plaza. "As I have myself, señora."

Tichi had put her arm around her, then, and had drawn her away

8

from the window. "La señora should never watch a flogging," she had said. "Nor even the face of one who watches."

And Tichi was right, she thought. She must put the flogging out of her head. But she could not put the memory of Don Pedro Villasur's face out of her head—nor prevent her mind from making its comparisons, as her eyes might compare the hues of two ribbons, or her tongue the flavors of two sweets. And so, looking over the candlelight at Don Antonio now, she saw sharply and clearly the pitiful thing he had become. She said to herself again, sadly and—since the threads of their lives had been so long entwined—a little fearfully: Here, indeed, is a man who is all but finished.

She marveled that she had not read the signs before—they were so plain and so many. She asked herself how she could have been blind so long to something that—as Tafora's letters should have warned her—even the Viceroy in México suspected. And then, above all else, she wondered that so great a change could have come over this man who had found her—eighteen then, and filled with hunger and despair—in a little Spanish inn, and had carried her to this wild and wonderful and terrible Kingdom of New Mexico.

2

She had styled herself "La de los Ojos Verdes"—She of the Green Eyes—in those dreadful days, having dropped through fear and shame the title of La Sola by which she had become known and almost famous in Madrid.

And that is what Don Antonio Valverde was told when he asked the keeper of the inn in Roa, "What is that one called, landlord? And what is she doing here?"

"They call her La de los Ojos Verdes," the innkeeper had answered. "She is with a company of players, stranded here like Your Excellency."

Don Antonio slowly finished his glass of Valdepeñas, watching the girl as she crossed the courtyard. He was a very bored man; and his boredom sharpened his interest, no doubt, in this slender young figure moving with such peculiar grace and dignity across the sun-soaked square.

She walks like an angel, Don Antonio said to himself, or a king's concubine. He asked the innkeeper: "Did you say they have lodgings here?"

9

"I had to take them in, señor," the innkeeper said apologetically. "The floods. They have paid for yesterday and today—eighty reales. Tomorrow—out they go, unless they can dig up another forty among them."

"Where are they from?" Don Antonio asked idly.

"They say Madrid. But I doubt it, señor. I doubt that they have ever seen the Capital." The innkeeper paused to pick his teeth with an ivory toothpick. "Except the one you have observed, señor. She has a certain something, no? I have not been able to figure her out. She is not easy to talk to. One would think from her airs, señor, that she was La Caramba herself—or the Maya."

"She walks well," Don Antonio said, with a slightly self-conscious smile. "I haven't seen her face."

"I wouldn't call her beautiful," the innkeeper said. "She's a little too thin for my taste. Personally, I like 'em——" He made elaborate curving motions with his hands and smirked. "Too pale, also, and she does not laugh. She has no gaiety, that one. Her eyes, however, are very fine—as you will observe later, sir."

"Later, landlord?"

"I am providing a small entertainment for my guests this evening," the innkeeper said importantly. "A play and a little dancing, eh? This little Caramba—I am assured by this troupe of vagabonds—is very good, señor."

"It will be something to pass the time, at any rate," Don Antonio said.

"It will have to be something better than that," the innkeeper said. "If it's good, they stay another day. If it's as bad as I'm afraid it will be——" He made a tossing gesture with both hands. "Out they go in the morning."

He laughed unpleasantly, and Don Antonio, still watching the girl, felt a sudden distaste for the fellow. He got up abruptly and went upstairs to his chamber.

At this time Don Antonio Valverde was somewhat of a lindo—not quite a dandy, but a man of fastidious taste in all matters relating to his personal appearance. But when, after a short nap, he began to dress for the evening, it was with such special care that his servant, a brash young Asturian he had acquired in Madrid, was moved to ask, "Shall I make preparations for the entertainment—of a lady, señor?"

You do better than read my thoughts, Salvador, Don Antonio said to himself. You anticipate them!

Now that Salvador had reduced the matter to such concrete terms, Don Antonio was a little surprised at his own intentions—almost as if he had caught himself in some surreptitious, and not quite proper, design. He also derived a certain amusement from the idea: that he should be planning the conquest—he must acknowledge it—of a woman whose face he had not even seen, whom he had only watched from across the courtyard as she walked past in the sunshine.

And, on top of all this, he was conscious of something too faint to be called an emotion, but disquieting nevertheless, and vaguely pleasurable, whenever he recalled her image. Perhaps if he had not dreamed of her in his nap, he thought; or if the boredom of the inn had been less colossal; or if the landlord had held his tiresome tongue; perhaps this rather ridiculous situation might never have developed. . . . Or if she hadn't walked across the courtyard.

"Some players have arrived here," he said to Salvador. "There's a young girl with them. Have you observed her, by chance?"

"There are three young girls," Salvador answered. "I have observed them all, señor."

"I am sure of that. Then, perhaps you can tell me——"

"Yes, señor?"

Don Antonio perceived that he was in danger of making himself ridiculous before his servant. He said carefully, and with an air of negligence: "This one is the primera dama of the troupe. I am told she is quite good-looking. What is your opinion, Salvador?"

"It is a matter of taste, señor. I know the one you mean. Myself, I prefer the other two. They are less beautiful, perhaps, but more cheerful."

"She is really beautiful, then?"

"In a way, señor—" Salvador made the very suggestion of a grimace —"but the others are gayer."

"And more accessible, no doubt," Don Antonio said dryly.

"All actresses are accessible to a gentleman like yourself, señor," Salvador said respectfully. "Provided the gentleman is resourceful."

True enough, Don Antonio assured himself. Then he wondered if this Salvador were finding amusement, perhaps, in his peasantlike preoccupation with a road-show dancer. It was a fashion with Spanish servants, he had learned since his return from New Mexico, to make sport of their masters nowadays. It was one of the new French ways that had come in with the Bourbons while he was absent: ways that sometimes made him feel strange and provincial—and a little lonely— in his own homeland.

He said to Salvador, with a touch of brusqueness, "Call the landlord."

"Yes, señor. Your cravat?"

"I'll tie it myself. Get the landlord up here at once."

Don Antonio, who had worn nothing but military garb for many years, was pleased to discover on his return to Spain that, under the French influence, the king's uniforms had taken on a new elegance and brilliance. They were now a delight to the eye—and to the astonishingly giddy women of the Spanish cities—and Don Antonio had been quick to adopt several of the more spectacular features of the new mode. One of these was the cravat he now placed around his neck. It was a wide and flowing length of white silk, elaborately embroidered and ruffled; and when he had tied it under his chin it billowed down for eight inches over his satin waistcoat. The effect was hardly military, but it was assuredly striking. And immensely pleasing to Don Antonio.

He gazed at his reflection in the glass with satisfaction. After twenty years in the outposts of New Spain, it was good to see oneself thus, dressed in the latest fashion of the civilized world. But the twenty years showed through the finery. Don Antonio still had the look of a soldier. He was no longer young—he was forty-one—nor quite as lean as he had been in the great days of the Reconquest. But no one who had campaigned with Vargas had come through without the look of a soldier; and Don Antonio had that look.

He had it in his eyes, which were either blue or gray, depending on the light, and possessed that misty paleness that comes from gazing into dazzling skies and across great distances; and the hardness that came from seeing the things that a soldier naturally saw in the Kingdom of New Mexico. He was not handsome, he considered, but neither was he ill-favored—as the ladies of Madrid and Seville had so generously attested.

Of all the marvels of Spain, Don Antonio thought fondly, the women were the most wonderful. Among the mestizas and mulatas and pueblo girls of New Spain he had almost forgotten what a real Castellana was like. He had claimed his share of the mestizas and mulatas and pueblo girls; and for a time there had been Consuelo, the sister of Don Diego Vargas' own mistress. . . . But ah! what were any of them compared to the women of Castile and Andalusia?

At first he had been almost frightened of the silken beauties who, luxury-mad and avid to ape the dissolute habits of the Court, had flocked into the war-disordered Capital from every corner of the Peninsula. The Spanish courtesan—for more than a thousand years the elite of Europe and Africa—had blossomed with a new profusion and splendor in the lax and pleasure-crazed climate of Madrid. And a new kind of woman had appeared in the city, also, since he had left it almost twenty years before. She was called La Petimetra.

Even the rumors he had heard in New Mexico about this fantastic creature had not prepared him for the reality. Perfumed, coiffured and gowned in the latest French fashion, she trampled in her high-heeled slippers and long silk stockings over all the old Spanish ideas of modesty and virtue. And no girl in Madrid, it seemed to Don Antonio, but tried to follow her. Every married woman, he heard, now had her suitor. And so low had Spanish morals fallen that wives practiced this custom without the slightest sense of shame—and, even more incredible, husbands tolerated it without jealousy.

It was plainly a deplorable state of affairs, but one to which, Don Antonio found, he could adapt himself without too much difficulty.

Don Antonio had denied himself few of the pleasures of the Capital —so few, indeed, that even his naturally robust constitution had at last cried out for quarter. But now, refreshed and rested after a fortnight's respite at Villa Presente, his birthplace in the mountains of Burgos, he was impatient to return to the pleasant fray.

It was this rising fever of anticipation, he reflected as he viewed himself in the mirror, that accounted for his altogether improbable interest in this incognita who called herself—what was it again that she called herself?—She of the Green Eyes. That and the boredom.

Don Antonio had been detained for three days at this small inn by the raging Duero: a long time in any country inn, but in this case a special trial. He had finished his business in Villa Presente—which was the sale of a large parcel of ancestral holdings to his uncle, Don Alonzo de Castillo Navarrete—and had set out, well satisfied with the transaction that had brought him halfway around the world. Over-eager, he had unwisely taken a short cut over the mountains, where he had been caught by the spring floods at Roa. And at Roa he still tarried, driven by the dullness to dressing as if for a royal hand-kissing at Aranjuez, while he plotted the seduction of a dancer in a third-rate troupe of players. He scrutinized his image in the mirror, suddenly less pleased with it than he had been. He unknotted the white neckcloth.

"Salvador!" he called. "The yellow one."

The lackey handed him a length of silk, embroidered and ruffled as before, but of a gay mariposa color. He knotted this under his chin so tightly, in the fashion of the time, that his rather pale face reddened. He smiled at himself.

"Better, no?" he asked over his shoulder.

"Yes, señor," Salvador said. "It becomes Your Excellency. It makes you look younger."

"Mother of Christ!" Don Antonio bellowed. "Did I ask for a commentary?"

Had he reached the time, he thought, when he must study to look young? He viewed his face critically. It had no longer the smooth and glossy contours of youth, he had to admit; but what soldier's did? He chose to see in the various lines and cockles, and even in the lavender pockets under his eyes and the down-sloping folds at the corners of his small mouth, simply the imprint of experience and character. Certain other unflattering signs—of self-conceit, cupidity, cruelty, and, despite his good birth, a native vulgarity—wholly escaped his perception; for Don Antonio, after all, was—Don Antonio.

And while he was thus endeavoring to deny the flight of his own youth, his mind was half-occupied with the memory of a young girl crossing a square in the hot Castilian sunshine, and of the movements of her slender body, and of her walk which was the very poetry of life's springtime.

A sudden impatience seized him and he growled at his servant, "Salvador, where is that fat big-mouth, the landlord?"

"I am here, Your Excellency," the innkeeper said. He had come in quietly during Don Antonio's communion with the mirror. "At your orders, señor."

Don Antonio burst into a great laugh that sprayed the glass with saliva. It was his amusement to abuse inferiors—except Salvador, whom he secretly feared—and there was something about the inadvertency of this particular insult that struck him as being exceptionally funny.

"Well, well! Speak of the devil——" he roared. His laughing, and the tightness of his neckcloth, made his face alarmingly red. He choked, caught his breath, and turned fiercely on the innkeeper. "Landlord," he demanded, "what have you got that's fit to eat?"

"Mutton," the innkeeper answered.

"Mutton!" Don Antonio groaned. "By the holy ribs of Christ——" He abruptly assumed a quiet and reasoning tone that managed to suggest something sinister. "Consider, landlord," he said, "I desire a dinner tonight for two persons. A dinner, you understand, of a special excellence. And for this dinner *mutton?* Let us think hard now."

"A kid, señor. A very young one—I could bake it——"

"I am not in a mood for joking," Don Antonio said coldly.

"Well, a turkey then," the innkeeper suggested doubtfully. "There is one I have had my eye on for His Excellency the Conde de——"

"The Conde can eat mutton," Don Antonio said, "or kid. I shall have the turkey. It is a young one, I trust——"

They fell then to an animated discussion of the dinner, which continued for a quarter of an hour, and ended with Don Antonio and the innkeeper on good terms; and with Don Antonio feeling very well toward himself also, as he always felt after the planning of a good meal, in that pleasant interval of anticipation before eating it.

He had almost forgotten why he was ordering so special a dinner; but he remembered now, and the recollection added an extra glow to his self-satisfaction. He placed his peruke carefully over his own rather thin, sand-colored hair, brushed up the ruffles of his cravat with the tips of his fingers, and extracted from his waistcoat pocket a snuff-box of gold and tortoise shell, adorned with the figure of a woman in a most obscene posture.

14

Opening it, Don Antonio took a pinch of vinagrillo—a snuff especially prepared for him with rose vinegar—between his thumb and index finger. Raising it to his nostrils, with the three idle fingers daintily curved, he applied the snuff to his nose with several rapid frictional movements. A few grains remaining on his fingertips, he blew lightly into the air.

"La de los Ojos Verdes!" he mused aloud, smiling. "It should be an interesting evening, Antonio. . . ."

3

Josefina stared wearily at a dog-eared script of the great Lope de Vega's play, *The Star of Seville*. Pepe had chosen *The Star* for tonight—or rather a scene from it; the one, of course, in which Estrella, dressed in her wedding finery, goes to receive her bridegroom, and receives instead her brother's corpse.

"It is necessary for us to make them weep," Pepe had said.

Besides, José Molina, the leading man, had drunk a little too much the night before and was fit, really, for no role but that of the corpse. So Pepe had decided on a scene from *The Star* and had given her the part of Estrella.

"What I mean," Pepe had amended, "is that it will be necessary for you, my dove, to make them weep. Otherwise it is doubtful how we shall eat or sleep after tonight."

"Trust me, papá."

"Especially the innkeeper."

"Don't worry, papá. I'll make that son of the great sow weep—I'll make him melt in his own tears."

She spoke bravely because she was sorry for Pepe. The luck had been against him—against all of them—for so long. There was nothing sadder, she thought, than a fat man who has lost his fat. And Pepe had been so fat and so jolly.

"I shall light a candle for you," he said, "to Our Lady of Atocha."

He was not jesting, she knew. He would light a candle for her, and possibly spend his last copper for it. But not for you, Josefina, she said to herself. For success tonight in making them weep.

Pepe stood there, looking at her tenderly, his face made melancholy by the folds of loose skin; and she hoped he would not smile, because there was something gruesome about his smiles of late.

15

He asked abruptly: *"Who are you, my daughter?"*

He had asked that question only once before—when she had first begged admission to his troupe, at the beginning of the winter. She had given him an evasive answer then; now she laughed and gave him none at all.

"Go light the candle," she said, "and leave me alone. Tell the others to keep away also." She made a little grimace of distaste. "Especially José!"

He left on tiptoe. She was sorry for him, now that he was sick and luckless; but not with her whole heart. When he was well and fat, he had not always been so gentle with her.

"Let us save a little of the pity for ourselves, Josefina," she said.

She returned listlessly to the script. It was not easy for her to concentrate on the lines: it never was. She was not at home, really, in the acting of parts. Her talent was for those between-the-acts entertainments, intimate and salty, that were the delight of Spanish audiences. And for the dance, which had made her almost famous in Madrid.

But now, as she closed her eyes and tried to recall the words of Estrella's somber grief, the lines came even harder than usual. She was bothered by a kind of lightheadedness, almost a giddiness—the result, probably, of too little sleep and too many meals of bread and cold garlic soup—and a deep lassitude came over her, making it all but impossible for her to think.

Josefina lay her head back against the wall and tried to remember Estrella's words. They came to her in short, disjointed fragments of sentences. They drifted away from her, the fragments; and sometimes she could recapture them for a moment . . . then they would be lost again. Suddenly her mind slipped into that mystic plane of thought, somewhere between sleep and consciousness, in which time becomes nondimensional; and she is dancing in the empty patio of La Greca's house.

She is alone in La Greca's flowery patio, and she is dancing the solitary dance of Andalusia that her mother had taught her. There is music, and she is thirteen, and so she is dancing.

The musicians are playing in the sala where the guests are sipping strawberry sherbets. La Greca has brought them up from the Capital; for this is a very special entertainment she is giving for some friends—powerful at the court of the new king—from Madrid. And La Greca, whose extravagancies had been notorious in those days when she was young and the darling of the Spanish stage, could still manage a lavish party occasionally.

Because this is one of such importance to La Greca, Josefina has been sent for to help in the kitchen. She has been instructed by La Greca's housekeeper to keep out of sight; because, as that unfeeling old woman has pointed out, she is thin and poor, and (although she has washed and mended for hours) has the appearance of a hungry gypsy.

That she is hungry is true enough (she could hardly remember not knowing hunger in those days). But she is young also, and so, whenever she is given a little chance, gay. And now, as she steps into the patio on some errand and hears the music coming from the sala, she cannot help but stop and listen.

When La Greca was the reigning comedienne of Spain, it was part of her legend that the usual was never to be expected of her; and now in her retirement she is still at some pains to preserve this reputation. So her guests are hardly surprised when, after the musicians have performed the customary polite compositions by Narvaez and Mudarra and the rest, La Greca introduces a ruffian who styles himself "The Little Angel," and plays the guitar like one.

"Olé! Olé! Jaleo!" the guests cry enthusiastically, beating the palms of their hands softly together. "Bueno, chico! Otra, otra!" As if they were gypsies of Triana themselves.

And Josefina, hearing this playing of Angelito's, can no more move from where she stands than could the little bronze statue in the center of the fountain. The music—low and melancholy, full of strange and startling pauses—creeps into her limbs and stirs her blood: she shivers, frowns, and then, after glancing swiftly around to make sure that no one is watching, begins to dance.

Her mother, Eva Helena, has taught her how—how to make her arms wind upwards, and how to lower them and beat her palms together—how to answer the strings with the slow, soft cadences of hips and arms and torso—how to freeze her body stiffly in a sculptured rigor. She knows, also, how to stamp her heels, and frown, and utter the low husky exclamations that are almost moans, and how to use the castanets.

She has no castanets, so she snaps her fingers: now softly, almost silently beside her hips, now in a shower of staccato notes above her head; and her arms move in the slow, hieratic gestures that were known to Hadrian and Tiberius. She is not woman enough yet for the Spanish dance: she is too young and too thin, and she has never loved. But her mother has taught her well; and something that could not be taught has been passed on to her in the blood by those older— by those two thousand years older than she, and more woman, and infinitely wise in passion. So Josefina dances, at first timidly, then joyfully, and at last with abandon.

"Bueno, chica!" she hears a low, strong voice say. "Niña!"

She freezes in terror and crosses her arms over her breast, as if she had been come upon naked. A man, half-concealed by the fuchsias, is watching and smiling and applauding softly. He is a tall man, elegantly dressed in black, with a beautiful white beard that makes him the more terrifying.

"Más!" the man says, nodding and smiling. "More, chica!"

But at that moment Angelito's music stops abruptly. She utters a little cry, wrenches herself free from the paralysis that holds her, and flees. She can hear the man calling after her. . . .

Josefina's head bobbed over the script of *The Star of Seville*. She opened her eyes wide and shook herself. It had been the matter of a moment—of less than a moment, perhaps. She dully picked up Estrella's speech in the middle of a line, where she had dropped it for this dancing in La Greca's garden.

"You had hunger then, Josefina," she said to herself wryly. "Well, you still have it."

She struggled along with her lines, weary of Estrella's grief and bothered by the giddiness that made it so hard for her to remember. Her mind kept wandering away from the script—to Lope de Vega again, with a certain resentment because he had written all these words that she must commit to memory. He had written two thousand plays, Pepe had said, and every play in three acts, no more or less. . . .

Like her own life, she mused. Her life was much like a play—like one of Lope's plays—in three acts, no more or less. . . . She had never thought of it before, but when she was weary her mind sometimes turned to numbers—numbers filled her head—she counted and divided and made groups of numbers, and counted over again: and now she was drowsily amused to discover how plainly her life also divided itself—exactly, for instance, like *The Star of Seville*—into three parts: and how neatly—like one of Lope's curtains—the first part had ended on that afternoon when the elegant señor with the white beard had watched her dancing from behind La Greca's fuchsias. . . .

4

It had begun, of course, with the accident of her birth in Ávila, the City of the Knights and of Santa Teresa.

That had made her a Norteña, a daughter of the North. Yet there was only southern blood in her veins; and it was only by a notion of fortune that, on a bleak October morning of the year 1692, Eva Helena

Torres, her mother, had happened to bear her first child in the old walled city of Castile.

During all their lives in Seville, Eva Helena and her husband, Miguel, had never so much as heard of Ávila. But they had heard much of Madrid. They heard of it unceasingly from Tío Chepe, an uncle of Miguel's, who, having gone north in the 80's, had returned to Seville for a visit with his nephew.

Tío Chepe could not say enough in praise of the capital. He laughed at the old saying, "Who hasn't seen Seville has never seen a marvel."

"If you believe Seville is a marvel," he said contemptuously, "you are but confessing that you have not been to Madrid."

"I like it here," Eva Helena said.

"You have been nowhere," Tío Chepe said. "If you have not been to Madrid, you have been nowhere."

"It is said to be cold up there."

She did not like this talk of Tío Chepe's. For that matter, she did not like Tío Chepe very much either. But she could say nothing of this to Miguel, who appeared to be fond of the old man.

So she listened to Tío Chepe while he told of the wonders of the Capital: of the Puerta del Sol, of course, where all Madrid met and gossiped, and the soldiers strutted and ogled the girls, and the courtesans went to Mass in the church of Buen Suceso; of the Paseo del Prado, that great dark promenade frequented by lovers and murderers; of the Christmas and autumn fairs, the bull feasts, the great church holidays, the seven hundred fountains of Madrid; of the hangings and beheadings and garrotings in the Plaza Mayor.

His talk was that of a windy, morbid, ignorant old man, and it had no effect on Eva Helena but to make her love Seville all the more. With Miguel, however, it was different. He was of a restless and not very steady nature. Eva Helena could see how Tío Chepe's talk disquieted him, and she prayed to the Virgin that Tío Chepe would go away. But he stayed, and drank Miguel's brandy, and talked; and after a while Eva Helena could see that Miguel was wanting only a good excuse for proposing that they themselves go to Madrid.

One day he said to Eva Helena: "Querida, this is a hard place, where every second man is a maker of tiles, to get ahead."

"We are doing well enough," Eva Helena said. "What has Tío Chepe been telling you now?"

"Only what is plain to any sensible man. Here there is an abundance of tiles, but very little money."

"There is very little money anywhere in Spain today."

"But here it is worse—because of everybody making tiles. It would be better to go where there are fewer tiles and more money, no?"

"I suppose you mean Madrid?"

19

"Well," Miguel said with a judicious air, "it is well known that the products of Seville are very popular in the north."

"Ay, caramba, that Tío Chepe!" Eva Helena said sadly.

She was pregnant and easily depressed. She had no desire to leave the sunny, smiling land of Andalusia. That seemed a mad, impossible thing for anyone to do; and the very thought of it made her heart heavy. She felt also the sadness of any young wife when she begins to see a little more plainly the man she has married.

Eva Helena and Miguel Torres had been married at this time for a little more than a year. It had been a happy enough marriage—a true love match, both Eva Helena and Miguel thought. For neither suspected that it had, in fact, been arranged by the Condesa de Mora—for reasons that could never be known to Eva Helena, but were very plain and compelling to the Condesa.

Eva Helena had been born into the Conde de Mora's house. Her mother, a Sevillana named Juana Velez, served the Condesa as a housekeeper. It was rumored, also—as was inevitable, since she was a beauty—that Juana's relationship to the Conde was considerably more intimate than that of servant and master. And this gossip went so far as to include, after Eva Helena's birth, the infant herself.

In the Spain of Charles II, however, such a circumstance—even if true—was nothing to agitate anyone unduly; and the Condesa herself was coldly indifferent to the sly intimations of her friends and enemies. That great and gracious lady, in fact, not only continued to treat Juana with her natural kindness, but bestowed a special, almost maternal affection on her child.

"She is so completely beautiful!" the Condesa said, a little wistfully. "She compels one to love her!"

So Eva Helena grew to childhood in the Conde de Mora's great house, and played with his children, and attended lessons with them, studying the arts of reading and writing—the latter at the Conde's own express wish. From her mother, Juana, she learned other useful things: how to play the guitar of Andalusia and sing the sad-gay songs of that province; how to dance the sevillanas; and how to cook a good puchero.

She was an accomplished young woman at the age of fifteen, tall for the South, but showing a fine, full development of hips and breasts. She had beauty and charm—and even dignity—beyond that of the Condesa's own daughters: and—as none had failed to observe—eyes of the same striking emerald color as the Conde de Mora's.

It was at this time that the Conde's eldest son, home from the wars in Italy, became suddenly and acutely aware of Eva Helena's disquieting presence. And it was at this time, also, that the Condesa de Mora

20

decided that her lovely and fascinating young protégé should be provided—and quickly—with a suitable husband.

The details were not difficult for the Condesa to arrange. What could be more natural than Eva Helena's falling in love with the clever and handsome young man whom the Condesa had engaged to build a fountain of glazed tiles in her private garden? Or that Miguel Torres, the young man, should develop a swift passion for the beautiful girl on whom (the Condesa let it be known) a dowry of twenty thousand silver reales had been settled? Within a week Miguel had made his proposal in proper form; and the marriage was brought off by the smiling but somewhat anxious Condesa as hastily as the laws of Holy Church would permit.

It had been a happy marriage and, until the advent of Tío Chepe, quite free from even minor disagreements. Eva Helena became a serious, thoughtful, and capable young wife. She frequently displayed a firmness remarkable in one so young and pretty. She was exactly what Miguel Torres needed, in fact; for Miguel was a little too pleasure-loving perhaps—even for an Andalusian.

"Listen, Miguel. It is beautiful to hear you play the guitar, but Don Francisco is expecting his flower jars tomorrow, no?"

"He shall have them, sweetheart." (M-brum-brum, m-brum-brum.)

"Are they finished, then?"

"All but the firing." (M-brum-brum.) "That I shall do this afternoon."

"That you shall do now! Give me the guitar, Miguel."

"One moment, sweetheart." (M-brum.)

"Give me!"

"Here, then. Where is my hat? And a kiss, querida. . . ."

Yet he was so skillful in the designing and making of jars and bowls, gallipots and plates, and all descriptions of pottery decorated with flowers, birds, animals, human and saintly beings—and of tiles showing the lives of the saints, the Virgin and Child, and scenes from the Passion—that his workshop, which he had bought with Eva Helena's marriage portion, flourished; and even in that time of widespread distress in Spain, Eva Helena and Miguel wanted nothing. It was only when Tío Chepe came that trouble arose.

"I have decided to sell the shop," Miguel said one day. "I have been offered a very good price for it."

"But Miguel——!"

"The profit will be four hundred reales."

"But have you thought, Miguel——?"

"I have decided," Miguel said. Like most weak and irresolute people, he had a deep-buried streak of stubbornness. "There is nothing to talk about."

Even though she could smell the brandy on his breath, Eva Helena was shocked at the look in Miguel's eyes. It was a look at once foolish and mean, and she had to fight against a sudden impulse to weep.

"And what do we do now?" she asked quietly.

"We are going to Madrid."

"Good then, Miguel." She made herself smile. "Let us pray that we shall be happy there also."

She went, without saying anything more, to her tasks in the kitchen. But when Tío Chepe came in a little later, sniffing at the baked peppers, she turned on him in a sudden fury.

"Fool!" she cried. "Old, drunken fool! Why do you stick your long nose into other people's lives? Why don't you go away from here?"

But she made no further protest to Miguel; and so, on the twenty-second day of July, 1692, she found herself, as if in a dream, crossing the Manzanares on a jolting cart piled with such household goods as they could take with them. They crossed the river, passed through the Royal Toledo Gate, and found themselves in the city of Madrid.

5

It was not, they quickly discovered, quite as Tío Chepe had described it. Madrid was but a filthy jumble of singularly mean one-story houses, ugly churches, and great sprawling public buildings, baking in the intolerable heat of the Castilian plain. By all odds the dirtiest capital in Europe, it was now in an especially foul state, due to the neglect and disorganization caused by the new war with the French.

Where, Eva Helena asked bitterly, but of herself only, for she had resolved to complain of nothing, where are all the marvels, Tío Chepe?

For here, in place of the old man's grand promises, was a revolting maze of narrow streets and alleys, calf-deep in mud when it rained, choked with clouds of fetid dust when it was dry, into which she had not the courage to enter, even with Miguel. Filth ran through them in open sewers. Garbage and slops were flung on one from doors and windows, so that all must wear big hats and long cloaks for protection. Coachmen and pedestrians cursed and fought—sometimes to the death—for the right to pass. The stench from doors and vestibules was unbearable; and, since there was not a public privy in all Madrid, one occasionally encountered a shamefaced traveler squatting perforce in some corner or portal.

22

Because she was six months with child, all this was abnormally depressing, perhaps, to Eva Helena. Certainly it was less so to Miguel. There was hardly a bullfight, an execution, or an auto-de-fé in the Plaza Mayor that he did not attend; and sometimes he made an excursion outside the walls to see a burning. He was faithful in the observance of every fiesta—of which there was no end in Madrid—and he never missed a fair.

At times he even took Eva Helena with him. They visited the gardens of the Retiro together. Miguel rented straw chairs at four cuartos each, and they sat sipping raspberry water as they watched the Madrileños promenade. A sedan chair passed, swaying between its bearers.

"I wish," Eva Helena said, "that I could be carried in one of those."

"They aren't as comfortable as they appear to be," Miguel said. "Besides, they cost two reales a trip."

Miguel was not as free with money as he had been at first. But there were many pleasures in Madrid that cost nothing, and some of them he allowed Eva Helena to share with him. Of these, she enjoyed most the famous Fair of Madrid, which opened each year on St. Matthew's day and lasted until the fourth of October. Here, at least, was something almost up to Tío Chepe's boasting!

It was a gay, joyful, wonderful time, this Fair of Madrid, when the whole city—and most of the countryside too, it seemed—flocked to the Plazuela de la Cebada; and even the thronged avenues of the Prado were for once deserted. Perhaps, Eva Helena thought, the people loved it so because it was but a small fair—a small fair crowded hilariously into a single plaza, so that it overflowed into all the neighboring streets; and where only things of little value were offered for sale.

Everything was stacked pell-mell in the square and the streets: shoes, slippers, candlesticks, swords, wigs, fine porcelain clocks, pictures, old coats, skirts, couches, sofas, damask-covered chairs, mats, pots, kettles, brooms, books, laces, and jewelry and finery of every sort.

"One could furnish a whole house, Miguel, for a song!" Eva Helena said.

But, because they had as yet no house, they bought nothing at all. They merely looked and listened and marveled at the barkers and the people and the sights; and then, caught in the irresistible currents of the crowd, they found themselves out of the plazuela altogether. They were in a small street where toys of all sorts were brightly displayed—a special street of toys; and they were looking into a tiny shop whose walls, ceiling, and floor were covered with more playthings than ever filled a child's dream of heaven.

"Look, Miguel!" Eva Helena exclaimed, and clutched her husband's arm. "Will you look at that!"

23

It was a doll she was pointing at, a doll of indescribable beauty, with pink porcelain cheeks, and blue porcelain eyes, and hair of a heavenly blondness; and its dress was of a richness that an infanta herself might have envied—although of that certain, vaguely foreign appearance characteristic of dolls' dresses.

"Inquire of the shopkeeper about the price," Eva Helena said.

"It is probably very expensive," Miguel said doubtfully.

"But ask him."

"Of what use is a doll to us?" He caught the sudden flash of exasperation in her eyes, and faltered. ". . . Perhaps it will be a boy," he said lamely.

She did not bother to answer him. "Señor," she called to the shopkeeper, "what is the price of this?"

"Twelve pesos," he said. "It is of German manufacture—very fine, no?"

"Really, señor, I am serious."

"Well, what will you give for it, señora?"

She drew Miguel aside and said to him in a low voice, "I shall offer eight, but we will pay ten."

"No," Miguel said firmly, "we cannot afford to throw away our money for toys."

Something took hold of her—something that may have reached out of the past, or perhaps out of the future: she knew not which or what—and she was overwhelmed with a fierce desire to own this little image of a child.

"It is something I want very much," she said quietly. "I shall be unhappy without it, Miguel."

She knew how difficult it would be for him to hold out against the superstitious belief that to cross an expectant mother was to leave a devastating mark upon her child.

"It is like the time I wanted the green pickled almonds," she said. "Only much worse, Miguel."

"Oh, well——" he said. But he was surly and unsmiling about it.

So they bought the doll for nine pesos, and Eva Helena took it home and put it away in the bottom of their big leather traveling wallet, among her linens and Granada laces.

"For Josefina," she said. For she was sure that her baby would be a girl; and she had decided to call her—simply because she liked the sound of the words together—Josefina María del Carmen.

At this time almost three months had passed since they had left Seville; and Miguel was still looking—like the conquistadores in the Indies—for the gold that Tío Chepe had promised. He assured Eva Helena, at any rate, that he was searching diligently for the opportunity to buy a shop. Or even, if he could find no shop to his liking, for employment worthy of his skill and experience. And what he was seeking, it appeared, was always about to fall into his lap in a day or two.

In the meantime, the money of Eva Helena's marriage portion melted away. Money, Eva Helena learned, reduces all things to tangible and specific terms—to something that can be measured, and counted and watched. And, as she saw the nineteen thousand reales that Miguel had got for the shop in Seville (he had not made a profit, really, but had actually lost a hundred reales or so) shrink to less than fourteen, she could measure the declining brightness of their situation.

"I did not think it would be so hard to get money in Madrid," she said innocently.

"All the money in Madrid is in the pockets of the Catalans," Miguel said glibly.

He was never at a loss for an excuse and—since he strove to act and talk like a true Madrileño—he blamed the Catalans, and added that they were "the Dutchmen of Spain." But one night he came home with an important and confident air, and he made an announcement.

"Tomorrow," he said, "I am going up to Ávila."

An acquaintance, a pothouse crony, actually, had informed him of a small but flourishing pottery that was for sale there. It appeared, Miguel said, to be exactly the kind of proposition he had been looking for, a good example of the fact that, if you knew precisely what you wanted, and only waited long enough——

"If you are going up to Ávila," Eva Helena said, "I am going with you."

"But that is impossible, my dear."

"Impossible or not, I am going with you."

She was wearied beyond further endurance of Madrid and its filth; and of the squalid rooms in which they had been forced to lodge; and of the waiting. Even small things, such as the cries of the street-hawkers—particularly the "Aite! Aite!" of the oil-sellers—drove her to distraction lately.

"You cannot leave me here alone," she said steadily. "It would be more than I could stand. . . . It would mark the baby, surely."

This had worked in the case of the doll, and it worked again now, but less easily. Eva Helena had to resort to tears and a small fit of hysteria before Miguel would give in. But in the end he said, "Very well—you are insane," and she went along. Miguel, however, stubbornly refused to speak to her during the whole of the first day on the road up to Ávila.

Near the end of the third day they came in sight of the ancient city of Santa Teresa, huddled inside its dark granite walls on the broad back of a ridge sloping down from the Guadarramas to the River

Adaja. They saw it through an icy blur of autumn rain that beat through their woolen cloaks and wet them to the skin.

Eva Helena sat beside Miguel on the seat of the pitching cart and wept because her pains had begun, and because Miguel was so glum, and because they were so far from home. She wept and hoped, at least, for an hora chica.

She did not have the hora chica, the "little hour" she had prayed for. She had a long, hard time of labor, but she bore her baby safely the next afternoon. Miguel, exhausted and elated, and a little the worse for drink, had a misa de parida—the Mass for one who has just given birth—said in the Church of Santo Tomás. But Eva Helena, not knowing why—from simple weakness, perhaps—wept a little as she gave her baby her breast for the first time.

"Josefina María del Carmen," she whispered with a kind of wonder. "My poor little girl!"

6

For the first fifteen years of her life, the medieval fortress city of Ávila of the Knights was the whole of Josefina's world.

Its turreted walls encircled all her memories of girlhood—except a few that crept, like truant children, out upon the rolling boulder-strewn plain where the sheep grazed, and the gypsies camped, and the cloud shadows swept across the grass. The granite walls of Ávila made a great, high fence around her joys and griefs, around the dreams and bewilderments and terrors of her childhood.

From the time she first became aware of Eva Helena's shadowy and infinitely comforting presence, until she was six years old, this world of Ávila and the girding walls was not an unhappy one for Josefina. Her premature and unexpected birth in the town of Santa Teresa had seemed a kind of good omen to Miguel and Eva Helena, an occurrence that gave a certain stamp of permanence to their being there.

"Perhaps it is a sign from God," Miguel said. "Who knows? Besides, I have looked at the pottery, and it is not bad. It is small but not bad. I think it is worth twelve thousand reales."

"Well, let us decide to live here then," Eva Helena said indifferently. "It cannot be worse than Madrid!"

So Miguel invested most of their remaining capital in the pottery; and, after a little initial difficulty with the local clay, he began very successfully to turn out the tiles, plates, jars, and gallipots of Seville.

For his family he rented rooms in a large and decent apartment building.

"Now we march ahead!" he said. "Why not? There is not a potter in Castile who is my better!"

In this he was possibly correct. When he was working smoothly, few could surpass him—particularly in tiles of the popular pisano style adorned with the figures of saints or (on order) effigies of the dead, and bordered with the most delicately drawn decorations. And none, perhaps, could exceed the purity of his glaze colorings—the light and dark blues, with touches of orange and honey-yellow—that were the special glory of the Sevillian school.

And Miguel was working very smoothly now. He had become his ebullient self again, confident and gay—and a little boastful, of course —and if he played the guitar and sang a good deal, it was not at the expense of his work. His business prospered and his reputation grew: he became known to lovers of the pisano style even in Madrid. And life was pleasant for Eva Helena once more—as pleasant as life could be, perhaps, for a woman of Andalusia hemmed in by the granite walls.

More children came, almost as rapidly as nature would allow. Three were born in less than four years, and all daughters: María de Jesús, Concepción, and Rafaela. Of these, Josefina was to remember only María de Jesús and Concepción in later years; for Rafaela died while she was still a baby, leaving behind her only the faint, uneasy memory of her death.

In Josefina's mind this very early memory was linked vaguely with another of a tall, incredibly vast apartment house near the central plaza of the city. And here there began to emerge from the confused, mysterious middle-world of babyhood the first clear and lasting impressions of unfolding life: memories of a big balcony-encircled patio—an endlessly astonishing four-sided universe of blinding light and cool, deep shadows; of climbing, crawling, and trailing foliage with giant, strong-stemmed leaves; of sounds—the constant splatter of water, the twittering of birds in cages, the chatter of women, and the laughter of young girls. There were huge burning flowers, and many cats, and children who played hopping and dancing games around the faïence fountain. Sometimes there would be the soft-strident sound of a guitar and singing in a strong, low voice; and sometimes the harsh, frightening cries of serving wenches quarreling at the fountain. The days were long here and filled with wonder. It was a happy, bewitching, contenting world—by far the happiest and most contenting that Josefina was ever to know.

Beyond it to the granite walls spread the town into which, later on, she ventured occasionally with her parents to see some marvel—the slow, solemn passing, perhaps, of a sacramental procession in all its terrible beauty of bejewelled images, and smoking candles and the dark, set faces of the marchers and image-bearers; or the going out of a troop of soldiers with banners and gleaming morions, and every horseman with the proud appearance of a prince or some other great personage; or maybe only the flower stalls on the plaza, and the unforgettable spicy fragrance of the huge carnations.

To Ávila in those days still clung some of the glory and color of its great Spanish past. The nobles of Castile maintained their medieval townhouses there, and Josefina sometimes saw them come clattering up from the Capital in their sumptuous coaches. They had given the town its name in the old days—"Ávila of the Knights"—and their occasional presence now was like an echo of the old knightly Spain.

Her child's ears were quick to hear such echoes, and her heart to keep them. Josefina heard and remembered, too, the gentle fall of Santa Teresa's footsteps in the cobbled streets of Ávila. The saint's house stood there still, the house in which she had been born: Josefina had seen it, and touched its time-soiled walls, and once she had sat for a little while on its very doorstep. From this house, two hundred years before, young Teresa de Cepeda had gone on her passionate and heroic search for mystical union with God. But so good, so real, so much a woman was Santa Teresa de Jesús that she had never left Ávila actually: she lived there still—a very great saint, but yet a simple peasant girl of Ávila, as all in that city felt and understood.

Such things of the past were Ávila—as much a part of Ávila still as were its ancient churches of San Pedro, Santo Tomás, and San Segundo, and its grim cathedral built like a buttress—which indeed it was—into the walls of the city; or its spacious plazas washed in mauve and ochre light, and the public fountains where brown-armed women came and went with water jars on their hips; or the immense mass of the Guadarramas. And, as she grew taller and her eyes contemplated gravely a wider and wider circle of the world's wonders, all of this— all of Ávila's form and life and history—became a part of Josefina also.

But Eva Helena, it seemed, became ever more the Andalusian. "It is better to live in Seville," she said. "It is always warm there, no?" She had never accustomed herself to the bitter Castilian winters. She was wearied also with childbearing; and Miguel had begun to disquiet her again. It was more than the warmth of Seville that Eva Helena remembered and missed: it was the quiet security of a time that could never, it seemed, return to her.

"What is it like there, Mamá?" Josefina would ask. "Tell me again about when you were a little girl."

"It was a very happy place: everybody there was happy. I lived with my mother, little daughter, in a very big house—a very big white house with a fountain, and many flowers and orange trees——"

"Where was your papá?"

"He was far away," Eva Helena said. "He went away to the wars in Italy, and he did not come back. I never saw my papá, 'Fina."

"Oh," Josefina said soberly. "Well, tell me some more, Mamita."

Jesusita and Concepción listened also as Eva Helena told them of the warm and sunny South where everybody was happy; but not with the same absorption as Josefina. Neither of them sighed as Josefina did when Eva Helena had finished.

You are most my daughter, 'Fina, Eva Helena said, a little sadly, to herself. You are most like me.

The others resembled Miguel. They had their father's dark eyes, soft now in childhood but inclined toward a bright, gypsy hardness. They were flighty, also, and either wept or giggled a great deal; and they were much closer to each other than to Josefina.

"It does not matter," Josefina said when her sisters kept something from her. "I have a very great secret of my own."

What her great secret was, she herself did not know exactly. It was only something that she felt about herself—some difference between Josefina and her sisters, between Josefina and every other person in the world: a difference vaguely but strongly felt, like a kind of faith.

One day, in the summer before she turned six, a very great lady visited Ávila—the young and incredibly lovely Doña María Francisca de Ariza y Lazan—and Josefina glimpsed her in her glittering coach. For a long time that night she lay awake, excited as with a shining vision, and struggling with a question that had come to her: "If it were possible, would you be that lady instead of Josefina?"

It was not a matter of her merely exchanging places with Doña María Francisca: of growing up, say, and becoming the beautiful daughter of a duchess, and riding into Ávila in a golden coach—but still remaining herself, Josefina. It was a graver matter than that, and she shaped her question with inexorable Spanish logic: "To be her, would you give up being Josefina?"

She lay uneasily for a long time in the darkness, a small, thin child with the image of a golden woman in her mind, searching for the answer she somehow had to find. And after a time she had it—for all her life, she knew—and she sighed and fell asleep: *I would rather be Josefina.*

She was a serious child, sedate and withdrawn, and possessed of an almost adult dignity; but capable also of sudden bursts of energy and passion—and sometimes of violent gusts of temper. She was like

29

her mother, but less gay, less Andalusian, as if the austere climate of Castile had chilled a little the warmth of her southern blood.

Still, of all the children, she was indeed most Eva Helena's daughter. She looked and acted—and no doubt thought and felt—like her mother. She had Eva Helena's voice, warm and soft, with a very slight and not at all unpleasing metallic quality. And her golden skin—of a depth and richness rather deeper than golden. And, most striking of all, the same large, heavily lashed, clear green eyes: true ojos rasgados, so much admired in every province of Spain, like Eva Helena's.

It pleased Josefina to know that she resembled her mother so much. She thought that Eva Helena was the most beautiful woman—not even excepting the Virgin Mary—that had ever lived. And she loved her in the same way that she loved the Virgin, but more deeply.

Her father she did not love at all. Not even when he sang and danced to make them laugh could she feel more than an amused fondness, oddly mixed with a kind of embarrassment, for Miguel. She sensed in him some lack of dignity. And occasionally there was a strange "crazy" quality about his gaiety that puzzled and frightened Josefina. It perturbed her mother also, she knew; sometimes it made her weep.

It was Eva Helena who was the source and center of all that made their little group of human souls a family: a safe little island in the center of a vast unknown. Childbearing, and exile, and sorrows that Josefina could as yet neither know about nor comprehend, had saddened her beauty somewhat. But she still remained a young woman of arresting face and figure: she still had some of the Sevillana's flashing spirit, and all of an hidalga's poise and dignity. She was by nature—and perhaps by birth—a great Spanish lady.

From her, Josefina learned how to speak with care and precision and with a pleasing voice; how to carry herself with pride; how to walk and sit well; how to use a fan . . . and all the other things that Eva Helena herself had learned in the house of the Conde de Mora. Among these were the arts of reading and writing; of singing and playing a little on the six-stringed guitar of Andalusia; and of dancing the dances that every child of the South learned, almost with walking. Eva Helena taught her also a proper Spanish love for God—for Jesús, María and José—and for all the saints, particularly the good Santa Teresa de Jesús.

"You learn so quickly, my little daughter!" Eva Helena smiled a slow, reflective smile. "But I think you learn the sevillanas more easily than you do your catechism, no?"

"I cannot help it, Mamita. God has made it easier for me to dance."

"Well, good. Let us dance to His greater glory then!"

Those were not unhappy years—those earliest years of her life, in

30

which the teachings of her mother, and the ancient ghosts of Ávila, and all the old and fearfully complicated urges of the blood were shaping out of obscurity and uncertainty the beginnings of a woman and a Spaniard called Josefina.

They were long, crowded, good years; and it was not until she was almost seven that Josefina began to feel—with the bewilderment and shock that only a child can experience—the presence of evil in the world: in her parents' house.

7

It was not success that ruined Miguel, as Eva Helena had feared it might. Success had provided him with better wine, and more time for dancing, and, no doubt, handsomer wenches; but it had not ruined him as a man. As now adversity did.

The clouds of misfortune gathered swiftly. One night, when neither of them could sleep because of the heat, Eva Helena asked, "Was Don Manuel pleased with the designs for his tiles, Miguel?"

She had heard a great deal from Miguel about those tile panels that Don Manuel, the Marqués de la Peña, had ordered for his new townhouse. They were to be in the latest style, depicting bullfighters, carnival revelers, soldiers, and card-players. Miguel had spent many days on the drawings: they were to be his masterpiece, really.

"He has not approved them yet," Miguel said.

There was a certain heaviness in his words that caused Eva Helena to turn to him quickly.

"Miguel," she asked, "has something gone wrong with the tiles?"

"No, nothing," he said gruffly. "Go to sleep now."

But something is wrong, Eva Helena thought. Something is wrong, but he does not want to admit it. She wondered why. Is it because he is dejected—or frightened, maybe?

It was both. Actually, the Marqués had withdrawn his commission for the panels, without any explanation. He was a marqués and was not required to explain. But that was not all. Others had followed the Marqués's example.

"I do not understand," Miguel said one day. "For no reason at all, my work is no longer wanted." He repeated dully, "For no reason at all."

But this was not quite true. That the popularity of Sevilla and Talavera ware had suddenly and sharply declined was something that other potters besides Miguel had discovered. Not, however, without a reason.

An unheard-of thing had happened in Spain: a Frenchman had been crowned king. And with his ascent to the throne had come an abrupt and radical change in national taste. Now to be fashionable, one must be French. One must take snuff in the French manner, and sup at nine o'clock, and wear the tricorn hat. And soon nobody wanted the beautiful old-fashioned Spanish tiles and plates and pitchers. Almost overnight the rage was for delicate and minute flowers and foliage and scrolls like point lace, and cherubs with purple wings, and fanciful little creatures with leaves sprouting from their heads.

"Jesús, María, and José and all the family!" Miguel groaned in disgust. "That such trash should be allowed in Spain!"

It did not help matters, however, to be indignant. As if word of the Marqués de la Peña's conversion to French ways and tastes had got around, more and more orders were canceled, while new commissions became fewer and fewer.

One day Eva Helena said hopefully, "Perhaps, Miguel, you also could work in the new style."

At this he turned on her with a sudden, savage vehemence. He had a rather small, dark face of an almost gypsy swarthiness. It had a kind of winsome charm when he was happy and smiling; now, twisted in unexpected rage, its ugliness struck Eva Helena like a blow.

"Ungrateful woman!" he shouted thickly. "Is this what you ask of me now? That I, Miguel Torres, make myself one of the French whores? Like an ordinary puta, eh? You would like that, no? It would bring in the money, eh?"

With each question he advanced a step toward her in a threatening way. She expected him to strike her finally, but she could not move. He grew more violent and obscene. Then he abruptly spat on the floor, whirled about, and left.

"Poor Miguel!" Eva Helena said, when she had recovered a little from her fright. "He is frightened. He feels that he is too old to learn the new style."

It was at this time that Josefina began to see in her mother's face that something bad was happening. Something was happening to them all—and it must be kept hidden and secret like some unmentionably ugly thing. So, whenever she heard her parents' voices become high and harsh, or when Miguel walked unsteadily like a baby and muttered strange words, she suffered a child's helpless fears and imaginings. She would go away and hide herself somewhere. Once, when she found Eva Helena weeping quietly by herself, she sat down beside her mother and wept also.

But there were happy moments, too. Miguel was not always strange or stupid with drink, and when he was not, he sometimes made a special effort to ingratiate himself with his daughters. He was fond of them all, and especially of Concepción, who was plainly his favorite. It gave neither Josefina nor Jesusita pleasure to hear him say tenderly, "Ay, Conchita! You are your father's jewel!"

Sometimes Miguel would bring them small gifts, such as roasted chestnuts, still hot from the vendor's brazier, wrapped in his handkerchief. At these times Eva Helena would come as close as she ever did to drawing aside the veil that hid the Evil.

"Pobrecito!" she would say, as if speaking of a child. "He is having so much trouble—the business is such a worry to him. Let him see that we love him, children."

So Josefina tried, but not very successfully perhaps, because she could not love Miguel really; and it was not unlikely that he, in turn, sensed this and resented it.

"Ay, those green eyes!" he said at one time in a mood of pique and self-pity. "I'll wager no man will ever find much love in them. Not even your poor father, eh?"

8

When she had reached the age of six, Josefina was given Yolanda.

One does not ever forget such a wonderful thing, and Josefina was to remember it all her life, even to the smallest detail. She was never to forget the kind of day it was—a flashing October day, flower-scented and filled with the music of voices and a single guitar in the patio below; and with the singing of the caged birds on all the lacy balconies. The sun streamed through the latticed window and made a pattern of graceful scrolls and curlicues on the red tile floor and halfway up the whitewashed wall. And Eva Helena's face was alight with some gentle inner excitement.

"Now close your eyes, little daughter," Josefina would forever hear her saying, "and keep them closed, no? Until I tell you 'Open.'"

She goes now to a great chest painted with red, yellow, and green designs. She places the key in the lock, turns it, and lifts the long iron hasp: there is a clanking sound. She looks quickly over her shoulder, and Josefina closes her eyes again, just in time. Josefina hears the hinges creak as Eva Helena lifts the heavy lid.

"Are you peeping?" Eva Helena asks.

"No, Mamita."

This is almost the truth. She can see only very vaguely, through her

33

thick lashes, the shadowy form of Eva Helena bending over the great chest. She waits forever.

"Madre de Dios!" she murmurs to herself in an excess of eagerness. "What can this be, Josefina?"

Her mother has taken a large bundle out of the chest and is unwrapping it now. Josefina suddenly clamps her hands across her eyes. She stops breathing.

"Look!" Eva Helena says. "Look now, my daughter—my little mother."

So Josefina uncovers her eyes, and looks, and what she sees is an impossible thing. It is a kind of dream—the dream of a doll of indescribable beauty, with pink porcelain cheeks, and blue porcelain eyes, and hair of a heavenly blondness. Its dress is of a richness that an infanta herself might envy—although of that certain vaguely foreign appearance that sets all dolls apart from things of the ordinary world. . . .

Eva Helena holds out this apparition to Josefina, who can only stare with enormous eyes and say nothing. Then Eva Helena places it in her arms, and Josefina holds it and begins to cry.

"So!" Eva Helena says. "Is this how you show that you are happy, simpleton?"

But now—nothing is improbable here—Eva Helena is crying too. They both weep, holding to each other, and the doll between them, until suddenly they are smiling. Then Josefina asks, "May I call her Yolanda?"

"Surely, my dear. I love Yolanda. It is a lovely name."

"I knew you would like it," Josefina says contentedly.

And that is exactly how she would have remembered it all her life—as one remembers any moment of complete and perfect happiness—had Miguel allowed it.

Josefina had not heard him come into the room. But she saw her mother look up with a startled, almost frightened expression. Then she heard her father say, "What are you doing in the chest, Evita?"

"The doll," Eva Helena said. "I have given Josefina the doll, Miguel."

"Ah, yes, the doll," Miguel said. "For which we paid the nine pesos."

"Do you remember, Miguel?" Eva Helena asked eagerly. "At the fair in the plazuela——"

"How could I forget?" Miguel said caustically. "It was something that you had to have—you could not do without it—like the green pickled almonds, eh?"

"But surely, Miguel——"

"You took advantage of me," Miguel said. "By the five wounds of God, Evita, you always take advantage of me. You get the best of me. Everybody gets the best of me."

34

His words had no meaning for Josefina; but she could feel some deep and bitter grudge they carried.

"You are not well, Miguel," Eva Helena said. "Why don't you go now and sleep a little?"

"Let me see that doll," Miguel said, stepping toward Josefina, "that doll of nine pesos."

"Miguel!"

Her mother was standing in front of her—between her and her father. Her back was very straight, and she looked extraordinarily tall to Josefina.

"Go away somewhere," Eva Helena said in a low, steady voice. "Leave us alone now."

Over her mother's shoulder, Josefina saw her father blink a couple of times; then a stupid smile spread over his dark, smallish features.

"Good!" he said, and it seemed that he was trying to make his words imply some threat. "Good! I'll go away, Evita." He added a shocking and senseless obscenity, turned stiffly, and left them alone.

"Pobrecito," Eva Helena said softly, with a kind of hesitant pity. He had done them no harm, really. He had hurt nothing but a memory.

9

Josefina was ten when Miguel finally lost his business. It became necessary, then, to leave the airy apartment on the big, noisy, flowery patio, and Miguel moved his family to new quarters in a mean section of the town close under the city wall. He hired out as a potter for a while, then turned to various odd jobs. He was successively a porter, water-carrier, muleteer, hawker of straw mats, and porter again. But much of his time was spent in taverns and pothouses where he drank away or lost at cards and mora most of his meager earnings; and Eva Helena and her children sometimes lacked enough to eat.

There was an old Spanish saying that poverty is no disgrace. But when Josefina saw her mother's face as she divided among them a few roasted acorns and a little bread for supper—keeping the smallest portion for herself—she knew better than the proverb. She understood that poverty was wholly an evil and shameful thing, to be feared and hated with all one's will. But something, also, to be borne as best one could while it lasted.

"It is necessary to have courage," Eva Helena explained to them, "and even to be a little gay, if one can. Because, children, this is not to last forever. We shall see good times again, never fear!"

Her daughters believed her, not only because of the braveness of her words, but because she managed somehow, in everything she did, to impart a gracious dignity—even a certain gaiety—to their sorry existence. She had a way of turning a few peppers and a little garlic, fried in oil, into a feast. She could create a small holiday out of a few cuartos earned by her needle. She almost—but not quite—made the old proverb come true.

It was during these drear days that Eva Helena began, for the first time, to talk much about her own childhood in the Conde de Mora's house. She made her stories rich with the small details that children love.

"In April, children, all the orange and lemon trees in that patio burst into blossom in a single day. And a hundred other kinds of flowers also bloomed. We wore the roses and carnations in our hair. The perfume of the garden made us faint. . . ."

Or——

"First came the chocolate, and then the white French bread, and the cakes. And then the sweets of so many kinds that I cannot remember them all. But shall I try, children?"

"Yes, try, Mamita!"

"Well, there was cinnamon candy, and orange-blossom bonbons, and bonbons perfumed with amber water, and sugar-coated almonds, and violet drops. . . ."

"And then?"

"Oh, yes. Then—" very fast—"candied limes, oranges, pears, apricots, peaches, rose leaves, jelly, caramelos, and—" very slowly—"little colored candies made of anise seed."

Or simply——

"All of señora's chemises were of silk, niñas, and all of them were edged in black-blonde lace. . . ."

How wonderful to hear these beautiful things from one who herself had known them! What a delight to imagine in one's own mind such marvels as the Conde's chapel and its silver statue of San Blas: "Its face was painted in the colors of life, and it had blue eyes and gilded hair." Or the Condesa's two hundred fans, each with a different scene painted on its silk—Diana's bath, or Leda and the Swan, or The Earthquake and Attack of the Moors on Orán. . . .

"Shall we ever see such miracles, Mamita?" they would ask her.

"Everything is possible, little daughters," she would answer, "if you but wish hard enough."

For all she told them was with a purpose, was designed to make her children feel a kind of mystic link with a world unknown—even in

36

imagination—to most other children. A world of gentle people and pleasant living and beautiful things—yet also a proud, exacting, relentless world—to which, if they but wished hard enough, they would surely belong one day.

She was brave, resolute, strong, cheerful, and even gay for them; and Josefina accepted without question her assurance when she said, "You will see, children. This is but a little rain that will blow away—and ay! how lovely the sun will shine for us then!"

Josefina studied hard to become good in all the things that Eva Helena taught them. She learned how to sew, and embroider with a frame, and cook; and as she grew older, she applied herself industriously to the studies she had begun as a little girl—to the reading of books, and writing of letters, and accompanying herself on the guitar when she sang, and to the Andalusian dance. She was very apt and learned more quickly than her sisters; and she had a special talent for the seguidillas.

"Niña! Ea!" Eva Helena murmured softly as she watched with what serious precision Josefina performed the gracious, yet rigorous, almost ritualistic movements of that ancient dance. "You do very well, my daughter." And then, aloud, "More softly now with the castanets—and slowly, no?"

Next to dancing, which was her great love, Josefina was fond of reading. There were no books in Miguel Torres's house, but Eva Helena—by what means she alone knew—procured a few. A volume of verse or tales, perhaps, a novel in the pastoral style, or even some of the plays of Lope or Calderón. But mostly they were books on religious subjects and very dull—except those mystic raptures of Santa Teresa, so simple, so natural and vivid, but yet so beautiful they made one weep.

Then Eva Helena brought home *The Quixote* one day, and it was as if the moon had suddenly come out from behind a cloud and flooded with light a silvery, magical landscape—a vista filled with windmills, and strange processions, and castle-inns, and mysterious forests through which the Knight of the Woeful Figure rode in mad and wonderful dignity. It was, for Josefina, as if she had made a discovery no less miraculous than Colón's finding of the Indies.

And of all the fascinating people who thronged that marvelous land, she liked best Marcella, the lovely shepherdess for whom Chrysostrome killed himself. She could not feel much pity for poor Chrysostrome: she thought him merely obstinate, if not stupid, in acting as he did. But *Marcella*—ah, what sorrow, what sweet sorrow, to be cursed with beauty as tragic as hers!

Josefina stood before her glass and thought of herself as that ravishing star-crossed girl; and she repeated softly aloud: "I am a distant

37

flame and a sword far off. . . . Heaven has not yet willed that I should love by destiny. And it is vain to think that I shall ever love by choice."

She stood there before her mirror and gazed at herself with great shadowy eyes as she recited Marcella's words, and tried to look very tragic indeed.

"Shall I some day love by destiny?" she asked herself. "Or will it be by choice?"

She regarded herself gravely and intently, with something near to curiosity. She seemed different—almost strange—to her very self these days. It was sometimes as if she were someone else—someone apart from Josefina María Torres. . . .

The world about her had also taken on a certain difference—a mysterious and secret newness which was not unlike the silvery, magical spell of Don Quixote's dreamy universe. And, like the Knight of the Woeful Figure, Josefina knew that in such a world there was nothing, really, that could not take place . . . if one only wished it hard enough.

10

One's life, she began to learn, is shaped by a multitude of small, even unnoticed events, and by a few great ones. And now there occurred a series of great events that were to mark her mind and soul so deeply that she was never to free herself from their disfigurement.

The first of these was the death of her youngest sister, Concepción.

In August every year the intermittent fevers killed a number of people in Ávila. They recurred with such regularity that the inhabitants of the Castilian plain had become quite accustomed, if not resigned, to them. But familiarity had made them no less terrifying; and when Eva Helena detected the first dreaded symptoms of the disease in her own child, she gave way to an unexpected panic.

This was the first time that Josefina had ever seen her mother so distraught, so bereft of self-control. And this frantic anxiety—this sudden and utterly improbable disintegration of her mother's inner strength—shocked and alarmed Josefina even more than the horrors of her sister's illness. She felt something slipping away from her, and she prayed to God and the Blessed Virgin to help them all.

But Eva Helena steadied herself as the fever ran its course, one day a frightening delirium, the next a quiet, bright-eyed languor. She did what she could to make Concepción comfortable and to give her, in the lucid intervals, hope and courage. No doctor came to see Concepción, because the price of a doctor's visit was one real of silver; and there was not one real of silver in the house.

Twice Josefina went to the surgeon, nevertheless, and begged him to come. The first time he was playing dominoes with an elegant young abbé who tried to make sly jokes with her: that time she burst into tears and ran away. The next time the doctor was about to go on a visit to a patient who had money, and he disdained even to speak to her. But the third time she had money also.

She wondered why she had not thought of Yolanda before. There was a tiny shop on the market square where one might buy, or sell, any small thing. She carried Yolanda to this shop. At the entrance she quickly kissed her china cheek and straightened her dress.

"Good-by, my heart," she said. "In any case, you are now too old for dolls, Josefina."

The shopkeeper gave her five reales for Yolanda. Of these the doctor demanded two, although his ordinary fee was one real. But he came, at any rate, dressed in black and riding his mule, and he bled Concepción in the foot to purge her of the humor that was making her sick.

"If the fever does not subside by tomorrow," he said impressively, "it will be necessary to drain away more of the excess fluid." He added generously that the price of the next visit would be only one real.

"Go with God," Eva Helena said dully.

She seemed to know that there would be no need for another visit from the doctor, for any more letting of her daughter's blood. She sat quietly beside Concepción's bed during the long, stifling night, doing whatever small and futile offices one can perform for the dying. At daybreak she awoke Josefina and Jesusita. She sent Jesusita for the priest, and to Josefina she said, "I think that God wishes Conchita to leave us soon, my little daughter. It does not seem proper that her father should be away now. Perhaps you can fetch him?"

She ended on a question and a note of hopefulness. Miguel had been away for several days, none of them knew where. Yet it was not his nature to stray far from home: Eva Helena named some neighborhood taverns where he might be found.

"Be at rest, Mamita," Josefina said. "I shall find him and bring him home." She kissed her mother's pale mouth. She suddenly felt greatly older—almost a woman.

Still, she was frightened a little when she went out into the gray, hushed streets. She had never been abroad at such an early hour before: what could one expect to meet with at such a time? It was impossible to tell.

She passed long rows of tall, stained houses, each with a dark and evil-smelling street entrance from which a narrow staircase ascended to the upper floors. Once a rough voice reached out for her from one of these cavernous openings. She hurried past such fearful places, darting along the crooked streets in the gloom of lowering balconies. Several times she passed the entrances of what, from the shouts and songs inside, she took to be taverns; but she did not have the courage to inquire for her father.

Then, as though a great light had been struck, the sun suddenly cleared the Guadarramas and flooded the whole town with its full, direct rays. Almost immediately, it seemed, Ávila began to bestir itself. A peasant with a dozen brace of partridges slung over his shoulders passed Josefina on his way to market, and gave her a curious but friendly greeting. A cart loaded with wood forced her into a foul entranceway. A serving wench shouted a warning and heaved a bucket of slops from an upstairs window. . . .

Josefina scurried to the protection of a sheltering balcony. Here she dared to stop and look about. She realized that she had been hastening blindly through strange streets. Now, finding that she had come a considerable distance from home, she endeavored to return to the Street of the Two Friends, in which she lived.

Only a few steps from her own door she found Miguel.

At first she did not identify the man in that dark doorway as her father. She saw only a drunken man propped against the wall, his head sagging on his chest, his legs sprawled grotesquely—like the legs of a doll or a dead man—on the pavement. But some vague flicker of recognition caused her to bend swiftly and examine his face.

"Papá!" she cried out. It was a cry of incredulity and horror. "Papá —what has happened?"

No answer came out of the sagging, slavering mouth. Josefina had to shake him vigorously, for a long time, in order to awaken him. At last he raised his small, dark, bristly face and opened his eyes. They were blank and bloodshot, and they stared at Josefina for a while in stupid incomprehension. Then Miguel smiled dreadfully at his daughter. He muttered a string of unintelligible sounds, among which Josefina could distinguish only one:

"Conchita . . ."

Someone has brought him word, she said to herself. He has been trying to find his way home.

The thought struck her like a wave of nausea that now she must take him to that dim, quiet room where his favorite daughter was dying. A terrible thing was happening to her sister in that room; now it must become an utterly ugly thing. She thought of Eva Helena's strong, pale, grief-composed face, and she cried aloud, "Mother of God! What shall I do?"

A passing crockery vendor looked at her curiously and made a ribald jest. Miguel rolled his eyes upwards and smiled at her again. Then his head flopped suddenly down on his chest. From one leg of his ragged breeches a trickle of urine spread and formed a dark pool on the pavement.

Josefina found herself running wildly along the street, as if pursued by some horror. She passed her own door without seeing it and continued down the narrow, twisting Street of the Two Friends. When she came to the Church of San Segundo, she darted into it blindly—as a criminal might, seeking sanctuary.

The Church of San Segundo was very old, and even darker than most small Spanish churches. At this early hour its gloom was broken only by the ruby glow of the altar light, and it was completely empty.

Josefina dropped to her knees on the stone floor and, sitting on her heels, buried her face in her hands. Automatically, she began to pray. And her prayer—perhaps in response to some profound and desperate instinct—was not to God but to His mother.

"Hail Mary, full of grace, the Lord is with thee. Blessed art thou amongst women . . ."

But the nausea seized her again, this time with appalling violence. She left off her prayer to the Virgin and was wretchedly sick.

11

Concepción's death appeared to sober Miguel for a while. He even obtained steady work as a driver of carts, and brought home a little money occasionally. And he was not so often drunk.

Eva Helena made much of Miguel's recovery; but it could be seen from the start that it was not likely to last. For Miguel was little more than a remnant of the man he once had been. He had even lost his love of a good time. He had become morose and sullen, and was given now to swift and unreasonable outbursts of anger.

Josefina felt in him a special resentment toward herself. She sensed that, in some vague and muddled way, Miguel held her responsible for his failure to reach his Conchita's deathbed in time. His presence in the house was not a happy thing for her, although Eva Helena tried to make it appear as something good and hopeful.

"Look!" she would say, showing them the small hare Miguel had brought home. "Look!" As though he had performed some miracle. "Your father provides well for us, no?"

But not even Eva Helena's boundless hope and faith could save them from the pattern of their destiny. It was not long before Miguel began to disappear again, more and more often, and for longer stretches of time. He provided them with nothing but shame and misery, really. They all suffered once more from hunger and cold and the simple, dull pain of poverty; but Eva Helena also from a secret distress: she had become pregnant again.

Then, like some ugly and obscure alley-happening, in the evil darkness of the night, there occurred the second great event that was to scar the mind and heart of Josefina forever.

One night Miguel came home while they were all asleep. They were awakened by his pounding on the door and shutters, and by his cursing, and by another shrill, high sound they could not understand. It was frightening to hear this strange uproar in the darkness, and Josefina began to cry.

"Hush," Eva Helena said. "He means no harm. Let us just remain quiet, no?"

"Do not let him in, Mamá," Josefina begged. She was trembling, as if with a chill. "For the love of God, do not open the door!"

"Perhaps if we remain quiet, he will think we are asleep and will go away," Eva Helena said.

But he did not go away, and soon those living nearby were awakened by the din and began to shout violent threats and imprecations. Eva Helena and the girls sat huddled in the cold darkness, hoping desperately that the horror would end at last; but finally Eva Helena said, "This is too heavy a disgrace, even for us, children. We shall have to let him in."

She lit a candle and they all dressed hurriedly, as if they had been roused from sleep to go somewhere. Then Eva Helena crossed herself and opened the door; or Miguel, rather, opened it with a violent kick as soon as she had drawn the bolt.

"Blood of Christ!" he shouted, so that all in the neighborhood must have heard him. "Am I locked out of my own house?"

They saw then that someone was with him—a bedraggled gypsy slut who stared at them with black, glittering, insolent eyes. It was her laughter they had heard, mixed with Miguel's pounding and cursing.

"Do you see, Chata?" Miguel said to her. "I am not wanted in my own family. They are ashamed of me, no?" He stepped aside and bowed like a grandee. "But enter, chica."

The gypsy sauntered forward a step or two; then, finding herself confronted by Eva Helena, hesitated. A look of mixed arrogance and uncertitude flickered across her dark features. She rasped at Miguel, "Son of the Great Whore! I am not welcome, eh? Do you stand there and see me insulted, then?"

"Allow her to pass," Miguel said, with a drunken gravity.

"No, Miguel," Eva Helena said. "In God's name, do not bring any more shame on us. Don't make any more disturbance, Miguel. Go away now."

"That I go away now!" Miguel shouted. "Do you hear that, Chata? This great lady—this hidalga—does not wish me in her house. I am not good enough for her, eh?"

He appeared to be in a simple, drunken frenzy; but, even in her terror, Josefina could see that something stronger than drink had hold of him—something old and very deep and bitter, and too powerful to be held in leash any longer. It had broken free at last, this ugly thing, and it showed itself now in every twisted line of her father's face.

"I am not good enough," Miguel said, very slowly and heavily, and with some malignant private irony.

"No, Miguel!" Eva Helena begged.

"I am not good enough for the bastarda of the Conde de Mora."

It may have been that Eva Helena struck him then. To Josefina, this nightmare, like all nightmares, had no beginning but only a sudden, shocking, paralyzing culmination. She was to remember nothing whole: only—and forever—the dark disordered fragments of the dreadful dream:

The long swinging shadows that sprang suddenly across walls and ceiling—the gypsy's eyes glittering in the flaring candlelight—her mother's huddled form, turned toward the wall as if to protect something in her arms from harm—the soft, terrible sound of Miguel's blows—— And then her mother's moan:

"For God's love, Miguel, the baby. . . ."

Josefina flung herself at her father, tearing and clawing at him until, in a momentary flash of clarity, she saw his face turn toward her and his fist shoot out. He struck her once, savagely on the mouth, and she sank to her knees in a pool of blackness.

When her head had cleared a little, she saw Miguel kicking at a huddled shape in the corner; then she heard the strident, suddenly urgent voice of the gypsy; and then all was quiet again but for Eva Helena's sobs. Josefina pressed the back of her hand against her mouth and tasted the salty, metallic taste of her own blood.

Daylight came at last, hard and cold on Eva Helena's gray, sweat-beaded face; and with it came the final horror of that evil night. Some women of the neighborhood—drawn by compassion and a neighborly curiosity, no doubt—arrived and forced Josefina and Jesusita to leave, while they remained with Eva Helena. It was not until the end of the day that the girls were allowed to return home to their mother.

Eva Helena lay under a thin blanket, her eyes closed, her face the color of a corpse's in the dim light of the whitewashed room.

"Is she dead?" Josefina asked.

"She is asleep now," a thickset woman with a heavy mustache said. She wiped the sweat from her face with a big handkerchief and smiled obliquely at another neighbor. "Let us pray that she sleeps well—and that we have some peace tonight!"

Josefina was to hate this woman, and her memory, for the rest of her life.

12

Two months later Eva Helena had just begun to recover from shock and the loss of her baby. They were months that would have been unsupportable, except for the money that Eva Helena received in response to a letter she had written to the Condesa de Mora. It was the first time she had ever appealed to the aging Condesa for help, and it was to be the last.

"You see, children," she said, "there are still some people in the world who are good and generous."

That seemed to mean more to her, almost, than the money itself. But Josefina, for the first time in her life, did not feel a warming response in her own breast to her mother's simple hopefulness and faith.

Ay! that may be so, she said to herself, with a new bitterness, but they are so very few, Mamita.

They were spared, at least, the dread of Miguel's intermittent appearances now. He had left Ávila, they heard, and had returned to the Capital: at any rate, he bothered them no more. And when, at last, they learned that he had been taken in a clumsy attempt at robbery and shipped off to the mines of Asturia, the news cast no shadow of tragedy, or even of sorrow, over his family, but only a feeling of release and relief.

Eva Helena cried a little, but more for lost hopes and crumpled dreams than for the weak and drunken man who, for so many years, had brought them little but misery and disgrace.

Yet now, deprived of even the pitiable support that Miguel had provided, she and her children must face a saddening new side of poverty: to the nagging ache of actual want was to be added the unhappiness of separation. For Eva Helena, in desperate lack of anything better, now hired herself out as a servant in the house of one Doña Petra Baca, called La Greca, a superannuated actress who had once

44

been the rage of the Spanish theater and was now an almost equally famous virago.

"Always give the road to winds and madmen," they said of her, "and to La Greca."

Doña Petra still called herself, and obliged others to call her, La Greca, the name that had been so widely—if not irreproachably—famous a dozen years before. She was a willful, grasping, vain old woman who would not let go of her past.

La Greca paid Eva Helena little and abused her much. Each time Josefina saw her mother, she observed how the lines of fatigue and sorrow—and, most pitiful of all, of defeat at last—were making her once serene and lovely features heavy and almost ugly. And her heart ached.

This is a thing that can happen to me also, she thought. I am so like my mother. Then, with a hardness she had come to feel of late within herself: Let us make sure that it does not, Josefina!

She and Jesusita did not live with their mother in La Greca's house, which was very elegant but rather small. They were lodged—for ten cuartos a month taken out of Eva Helena's wages—in a nearby hovel owned by the actress. And Eva Helena was now allowed to see her daughters only when La Greca permitted.

In their dingy little room Josefina and Jesusita had neither bed nor table nor chairs, but only a dilapidated brazier and a tiny altar adorned with paper flowers and dedicated to the Virgin Mary. They slept on a small heap of straw, and covered themselves in winter with a single tattered blanket.

Over the brazier—whenever they could get any charcoal—they cooked a poor puchero without meat; or, if they were especially lucky, fried an egg. But often their meal was only a mess of chick peas, or a handful of roasted chestnuts and a couple of ounces of bread, or a lettuce salad perhaps with a little rancid oil. And sometimes they did not eat at all.

From La Greca they received at rare intervals scraps of castoff clothing; and from Eva Helena whatever small sums she was able to extract from her miserly mistress, or whatever bits of food she could smuggle out of La Greca's kitchen.

"I do not feel that it is wrong for me to take this, children," she would say apologetically, unwrapping a few cakes, perhaps, that she had carried away in her handkerchief, "because señora does not pay me all she owes."

Then, to herself, as she watched with what famished eagerness her daughters devoured the stolen food: But I would not do differently, in any case!

Josefina and Jesusita, as they grew older, also began to earn a few cuartos for themselves occasionally. They wrote letters for their less literate neighbors and read the newspapers for them. They carded wool of the Merino sheep that grazed the hills around Ávila—hard, disagreeable work that made their fingers bleed. They made bobbin lace, and helped with the great linen-washings of the hidalgas, and welcomed any other task that might earn for them the ingredients of a cold soup or a half-loaf of bread.

And sometimes they went up to La Greca's house to assist their mother in her work.

These, of course, were great occasions in their drab and meager lives. La Greca paid them nothing, but they brought back from her house something more precious than the few coins that another, more generous, might have given them. They carried away memories on which they lived for days: of a dreamlike patio paved with majolica and cooled by a faïence fountain; of a great dim-ceilinged sala thronged with ladies and gentlemen elegant and exotic in the new French dress; of music, and card-playing, and dancing, and laughter, and gay talk they understood hardly at all; and, if they were fortunate, of stolen sips of water ice or nibbles of sweetmeats.

"This," Josefina said wistfully, "is what it must have been like in the Condesa's house."

But Eva Helena was at pains to correct her. La Greca may have been a great actress, she explained, but she was not a great lady. Her parties, if not frivolous or even downright vulgar, were hardly to be compared with the Condesa's brilliant entertainments. And of the guests who frequented them—perhaps the less said the better!

Josefina and Jesusita talked this over, trying to determine in their own minds the exact difference between life at La Greca's and that in the Condesa de Mora's house—which, alas, they knew only from Eva Helena's descriptions.

"It is the difference between La Greca and our mother," Josefina said at last. "It is a hard thing to find words for, but very easy to see."

"That is true," Jesusita agreed. "But it may also be true that Mamá has become a little old-fashioned."

"Perhaps you are right. It is difficult for many of the older people, I have heard, to become used to the modern ways."

"Myself, I find La Greca's parties very amusing," Jesusita said, with an air of sophistication. "For example, the time I came on the fat captain and that dancer, La Tirana, behind the palms——"

"That you spare me that again, Jesusita!"

"Mojigata!" Jesusita mocked.

It was a word that meant prude or hypocrite, or perhaps merely one excessively fastidious, as Jesusita used it. But it did not please Josefina. She arose abruptly and left the room.

46

Well, 'Fina! Jesusita thought. What is there to upset you so?

She did not understand her sister any more. Sometimes she believed that Josefina was indeed a prude; but she suspected, also, something more complicated than simple prudery. She could not guess what: they had grown a little strange with each other. Sometimes they quarreled now, and occasionally their quarrels were violent.

But they loved each other, nevertheless; and it was fortunate that they had each other, and that they were young. It helped to make the burden of their bleak existence supportable. They had the courage, even, to make wry jokes about their poverty. For example, they called their miserable stylike room La Casa de las Tres Bellotas: the House of the Three Acorns. Because, on one occasion they had been reduced to only that—to three roasted acorns—for supper.

But it was not the actual hunger and cold and the utter cheerlessness of their environment that hurt most. Far harder to bear, for Josefina at least, was the stark indignity of being poor.

When you are in rags, and have no money, nor any friends with money, you must suffer quietly all sorts of insults and slights—unless, of course, you are a beggar, in which case you have God on your side and no one dare offend you—she discovered. And if you are a young girl living alone with your sister, and just coming into womanhood, and of a rather extraordinary beauty, there is no end to the affronts that one may expect.

"Oh, don't take it so much to heart, 'Fina," Jesusita told her. "Be like me. Make a joke of it."

She had come home to find Josefina sobbing on the pile of straw they called a bed: a buyer at the market square had put his arm around her and slipped his hand beneath her bodice.

"I don't want to be like you!" she wailed. "He was a filthy, low wretch—but not too low to dare treat me like a whore."

My poor sister! Jesusita thought. She will not have an easy time of it. She has too much pride and she is too pretty. I wish I had such beauty—I would know what to do with it!

Jesusita, as she herself realized, was unlike Josefina in many ways. Physically, she patterned after their father. She was dark, slight, and wiry; she talked and walked fast; she had snapping black eyes, jet hair, a large mouth, and teeth that flashed arrestingly when she smiled. She left an impression of energy rather than beauty. Still, she was not unnoticed by the young men of the neighborhood.

Of this Jesusita was neither unconscious nor unappreciative. She accepted the rough attentions of woodcutters, water-carriers, and even sheepherders—so long as they were good-looking and not too dull-witted—in a way that puzzled and sometimes shocked Josefina.

It was as if some strange inner change was taking place in her sister at the same time that her body was changing from the body of a child to that of a woman. . . . It was, Josefina thought, as if all at once Jesusita were no longer the daughter of Eva Helena.

Look at her! she said to herself, watching her sister tussle playfully with a young water-carrier at the public fountain: That she should allow such a one even to talk to her!

As for herself, the young men had learned to leave her alone. But it had taken several lessons to teach them the wisdom of controlling their tongues and hands. They looked at her now with an odd mixture of respect and resentment and longing. There was something unfair, it seemed to them, in such a withholding of God's blessings; and something frightening, also, in the suddenness with which such serenity could erupt into fury. It was perplexing even to Jesusita.

"What harm is there in it?" she demanded. "It is amusing to tease these dolts."

"They don't amuse me," Josefina said. "They revolt me."

"All of them, 'Fina?"

"Yes, every one."

"Alexo also?"

Alexo Sedano was a handsome young carpenter with an easy smile and excessively long sideburns, whose shop Josefina and Jesusita often passed on their way to the market plaza. He had, Jesusita decided, fallen fatally in love with Josefina on sight. Of this she had many signs and proofs—among which was a small, low chair Alexo had made for them in violation of the law, which prohibited a carpenter, of course, from making furniture.

"Alexo most of all!" Josefina said.

Jesusita observed the flush that had suddenly warmed her sister's skin, and she wondered whether it was caused by anger, or embarrassment—or was Josefina, perhaps, keeping something from her?

"Excuse me, 'Fina, I do not believe that," she said. "I think you are a little gone on him. How, for instance, do you feel when he smiles at you like that?"

"I feel nothing. I only think. And what do I think? I think he acts like a fool."

That is not the truth, Josefina, she added to herself. You do feel many things. You feel excited. And angry. And a little sad. And you think that maybe you are in love with this Alexo and maybe you hate him. And your knees become weak.

"Well, if he smiled at me in that way, I should feel plenty!" Jesusita said.

"I am not you. I am Josefina."

She was not sorry that she was Josefina. Never since that golden duchess had ridden into Ávila in her glittering coach had she ever

48

wished to be anyone else. But it puzzled and disquieted her that she should be so unlike her sister in certain ways—so unlike every other girl she knew. She got no pleasure from this odd hostility that all men seemed to arouse in her; and she was concerned that there should be this thing about herself that she could neither name nor understand.

There developed a certain strangeness—the sort of separateness that is never so wide and deep as between sisters—in Josefina's and Jesusita's relationship. Yet they remained loyal to each other and gave each other the courage to bear the dreadful indignity and depression of their poverty. And, together, they even contrived to find a little happiness in their miserable lot.

Like all Andalusians—which they were by blood, if not by birth—they loved to dance. They had no music, but Josefina had saved a pair of castanets that Miguel, in one of his propitiatory interludes, had given her. And this was all the accompaniment they needed.

Over and over, in the shuttered seclusion of their little room, they practiced the Andalusian dances that Eva Helena had taught them. They corrected each other, applauded and encouraged with beating of the palms and with soft, throaty exclamations—*Chica! Otra! Otra!*— and strove to remember what their mother had taught them. And when Jesusita was tired or lost interest, which she did rather easily, Josefina would continue alone for hours.

Besides the seguidillas, they learned new dances also at the fairs and fiestas: the seductive and voluptuous ones of the city of Cádiz, whose dancing girls had been esteemed so highly by the Romans; and the gay, bouncing Aragonese jota, which Josefina came to love almost more than the amorous dances of the South.

Once, when Josefina was fourteen, there came to Ávila a celebrated dancer to perform at the feria. Her name was Mariá de la Chica. She was small and ugly and vulgar; but such was the fire of her nature, and so truly great was her art, that all who saw her forgot everything but the passion and brilliance of her performance. Until she saw Mariá de la Chica, Josefina had thought of the dance in terms of itself alone; now she thought of it in terms of the dancer—of the great artist who could shape and dominate it. She was on fire to be like María de la Chica some day.

On several occasions, too, Josefina and Jesusita stole beyond the walls of Ávila and, from the concealment of the boulders that strewed the plain, watched the gypsies dance their own dances. They were wild and sensual things that stripped the beautiful Andalusian dance of all its impersonal and abstract dignity and gave it, instead, a passionate intensity without discipline, without pride. It was also wicked, as the gypsies danced it. They laid aside their long, smocklike dresses at last; and Josefina could understand why Eva Helena had not taught it to them! But she studied it, nevertheless, watching from behind the granite boulders, and practiced it in the little shuttered room; and finally she learned to dance it like any gypsy. . . .

She had been fifteen then, and thin, and often sad, and almost always hungry. But now—now as she sat here, three years later and hungry still, in this miserable inn at Roa, drowsing over a dull part in a dull play—it seemed to her that life had not been wholly bad in Ávila. For she was fifteen then; and nothing—an old Spanish proverb declared—nothing is ugly at fifteen.

13

A patch of sunlight had lain like a rug on the tiled floor when Pepe went away: now, as he returned, it had moved halfway up the whitewashed wall. Yet, Josefina still sat where he had left her, with the script of *The Star of Seville* lying on her lap.

"Ah, my little dove!" he exclaimed. "I see you have been obedient to your Uncle Pepe. You have been diligent, no?"

She raised her eyes and gazed at him with a kind of patient distaste, and said nothing.

"Look!" Pepe said. "Look what Uncle Pepe has brought—see how he rewards you!"

He placed a small brown-paper package on the table and ceremoniously opened it. The package contained a large white roll and a length of sausage. The spicy, smoky fragrance of the sausage caught at her very stomach.

"For me, Uncle Pepe?" she asked, with a not very successful indifference. "Where did you get it?"

"Pepe has ways!" He carefully cut the sausage into short cylinders and removed the casing. "He does not often fail his children, eh?"

He broke the roll and handed her a piece of the creamy Spanish bread and a section of the sausage. She munched zestfully and smiled at Pepe with something like affection.

"Do you love your Uncle Pepe?" he asked, sensing the propitiousness of the moment.

"It is natural," she said, "to love those who feed you."

"Well," Pepe said, "it won't be easy to make those bastards weep on an empty stomach."

"So!" she laughed. "You feed me as one feeds a nag before a hard trip. Is that right?"

"Yes, that is right, my daughter."

"Well, I no longer love you then."

"That grieves me," Pepe said. "But it is not important in the larger view. The important things are, first that you have been fed, and second that you have learned the part."

"I have studied the part with all my mind and strength——"

"Good! Let us go over it now."

"But I cannot," Josefina said. "I do not know it, Uncle Pepe."

Pepe let his mouth fall open and stared at Josefina in tragic unbelief. "This," he said heavily, "cannot be true."

"But it is," Josefina said miserably. "I cannot learn those stupid lines. I cannot memorize, Pepe. Even when I was a little girl, I could not get my catechism by heart."

Pepe gazed across an imaginary proscenium at an unseen audience. "She speaks of catechisms," he groaned. "Of catechisms! Perhaps she can recite the catechism tonight!"

She said contritely, "I am sorry, Uncle Pepe. I am good for nothing, really, but to dance."

"Perhaps that is so," Pepe agreed. "If even for that."

He began to pace the room. Josefina did not watch him. She listened to his anguished breathing, and she thought: This is indeed ridiculous, Josefina. But do not laugh. That you should weep, rather! What you have come to, La Sola!

Suddenly Pepe whirled about and rushed over to her. "Estúpida!" he screeched at her. "Half-wit! Mother of Christ, let me not kill her!"

She knocked over her chair in getting out of his reach. She retreated a few steps, turned, and hurled the script of *The Star of Seville* at him.

"Beast!" she said coldly. "Old ugly beast! Don't touch me, beast, or I shall scratch your eyes out."

He stood there looking at her with the pale, watery eyes she had threatened to scratch out—a thin man with sagging skin who had once been fat—a sick, forlorn man who had once been lustful and jolly. His mouth quivered, and he seemed about to cry; but he summoned up his dignity, and said, "Forgive me, daughter. I have had nothing to eat since yesterday's breakfast."

He said it so sadly, so pitifully, that she wanted to laugh. Yet, knowing that it was probably true, and thinking of the bread and sausage, she wanted to cry too. She flung her arms about him—how thin and bony his shoulders felt beneath his shirt!—and comforted him as one would sooth a sobbing child.

"Poor Uncle Pepe!" she said. "That my stupidity should have caused you this grief!"

"It is nothing," Pepe said. "It is nothing that can be helped, anyhow."

51

He added, with a somewhat pathetic attempt at briskness, "Let us consider now what to do."

Ah, yes, let you consider, Pepe! she thought, with a sudden pang of pity. There is little else for you to do now. You are sick and hungry —and you are frightened that the lousy innkeeper will not like our entertainment. He will throw us out then, and where shall we go next? She paused in her thoughts and smiled a faint, dry smile. Perhaps you had better consider a little also, Josefina. Here is Uncle Pepe. He is a man and—like all men, no?—he is vain and deceitful and he thinks of nobody, really, but himself. . . .

"A song, maybe——" Uncle Pepe said.

Josefina did not hear him. She was gazing at him with a dreamy objectivity; but her thoughts about him were shaping into simple, solid words.

Pepe is always acting, she was thinking. He acts to hide his weakness and fear—not only from the rest of us, but also from himself. Yet, what man does not? Look how wretched he is! He took you in, remember, when nobody else would: and if he expected a little payment—well, he did not get it, after all! And he did give you the bread and sausage. And he is sick now, and frightened——

"Listen," she said suddenly. "I have something to tell you."

"Ah, you have a better suggestion, no?"

She gazed at him with the steady, reflective look that, by itself, expresses—and asks—confidence. She said: *"I am La Sola."*

He had inquired only twice about her identity. The first time was when she had joined his troupe. She had told him then, "I am called La de los Ojos Verdes." And he had said, "Good—little Green Eyes— that is what we will call you here." And no more.

The second time—only this afternoon—was when he had asked her abruptly, "Who are you, my daughter?" She had ignored his question then, and had told him to go and light his candle to the Virgin of Atocha.

Between these brief inquiries, he had displayed no curiosity at all about her past. He had never been a prying one, at any rate. And now, when she told him, "I am La Sola," there was no sign of surprise in his melancholy eyes.

"My daughter," he said, "I have known that for a long time."

If he is acting, she thought, he is doing a very good job of it. If he is telling the truth, it is even more remarkable. Well, in any case——

"Then," she said, "you know what my talent is—what I do best, no?"

"Everyone knows that," Uncle Pepe said, with a small bow.

"It is not acting, eh?"

"But acting is less dangerous," Uncle Pepe said. "It is less dangerous than dancing—for La Sola."

This was true. It was far easier for her to disguise her face than her style. She could make herself look like someone else, but she must always dance like La Sola. This was true, but what did he mean?

"And so, Uncle Pepe?" she asked.

"If I have never asked you to dance," he said soberly, "that is why."

Either you are the greatest of liars and hypocrites, she said to herself, or you are an angel.

"Well, tonight I shall dance for them," she said. "I won't make them weep, Pepe. But maybe I can do even better than that, eh?"

"Someone will surely recognize you——"

"Quiet, Uncle Pepe! You worry like an old woman. Hurry now—fetch Jacinto and his guitar."

She let her arms drift languidly upwards and her fingertips made pito. She turned her clear green eyes on Pepe and smiled absently.

"Ay, caramba!" she said, and her voice was low, softly strident, almost Moorish. "They shall see what it means to dance the seguidillas!"

Suddenly she felt released and carefree, reckless and young, and filled with an exhilaration she had not felt since that miraculous afternoon when—she was fifteen then, and thin and poor, but sure of her beauty—she had danced in La Greca's garden for La Maya. She felt again how the trembling had rushed along her limbs, and how the smooth weight of the great Maya's own castanets had lain under her curled fingers—and how the Maya's arrogant, dark-glancing eyes had smiled ever so faintly. . . . And now——

Angelito's hand brushes his guitar. She bows her head and listens to the music, her body still, her young forehead cleft by a little frown: the music takes possession of her like a spell, like a mood: her castanets float upwards and she begins her dance.

"Olé!" La Greca murmurs softly, then flushes and is silent. She is glanced at reproachfully; all watch the Maya's face for some sign of her reaction. But the Maya's face is expressionless; her dusky eyes are fixed in a preoccupied stare—as if at something far away; she says nothing. . . .

The dance is finished. Josefina sinks to the floor in a deep curtsy, head bowed, arms outstretched, as Eva Helena had taught her. Still the Maya says nothing. There is an interminable moment of silence, of emptiness, of terror. La Greca clenches her dark-veined hands and turns her face away. Josefina knows that she can never rise, that she is about to faint—perhaps to die of shame. Then the Maya says softly:

53

"Ea! You have everything, my child!"

There is a little burst of applause and talk then, and an inclination of heads and fluttering of fans; for when the Maya said that, it was almost as if the Virgin de la Soledad herself had spoken.

"Of a certainty," the guests repeat. "She has everything!" And they nod, smiling, toward the Maya.

Manuela Maya had never been beautiful, and she was no longer very young; but she was still the dominating personality of the Spanish theater. Her mere appearance on the stage called forth applause so violent as to frighten women and provincials. When her sedan chair appeared on the streets, a great and sometimes disorderly crowd always collected. She had as lovers a succession of grandees, soldiers, poets, bullfighters and churchmen that included some of the most arrogant names in Spain.

So it was a great coup for La Greca when, with Lujan the critic and several other personages of the theater, the Maya came up from Madrid to attend her party—a tribute, as all must see, to her own former glory. And there was nothing, of course, that La Greca had omitted to make her entertainment agreeable to her famous guest.

Yet, as it had turned out, nothing in all of La Greca's elaborate preparations—the profusion of delicacies, the water ices and sorbetes cooled with snow from the Guadarramas, the spectacular flower pieces, Angelito's music—none of these had pleased the Maya so much as the dancing of her serving-woman's daughter.

La Greca could not know what the Maya was thinking as, with those smouldering eyes, she watched Josefina.

Ay, Manuela! the Maya was thinking. *There you are again, no? You were as thin as that, and as frightened—and as hungry, no doubt. Do you remember, Manuela?*

But La Greca could see that the actress (who had displayed some disturbing signs of boredom) was oddly interested in, even affected by, Josefina's performance. And she congratulated herself on having given way to Don Gaspar's rather droll whim.

For it was Don Gaspar—he of the elegant black clothes and terrifying white beard—who had happened on Josefina in the patio, had watched her from behind the fuchsias, and had sent her flying like a frightened rabbit to the sanctuary of the kitchen.

"Really, Greca," Don Gaspar had said, "it was remarkable. It is something the others should see also!"

"You are joking, Don Gaspar. Or you have had too much of the punch."

"I am serious, Greca. It was astounding. It is a thing the Maya should see."

54

La Greca recalled, with a little spasm of fright, a glimpse of the Maya yawning behind her silver fan.

"Very well, Don Gaspar," she said, with a bare hint of professional irony. "Anything to amuse the Maya. But if you are having sport, Don Gaspar, I shall surely kill you."

Don Gaspar bowed. "It is understood, madama."

"Good. Now, if we can only find this protegida of yours——"

She laughed, but almost immediately she reproached herself for having fallen in with Don Gaspar's crazy idea. It was too late to retreat, however. She had her own reputation for madness to maintain. . . . Besides, there was that yawn behind the silver fan.

They found Josefina hiding in the linen press. Don Gaspar was kindly and suasive with her, La Greca fierce. They had taken her to the sala, too frightened to protest, and had thrust a pair of castanets —the Maya's own—into her hands.

"My dear friends!" La Greca calls gaily to her guests. "We have a surprise for you!"

She assumes a half-serious, half-amused air, presenting Josefina with a little recital of Don Gaspar's adventure in the patio, and commands Angelito to make music for the seguidillas. After that she can only sit, and squeeze her fists together, and wait for Josefina's dance to end and for the Maya to say something. And when it is over:

"Ea!" the Maya says. "You have everything, my child."

"Of a certainty," the guests repeat. "She has everything."

Then, when the applause and chatter and the sudden flutter of fans has died away, the Maya adds: "And you know nothing."

"That is true," the guests say, almost in unison. "She has a great deal of talent, but she knows nothing really."

Josefina raises her head and draws herself upwards until she stands, with an odd rigidity, before the great actress. She takes command of herself and forbids herself to flee or burst into tears, and she meets the Maya's dark gaze steadily with her own clear green eyes. The Maya smiles slowly and makes a gesture with her fan.

"Come here," she says. "Sit here beside me."

Josefina does as the Maya bids. The actress strokes her hair gently with her slim fingers. Without so much as a word or a sign, she dismisses everyone in the room. It is as if the two of them—Josefina and the Maya—are alone in the sala. And Josefina hears the Maya say, dreamily and enigmatically:

"One should never forget, no? . . . That you come with me, my child . . . that you come to Madrid with Manuela Maya."

14

For almost three years Josefina lived in Madrid under the Maya's protection.

Only the actress knew why she had chosen to thrust this frightened child into a dress of sea-green satin (La Greca's), bundle her into a lacquered coach (Don Gaspar's), and carry her down to the capital of the Spains. Only the Maya knew. And nobody, not even Josefina, wondered: it was one of the Maya's whims, simply.

One no more questioned the Maya's whims than one questioned the weather. The Maya was known to be an impulsive, passionate, unpredictable woman; and a great enough artist to do as she pleased. She was known also to be capable of cruelty on occasion, and of shameful rages; but these too were allowed her because of her great talent.

"I shall try to treat you well, my child," she said to Josefina, "and to teach you what a woman needs to know in this miserable reign. You can thank me for that sometime. I shall probably beat you also. And for that you can forgive me."

Josefina bowed her head ever so slightly and murmured, "Señora."

"That was very good," the Maya said, with a faint note of surprise in her voice. "You did that well."

She held up her hand mirror and placed just below the outer corner of her eye—a position known in the terminology of the beauty patch as "passionate"—a tiny black star.

"Now the gesture, no more."

"Perdón?"

"The obeisance," the Maya said, a little impatiently. "I wish you to make the little bow again, but in silence."

Josefina inclined her head, a shade more stiffly than before.

"Good! Now the speech alone." The Maya waited, frowned; she said harshly, "The speech, estúpida! This time without the bow."

There was a flicker of green flame deep in Josefina's eyes. She gazed at the Maya steadily for a long interval before she repeated:

"—Señora."

The Maya laughed. She thrust the silver-gilt mirror out at arm's length and inspected her handsome, arrogant face. She made a little grimace expressing something less than complete approval, and handed the mirror to her maid, a huge, mustached woman named Serafina.

"That was good, also," she said to Josefina. "You have told me with

one word and one gesture all that you wish to tell me—and all that I
need to know, eh? You have said that you accept what the Maya
offers—because you have no other choice. But your submission is made
with pride. It is made with spirit. You reserve the right to hate me a
little, no?"

"I do not wish to hate you, señora."

"I think you have a certain talent," the Maya continued. "It would
have been better if the word alone—or the gesture alone—had sufficed.
But perhaps that will come later."

She drifted her creamy arms out and Serafina slipped a blonde lace
mantón about her shoulders.

"You must consider these things, my child," the Maya said, smiling
a little. "You must study the effect of everything you do or say—even
the smallest thing—how it will advantage you. Above all, do nothing,
say nothing from the heart—that is fatal."

The Maya kicked the heavy flounced train of her dress behind her,
a swaggering, slightly vicious gesture familiar to every theater-goer in
the Capital.

"That is something you must always remember," she said. "Even
when you are in bed. Especially when you are in bed. It is the first
thing you must learn if you are to survive, no? . . . The first of many
things."

Josefina made the Maya a deep bow, full of respect, this time, and
a little awe.

"Thank you, señora," she said gravely. "I shall remember."

She remembered this and everything else the Maya told her; for
now, more than anything else, she desired to be like the Maya—cold
and impregnable and unhurtable. Just as she had studied with all her
heart when younger to be like Eva Helena—warm and gay and
hopeful—so now she applied herself to the emulation of Spain's greatest
actress and courtesan.

Even before the Maya carried her away from Ávila, this change in
Josefina had set in. She had begun to feel oddly insensitive to almost
everything that had once touched her heart: and she observed this
slow mutation with a curious detachment.

You have become like Jesusita, she mused. But no. Your sister talks
like a maja and mocks at everything, yet actually she is of a soft and
impulsive nature that will one day get her into trouble. You, on the
other hand, are really cold and hard inside. That is something, Josefina,
that you must never forget—how hard and cold you are within yourself.

Yet, one must never appear so. One must be like the Maya—gay and
impulsive and always much woman. The Maya, better than any
woman in Spain, perhaps, knew what was required of one to survive
in the mad, disordered world of war and duplicity and masculine

57

brutality that was the reign of Philip V. And this, she taught Josefina, was the first necessity of all: the knowledge of how to deceive everyone—but never oneself.

The Maya taught her many other things. The modes of defense, for instance, against men and—even more important—against other women. The ways of winning favors from the great and of rejecting the advances of the uninfluential. How to be cruel graciously and gracious cruelly. When to be discreet, when bold, when serene, when angry in the most violent and terrifying manner imaginable. When to weep.

The Maya instructed her, too, in a thousand small details of la coquetería: how to use her eyes, her mouth, her fan, and her mantilla; how to walk, sit, rise, turn her head, expose the tip of her slipper. She spent almost an hour demonstrating the tapado de medio ojo—the art of so arranging the mantón as to reveal only one eye (and always the left one) in the most mysterious and seductive fashion possible.

Some of all this she taught by precept, some by example, most by the subtle signals that pass between women, conveying all—and no more—that needs to be told. And Josefina learned quickly and well.

She served the Maya in various small and intimate ways: assisting the maids, the hairdresser, the dressmaker at her mistress's toilette; running errands; performing a thousand casual—and often very private —offices; and commonly accompanying the actress to her theater, the Príncipe. From the very start, she occupied a position of rather special privilege in the Maya's ménage. Before the end of the first year, she had become so much her confidante that there was little of the Maya's colorful—and frequently scandalous—personal life that she did not know about.

"You know enough to hang me, eh, chica?" the Maya once asked her. "But never fear, my child—I should hang you first!"

For the most part, she treated Josefina with kindness, even affection— as a mother (if one could imagine the Maya as a mother!) might treat a daughter. But she was given to sudden, and ugly, rages; and at times Josefina was caught in the storm of her fury. The Maya would pelt her then with curses and obscenities, and would beat her with small, hard fists; and once in a frenzy she struck her with a jet statuette of Santiago, knocking her senseless. Josefina awoke to hear her wailing enigmatically: "Ay, Manuela! What have you done to her? What have you done to our little Manuela?"

Josefina endured the Maya's abuse patiently, even cheerfully. At least, she told herself philosophically, I am getting something in return for these blows. The Maya clothes me and feeds me—although there have been some days of bread and garlic—and lets me sleep in her alcove. And these are but the least of her kindnesses to me.

The Maya's favors were indeed many, and the most precious of them all, Josefina well knew, was the instruction which, towards the close of the year, the famous actress began to give her in the hard, harsh art of the Spanish theater.

"Ella es la protegida de la Maya."

Sometimes as she struggled through the thronged Street of the Prado, in the wake of the Maya's sedan chair, to the stage entrance of the Príncipe, she would hear someone in the crowd say this—"She is a protégée of the Maya's"—and she would find it hard to believe that the words were about herself. That she, Josefina María del Carmen Torres, so recently the poorest and most obscure and most miserable of creatures, should hear herself thus pointed out by the Madrileños as the pupil of the great Maya! Really, that was almost too much!

The Maya was the hardest and most relentless of instructors—one who drove herself to exhaustion, and expected no less from others. Every morning, winter as well as summer, she arose at four o'clock to study her roles; and so prodigious was her memory that she could get an entire comedy by heart in three readings. At eight, after a single cup of chocolate, she was at rehearsal. At half-past two she appeared at the Príncipe, fresh and vivacious, for a solid three-hour performance.

"It is easy to become a famous actress in Spain," she told Josefina. "It is required only that one have the beauty of a Melibea, the energy of a Lope, and the constitution of a horse."

Through the possession of these virtues—except the beauty, for she was too vital to be beautiful—the Maya had made herself the reigning comedienne of the Capital. The government provided the sedan chair in which she was carried to the theater. She earned twenty thousand reales a year.

Although the distinction was later claimed by Teresa Garrido, the Maya was actually the first to sing tonadillas—those musical interludes so loved by Spanish audiences—alone with the guitar. She was the only actress in Spain who could compete with the best professional dancers in the fin de fiesta after the third act. (So good—and so scandalous— was her performance of the saraband that it was officially forbidden at last.) And no one—even her enemies admitted—could rival her in the roles of maja, flower girl, bawd, chestnut vendor, and other types from the lower classes of society: no one could portray vulgarity and ribaldry with such faithfulness—or with so much charm.

"For me to take these parts is but to be myself," the Maya said. "It is not an imitation that I give them, but the thing itself."

Josefina heard her say this with a certain heaviness of the heart, which was followed immediately by a sudden feeling of antagonism. Almost six months had passed since the Maya had begun to instruct her in the arts of declamation and the singing of tonadillas, and she was quite worn out. She was unutterably weary in mind and body from poring over greasy scripts, and practicing a thousand times how to open a fan, or how to lower one's eyes or rise from a hand-chair.

Worst of all, she could do nothing well. She could never, she was certain, do anything at all well—not even the simplest lines that were so easy and natural for the Maya. Everything was easy and natural for the Maya—for herself difficult. No, not difficult—impossible.

So Josefina believed—forgetting the thousands of times the Maya had opened a fan, or lowered her eyes, or got herself up from a hand-chair—and she felt this sudden rush of depression, mixed with anger, when she heard the Maya say so airily: "For me, to take these parts is but to be myself. . . . It is not an imitation that I give them, but the thing itself."

"That," Josefina said sadly, "is why I am a failure, señora."

"What is that you say?" the Maya demanded. The very word failure —even on the lips of another—irritated her, seemed to frighten her.

"That is why I can never succeed," Josefina said. "I have nothing to give. I have been nothing. I am nothing."

"Have I said that you do not succeed—that you are a failure?" the Maya wanted to know.

Josefina ignored the question. "I can never act," she said. "I think I should return to Ávila."

In an era when even women of the highest rank were noted for their scabrous language, the Maya was famous for her tongue; now she uttered some of her choicest obscenities.

"Besides," Josefina said, "I cannot learn the lines."

"You are an idiot," the Maya said coldly. "Perhaps you should play only the parts of idiots."

She had begun to pace the room with long, swift, catlike strides. Her face, it seemed to Josefina, grew physically darker; the Maya was small, but she could be terrifying.

"Ingrate!" she said, advancing slowly toward Josefina. "Ungrateful perra—slut—thankless bitch!"

There was something strange—unnatural—about the Maya's anger. Something oddly personal and private—almost as if this particular tirade were an explosion of her own disappointments and frustrations.

"Perhaps you are right," she rasped. "Maybe it is better that you go back to Ávila . . . that you go back and rot in Ávila."

"Please, señora——"

"But first," the Maya said, "I shall give you something to take back with you. Something to remember the Maya by, no?"

She slowly picked up a fan from a small table. It was a lovely fan—

one of the Maya's choicest, its ribs of ivory, its silken surface painted to show the annual fair in the Plazuela de la Cebada. Josefina had often watched the Maya use this fan. In all of Spain no one could manage one like Manuela Maya. A thousand times Josefina had seen her, on the stage or in her own sala, set the painted semicircle of silk in tremulous suggestive motion, or twirl it languorously between her fingers, or close and display its folds in quick eager flashes, or slowly incline it unopened in cold dismissal—each gesture with a meaning beyond the meaning of mere words, speaking a language that only the Maya could make a fan speak. But never had Josefina watched with such fascination as now the Maya, flicking this fan of the Plazuela de la Cebada open, gazed over its edge with black, malevolent eyes. The fan fluttered ever so faintly, as if with the Maya's quick breathing.

"Bastard of a bastard," the Maya said softly, "I shall teach you to mock at me."

The fan snapped shut with a slapping sound of its ivory ribs. Josefina felt the sharp, infuriating pain of its impact on her cheek and nose. She bowed her face into her bent arms, her hands clutching the top of her head. The Maya's blows fell in silent fury on her fingers, her ears and neck and shoulders. Josefina sank to her knees, sobbing, enduring the stinging blows until she felt a sharp, vicious kick in the side, and she knew the beating was over.

"Get up, perra," the Maya demanded.

Josefina arose, sick and shaking, and faced the actress. The Maya's features were pale and damp; the faint mustache on her upper lip was beaded with perspiration; her eyes were dull and cold.

"Ea! Get going now," she said. "Before I feed my cat your entrails." She paused, panting, to catch her breath. . . . "My little hija de puta."

She smiled as she said this, which made the insult to Josefina and to her mother even more deadly; and Josefina flung herself not so much at the actress herself as at that smile on the pale, dark face.

The Maya was like a writhing cat in her embrace; but the advantage of surprise was with Josefina, and she pressed it savagely. She felt the Maya's teeth puncture her shoulder. She cried out in pain and astonishment, and struck at the actress's distorted mouth with all her force. The blow knocked the Maya over a low brazier, sprawling her on the tiled floor. She did not get up at once; she lay, half-stunned, gazing up at Josefina with incredulous eyes.

"Por Dios!" Josefina whispered. "I have killed you!"

The Maya shook her head a few times, slowly—as if to clear her mind; then she pulled herself to her feet. She stood looking at Josefina for a long interval, with an odd, indefinable expression.

"No, chica," she said gently. "The Maya doesn't kill so easily."

"I'll call the surgeon——"

"Little fool!" the Maya said. The expression on her face turned into one of amused curiosity. "That you should have done it!"

She seemed almost pleased. She crossed the room and picked up a tiny gold snuffbox. She applied a pinch of son to each nostril, paused anticipatively, sneezed voluptuously.

"Now," she said. "What is it you want?"

"I want nothing, Doña Manuela—except to return to my mother."

"Nonsense!" the Maya said. "That is impossible. You have too much spirit for that. You are too much like me. In certain respects—no?—you are very like me. I think so. Except for the men, eh? And the acting——"

The Maya's speech, Josefina thought, was oddly fast and jerky. She had never heard her mistress talk like this before; it puzzled and frightened her a little.

"There is no other like the Maya," she said flatly. "Why do you laugh at me, señora?"

The Maya came over to Josefina, grasped her shoulders, and turned her face towards the light.

"Look at me, chica," she said. "Am I laughing at you? I wish only to know what is it that you want?"

The starkness of the Maya's question—and the hypnotic intensity of her gaze, perhaps—was like a probe reaching down into the past, into the depth of desire. Without reflection, without thinking, Josefina answered:

"I wish to dance, señora."

She said this so simply, with such a flat, childlike definiteness—that the Maya laughed, a little sadly perhaps; then threw her arms suddenly about Josefina and held her in a tight embrace.

"Ay, my little daughter," she murmured. "You do not have to tell Manuela Maya. She comprehends well. She understands, but she forgets, no?"

"You forgive me, Doña Manuela?" Josefina asked, bewildered by this strange talk.

"Ay, chica! It is I that ask forgiveness," the Maya said. "I shall tell you something."

The actress was interrupted by a delayed sneeze, produced by the snuff she had taken earlier. She crossed herself and said, "Jesús!"

"I also hate those stupid lines," she continued. "Lope's, Calderón's, all of them. There is no pleasure in what one says with the mouth—only with what one says with the body, no? It is better to dance one good seguidillas than to play a thousand silly parts."

"That is true, señora," Josefina said inadvertently.

62

"It is better to love," the Maya said, with a wry smile, "than to talk about it."

She was pacing the room again in her restless, catlike fashion. When she began to speak, it was without looking at Josefina, as if to herself.

"I would rather be Spain's greatest dancer," she said, "than the Queen herself. That is something I told myself when I was young—even younger than you, chica."

"But you are a great dancer, señora."

"There are some greater. There is no actress in Spain to compare with the Maya; but of dancers there are Mariana Alcazar, La Catuja, Teresa Garrido, María la Buena . . ."

"You are more famous than any of them, Doña Manuela."

"Ay, that is the very point," the Maya said, almost impatiently. "Manuela Maya, the actress, possesses more than Manuel Maya, the dancer, could ever hope for, no? The cheers of the pit and twenty thousand reales of gold a year, and lovers of the highest rank. And of the greatest wealth."

What is she getting at? Josefina asked herself. She felt on guard, oddly distrustful. What passes here?

But the Maya, for once—if with a kind of maudlin coldness—was speaking from the heart.

"One is never free," she said, "except to feel. One is thrust about—onto roads one has no wish to travel . . . into unwanted roles . . . and into strange beds. One learns too late to trust only one's feelings. . . ."

She smiled at Josefina with a look in her dark, half-hostile eyes that was as close as the Maya ever came to tenderness.

"If you wish to dance, chica," she said, "you shall dance. And perhaps you will be great. Quién sabe?"

15

If she was not yet great, at least she was very good.

By the end of the year she was so good that one heard the name of Josefina spoken quite often on the plazas and in the salas of Madrid. An article in the *Correo* said of her: *La Señorita Torres deserves encomium . . . Let us not be deceived. This comely young artist will one day dominate the dance.* The dancer La Catuja paid her the compliment of a waspish comment on her castanet work. And, most important of all, the people liked her.

"You are even better than I am," the Maya said to her one day. "I have taught you all I know. It is time now for you to go to Soriano."

So, every morning at daybreak thereafter, she appeared at the bleak "Academy" of that dark, fierce, horse-faced little dancing master, and began all over again to learn the rudiments of the Spanish dance—as José Antonio Soriano understood and taught them. Very few of Soriano's pupils could resist for more than a few months a rising compulsion to strangle the small sadist; but Josefina actually rejoiced in his abuse and insults: for she, too, was in deadly and sometimes ill-tempered earnest.

Soriano not only taught her the Spanish dance—he gave her eyes to see its glorious past, and a heart to feel it. He told her of the Gaditanas—those dancing girls that Old Cádiz sent forth to charm and fascinate the ancient world. And of the greatest of these, Telathusa.

"Imagine that you are a Gaditana," Soriano would bark. "Think that you are Telathusa. *Feel* that you are Telathusa—in your arms, your hips, your legs, in your guts, no? Good! Now let me see you try to dance. . . ."

And so, in Soriano's cold, bare Academy, she drove herself to be not *like* Telathusa, but the Great One herself. And at last——

"Get out!" Soriano said to her. "You are wasting your time here. You will never learn to dance—that is clear."

"Is there no hope for me, maestro?"

"None whatever. You have nothing but a style."

So she kissed the fierce little man an affectionate adiós, and studied no more with Soriano nor any other master, but drove herself even harder, and added another half-hour to her predawn exercises with the castanets.

She had, in fact, brought something new and fresh to the dancing of her time. She possessed, as even Soriano had acknowledged, a style. It was a style that revealed itself in an odd and surprising combination of sadness and gaiety, of reserve and abandon. The Madrileños were always fascinated, and a little startled, when this frowning girl passed from a mood of decorum and solemnity to one of such passionate intensity—of such swift and desperate fury—that they, at the end, were almost as exhausted as the dancer herself.

"Ella es de hielo y fuego," they said. "She is ice and fire." And they found it to be an interesting mixture.

Josefina performed at the Príncipe, where the Maya gave her small parts in the comedies. She played these with no little grace and skill. She also sang in the tonadillas, and sometimes alone between the acts, accompanying herself on the guitar.

The Madrileños loved her almost as much for these incidental songs —light and topical and often sharply satirical—as for her dancing.

There was a kind of charming incongruity in her grave manner of singing an amusing and not quite decorous parody on the foibles of the French.

"She is very droll," the Madrileños said. But the critic Luján observed, more astutely, "She scatters her laughter sadly."

She was fortunate enough, also, to be beautiful. It was surprising, Josefina discovered, how few of the actresses at the Príncipe were so favored. Some—and among them several of the most talented and popular—were downright ugly without paint, wigs, and the artful padding of their figures. Some, like the Maya, were of a handsome and striking appearance, but by no means lovely.

"You alone among us, chica," the Maya said, without envy, "are really beautiful. A little strange perhaps, but beautiful. Let us pray that it does not ruin you!"

She was also young. In the year 1711—the year in which all Spain was still celebrating the expulsion of Stanhope from the Capital and his great defeat at Bruhuego—Josefina was seventeen. This is the age at which a lovely Spanish woman is most lovely: it is her high, brief, sad moment.

Josefina, at this age, was described by the critic Luján, a trifle exuberantly perhaps, and possibly with a touch of erotic bias (for Luján had come to feel a powerful personal attraction for the young dancer, whom he now considered to be his own discovery—or at the very least his and the Maya's jointly). He wrote in the *Gaceta*:

> Señora Torres, as all who have patronized the performances at the Príncipe this summer agree, is a dancer of great talent and distinction. It gives me pleasure now to speak of her equally great and distinguished talent for being a beautiful Spanish woman.
>
> The quality of her beauty is to be seen in the incomparable loveliness of her complexion, fair yet possessing that warm and golden patina that is the special glory of the Andalusian woman's skin. How shall I describe it, save in the words of the immortal Cervantes: "a skin as smooth as a burnished and polished sword!"
>
> And what of her splendid eyes, by far the most unusual feature of her beautiful face? It conveys little, as all who have seen Señora Torres know, to say that they are of the deepest green, and extraordinarily large, and heavily lashed: two emeralds, to use the classic phrase, burning in smoky flame.
>
> For it is not so much the color and physical quality—striking as these are in contrast to her flawless skin and ebony hair—that give Señora Torres' eyes their peculiar fascination. It is rather the quality of their gaze—clear, steady, with an almost hypnotic calm in repose, but animated with a jewel-like fire when aroused. He who has never seen the play of Señora Torres' eyes in the seguidillas has seen nothing!

65

Thus, on and on, Luján—a little carried away by his enthusiasm, no doubt, as critics sometimes are, and forgetting to mention several minor faults that, even her most ardent admirers conceded, detracted a little from Josefina's beauty.

Among these were: a slight irregularity of the nose—a characteristic not uncommon among Spanish beauties; a habitual small frown, hardly discernible, yet marring a little the serenity of her fine forehead; and (although some counted this among her attractions) a pronounced dimple near the outer tip of each shoulder.

Still, there were more who agreed with Luján than cared to dispute his judgment; and it might be asked, as many in fact did ask: "Is it possible that a girl with so many charms could lack lovers?"

The age was one whose morals were summarized with diabolic naïveté in the monk Tirso de Molina's famous line: "Everybody says there are virgins, but nobody has seen one." Prostitution, adultery, and sexual promiscuity were, as another writer of the time observed, "the whiplashes of the epoch." It was not a very virtuous moment in history; and the Maya, perhaps, could be forgiven the utter unbelief with which she asked her lovely protégée:

"Are you in truth a doncella?"

"Yes, señora," Josefina said.

She had just come to the Maya; and, although, she tried to sound defiant, there was a certain quality of embarrassment, almost of shame, in her answer. At that moment, under the Maya's incredulous eyes, she felt a kind of guilty lack of pride in her so-rare virginity.

"That I should have lived to see it!" the Maya exclaimed: then gently, and with a small, reflective smile. "But I am sorry, chica. I do not mean to make a joke of it."

"I forgive you, señora."

"Sit down here beside me," the Maya said: she patted the surface of the hard Spanish bench, one of the few pieces of furniture in her bare, austere apartment. "Your Tía Manuela has something to tell you."

Josefina seated herself somewhat stiffly beside the actress. She waited awkwardly to hear what "Aunt Manuela" wished to say. The Maya took snuff, and half-closed her eyes.

"Now you have come to Madrid," she said, "the Capital of the Spains. It is wonderful, no? But wicked. All capitals are wicked—Madrid more than most. And cruel—especially to women, chica. It is hard for a woman—even for a woman of beauty and talent—to survive in Madrid. There is but one way."

"Los hombres?"

"Yes," the Maya said, with a note of surprise in her voice, "the men: although that is to make it rather too simple."

"I have known them only as the ruin of women, señora."

66

"I know of that," the Maya said, without any show of compassion however, "from La Greca: that gruesome old woman. It is something you will have to forget."

"I do not wish to forget," Josefina said.

"Well, even bitterness can be useful. You can make the memory serve you, then."

"I try to," Josefina answered. "I try to make myself hard—like my sister Jesusita. But I do not succeed."

"You will have to succeed—" the Maya's eyes darkened—"or you are lost, chica. You will have to succeed—*as I have.*"

"I shall pray to Santa Teresa to make me like steel," she said; and, to herself, with a mystical comfort in the words, she added, Like a sword far off.

"I think the saints help those who help themselves," the Maya said dryly. "As they say of God. We must find you a protector here below."

"But you are my protector, señora."

The Maya gazed long at Josefina, with a curious and detached interest. "Pobrecita!" she said softly. "My poor little one!"

She suddenly arose and began to pace the tiled floor. Her heels made little clicking sounds up and down the room. She paused and said: "Listen, Josefina mía, to what I am about to tell you. Listen to your Tía Manuela."

She resumed her restless promenade and began to speak in a rapid, precise manner—almost as if she were declaiming a part. Occasionally her smouldering eyes shot a dark glance at her protégée.

"This is something I did not think I should ever have to explain to any woman," she said. "But apparently your mother, who taught you many useful and charming things, was negligent in this particular. Also, you must yourself have been very unobserving of life. But perhaps things are different in Ávila. Now, at any rate you are in Madrid, and you should know that there is but one way for a woman to save herself from sinking to the bottom of this fine cesspool of humanity which is the pride of the two Castiles."

Los hombres! Josefina said again, but to herself. The men are the answer to everything!

"I speak, of course, of women like ourselves—like you and me, chica. For others there is still marriage. Although—" the Maya said in the manner of a stage aside—"it seems to me that this is an institution that is rapidly dying out, except among the lower classes, where the men have nothing to lose by it. . . . There are also the nunneries."

"I have no vocation," Josefina said.

"That is just as well. God has little need for your particular talents."

The Maya fell suddenly, as a child might, into a kind of reverie. It was a habit of hers to do this—to become abruptly silent in the midst of animated talk, as she did now, striding back and forth across the clicking tiles and lost in frowning contemplation of some memory or sudden notion.

"What is it, Doña Manuela?" Josefina asked respectfully. "What is this one thing that I should know?"

"You have already answered that," the Maya said. "Which leads me to suspect that you are perhaps less innocent than one would suppose."

"But what must I do, señora?"

"You must find a man—and soon—who is rich and powerful and who will not treat you too badly."

The Maya paused before Josefina and swept her with a dark, appraising glance.

"That should not be too difficult," she said. "But there is no time to lose. *Time is never on our side, chica.* Now let us consider——"

"There are already some," Josefina said with a certain hauteur, "who eat me with the eyes."

"For example?"

"Well, Don Diego, the tonadilla composer, for example—although I find him repugnant. The others also, for that matter. I have no desire for a lover."

"I can see," the Maya said, "that you have absolutely no understanding of what I have been saying. Have I said anything about lovers? Lovers are very well. They are a necessity (although I believe I could live without Don Diego!). But they are also a luxury. I am not speaking of luxuries, my child. I am speaking of survival."

She stood before Josefina like a priestess instructing a novice in the mysteries of an ancient cult. And this, in a sense, she was. For, of all the women in Spain, Josefina was aware, none could speak so deeply of certain things as Manuela Maya.

She had been the mistress of many men—of more than she could, or desired perhaps, to remember; and among her lovers had been some privileged to stand uncovered before the king. But in addition to the grandees, the condes and marqueses, there was a heavy sprinkling of soldiers, bullfighters, clerics, and others without rank but possessing richly those natural qualities prized by the Maya in her amantes.

"Money and the Maya are very catholic," the Madrileños said, embroidering an old proverb.

She had settled down now—with only minor lapses—to a quite conventional, almost domestic liaison with Don Lorenzo Casteneda, Conde de Vega. But it was not the docile mistress of the great Vega that stood before Josefina now. It was, her protégée sensed, an earlier,

68

a much earlier Maya—a very young girl called simply Manuela per
haps—who was saying again:

"I am not speaking of luxuries, chica—or of love. I am speaking of
la supervivencia . . . of survival."

Her words were accompanied by a look that was like a sudden
strong light revealing, but for an instant only, the mysterious contours
and hollows of a dark, unfamiliar place.

Madre de Dios! Josefina said to herself. Even she has been at one
time frightened. Perhaps she is still afraid. But what could the Maya
be afraid of?

Then the Maya answered her.

"There is a dream, chica, that I cannot be rid of. It comes back to
me—sometimes the same, sometimes a little different. But it is always
about a piece of bread. I have got this piece of bread, and I am running
with it—as if I am being pursued. I have stolen this bread perhaps, I
do not know. I am afraid, but I am also hungry, and I stop at last under
a bridge where there is water running. . . .

"The bridge," the Maya said, with a frown of concentration, "is one
of those in Ronda, where I was a child. But whether it is the new
bridge, or the old one, or the one called after the Romans, I cannot
remember. It makes no difference, really, but I should like to remember
which one it was. . . .

"I stop in my dream, however, under this bridge. I take my piece
of bread and I am about to bite into it when, alas, it slips from my
hands and falls into the river. I do not jump into the water after it, but
I am able to restrain myself with only the greatest difficulty. And this
terrible effort wakes me up."

The Maya closed her eyes for a little while and smiled faintly. When
she looked at Josefina again, her gaze was hard and impersonal.

"I do not mind having this dream," she said slowly. "It is a cruel
dream and after I wake up I am afraid—I sweat with fear. But then
I think: It is a good thing for you to have this reminder, Manuela.
That you should be thankful for what you have. That you should be
thankful even for the Conde de Vega!"

"I also have a dream," Josefina said slowly.

"I know, my child," the Maya said. "There are few of us who do
not. But let us drop this dull subject of dreams now. Let us try to
think of a rich and powerful man who has the reputation of treating
his amigas well."

"But, señora——"

"It seems to me," the Maya said, warm and smiling and cheerful
again, "that young Don Nicolas de Dueda y Pelayo might serve very
well. . . ."

16

The "protectorship" of Don Nicolas—a well-born, deeply religious, and somewhat effeminate young man—did not last long. It began badly, with an hysterical scene in Don Nicolas's apartment that so astonished and unnerved Josefina's first lover as almost to wreck the Maya's fine project at its inception.

"Pitiful Mother of Christ!" the Maya stormed. "What is this impossible thing that Don Nicolas has been telling me? What does it mean? Is this how you repay me—by making a fool of me? Don't stand there like the stone Mariblanca. Answer me, estúpida!"

"I am sorry, señora," Josefina said miserably. "It was something that happened to me. I could not help it, Doña Manuela. I shall try again—if Don Nicolas wishes."

Don Nicolas was forgiving, almost patient, and for a whole fortnight Josefina succeeded in making him hope that his ardor (for Josefina was only his second mistress and he was all but in love with her) was being reciprocated. But then it was as if a dam holding back the strange fury of her emotions burst; and Don Nicolas fled in dismay and bewilderment to the comforting arms of his wife. "Jesús María!" he wailed to the Maya. "She is not a woman, but a demon!"

And Josefina, physically ill and unutterably wretched, made her bitter preparations for leaving Madrid and the Maya.

"It is of no use, Doña Manuela," she said dully. "I try, but I cannot withstand the thing that comes over me. I have begged God and His Holy Mother in a hundred ways to help me. But neither they nor Santa Teresa—who has often interceded for me—will listen to my prayers. I am sorry, Doña Manuela, and ashamed . . . but I do not seem to be like other women."

She waited for the Maya to pour her wrath upon her, perhaps to beat her, or even to kill her where she sat beside her traveling wallet. She waited a long time in a dreadful silence.

"Pobrecita!" the Maya said at last. She sank to her knees beside Josefina and put her arms about her shoulders. "Do not grieve, child. It is not because you are less a woman that this happens. It is because you are more woman than most. You do not understand that? Well, don't try, chica!"

"You forgive me, señora?"

"There is nothing to forgive, my child. There is nothing I do not understand—and so there is nothing to forgive. But you will not lose hope, eh? You will pray to God and the Virgin and Santa Teresa to assist you. And you will strive to succeed, no?"

"With God's help, señora."

"Good! I shall pay for ten masses at the Church of Buen Suceso for your intention."

Josefina burst suddenly into tears. It was the first time in all her life that she had wept so earnestly. When she was a child, she had sometimes hid herself in a corner and cried in sorrow for her mother. But she was not given easily to tears; and not even when her sister Conchita died, nor when her mother lay pale and deathly still after the horrible thing that Miguel, her father, had done to her—not even then had she wept as she did now.

"Caramba!" the Maya exclaimed. "You flow like the Fountain of the Four Seasons. Well, weep, chica. It is not good to weep too often—but when you do, weep hard!"

Josefina did not go back to Don Nicolas who, in fact, was too terrified of her to make that possible—even though he half-wished for it. But there were others toward whom, out of gratitude to the Maya and because she had come to accept this now as a kind of thing willed by destiny, she gave complaisance.

It could never be called more than that. There were no more hysterics, no repetition of the scenes that had shaken Don Nicolas so badly. She drew on the hardness that she felt at the center of her soul—the cold will and instinct for survival that the Maya had awakened—and, while looking at her lovers with a certain hostile detachment, as the Maya did hers, she even strove to please them.

But none gave her pleasure; and none—except one—awakened even the vague stirrings of disquiet that the carpenter lad of Ávila—when she was so much younger—had succeeded in arousing. And so, most of her liaisons were brief, and ended usually with the sudden and sullen withdrawal of her perplexed partner. And with a little shock each time to herself—a vague sensation of frustration and disquiet that left her moody and a little sad for days.

You are indeed a distant flame, Josefina, she said to herself, but without the faint romantic flutter the words had once given her. Before long there will be none who will want you!

Yet while she had, in fact, acquired a reputation for a strange hostility toward her lovers, there was none who would not agree that she was "much woman." She was ice and fire, in Luján's words; and so powerful was the attraction of her odd beauty and the electric lines of her body, that some of the most influential figures in the Maya's circle sought the favor of her eyes.

Among these—among the first—was Luján, the critic. He was a mild, affected man, reeking always of Norwegian water, who, as it turned out, was more competent—and also more content—to write of Josefina's charms than to enjoy them. He appeared satisfied, after a little time, to be counted among his beautiful protégée's ex-lovers—considering this, no doubt, a certain enhancement of his own reputation as a man of parts—and he continued to write complimentary pieces about her in the *Gaceta*.

"That is very good," the Maya said approvingly. "It is like receiving free rents or interest. You have nothing to do but smile at Luján in public now, and he continues to praise you. He makes you famous. That is good, chica!"

The Maya had a very practical point of view on such matters; and Josefina, as the days passed, grew to understand it a little better and, at last, even to share it. She was grateful to Luján for what he had done for her. Later she was also grateful to the painter Juan de la Hoyo.

To be painted by Juan de la Hoyo was an even greater distinction than to be written about favorably by Luján in the *Gaceta*. At the palace—which was full of French painters—he was the only Spaniard who had won the attention of Philip. He had painted the king and his family, and had commemorated various events in Philip's life with a famous series of fan designs. But of all his paintings, the one most talked about—for few had seen it—was a portrait of Josefina called *La de los Ojos Verdes:* "She of the Green Eyes."

A prudent respect for the Inquisition, which had been known to condemn even pictures of the Virgin Mary as indecent, had caused Hoyo to keep this canvas in semiconcealment at his studio. Some said that he had even painted another picture, identical in every respect but fully clothed, to exhibit in event of a visit from the Holy Office.

Actually, there was nothing in Juan de la Hoyo's painting of Josefina to offend any but a most fanatical sense of morality. Himself a young man of stern, almost ascetic austerity, Hoyo painted with a cruel Spanish eye for the realities. Among these he noted—and painted with a superb technical competence—the warm ivory-and-gold flesh tones of Josefina's skin, the sure-flowing lines of her unhampered body, the lovely asymmetry of her features, and (with such striking effect as to give the picture its name) the strange fascination of her eyes.

But Juan de la Hoyo saw deeper than all these; and he managed to impart to what might otherwise have been simply another striking nude a quality of remoteness and aloneness, a suggestion of spiritual continence, that lay like a cool repressive glaze over the sensuous charm of *La de los Ojos Verdes*.

"Juan de la Hoyo has painted a chaste frivola, a voluptuous virgin," the Bohemian painter Mengs observed. "More than that, he has painted a woman in torment."

Of those who, during this period, offered themselves in the role of protector, only Juan de la Hoyo—that simple and sturdy young peasant-painter from the brown-and-red wastes of Murcia—offered her also tenderness, compassion, and uncomplicated love.

When she was with him, those vague fears and loathings that seemed always to lurk on the rim of her consciousness drew back, sometimes almost to nothingness: and she, who could never quietly pleasure in anything before, began to feel a kind of sweet content in Juan de la Hoyo's arms. The Maya, whose dark eyes missed so little, observed the signs of this change in her protégée. She said: "You are in love, chica. I think you have discovered how to love, no?"

"I do not know, señora," Josefina said gravely. "But I am no longer afraid."

"Is that all, child?"

"He gives me happiness—and pleasure. Is that love, Doña Manuela?"

"Ah, my little one," the Maya said, with a certain sadness. "I am not sure I can answer that. I am not sure that I know truly what love is. . . . But I think that this is one of the signs: that a woman who is in love seeks to satisfy neither her own pleasure nor her own will, but only her lover's."

"I think then," Josefina said pensively, "that I am a little in love, Doña Manuela."

"But this," the Maya went on, not hearing her, "seems to me to be a deadly thing. Such love is like a fever that is wholly destructive. It devours even itself. It is called beautiful, I know, but to me it appears only evil."

There was suddenly such a bitterness in her voice that Josefina thought, ay, Doña Manuela—this is another wound you hide!

The Maya, with exact, disciplined steps, began to pace the floor in her fashion when agitated or deep in thought. She said, looking straight ahead, as if speaking to herself: "A woman can stand only one such love in her life. It is better not to know it at all."

She ceased abruptly and said no more, then or afterwards, leaving Josefina to wonder—as did so many others—about the dim, early reaches of the Maya's past. But later, when Josefina saw her at her bath, disrobed, she noticed that the Maya's breasts were the breasts of a woman who had borne a child.

Ah, Josefina, she said to herself then, remember always that Doña Manuela protects you, and seems to love you, and that you should be like a good daughter to her.

She tried hard to please the Maya in every way, serving as a kind of

73

supervisor of her household, attending her to the theater, practicing through long hours of dawn or dusk to achieve a perfection in the bien parado or the vuelta volada that would win a soft "Olé!" from her mistress. She had but little time for Juan de la Hoyo.

"You are giving me the pumpkin," he complained, which in his strange Murcian dialect meant that he felt himself neglected—and was also a little jealous. "You think less of me than a good *tok* of your castanets!"

"That is not true, Juan. But I have noticed that you, on the other hand, put nothing ahead of your painting."

"My painting," Juan said a little stiffly, "is for the centuries."

"Well, it is just as difficult to dance as to paint," Josefina said stoutly. "It is a great art also. And—" there was the faintest suggestion of mockery in her smile—"the people like it better than pictures."

"It is a gypsies' pastime!" Juan said contemptuously.

Juan was changing. Even his solid peasant character had not proved wholly impervious to success and flattery. He had adopted an air of arrogance, fashionable at the time but ill-befitting his simple country nature. In other ways, also, he was suddenly different.

But Josefina bore patiently enough, although with a questioning heart, the strange new aberrations of Juan's incomplex personality, and particularly of his lovemaking: until a dreadful night when, stripped down by wine to the crudest remnants of his peasant origins, he turned loose again the wild, uncontrollable flood of her terror and fury. It was all the more violent for having been dammed up so long, but Juan de la Hoyo was not Don Nicolas. He was strong, stubborn, and brutal when drunk; and he imposed on her the ultimate insult and injury of his overpowering animal strength.

For a long time, Josefina carried on her skin the deep purple marks of Juan's victory. She hid them from the Maya, and said nothing. She became very quiet—quiet even for Josefina—and spent herself fiercely on her work. So fiercely that the Maya became concerned.

"Caramba, chica!" she asked. "Do you want to kill yourself?"

"I would not mind, Doña Manuela."

The Maya looked at her sharply. "I think you require a rest," she said. "You should have a little holiday, no?"

"I would not mind."

"Well, good," the Maya said. "Let us think of something. Let us think of some place to go in the spring. . . ."

"I should like to go for a little while to Ávila."

"Ah yes, of course! That will be easy to arrange, my child. It is beautiful in the Guadarramas in June."

"I have a great longing to see my mother, señora."

74

"Well you shall see her," the Maya said, "this very week. But there is one thing you must promise, no?"

"Whatever it is, Doña Manuela, I promise it."

"That you will return to me."

"Ay, Doña Manuela!" Josefina said, and it was necessary for her to struggle against the embarrassment of tears. "Why do you endure me—why are you so good to me?"

"It is a thing that I sometimes wonder about myself, chica," the Maya said, smiling. "But you will come back to me?"

"I promise, señora," Josefina said into her handkerchief, for the tears had come nevertheless.

17

For the journey to Ávila the Conde de Vega provided his own coach, with four mules, a driver, and runner. More than that, the grandee himself handed Josefina into this fine conveyance and bade her an elaborate farewell.

"Go with the Virgin," he said, with a downward sweep of his new-fashioned French hat. "May she protect the glory of your eyes. We shall count the hours until you return to us, our little jewel. . . . No, Manuela?"

The Maya, who had been listening to her lover's effusions with a bored air, gave him a small smile and said, "In Christ's name, Lorenzo, let her go now!"

Sometimes, Josefina thought, the Conde's banter did not amuse the Maya overmuch. He had acquired this habit of exhibiting an exaggerated tenderness toward her. It was a kind of game they played at together, the Maya laughing (with a certain reserve) at the Conde's gallantries, and Josefina rather enjoying the sport of extricating herself from his feigned advances.

The Conde, however, was not a man of wit or grace. He was simply a middle-aged nobleman who, like most of the aristocracy of blood, concerned himself with little save religion, valor, and love for the king. A vain, stupid man, in short, and his ponderous make-believe flirtation amused neither the Maya nor Josefina half so much as himself.

"No, no, Manuela mía," the Conde said with heavy jocularity. "Let us savor rather this sweet parting."

"Mother of God!" the Maya said simply.

Josefina glanced swiftly at her. Their eyes met. The Maya's were expressionless; but her lips smiled, revealing her strong white teeth, and she made a little gesture, half of exasperation, half of farewell.

"Adiós, chica," she said shortly. "Until we see you again."

"Adiós!" Josefina called from the moving coach. "Adiós! I love you!"

She felt a sudden, almost violent, surge of aloneness and a kind of dread, vague and indefinable, but somehow connected with this departure for Ávila. She drew her traveling cloak more closely about her and lay her head back against the silken seat of the Conde's coach; she closed her eyes and made a small prayer to the Virgin and San Cristobal for a safe journey.

It was good to lay one's head back against the silken padding, and close one's eyes, and think of nothing at all. Or to gaze out of the window at the flowing Castilian plain, and breathe the spring-scented air, and feel one's spirits rise with the sight of so much loveliness and such a stainless blue sky. . . .

The half-league roadmarkers seemed to fly by. Shepherds and shepherdesses waved at them from the flowery lower slopes of the Guadarramas, and Josefina waved gaily back. There was something exciting about their swift, fine progress. When, at one of the royal posthouses, they paused and Josefina looked down at the distant city of Madrid, she felt a kind of goddesslike elation—a giddiness induced, no doubt, by the high air and youth and unaccustomed luxury, as she herself might have suspected. Yet she whispered to herself:

"Ay, Madrid! I am not afraid of you up here. I think I even love you a little. Perhaps you will love me some day, Madrid! Who knows!"

Late in the afternoon they came within sight of the monastic palace called the Escorial, a grim mass of granite on a bleak height, and almost an hour later drew into the small village adjoining it. The Conde had arranged for accommodations in La Fonda del Escorial, one of the less miserable inns of the town. Here Josefina, a young woman traveling alone, prudently locked herself in her cold, verminridden chamber and endured a wretched night. She was glad to be on her way again, immediately after chocolate.

"It is but a short step from pigsty to palace here," she observed to her driver. "Those who attend the king in this place are welcome to that privilege."

"Below the king, all men are peers in El Escorial," the driver said. "As any louse can tell you, señora."

"Have you been to Ávila?" she asked suddenly.

"Certainly, señora. Twice."

"On market day?"

"Once, señora."

"Ah," she said. "It is wonderful, no?"

"It is not so much," the driver said. "It is nothing, really, compared with the markets of Salamanca and Segovia and——"

"If you are trying to impress me with the extent of your travels, mule-driver," Josefina said tartly, "you may save your breath. A person can travel as far as the Indies and still remain blind and a fool."

"You are no doubt right, señora," the driver said, touching his hat. "I am mistaken about the market at Ávila. It is a fine market. It is certainly the finest market in the two Spains." He smiled broadly and winked at his companion.

"Estúpido!" Josefina spat out. "You have eyes only for the rear ends of mules."

She shook her shoulders as she settled back into the coach. She was a little ashamed of herself and wondered why the driver's chaff should have upset her so, why she felt so edgy and irritable—and why she experienced a vague uneasiness also that bordered on apprehension.

"It is like fear of the pit," she thought, groping in the idiom of her new life. "You have stage terror, Josefina!"

The road staggered upwards from El Escorial, past half-hidden red-roofed mountain villages, through the long still-snowy Guadarrama pass; then it slipped steeply down to Ávila. A league away Josefina saw the tip of its cathedral tower: moments later, with almost magical abruptness, the whole of Ávila—all of the ancient walled and turreted City of the Knights, and of Santa Teresa de Jesús . . . and of Josefina María del Carmen Torres.

For in that same instant there rushed over Josefina a sharp, almost aching awareness of her identity with this austere city of her birth. And with this sudden feeling of oneness—of coalescence with all the forgotten parts of her past—she experienced a deep, strangely intensified sense of self. Only once before had she known this feeling quite so strongly: once a long, long time ago when she, a child lying in the darkness with the image of a golden woman in her mind, had sighed at last and said, *"I would rather be Josefina."* She had forgotten that incident quite completely; but now, for some reason, she remembered it again. She smiled and repeated the phrase softly to herself.

The rumble of the carriage wheels on the Roman bridge broke through her musing. They plunged into the shadows of the towered gate, and emerged in a maze of twisted streets and hemming walls and the lowering cliffsides of churches. All at once a thousand forgotten images and impressions choked her memory. Suddenly, fiercely, fearfully, she was back in Ávila again. She was back in the city of her birth and childhood, and she had never felt so strange and so alone.

18

"I have heard that the dying sometimes say strange and cruel things," Eva Helena said. "They say outrageous things that hurt those they love most. If I should do this, my daughter, you will know that I do not mean what I say, and you will forgive me, no?"

"I shall remember, Mamita," Josefina said quietly. "I shall know that, whatever your lips may say, there is nothing but love in your heart. So be at ease now."

"Good. I am sleepy again."

She closed her eyes and smiled a faint smile that was like a grimace on her wasted face. Twilight was beginning to make. Josefina picked up her rosary and, sitting erect and immobile on the wooden stool beside her mother's bed, told her beads and waited for Tichi to arrive.

What, she thought, would have happened to her mother without Tichi?

For it was Tichi who had demanded, and had got, from La Greca this small room for Eva Helena. It was mean and miserable, but it was a place where she could bear her illness quietly and alone, and with a certain dignity. It was Tichi, too, who had come here every night to sleep near her; and who had stolen away from La Greca's house, where she served as housekeeper, to bring her a little soup or a half-loaf of freshly baked bread. And it was Tichi who, when Josefina had arrived in Ávila and had gone straight to La Greca's house to find her mother, had met her at the entrance and had said:

"So you are Josefina! Well, it is a good thing you have come at last. It is a good thing, indeed."

"What has happened?" Josefina asked, suddenly alarmed. "Where is my mother?"

"Remain here for a moment, please. I shall take you to her."

"But is she not in this house? Where is señora—where is La Greca?" Tichi spat.

"You do not wish to see La Greca," she said, with a strange, hard finality. "One moment, señora. I shall accompany you."

She closed the door, reappearing shortly in a decent black dress and mantón and carrying one of the striped pannier bags that the women of Ávila were never without. Josefina gave her a quick anxious scrutiny.

Tichi was a woman—a Gallega, probably—of compact peasant build, with soft brown eyes under strong black brows. Her face was broad, pleasant, and serious; her hands large and fine; she walked and moved with an easy reserve of strength and grace. Josefina guessed her age to be near thirty.

"She has only the small daughter of my brother with her now," Tichi said apologetically, as they started down the narrow street. "I was obliged to leave her for a little while."

"Is it the fever?" Josefina asked.

"No, señora. Nobody—not even the surgeon—knows what it is. But it is very bad."

They came quickly to a mean, narrow house—hardly more than a roofed-in space between two taller buildings—with one small window and a rotting door. It flashed through Josefina's mind: "This is the House of the Three Acorns—or even worse." Tichi rapped on the door; it opened cautiously and a small worried face peered out.

"Thank you, 'Nita," Tichi said. "You may go home now. How is the señora?"

"She is sleeping," the little girl answered gravely. She held the door open for them and, after they had entered, bade them good-by with adult courtesy, and left.

"She is but nine and already a woman," Tichi said, as if for want of something else to say.

It was so dark in the narrow, cell-like room that Josefina could not distinguish at first the form of her mother, lying still and flat, on a pallet against the far wall. But in a few moments her eyes adjusted themselves to the gloom, and she could see Eva Helena clearly. She could see a strange face that, in a vague shocking way resembled Eva Helena's—that must in fact be Eva Helena's, she told herself, for Tichi had said it was so.

But there was little left in it of the serene and madonnalike beauty that had once been her mother's: only some of the dignity, and even that transformed into a kind of inert, passive thing—the hollow dignity of the dying. Eva Helena lay as still and thin as a stone effigy in a church; she seemed to be without lips, and under her purple eyelids there appeared to be two round, hard objects, half-sunken in the parchment-colored face.

"She has eaten nothing for three days," Tichi whispered.

"Does she suffer?" Josefina asked.

"It is hard to tell," Tichi said. "She says nothing, so it is hard to tell. But I don't think so."

After a while the purple lids raised slowly and revealed the round, hard objects beneath them: two dull, dark balls that had once been the

79

lovely eyes of Eva Helena. They turned slightly without the head turning at all, in the direction of Josefina.

"Jesusita . . ." Eva Helena whispered slowly.

"Mamita!" Josefina slipped to her knees beside the bed and, grasping the hard wooden frame with both hands, lay her forehead against it and wept silently.

"She thinks you are Jesusita," Tichi said. "She has asked often for Jesusita; even more than for you, señora."

"Well, where is she?" Josefina demanded, with the sudden unreasonable anger that sometimes flares out of the feeling of helplessness in the face of oncoming death. "Why don't you bring her?"

"I don't know where she is," Tichi said. "And I have had no time to search. . . . Quiet, señora: she is asleep again."

Eva Helena slept a great deal. But often, for long periods, she lay awake, staring at the small, dim window and fingering, with a horrible ceaseless industry, the hem of her camisón. Sometimes, in the morning or toward evening, she seemed to gain strength and would begin to talk a little. Much of what she said was merely the strange nonsense of delirium—often about Jesusita and her dead children, sometimes about the Condesa de Mora's house and that patio where the orange and lemon trees burst into blossom on a single April day; but never, strangely, of Miguel.

She has put him out of her mind, Josefina thought. And out of her heart. As I have also.

Occasionally, however, Eva Helena spoke with startling energy and perspicuity. The priest had already come and given her the last rites of the Church. She was at peace and unafraid; but she desired strongly to perform her last act in life with dignity and decorum, and without trouble or hurt to others; and so she whispered anxiously now to Josefina:

". . . You will know that I do not mean what I say, and you will forgive me, no?"

Josefina sat beside her in the dusk and told her beads and thought.

She thought that she would like to kill La Greca for the shameful way she had dealt with Eva Helena in her trouble. "It would give me much pleasure," she said to Tichi, "to scratch that ugly old whore's eyes out." Her fingers curved and contracted: she was not speaking figuratively.

She thought of Jesusita. What had become of her sister? Tichi knew, no doubt; but when Josefina questioned her, Tichi offered only a somber look and a shrug of her strong shoulders. Josefina did not inquire of anyone else about her. There is enough grief for the time, she said to herself. I shall find out about Jesusita later.

A few times, bitterly and with a kind of lingering terror, she thought of Miguel, but for whom all this sorrow and suffering might have been spared Eva Helena. She remembered none of the small, pleasant things about her father—she had no wish to remember them. She recalled only the nightmarish flashes of horror—with always her father's face thrusting out of the darkness—that had shot through the sunny reaches of her childhood.

There was the time of Yolanda. And the time of Concepción's dying. And, most terrible of all, the time of the gypsy, with her black eyes glittering in the candlelight. Josefina counted her beads very fast and remembered.

"Mother of Christ!" she cried aloud, with such vehemence that Eva Helena turned her head and looked at her with her dull eyes.

She tried not to think of Miguel after that. But she thought much of herself, and of what a poor daughter she had been to Eva Helena. And she put her face into her hands and wept a little, as children have so often wept, briefly at least, in such periods of remorse. Then the hard and urgent consideration of money edged its way back into her thoughts and she wondered, a little desperately, what she could do about it. Because she had counted on remaining in Ávila for only a short time, she had brought but a few reales—mostly supplied by the Maya—with her; and now, after three days, there was little of that left. She was frowning over this problem—while she told her beads—when Tichi returned.

"Has she rested well? Has she had pain?"

"Who can say. The sick are often like the dead: they do not tell."

"And you, señora—how do you feel?"

"I do not feel gay."

Tichi sighed. "I accompany you in your grief," she said. "That I could make it less!"

She stood at the foot of Eva Helena's bed, her plain peasant features softened by the dusk and by the compassion that only the humble can feel for the humble, murmuring a brief prayer that ended with a quick sign of the cross. Impulsively, Josefina embraced her.

"Ah, Tichi!" she exclaimed. "All day long I thank God for you!"

She turned away abruptly and took down from a peg set into the wall her basquiña—that rich, always black garment without which no Spanish woman would venture into the street—and put it on over her skirt; then—since she was going out alone—she arranged her mantón so that it covered the lower part of her face.

"I must go out for a little while," she said. "On a certain business, Tichi. But I shall return soon."

The business was that of raising money. It was necessary, she considered, to obtain at least a hundred gold reales. She had cast up the total with a grim and aching practicality: for Eva Helena's burial, sixty reales; for masses for the repose of her soul, ten; to reimburse Tichi for fees she had paid the surgeon, six; for her own expenses in Ávila and on the journey back to Madrid, fifteen; for a second-hand brazier and charcoal to heat Eva Helena's chamber, a castoff cowl of the order of St. Francis in which to bury her, and other small but necessary items, the remainder. . . . A hundred reales of gold, no less: what a staggering sum to come by!

First I shall demand it of La Greca, she said to herself. A loan of this money. Surely, even she cannot refuse.

But with the first sight of La Greca, her assurance faded. The aging actress seated on a heavily carved tall-backed chair, regarded her visitor coldly and without greeting.

"God grant you good days, señora," Josefina said.

"May He give them good to you," La Greca answered mechanically.

The old woman's face, whitened and stiffened by lotions and unguentary plasters and toilet waters laced with corrosive sublimate, was as expressionless as her words. Her eyes, glittering darkly in the candlelight, were even less responsive. She was like a great wooden doll, Josefina thought—an ugly wooden doll decked out in a French deshabille and a ridiculous coif.

"I am Josefina María Torres, at your orders, señora," she said. "The daughter of Eva Helena."

"I should not have recognized you," La Greca said dryly.

How repulsive you are! Josefina thought. How pitiful! She marveled that she should once have held this creature in a sort of awe—that it was less than two years since she had scurried, like a frightened wild animal, from the approach of this great personage, for whom she now felt only contempt.

"But I recall you now," La Greca continued. "We dug you out of the linen press to dance for the Maya. She carried you back to Madrid with her, I believe—as her servant, no?"

"I am her friend, señora. I perform with her at the Príncipe."

She knows everything about me, Josefina thought. There is nothing she doesn't know. But she will not admit it; because she wishes to reduce me to littleness. What cruel eyes she has!

"Ah, the Maya!" La Greca exclaimed, with a sudden show of animation. "How does she do?"

"Very well, señora. Doña Manuela is worshiped by everyone. She is the primera dama of Madrid."

As if you didn't know! she added to herself. As if anyone, least of all you, had to ask: "How does the Maya?" Then, remembering why she was there, in La Greca's house, she reflected that perhaps a little guile were more to her advantage than enmity.

"She speaks often of you, señora," she said shamelessly.

The old actress smiled at that; but her smile was a vain and foolish one, and not a smile of friendliness. It congealed suddenly, and La Greca rasped, "What is it you are after?"

"I am after nothing, señora," Josefina said slowly: remembering what Tichi had told her about La Greca's heartlessness, she must make herself speak slowly. "I want nothing for myself."

"Then why do you force yourself thus into my house at this hour?"

Sometimes pride surged through Josefina as rage or joy surges through other people. She felt its sudden onset now, an emotion as violent and uncontrollable as the anger and contempt mixed with it. She stood a little taller before La Greca and said evenly:

"I came here, señora, to ask a kindness of you in God's name and on behalf of my mother, who is sick and dying."

"I have already given her my house," La Greca interrupted. "What else does she want?"

"She wants nothing," Josefina said stonily. *"Nor do I, señora. If I myself were dying, I should ask nothing of you. Adiós, señora."*

"Slut!" La Greca roared in a voice startlingly deep and strong for a woman. She arose from her tall-backed chair and stood, stiff with rage, in her French deshabille, her black eyes glittering under the ridiculous cap bedecked with laces and ribbons.

"Careful!" Josefina whispered.

La Greca advanced toward her until she was an arm's length away. Josefina thought, why do I stay to hear her insults: why don't I leave?

"Get out of my house, puta," La Greca said. "Go back to the streets of Madrid and walk them at night. You perform at the Príncipe! Indeed! You——"

Josefina struck her twice, hard on the face with her open hand. La Greca staggered, recovered herself, and stared at Josefina with sagging mouth, too stunned, too incredulous to speak.

"Tomás!" she croaked at last. An ancient porter appeared at the doorway of the sala and blinked stupidly at his mistress.

"Tell him to go away," Josefina said. "I shall leave you now, señora. If you have any thoughts of doing harm to me or my mother, I advise you to change your mind. I have a notion, in any event, to ask Guerra to write a tonadilla about the one they used to call La Greca—and also many other names. I should like to sing that one. And Madrid would like to hear it, no, señora?"

"Tomás," La Greca repeated weakly.

"Or perhaps the Maya herself would like to sing it," Josefina said.

She drew her mantón over her head and passed one end of it across her face. Tomás stepped aside, almost respectfully, as she left the sala.

83

The narrow street was filled with the soft spring twilight. Josefina hurried along it, past the doorways of humble, flower-splashed patios toward the Plaza in the meaner quarter of town. Her bravado had drained away: she felt suddenly depressed and a little panicky. Yet, she experienced a certain exhilaration, also, when she thought of how she had struck La Greca—when she refelt the sting of the blow on her hand. She was glad of that. La Greca, she knew, would never dare to seek reprisal—not with the threat of a tonadilla (sung by the Maya, perhaps!) hanging over her grisly head. Josefina recalled that stupefied face under the laced and beribboned cap, and she laughed aloud. Then she remembered her situation, her need for money; and she was depressed again, and frightened.

Like all Spaniards, she had always in the back of her head a sense of the disaster that had befallen the Kingdom. Never, for as long as anyone could recollect, had times been so hard. The wealth of the Indies, it seemed, had brought only a ruinous inflation to the land. Poverty, hunger, and fear dogged every Spaniard—except, of course, the court, the nobility, and the clergy, who still lived in luxury and with a looseness that not even Philip IV (father of thirty-two bastards!) had surpassed.

In Madrid, in the Maya's milieu, under the Maya's protection, she had been sheltered from the universal fear. With the easy forgetfulness of seventeen, she had almost lost—she thought—the dread of poverty that had weighed like a load of heavy dreams on her early girlhood. She had longed for the blue sky and, in her innocent fashion, had been willing to pay for it: sometimes, it had seemed to her, she had even possessed it.

But now, back in Ávila, enwrapped by a sense of her indestructible identity with this ancient city of her wretched past, confronted by this frightening plight—this terrifying fact of utter want and aloneness—it had all swarmed back and over her: the old, old fear and shame and hatred of poverty; the old anxiety and dread that had lived, like an evil guest, with her and Jesusita in the House of the Three Acorns. And suddenly, everything she felt and thought came together in one terrible sentence:

They will bury my mother in el cementerio de los pobres y desconocidos, she repeated to herself. She will lie in the field of the poor and unknown.

She felt weak and warm, and wished that there were some place where she could sit down for a little while. But she continued to hurry down the narrow street toward the Plaza, past ever darker and more evil-smelling entrances, her eyes staring straight ahead through the opening of her disguise. By the time she had reached the square, around which the people of the neighborhood moved slowly—for it was

84

the hour of the evening paseo—she had made up her mind to do what she had half-resolved to do, even before calling on La Greca.

She stopped at the stand of a memorialista and asked for paper and writing materials.

"The charge will be eight cuartos," the letter-writer said, with a bored professional air. "Name of the recipient, please."

"I shall write it myself," Josefina said. "I wish only paper, pen and ink."

"The charge will still be eight cuartos, señora."

"Very well. Here, you have them."

She dropped the coins into the wondering scrivener's palm and dipped the quill into his inkpot. She wrote swiftly—for she had already composed the note in her head—a dozen bold, clean lines to His Excellency, the Conde de Vega:

EXCELENTISMO SEÑOR—

For the gravest of reasons, I am in urgent need of a hundred and fifty gold reales. Because I have nowhere else to turn in my distress— except to Doña Manuela, who is already my benefactress beyond the possibility of repayment—I find the courage to ask Your Excellency for help. . . . If you will, in your great kindness, send me the loan of such a sum, to the inn of San Luis, I shall be grateful forever. . . . Your Excellency's very obliged and very obedient servant,

JOSEFINA MARÍA TORRES

She added the customary cross at the top of the sheet, folded it, and handed it to the memorialista for sealing. At the Inn of San Luis, half an hour later, she gave the letter to Vega's coachman.

"You are not returning, señora?" he asked curiously, and with the undertone of insolence natural to coachmen.

"Later," she said imperiously. "I advise you to lose no time in delivering this letter to His Excellency."

"We shall leave tonight, señora."

"Good, then." She gave him a whole real—which left only six and a few cuartos for herself and Eva Helena.

She hurried back to her mother and Tichi, thinking furiously of what she had done in the fever of her despair; and wondering, too, now that the act had been performed, what its consequences might be. How would the Conde de Vega respond to her appeal? Would he feel resentment, amusement, compassion? . . . Would he show her letter to the Maya?

Ay, caramba! Josefina thought. There is something you should have considered a little, Josefina. For who can tell about Doña Manuela!

She was aware that the Maya was not precisely amused by the Conde's playful gallantries toward her. What, she speculated, would she think when she learned that her little protégée had begged a

85

hundred and fifty reales from her lover? And what, especially, if the Conde supplied them?

Vaya, vaya! Doña Manuela will surely understand, she reproached herself. I wonder how long I must wait for the money?

19

It took Eva Helena a long, cruel time to go. For six days Josefina sat beside her mother's bed, watching with a curiously detached anguish the slow, dull, undramatic approach of death.

Her grief, she realized with a little shock, was not really for Eva Helena. She could not see Eva Helena in this ghostly form that lay day after day, sleeping most of the time, but occasionally staring at her out of purple eye-sockets and fingering with that horrible, feverish haste the hem of her camisón. Neither her reason nor her senses could accept this pitiful specter as that Eva Helena of the emerald eyes, who sang the gay songs of Andalusia, and danced the seguidillas, and was the most beautiful woman—not even excepting the Virgin Mary—who had ever lived.

"Ay, madre mía!" she moaned. "You have already gone. It is not Eva Helena who is dying now."

"God will grant her an easy death," Tichi said comfortingly. "She will die beautifully."

An easy death! What could be harder than this? Josefina thought. Or uglier? Why must God be so cruel?

But then, on reflection, she knew that there were much harder ways of dying: as the Inquisition had so often demonstrated. And the Inquisition had ears in every wall; so she was careful not to express her grief-engendered, but nevertheless plainly blasphemous, resentments aloud. She merely whispered, "But it takes so long, Tichi."

Only once, during the last days, was Eva Helena fully conscious, and then but for a few moments. She moved her hand almost imperceptibly toward Josefina's and smiled the ghost of a smile, and repeated painfully, in thick, difficult words, the names of all her children, living and dead . . . Rafaela, Concepción, María de Jesús, Josefina. Then, after a pause, she added Miguel's name; and in that instant Josefina thought she could not bear her hatred for her father.

At other times Eva Helena was awake but confused, and she imagined herself or her family in evil straits, and fretted pitifully about it. Often, during these periods, she mistook Josefina for Jesusita; and

86

then Josefina must pretend that she was her sister, and make up all sorts of answers to Eva Helena's anxious questions. This was the hardest thing of all for her to bear. At last, worn out and unstrung by her long vigil, she turned savagely on Tichi and demanded:

"Where is my sister? I think you know, Tichi, where Jesusita is. In God's name why don't you tell me?"

"She is in Segovia."

"I think you are lying to me, Tichi."

"No, señora, I am telling the truth—as it was told to me by someone who saw her there."

"And what else?"

"Alas, señora, I cannot—I cannot——"

Tichi burst into tears and bowed her face into her hands. Josefina let her sob, watching her silently, feeling wooden and dry and without capacity for more sorrow . . . for anybody . . . or about anything.

Well, at least, she thought grimly, I shall have to wonder no more about Jesusita.

So she sat beside Eva Helena and watched, and performed the small and futile offices for the dying, and waited. She waited with dread and with a kind of angry impatience for what must come to Eva Helena. And, although she hardly permitted herself to hope, she awaited the Conde de Vega's pleasure.

Ay, caramba! You were out of your mind, Josefina! she rebuked herself. That you could have done such a thing! You will receive no money. . . . Neither can you return to Madrid now. Then she thought of the cemetery of the poor and unknown, and she was not sorry she had appealed to the Conde, but only downcast and hopeless.

"Do not despair, señora," said Tichi, who knew everything. "I have asked San Isidro to intercede for us. He will see that we get the money. He has never failed me."

"If God is against you," Josefina said wearily, "of what use are the saints?"

But that same afternoon, less than three days after she had sent off her letter to the Conde, a booted horseman arrived at the Inn of San Luis and inquired for Señora Torres. When Josefina, breathless and incredulous, arrived at the inn, this man bowed, handed her a small leather purse, and said only, "With His Excellency's compliments, señora."

Josefina counted the money in the gaping innkeeper's presence, signed a receipt for it, and left with the little purse held tightly against her breast. Instead of the hundred and fifty reales she had asked, it contained five gold coins worth a little more than two hundred reales. And a small, folded piece of paper on which was written in the Conde's hand, *With what impatience do we await your return! V.*

The next morning Eva Helena drew up her knees and lay, like a child curled up in bed, until evening. At dusk, although she was unable to speak, it appeared to Josefina that her mother was trying to tell her something; and, with that instinctive recognition of imminent death common to all mortals, she read Eva Helena's wish. So she and Tichi placed Eva Helena upon her back, her head raised a little, her hands—into which Tichi had thrust a small crucifix—crossed on her breast. Thus, decorously and quietly—and without trouble to anyone—Eva Helena made what Tichi forever after maintained was a beautiful death.

But it was not beautiful to Josefina. At the last moment she arose with a little cry, turned and covered her face, and pressed herself against the wall. And it was Tichi who murmured into the dying woman's ear the holy names of Jesús, María, and José.

20

Afterwards, it was Tichi, also, who looked to the numerous details attending even so simple a funeral as Eva Helena's. She appeared to have a natural talent for such things, and an astonishing experience of them; and Josefina was content to let her manage all, including even the purchase of a mourning dress for herself. So, modestly but properly, Eva Helena was buried in the Church of San Tomás; and the Conde de Vega's money bought ten masses for the respose of her soul.

Now she has gone, Josefina thought, and I am really alone. I am truly La Sola now!

As she and Tichi left the church, this feeling of aloneness had suddenly pierced her mood of grief and (she could not tell why) of bitterness. She had experienced loneliness often enough before: she could hardly remember when she had not known it. But this was something quite different. This was a new sense of isolation: of having no one close to her. Jesusita? Alas, my poor sister, have you not died also? The Maya? How can I be sure of Doña Manuela now? How can I be sure of anyone? A litte chill of fear passed up her spine.

"Ah, Tichi," she said, with a pang of self-pity that Eva Helena would never have allowed herself. "What could be worse? That one should have nobody to go to! That one should have no place to go!"

"That would be very sad, señora," Tichi said. "Let us hope that it doesn't happen to us."

"Alas," Josefina said, "it has already happened to me, Tichi."

"I don't understand, señora. You have me to go to. As for a place to stay, they'll take you at the inn."

"For a day and a night only. The law permits a woman, alone, to remain no longer."

"Well, that will be long enough," Tichi said. "Tomorrow we can be on our way to Madrid."

"We? What did you say, Tichi?"

"I haven't told you, señora, but it is my intention to return with you to Madrid. I have had enough of Ávila. Especially, I have had enough of the one they call La Greca. So I have decided to serve you, señora —in Madrid."

"That is impossible," Josefina said. "I have no need of a servant. In any event, I have no money to pay one."

"Nothing is impossible, señora. As your poor mother used to say, you have only to wish hard enough."

"Wishing brought her little. I doubt that it will bring us more."

"You are cast down, señora. Perhaps tomorrow you will feel better. Let us go to my brother's house now and have a little chocolate, and we will talk this over."

Her brown eyes, in her plain country face, were soft and smiling and somehow reassuring. Josefina gazed at her for a long moment over the fold of her mantón.

"Very well," she said at last. "It is impossible, I tell you, but let us talk it over."

At her brother's house, Tichi made hot chocolate with milk and served it with little cakes flavored with anise seed. Josefina ate with a kind of guilty relish, vaguely surprised that grief could be attended by such a robust appetite. Then she lay down for a little siesta, while Tichi went up to La Greca's house to gather up the few poor belongings that Eva Helena had left.

When Josefina awoke it was mid-afternoon. Tichi was still away, but her sister-in-law Juana had a puchero simmering on the coals against her guest's awakening. It was a rich, fragrant stew, flavored with herbs and saffron; and its like, Josefina knew, was not served often in Juana's poor house. But, when Juana placed this savory dish before her, Josefina experienced only a sudden revulsion. She wanted violently to leave the table, to leave Juana and her house. Stammering an apology, she cast her mantón over her head and almost rushed to the door. As she went out, into the street, she heard Juana's bewildered protest:

"Por Dios, señora! Why do you not eat the puchero? That you do nothing unwise!"

She smiled wanly. She had nothing unwise, no rash act of any kind, in mind. She wished merely to flee. From what, she was not certain.

89

Only from Juana and her puchero, perhaps. It made her feel better to hurry, almost to run, along the narrow, sometimes steep and tortuous streets of Ávila. She noticed nothing. She paid so little attention to what was around her that she froze in terror when a rough voice shouted into her ear:

"Dios! Dios! Can't you hear, estúpida?"

Then she was aware of the tinkle of a bell, coming nearer and nearer, and she saw that everyone around her—including now the hairy-faced mat vendor who had shouted to her—had dropped to his knees; so she knew that a priest carrying the Host through the streets to the house of a dying Christian was approaching. She spread her handkerchief on the stones, knelt and bowed her head until the sound of the bell had died away again, then arose with the others. She cast a contemptuous glance at the mat seller.

"My sympathy," she said, "for the great sow that bore you."

She disregarded the vendor's answering insult and looked around her with interest. It was as if her head had suddenly cleared, and she saw that she was in a familiar quarter of the town. She had come to that very old and crowded district in Ávila where she had lived as a child. She knew the street on which she now found herself, but not quite completely; she sensed a special, rather than an everyday, familiarity with it; and it was not until she had come to a certain small shop that the past leaped back to her, sharp and clear and tragic.

"Ah, Yolanda!" she whispered.

For this was indeed the same shop to which she had carried the doll Yolanda when Concepción was so sick and money was needed for a surgeon. And this was the same dingy door at which she had quickly kissed Yolanda's china cheek, and straightened her dress, and said, "Good-by, my heart. . . . In any case, you are now too old for dolls, Josefina. . . ."

Ah, what a long, long time ago! she thought. Yet not so very long ago: two years maybe, or three.

She stood peering into the dark, cavelike entrance of the shop. Suddenly the thought came to her—Perhaps he has Yolanda still!—and the idea itself seemed to take her into the shop, to bear her along with it.

Inside, nothing was different. There was the same damp, musty smell; the same dim glow of a few smouldering coals in a battered brass brazier; the same disorder of petty wares covering floor and walls and ceiling: caps, combs, tinders, toys, old newspapers, small paper altar pieces, odds and ends of pottery and kitchen ware, images of the saints, and dog-eared pamphlets with such titles as *Spiritual Dial which teaches how to carry God with us Every Hour* and *The Art of Living for Working People, Useful to all.*

The shopkeeper peered at her through steel-rimmed spectacles as she entered. He wore a flat cardboard collar covered with greasy linen. Josefina recognized him at once, and with a kind of start. For an instant, time seemed to rush backward: for that instant she was a desperate child, standing in this murky shop and holding out, to this very man in steel-rimmed spectacles, a doll called Yolanda.

"I wish to purchase a doll, señor," she said, almost timidly: she felt her heart beating fast, just as she had felt it race under Yolanda's tightly held form that long time ago. "Do you have dolls?"

"Assuredly, señora," the shopkeeper said. "Only a few, but of the finest quality."

"Let me see them."

He began to show her a decrepit puppet dressed in the faded costume of a chestnut vendor; one eye was missing.

"That is not a doll of the kind I wish to buy," Josefina said coldly. "Have you nothing better to show, señor?"

The shopkeeper looked at her sharply. Did he recognize her? Josefina refused to believe it possible; nevertheless, she drew her mantón across her face, as if about to leave.

"One moment, señora," the shopkeeper said hastily. "I do have such a doll as you wish to see. But it is so fine, señora, that my wife would not allow it to remain here in the shop. She keeps it in her bride's chest, locked up like a piece of gold brocade or a blonde mantón. You will understand why, señora, when you see this marvel—please, one moment."

He ducked through a low door at the back of the shop, leaving Josefina alone and thinking: It cannot be. Surely, it cannot be. But, if it is true, Josefina—let us conceal our feelings!

So she became absorbed in the examination of a jet-and-silver rosary, and turned an expressionless face to the shopkeeper when he returned; yet she could not hide from herself the excitement of her heart.

"Señora," the shopkeeper asked, beaming, "have I exaggerated?"

He held out to her a doll with pink porcelain cheeks, and blue porcelain eyes, and hair of heavenly blondness; and its dress was of a richness that an infanta herself might envy—although of that certain vaguely foreign appearance that sets all dolls apart from things of the ordinary world. And she was even lovelier than she had remembered.

"Look!" she heard her mother saying. "Look now, my daughter, my little mother."

She took Yolanda from the shopkeeper and examined her critically. The shopkeeper's wife had cared for her well; she was as clean and fresh still as she had been on that wonderful flower-scented day when Eva Helena had taken her from the great chest and had said:

"Now close your eyes, little daughter . . . Until I tell you, 'Open!'"

91

Josefina handed Yolanda back to the shopkeeper with an air of indifference. She picked up the jet-and-silver rosary and examined it again, languidly.

"How much for the doll?" she asked.

"There is not another like it in the Two Castiles. Ten reales, señora."

You gave me but five for it, Josefina almost said aloud. I remember well enough. I gave two of them to the doctor. Now you ask ten. You are a cheat, señor shopkeeper, as well as a liar.

She offered four reales. Half an hour later she paid six and left the shop with Yolanda beneath her mantón. It had grown almost dark. She clutched Yolanda to her tightly and—she knew not why—began to run down the dusky street. She ran blindly, without knowing in what direction she was going. Whenever she passed anyone she turned her head, so that it could not be seen that she was weeping.

21

Upon her return to Madrid three days later, Josefina thought she could detect a certain reserve in the Maya's manner; and in the Conde de Vega's attitude toward her a subtle difference: the addition, perhaps, of a vague, somewhat sly air of proprietorship to his courtly banter.

Do I imagine this? she asked herself, deeply troubled. Or is Doña Manuela really angry with me?

She was not afraid—as so many others were—of the Maya; but she was gravely concerned never to offend her. Toward others she had tried desperately to make herself hard and cynical and contemptuous of her own gentler emotions; yet she had tried always to love Doña Manuela. That she should be grateful to this dark, strange, fierce, and no doubt depraved woman, she never questioned. That she should ever be disloyal to her was unthinkable.

"What do you think, Tichi?" she asked. "Have you noticed anything?"

"I have noticed a good many things since we came here yesterday," Tichi said. "But I have no way of telling what they mean. Doña Manuela, for instance, appears to me to be in a very bad humor. But I may be mistaken. Perhaps it is her natural temperament, and indicates nothing."

"No," Josefina said. "It is her temperament to spit fire sometimes, like the volcano they have in Italy. But not to smoulder."

"I have heard of that volcano," Tichi said. "Nobody knows what to expect of it, and so nobody worries about it. Let us not worry about Doña Manuela. Let us concern ourselves with these pigeons."

"The baker has overdone them, no?"

"He has overdone the meat and overcharged us, señora. Fourteen cuartos for roasting four birds not half the size of my fist! It is outrageous—especially since we furnished the bacon."

"Well, this isn't Ávila," Josefina said. "This is Madrid, where everything is bought only at a high price. And not food alone, Tichi. Let us eat."

The Gallega served her mistress one of the pigeons, which had been sent by the Conde de Vega and which, since Josefina's small kitchen had no oven, had been roasted by a neighborhood pastry cook. She poured a small glass of wine and withdrew.

"Join me, Tichi," Josefina said. "Since this is somewhat of an occasion, I think we may eat together tonight."

"What is the occasion, señora?"

"A mistress should not be questioned by her servant," Josefina said, "but I'll tell you. This is my saint's day. It is also the occasion of the Conde de Vega's having sent us these pigeons. It is the occasion, also, of your coming to me—or, perhaps I should say, of forcing yourself on me—as my maid."

"In that case, I give you my compliments, señora, and accept with thanks. I do not approve of such familiarity, however. What I heard about servants in this city!"

"When you have overstepped, Tichi," Josefina said dryly, "I'll let you know. That you join me now."

Tichi served herself one of the birds and, in response to Josefina's gesture, poured herself a little of the wine. Her comely brown face was serene and smiling, her brown eyes almost luminous in the candlelight. She swallowed her first bit of pigeon and sighed.

"It is pleasant here," she said. "I am happy that I have come with you, señora."

Josefina also was content: sad and heavy-hearted, but in a manner content. She allowed her eyes to wander over the room in which they dined. It was a small room with plain plastered walls and a very high ceiling, furnished austerely, almost severely, in the Spanish manner, with a few simple pieces: a bench and two chairs, on which she and Tichi sat, a large carved chest, a cupboard, and, of course, a brass brazier in which some embers glowed. The embers and the two candles on the table cast soft shadows about the walls and upon the lofty ceiling; and, even in so small a room, there was an air of spaciousness and tranquility.

"It is good to have you here, Tichi," she said. "You bring peace to my house."

Peace and—although she would not admit it to her servant—order. For she was not an orderly person; and this small apartment, which she had acquired next to the Maya's much grander establishment, had never been very neat until Tichi came. Then an atmosphere of calm and relaxation had followed at once. It was something, Josefina reflected, that probably accompanied this pleasant young Gallega wherever she went. And why, she wondered, as she had wondered so often, why had Tichi chosen to share her own poor fortunes?

"But why did you come?" she asked.

"For many reasons, señora."

"For example?"

"The one they call La Greca," Tichi said. "I could endure no more of her."

"That," Josefina said grimly, "I can understand."

"And Ávila. The walls made me nervous, señora. Even when I could not see them, I could *feel* them. I could feel them closing me in."

"That also I understand," Josefina said.

"And so, señora——" Tichi shrugged her rounded shoulders. She dropped her eyes and examined a pigeon wing, turning it slowly in her fingers. Josefina regarded her silently for a little while.

"You have really told me nothing," she said at last. "Have you, Tichi?"

"Ah, señora," Tichi said. "How do I know why I do things? How does anybody know? There are no colts without mares, they used to say in Arzua. But the colt grows up and the mare is forgotten, no? It was very dull in Arzua. I do not expect much of life, señora, but I could not endure Arzua. Once, when I was a child, a troupe of players arrived there—they must have lost their way—and they performed some autos sacramentales on the square. Without doubt, they were shocking plays, señora. If you can imagine, in one of them our Lord came down from the cross, put on his wig and a coat, and smoked a cigar—and then, señora, he joined the other actors and danced a seguidillas!"

Josefina laughed. "I have seen almost as bad," she said, "at the Príncipe."

"Yet," Tichi said, "they are all that I can remember of interest in Arzua, those autos. There was an actress among the players that I remember particularly. She was a slut, no doubt, but she played the part of an angel in a golden wig, and there was something magical and exótico about her that I can still feel inside me when I recall her. Do not laugh at me, señora."

Josefina said, with a kind of start, "I'm not laughing, Tichi. I believe it!" She was thinking of another child and of a dancer who called herself María de la Chica. "And so, Tichi——?"

"Nothing, señora. Except that when I left Arzua at last, and got as far as Ávila, perhaps that is why I became La Greca's maid. She is a true bitch, and to live in her house long is impossible: but she was a famous actress once, and people of the theater still come to her parties, and there is a certain——"

"And that, no doubt, is also the reason why you have accompanied me to Madrid!" Josefina said dryly.

"I think that is so, señora," Tichi admitted gravely. "That, and because it is necessary for someone to look after you, and also because I love you as my child."

Josefina was embarrassed to know that her eyes, no doubt, were bright in the candlelight with half-formed tears. You have become soft of late, she said to herself reprovingly. Let us wait and see how she talks when there are no pigeons and Valdepeñas, but only a little bread and garlic soup and water.

But, if her mind misgave her, her heart did not. She had already grown to love Tichi, almost as a mother; and her doubts were but a way of affirming this. As for Tichi herself, no woman in all Spain, Josefina told herself as the days passed, possessed such a servant as this pleasant, competent, and discreet Gallega.

Some of those days were indeed days of bread and garlic soup, but Tichi did not complain of, or even seem to notice, them. She kept Josefina's small apartment clean as a new tile; performed minor miracles with a few cuartos worth of eggs, mutton, sea bream, or green peppers; and asked in return only that she be allowed to accompany her mistress to the Príncipe. From her own precarious income, Josefina gave her whatever coins she could spare, but no regular wage; by making bobbin lace for edgings and chemises, Tichi earned for herself more than Josefina paid her; and sometimes it was the servant, not the mistress, who provided the milk omelet for dinner.

"Without you, Tichi," Josefina said, aloud but to herself only, "I do not think I could bear the heaviness of my heart!"

22

The sadness and feeling of aloneness caused by Eva Helena's death did not lessen with the passage of time. It was still a dull, insistent pressure in her breast. But even that was not such an aching burden as the thought of Jesusita. . . . And, over these two great griefs, lay the heavy knowledge that the Maya had become cold, distant, with sometimes (Josefina thought) a flicker of hatred in her dark eyes.

If she would but rage, Josefina thought in desperation. If she would beat me!

But the Maya continued merely to treat her with a reserve so studied that Josefina could not help but feel in it a certain quality of anticipation, of waiting. It was as if the Maya were biding her time.

Like the second lady, Josefina thought, waiting for the primera dama to break a leg or become pregnant: she is that patient. Yet she could destroy me with a word, or even a gesture. Why does she torment me?

"She is a woman," Tichi observed, "with cruel eyes."

"They are not always cruel," Josefina answered, instinctively defensive. "They can be kind, also. I have seen pity in them—and even fear, Tichi."

"Well, perhaps." Tichi shrugged. "But I have noticed nothing but cruelty. Gypsy cruelty, Doña Josefina. And it is the nature of cruelty to take its time."

"Do you think she has in mind to do me harm?" Josefina asked, horrified.

"She is a Spaniard," Tichi said. "And a gypsy."

"But in God's name, why, Tichi?"

"Señora, I have heard that when the solano blows in Andalusia, nobody is accountable for his acts, since madness then possesses everyone. It appears to me that something like the solano is blowing through Doña Manuela's heart. Like the wind from Africa, señora, it has made her a little mad. I should be careful, Doña Josefina."

"Of what, Tichi?"

"Of His Excellency the Conde," Tichi said.

Josefina laughed, but not mirthfully. The Conde de Vega was something she still had to face up to. As in the Maya's manner, there was also a certain quality of waiting in the Conde's. Was it a seemly regard for her time of mourning? Or was it fear of the Maya's wrath, possibly? Josefina could not tell; and the atmosphere of uncertainty and foreboding in which she now constantly lived oppressed and dejected her.

To escape from it, she threw herself with an almost cruel intensity into her study and practice, and in her performances at the Príncipe there began to appear technical innovations that surprised and delighted the critics and even brought cheers from the pit. It was during this period, when more than ever her dancing was a strange and oddly stirring mixture of coldness and passion, that the appellation of La Sola became firmly attached to Josefina.

"What a pity," the Conde de Vega observed gently, "that one so beautiful and so gifted should be known even to the rabble as The Lone One. And how difficult to believe!"

The Conde had called without warning—a thing he had never done before—and alone. It was a fiercely hot midsummer day and, ever since the siesta Josefina had been drilling herself—unclothed, like the ancient gaditanas—in the fandango. Another she might have kept waiting in the heat of the street, but not the Conde de Vega. And so she received him, hastily wrapped in a silken Chinese robe that he himself had once given the Maya, perspiring, and a little short of breath. She found it hard to smile at him, even though, like any rustic calling on his girl, he carried a paper of violet drops under his arm.

"I heard castanets, no?" he asked. "My apologies, if I have interrupted. Pray continue, my child."

"I have finished, Your Excellency."

"You may call me Don Lorenzo," he said. "Or simply Lorenzo, if you wish. . . . That you continue with your practice, por favor."

She fanned herself vigorously, pushed back a strand of hair from her damp forehead. "The heat is too great," she said stubbornly. "I have had enough."

Unlike the Maya, who had once greeted her guests in nothing more than her silver-embroidered slippers and a huge pair of spectacles (which were at the time much in vogue), Josefina possessed an old-fashioned Spanish sense of modesty that not even the easy conventions of theatrical life in the Capital had much eroded; and it made her uncomfortable now to feel the Conde's gaze prowling discreetly over her thinly clad body. She was angry, too, that he should have found her in such a state of deshabille.

I must look a sweating slattern to him, she thought, gazing at him over her fan.

But the Conde was thinking only: It should be declared a mortal sin to have such eyes!

The Conde, even his enemies conceded, was a man of taste and discrimination. A vain man, perhaps, and a little stupid, and full of windy speech; but his collections of enameled glass and mudéjar ivories were quite enough—if proof, indeed, were needed—to confirm his reputation as a virtuoso.

In Josefina his sophisticated glance had been arrested by something more intriguing even than great beauty—by that certain piquant strangeness for which, after all, women are loved and art treasured. And his delight in this discovery was now quite perceptible in his eyes.

He looks at me differently when Doña Manuela isn't present, Josefina mused. I have no doubt his thoughts are the same; but his eyes are different. He is afraid of Doña Manuela, of course.

This was the first time that she had ever been alone thus with the

97

Conde. She observed that his manner, his way of talking to her, had altered also. He could not help being a little florid and elaborate in his speech, but now he dropped the game he had played when the three of them were together—the heavy gallantries and pseudo-amorous speeches that had so delighted him . . . and had so little amused the Maya. He wore a serious air; and there was nothing in his manner, his mood, or his deepset eyes, she observed with a little flutter of panic, that could be taken lightly.

The Conde kissed her hand with his accustomed flourish, and gave her the paper of violet drops. She made appropriate exclamations of pleasure, and offered them to the Conde, and he took one. He sat down on one of Josefina's two chairs and looked thoughtfully about the room.

"I have just had a long conversation with Luján," he said.

"With Luján, the critic?" she asked, curious.

"Yes, madamita, with Luján of the *Gaceta.*" He cleared his throat gently. "And I shall describe our conversation. But first——" He paused, smiling at her appraisingly.

"Yes, Don Lorenzo?"

"What is your rank at the Príncipe, my dear?" he asked abruptly.

"I am the fifth lady, señor."

"It is Luján's opinion that you should be the first—la primera dama," the Conde said carelessly.

Ah, yes, that is it! Josefina said to herself. That I should have the first place . . . that I should displace Doña Manuela, eh?

She looked with hard eyes—very like emeralds in their glacial gaze —at Don Lorenzo. For the first time, it seemed to her, she saw him clearly as a man: not as a grandee of Spain, a cousin of the king with the right to cover his head before the sovereign, but merely as a man. And a man, moreover, who wanted to be her lover.

That you remember who he is, Josefina! she warned herself.

He was one of the ancient ricos hombres, and his title had existed from time immemorial; its antiquity was graven on his long, dark face But so, also, was a hint of degeneracy—itself the product and penalty of too many centuries of privilege, perhaps—and, rare but by no means unknown among the Spanish nobility, a strong suggestion of vulgarity. With the Conde, pride was a habit, and dignity something he wore like his black military dress; and they served to conceal a mixture of superstitious piety, loyalty to the king, valor, cruelty, and ignorance—the latter glossed over by a superficial virtuosity—that was, in actual fact, the Conde de Vega.

That you remember! Josefina repeated to herself. For he can be your ruin.

The Conde passed his hand over his rather large and slack mouth, and smiled with an air he might have thought disarming. His eyes slipped downward to the point of Josefina's slipper.

"La primera dama," he said again. "Luján thinks you deserve it." He raised his eyes suddenly to hers. "Y cómo no?" he asked. "Why not?"

So he had come to it at last: to the simple proposition—the offer. He fixed her with his deepset eyes, smiling faintly, waiting for her answer.

By the Mass! she said to herself, aghast. It is not me, but Doña Manuela he ruins! So that his new mistress may be worthy of his name, he sacrifices the old. La primera dama! He could make me that, I doubt not.

Suddenly his face became a great swimming leer before her sickened eyes. She wanted so badly to scream insults at him, to spit at him, to scratch him with her nails, that the nausea rose to her throat and choked her. She got to her feet, cried weakly for Tichi, and fought desperately not to be sick. Then she felt the Conde's arms about her shoulders, and Tichi's under her knees, and she was being carried to her chamber.

"Ay, Dios mío! Let me go!" she cried, her strength returning. "Set me down!"

Wrenching herself free of them, she staggered to her bed and sat defiantly on the edge of it, her arms stiff behind her, the silken Chinese robe falling off her shoulders. Oblivious of her nakedness, she glared somberly at the dumfounded grandee.

"That you go now," she said. "I am sorry, Don Lorenzo, but I do not feel well."

She drew up her legs and lay on the bed with her head in the crook of her arm. Tichi covered her with the silken robe.

"It is the effect of the heat," the Conde said nervously, staring with a kind of fascination at the half-covered form on the bed. "The air is very heavy and oppressive today." He smiled fatuously. "I feel a slight faintness myself."

"Yes, señor, it is the heat," Tichi said, and added pointedly. "Go with God, señor."

"Perhaps we should send for a surgeon."

"There is no need of it, señor. She needs only rest—and a little quiet. Adiós now, señor—adiós!"

So the Conde left, but reluctantly. The shouts of his coachman and the rattle of wheels on the pavement echoed after his departure. Josefina lifted her head and listened.

"Has he gone, Tichi?" she asked.

"Yes, señora—at last."

"That he never return!" Josefina said wearily. "That he go straight to hell and burn forever!"

99

23

For the next few days she saw nothing more of the Conde de Vega. He appeared neither at the rehearsals, as was his custom, nor after the performances. For Josefina this was a welcome circumstance; but to the Maya it was obviously—and if one might judge from the shortness of her temper—a deeply disquieting development. She became the terror of the company, and even Guzmán, the good-natured director, curled up like a fat worm in the heat of her frequent rages. And often—so often that it was not unnoticed by the others—Josefina was the special target of the Maya's crackling rage.

"What would I give to strike you!" Josefina cried at last, in tears. "Across your mouth—hard, hard, Doña Manuela!"

The Maya came close, hands on her swaying hips, her eyes narrowed to glittering slits. "Por qué no?" she asked in a low husky maja drawl. "Why not, my fine little cheat? That I might tear your lousy eyes out! That I might dance on your body!"

Josefina had turned and fled that time, pursued by the Maya's mocking laughter. Yet she did not fear the Maya: she feared only herself— what she might in anger and desperation do against her protectoress. For, except in such moments, she loved the Maya; and never, not even in the thick of her abuse, had there occurred to her even the possibility of disloyalty to this strange, fierce, proud, pitiful woman.

Ay, Don Lorenzo! she thought bitterly. You great, stupid fool, what trouble you make for everyone!

To escape this burden of depression, she drove herself, despite the fierce heat that hung over Madrid, like a madwoman. She drove herself, from darkness to darkness, until Tichi begged her to spare herself.

"In God's name, Doña Josefina—see how thin you have become! That you rest now."

"Once more, Tichi. The zarandeo is not yet perfect. Observe the hips now."

She was fired with the possibilities of an idea that had come to her. Something new—a discovery—a thing that no tonadilla singer had ever thought of before. And something, she knew, that no performer in all Spain could do as well as herself.

Guzmán had given her to sing, between the acts of the comedy, a new tonadilla by Guerra. It was less biting than most of Guerra's verses (although some said there was a buried satire in the simple lines), and the tune was charming. Josefina sang it, accompanying herself on the guitar, with just that touch of remoteness and sadness that intrigued and delighted the Madrileños:

> "They say that you now love
>   another,
> They say that you now love
>   another,
> But none shall ever guess
>   my sorrow,
> Ay! None shall tell of my shame.
> See how I smile with my eyes!
> See how I laugh with my lips!
> See how I dance in my satin
>   slippers!
> While my heart hides its anguish,
> While my heart breaks. Ay!"

What had occurred to her—such a simple thing, yet never hit upon by anyone before, not even by the Maya, whose invention was limitless —was the idea of combining the verses with the dance. The lines cried out to her for it. "See how I dance in my satin slippers!" . . . She felt a sudden, rushing urge—such as a woman might feel to throw herself into a lover's arms—to interrupt the sad little song and dance: to say with her whole body what words—even Guerra's!—could only hint at.

"Let me do it, Chico!" she begged Guzmán. "That you let me do it for you, at least. Please, Chico!"

The corpulent director, whom they called Little One, lowered his great bulk onto an oaken bench and gazed at her with sweaty, melancholy eyes.

"Body of Christ!" he said mournfully. "On such a day as this you come to ask favors of Guzmán. Look at me, child. What do you see?"

"I see the greatest director, señor mío, of the Spanish theater."

She said it soberly, perhaps a shade too soberly, for Guzmán sucked in his lower lip and regarded her with a kind of sad suspicion.

"You see a man to be pitied," he said. "A man surrounded by idiots, asses, and ordinary bastards who call themselves actors. A man cursed by bad plays and stupid audiences. A man without faith or hope and, what is worse, without money. How am I to meet a payroll of five thousand reales—not to mention ration money—on Monday? Have you thought of that, little sweetheart? Ay, Dios! On a day of so much heat and so many troubles, why do you come to pester me?"

"Please, Chico. It will be a sensation. It will make you famous."

"I am already famous," Guzmán said reprovingly. "What I long for is obscurity, peace."

"There is never enough of fame, Chico. As for peace—some day when you are old, no?"

"Does the Maya know about this?" Guzmán asked.

"I haven't told her," she answered, wondering. "I had thought to keep it as a surprise for her."

He shrugged his shoulders and looked at her silently for a while with his small, sad eyes.

"You have talent, my child," he said, with a sigh. "But no sense."

"Señor?"

"Well, let us see—whatever it is you wish me to see," Guzmán said wearily.

She threw her arms about his fat shoulders and gave him a hasty kiss. She clapped her hands and shouted excitedly, "Luis! Luis! Pronto!"

A young man with damp, curly hair, carrying a guitar, dashed in from the wings. He was—not very secretly—in love with Josefina, and he could play a guitar in a way to make it talk. For these reasons, Josefina had chosen him from among the ranks of minor players and musicians to accompany her.

"Vaya! Vaya!" she said, her voice low and tense. "Give me some music, Luis."

They had rehearsed the song many times together. Luis inclined his head and tested the tuning of his instrument. "Good!" he said. "Anda, chica!" Josefina twisted the cords of her castanets around her thumbs and pulled them tight. She gravely announced the title of her song, "Better Shame on the Cheek than an Ache in the Heart," raised her arms, and showered down a few experimental notes from her castanets. The familiar frown passed like a shadow across her face.

"A surprise for the Maya!" Guzmán muttered to himself, and smiled.

Josefina began to sing. Her voice was sweet and husky and small on the great stage of the empty theater. The music was from an old tune. Guzmán closed his eyes and listened. He appeared bored by the familiar music and, even though it were Guerra's, the rather banal versification.

Then a sudden carretilla of the castanets brought him alert, eyes wide open and staring at something no one had ever seen on a Spanish stage before. The tonadilla singer was dancing!

There was nothing new about the dance itself. It was one of Spain's oldest, light, gay, lively, with the lower limbs active and quick, the body "serene," the arms widespread and scattering the staccato notes of the castanets. Josefina danced it superbly; but there was nothing new in that either—she had always done the seguidillas like an angel.

But who had ever heard of such a thing as this! Who had ever seen a tonadilla singer dance, or a dancer sing? Guzmán sat in a kind of daze, his eyes delighted, but his mind struggling to grasp the reality of a unique, utterly novel experience. He stirred his huge bulk and muttered a bewildered "Olé!"

And now the brief dance interlude ended with a sharp *tok* of the castanets and a frozen figure; and Josefina's sweet, husky voice took up the sad burden of the song, so oddly at variance with the gay spirit of the dance. Again and again, this strange counterpoint of dance and song, of gaiety and grief, was repeated; until, on the empty stage, with only Guzmán watching, the very first performance of a tonadilla with dancing ended on the low, sobbing, almost Moorish refrain:

"While my heart breaks . . . Ay!"

When it was over, Guzmán heaved his great bulk up and propelled himself toward Josefina. He wrapped her in his vast embrace, silently; he was crying too hard for words.

24

Josefina thought now of that far-off moment, and of the next afternoon, terrifying yet even more wonderful and unbelievable, and of the disaster that followed soon afterwards.

She sat before the broken mirror in the room the innkeeper had given them for a dressing room—a wretched hole next to the stable— and made herself ready for the entertainment that might earn them, if God were willing, lodgings for another day or so in this wretched inn at Roa. She applied a little green shadow under each eye and smiled at herself in the murky glass.

"Why are you smiling, señora?" Tichi asked.

"I was thinking of something," she answered absently.

She was thinking how incredibly naïve she had been. What was it Guzmán had said? Well, Guzmán was right. She had been a fool. Only a year ago, even less, and what an utter fool she had been. She looked at herself in the glass, and said with a kind of bitter drollness, "At any rate, Josefina, you are different now. You are really hard at last!"

She had thought of herself as hard then—had even worn a small dagger in a sheath on her garter as a symbol of her majalike hardness—but how mistaken she had been! And how helpless when the lightning struck.

A sort of sultriness, common before lightning, had hung over the Teatro del Príncipe, it had seemed to Josefina—a suffocating heaviness of the atmosphere that affected everyone, like an Andalusian soltano. Guzmán was nervous and irritable. She herself had turned to water. And the whole company of the Príncipe, she could have sworn, was watching her with stony eyes.

They know! she repeated to herself. They have spied. Or someone— Luis maybe, or Chico—has told.

As four o'clock, the hour of the performance, approached, Josefina's nervousness turned into something she had never experienced before on the stage—something close to terror. It was a deliciously cool day for early September in Madrid—a blessed change from the relentless heat of the Castilian summer—but Josefina was annoyed to find herself drenched in perspiration. She had Tichi sponge her all over with cool water and rub her down with spirits of roses.

"Pray for me, Tichi," she said, and not in jest. "That I may somehow get through with this!"

Foolishly, she had allowed herself a quick glance through the curtain at the many-headed monster which, rather earlier than usual, had filled the Príncipe: at her friend, her enemy, the noisy, fickle, cruel, terrifying mob that, in just a few moments, could—as if with a single mind—make her famous throughout the two Spains . . . or tear her to shreds.

Although it was still a half-hour before curtain time, she noted that the long gallery—called by some "the women's cage"—was already a solid rectangle of white veils and fluttering fans. High up, to the rear, the balcony was filled with black-garbed churchmen and the more sober play-goers. Even the boxes, reserved for the wealthy, who seldom appeared until the performance was half-over, were coming alive with the forms of ladies wearing high combs and mantillas and gentlemen in powdered wigs.

And in the pit, the mosqueteros had been standing for several hours in the midday sun.

Ay, los mosqueteros! Josefina gazed with the almost morbid fascination felt by all actors and actresses at the raucous throng milling about in the pit below.

"Whoreson wretches!" she said softly, aloud. "Sons of dogs!"

She experienced a sudden, unaccountable hatred for this noisy, dirty, evil-smelling mob of riffraff, soldiers and scoundrels who called themselves los mosqueteros, and who boasted—and made good the boast— that no play could succeed without their blatant approval. They were the terrorists of the theater, those great bullies of the pit, and no actress could outlive their enmity. So even the greatest of them—even the fabulous Juana García, and the Maya herself—must, from time to time, invite this vulgar rabble into their homes for cakes and wine.

This, to Josefina, had always seemed a shameful thing. She had never felt affection for the mosqueteros—as some actresses professed to—but only dislike. And yet, in spite of this—even because of it, perhaps—the mosqueteros loved her.

Ah, yes, but how quickly, like a pack of mad curs, they can turn on you and destroy you! she thought.

She remembered how little the mosqueteros favored change—how they clung to the old ways and viewed with suspicion all things new. Had they not pelted María Castillo with garbage for no other offense than appearing in a red dress?

A chill traveled up her spine, and she hated the mosqueteros even more intensely for what, a few moments hence, they could do to her—for what, she had come to believe in her agitation, they were but waiting to do to her.

As Tichi smoothed on her dancing slippers, she could hear the tumult from the pit, a foreboding rumble pierced by the sharp cries of the water vendors, "Agua! Hay agua! Agua fresca!"

The mosqueteros had been standing for a long time in the sun. They had come early—more than three hours ago—and they were growing restless. Fortunately, Josefina did not know why they had arrived even earlier than usual today: that Guzmán had spread a report that something unusual, even sensational, would be viewed at the Príncipe that afternoon.

Josefina sensed only that there was an extraordinary atmosphere of tension, a kind of irritable anticipation, permeating the audience. As she tightened her long silk stockings and adjusted her garters, she was filled with the awful realization that she would be the first to face whatever frightful thing was crouched, ready to spring, out there.

For Guzmán had decided that she should do her tono con baile as a prelude before the first act of the play.

The play itself, that day, was a dull comedy by one of the newest plagiarists of the great Molino. No one, of course, had come to see it. All had come to the Príncipe for the gay musical interludes between the acts, and for the fin de fiesta at the end of the play. And, particularly today, out of curiosity to see the novelty that, it was rumored all over Madrid, Guzmán would exhibit in the prelude.

The rough shouts of the mosqueteros came faintly to Josefina in her dressing room. Guzmán appeared at the door. He looked very warm and somewhat distraught—as if he himself, perhaps, were not quite free from fear.

"You go on in four minutes," he said, looking first at one of his watches, then at the other. "How—how do you feel, child?" Guzmán stammered a little when he was discomposed.

"I feel fine," Josefina said. Guzmán's agitation, strangely, seemed to steady her own nerves. She suddenly felt within herself a kind of defiant calmness.

"Remember, sweetheart," the director said, with an attempt at jocularity, "Guzmán's reputation is at stake this afternoon."

"Don't worry, señor mío," she answered, with a touch of scorn. "You will be no smaller after today."

Guzmán laughed, and when he laughed all of his huge bulk shook. "Good girl!" He coughed. "That we slay them!" A woman's voice called "Chico!" from somewhere, and he was gone.

Josefina pulled on her castanets, attaching them to her thumbs in the Andalusian manner, as Eva Helena had taught her to wear them. She never went through this little act without thinking, if only half-consciously, of her mother. She thought of her now.

That we please you, Madre, she said to herself. That we make you a little proud of us in heaven!

When her call came a few moments later, she suddenly realized that the Maya had not come to wish her luck. The Maya must have known—as who did not?—that something of a special interest surrounded her performance today. But she had not come to say, "Good success, my child!" She had not relented. The Maya, some said, was constant only in hatred.

Perhaps, Josefina thought, but not hopefully, perhaps she will forgive me when she sees it. God grant it!

She made the sign of the cross and arose to go. As she walked through the wings, she saw the other players watching her curiously. She saw Guzmán also, but he was not watching; his fat face was buried in his fat hands.

Ah, Chico, she said to herself, how you suffer!

Then she saw the Maya, whose face was a bronze mask with eyes of jet that looked at her stonily; and behind her, Don Lorenzo who smiled and surreptitiously blew her a hand kiss over the Maya's shoulder.

Then, without knowing how she got there, she was before the flimsy curtain, on the stage. Her eyes went mechanically—as did those of every actress and dancer—to the pit, where so many careers were made or broken. She waited for the applause with which the mosqueteros customarily greeted her.

But none came today. Apparently the mosqueteros, whose whims were like those of children, had decided to assume a judicious dignity. They frowned in portentous silence, waiting to see if what they were about to see merited their approval. And their taciturnity spread, like a jar of spilled water, to every cranny of the audience.

But Josefina smiled at them as she always did, aloof, perhaps even a little contemptuous—in a way that, by some strange quirk of perversity, had endeared her to them all. And while she smiled, she said in a voice too low for them to hear:

"Very well, you lousy canalla—let you go ahead and finish me!"

Luis sauntered on stage from the wings, carrying his guitar and a small stool. He took his place at a distance and waited with an air of bored expectancy. A low murmur came up from the pit: the mosqueteros had detected the first sign of something different to come, for La Sola had hitherto played her own accompaniment to her tonos. One or two even answered her steady, frowning smile with a low "Olé!"

Josefina advanced a few steps, raised her arms in a wide brazeo, and flung a single trill of her castanets—a sharp, imperious demand for attention—over the heads of her audience. Then, her face empty, expressionless at first, she began without accompaniment to sing Guerra's sad little song of lost love.

25

It was not until the second dance interlude that the mosqueteros—too astonished at first to show any reaction whatsoever—gave their verdict. What happened then was described by Luján the next day in the *Gaceta*.

No one can doubt that on the afternoon of September 15, 1712, La Señora Josefina Torres added a brilliant new page to the history of the Spanish theater. Her introduction of a new form of the tonadilla, combining for the first time the singing of a tono with the performance of a solo dance (in this instance a highly personal interpretation of the seguidillas) was an idea as daring in concept as it proved to be triumphant in execution. . . . In these days of decadence and vulgarity in the impoverished realm of our drama, how refreshing is the art, the originality, and the personality of La Sola! How she dominates the theater! What color, enchantment, and charm she brings to the dance! . . .

Thus Luján, in his usual style, and unable to refrain from adding (in his usual style also) a querulous note at the end of his column-long article:

Something, in this connection, must be said about the vulgar and disgraceful conduct of the crowd in the pit. The noisy and offensive behavior of the mosqueteros has long been a source of annoyance. But nothing has yet equaled the shouting, commotion and riotous disorder with which they demonstrated their enthusiasm for Señora Torres' performance at the Príncipe. It is time that the Mayor, or even the governor of the Council, took steps to prevent these unpleasant disturbances. Not even the great art of Señora Torres is sufficient excuse for such vexatious displays of approbation.

From what was undoubtedly one of the most famous theatrical tumults of the day, Josefina herself escaped only when encore after encore had exhausted her physically—when even the mosqueteros could see the impossibility of her continuing. Then Guzmán, weeping and babbling incoherently, half-carried her back to her dressing room. He embraced her wildly, then rushed away like a distracted duenna: the curtain, after all, was rising on *The Girl from Ronda*.

Breathless and pale, Josefina sat for a while, her hands clenching the edge of the bench, her head back against the wall, numb with fatigue—like a peasant woman spent by some colossal effort. Tichi dried her face and shoulders and began removing her perspiration-drenched dress.

"Now," Tichi said, "you are the most famous dancer in Spain. How does it feel, Doña Josefina, to be so famous?"

"Did Doña Manuela like it?" Josefina asked. "Did she give me some palmadas?"

"I don't know, señora," Tichi answered. "But I think that Doña Manuela remained in her dressing room."

"During all that great uproar also?"

"Doña Manuela has an iron will," Tichi said dryly.

She got Josefina into fresh clothes and threw a woolen manta about her shoulders as a precaution against catching a chill.

"There's one thing that's certain, señora—His Excellency liked it," Tichi said significantly. "Don Lorenzo gave you plenty of palmadas. Slay me, señora, but he outdid the mosqueteros. Actually, it seems to me that he made somewhat of a spectacle of himself."

Josefina made a little moue of distaste. "If you are telling this for my pleasure, Tichi," she said, "you may save your breath."

"I have to tell you still more than that," Tichi said, unperturbed. "I have to tell you that Don Lorenzo is much concerned about how you will manage to leave the theater safely. The crowds outside are frightening, and one cannot forget the time that Juana García's sedan chair was torn to pieces by the mob of her admirers, no?"

"Tichi, what are you getting at?"

"Why, nothing, señora. I am only repeating what His Excellency himself asked me to tell you. That he has arranged to have his own coach waiting for you, with a guard of his servants, at the women's entrance. And if you will but disguise yourself——"

"Tichi!" Josefina exclaimed. "Go find Don Lorenzo and tell him that I thank him, but I shall make my own way home."

"It is unnecessary to seek him out," Tichi said. "He will be here shortly, you can be sure, after he has completed arrangements for the entertainment at his house to celebrate your success, señora. Then you can tell him whatever you wish, with your own lips, Doña Josefina."

"The entertainment, Tichi?"

"Yes, señora—at His Excellency's house. And it is certain to surpass in elegance anything ever given for an actress in Madrid. Even—" she added, without expression—"even for Doña Manuela."

Josefina studied the comely and innocent face of her Galician servant. How, she wondered, had Don Lorenzo won her over? How, possibly, had he bought her? For it was plain enough that Tichi—whether for selfish or other reasons—was furthering the Conde's cause. She remembered the old saying that all servants are inevitably enemies; and she felt her first sorry doubts about Tichi whom she had trusted so deeply, and had even loved.

"You talk as if you were the Conde's procuress," she said bitterly.

Tichi laughed. "You are the first dancer of Spain now, señora," she said. "You can choose as you wish, and reject as you wish. But it is nice to have hidalgos and grandees courting you, no?"

"It was my impression that you wished to come to me as a servant, not as an adviser."

"And also advantageous," Tichi said, ignoring this, "particularly in the case of His Excellency the Conde de Vega who, as you know, has tremendous influence with the critics and possesses such power at court that he can even bring about the passage of rules, regulations, and laws governing the theater."

"Holy Mary!" Josefina exclaimed in amazement. "Who told you that?"

"The Conde's lackey," Tichi answered with composure. "Not ten minutes ago."

"Well, I can do without the Conde's power and influence," Josefina said. But she did not smile: she recognized the truth in Tichi's parroting of what the lackey had told her.

"But this coin has two sides, señora," Tichi said. "Anyone who can do so much good can also do a great deal of harm. And whether the rock strikes the pitcher or the pitcher strikes the rock, it is always the pitcher that gets broken."

"In that, at least, I agree with you," Josefina said. "And now, I think this is a good time for us to get out of here, no? Let us go, Tichi."

She stood up and passed the white-wool manta across her face. As she was effecting this simple but almost impenetrable disguise, there was a gentle rap on the door.

"See who it is, Tichi," she directed.

Tichi loosed the bolt and opened the door slightly. A swell of discordant sound surged into the room: the mosqueteros, apparently, did not like *The Girl from Ronda*. Tichi closed the door again, slowly, and turned a perplexed and distressed face to Josefina. She whispered:

"It is Don Lorenzo, señora."

Josefina dropped her manta about her shoulders; she looked around the little whitewashed room as if seeking some means of escape.

"Well," she said, with a shrug, "let him in, Tichi. What else is there to do?"

26

Tichi, flinging the door open almost spasmodically, slipped past the Conde de Vega into the corridor. The grandee glanced after her in astonishment, then stepped into the room, closing the door softly behind him.

"Señor mío?" Josefina said. She made it a question, rather than a greeting, keeping her face empty of expression.

"Madama," the Conde said, "I am at your feet!"

There were half a thousand years of breeding in the low, sweeping bow he made; in the easy dignity of his rather slight but well-knit figure, clothed in elegant black; in the almost ascetic, yet sensual contours of his dark hawklike face, with its deep eyes and large, loosely controlled mouth.

"I thank Your Excellency."

"*Don Lorenzo,*" the Conde said, "or, better yet, Lorenzo? Remember?"

"I thank you, Señor Don Lorenzo," she said, giving the "Señor" a little stress. Unconsciously, she took a step backward.

This is going to be difficult, Josefina, she told herself. That you control yourself now. . . . That you remember the rock and the pitcher!

The Conde tossed his tricorn hat onto a wardrobe chest—a gesture that was the equivalent of tossing off his dignity—and his lips parted in a sudden smile. He ate her, as the saying was, with his eyes.

"Not only am I at your feet, my dear," he said, "but all Spain is. You were magnificent! You were divine! You have surpassed La Catuja, my dove. Nobody speaks of anyone now but La Sola. All the others are forgotten."

Even the Maya, no doubt, Josefina said to herself, wryly.

"Mira!" the Conde exclaimed suddenly. "Look! I am at your feet in truth! I am the slave of your beauty—your art!"

He dropped to his knees, his arms widespread, his eyes looking up at her with an expression that, it passed through her startled mind, was not unlike those one saw in religious paintings, such as those of "The Greek." As she gazed down, astonished at the spectacle of the great Conde de Vega at her feet, his arms suddenly wrapped themselves around her knees. She tried to wriggle free, taking little steps backwards. In the struggle, the Conde's powdered wig fell off.

"Por favor, señor," she begged. "That you let me go. That you get up, Don Lorenzo." She grasped him under the arms, to help him.

He got to his feet with her assistance, brushed off his breeches, and replaced his wig. His dark features were flushed, and he looked a little shamefaced; but only for a moment. Almost at once, he caught her into a close embrace; she was astounded at the strength in his thin arms.

Do not struggle, Josefina, she cautioned herself. Let us, with God's help, find an easier way out of this ridiculous business.

She had no real fear of the Conde, although the quality of force, even of violence, in his rather farcical advances aroused in her a feeling near to panic. She was possessed by the odd sensation that something dark and ugly from her wretched past was reaching out for her through the Conde de Vega's greedily encircling arms.

"In God's name, señor!" she said, as quietly as she could.

"You are frightened!" the Conde exclaimed. "Body of Christ! My dove, why are you frightened of me? Do you find me so repulsive?"

He laughed at this conceit: but she missed the irony, and answered him seriously, even a little desperately.

"No, no, señor mío," she cried. "As all know, you are the kindest and gentlest of lords. What woman in the two Spains would not grant it? What woman, señor——"

The Conde murmured, "How foolish of you, my child, to struggle so!"

She had a sudden, odd feeling that this was unreal. That the Conde de Vega was reading lines to her—that they were both in a play, a bad play by someone like Aragón. She could almost hear the prompter's voice, so strong was the illusion.

Whore's son of a whore! she cried out to herself in silent fury. Let me go, you great pig! Let me go now!

"It is foolish for anyone to struggle against the Conde de Vega," he said with a reflective smile. "Or to refuse what he desires."

"What is it you desire, Don Lorenzo?" she demanded, thinking to force an end to it, to have it done and over with.

"Why, only what all Spain desires," Don Lorenzo said smoothly. "The privilege of worshiping La Sola."

"And, señor——?"

"And the honor, also, of paying her the tribute that great beauty and great talent deserve."

"I thank you, señor, but——"

"And the heaven—no?—of tasting her affection."

"You want me to be your mistress?" she asked abruptly. "You are proposing, Don Lorenzo, that I become your amiga?"

Nothing seemed to disconcert him or disturb his arrogant self-assurance, not even the cold, matter-of-fact brusqueness of her question; nor even its edge of contempt. He smiled and, without relaxing the firmness of his embrace, seemed to make her a bow. He said, almost formally, "It is my deepest and dearest wish, señora."

Loyalty is never a direct emotion. It is a thing that must express itself obliquely, in terms of other and simpler feeling: sometimes as anger, sometimes as pity, or resolution, or love, or even jealousy. What Josefina experienced at this moment was a violent, blinding sense of outrage.

"But Doña Manuela——" she said weakly.

The Conde de Vega did not relinquish his expression of gravity. He said, almost sadly, "Ah, my child, all things, even the most beautiful, must some day come to an end, no? He is a fool who resists the——"

The Conde did not finish this sentence. Abruptly, his mock-theatrical manner fell away, as a mantle might slip from one's shoulders. He seemed to be seized with a kind of paroxysm that contorted his face and made his speech thick.

"It is not Manuela I want," he said in a low choking voice. "It is you. Do you hear me, little bitch? It is you I want!"

He thrust himself against her, enwrapped her so tightly, pressed her to him with such a fierce and sudden strength that the breath, quite literally, left her body. She felt his mouth—and in the lightning flash of darkness, it seemed a great, monstrous thing of devouring lips and teeth—crush hers. She wrenched herself free at last, and stood clear of him. She was weak and strangely confused—as if without feeling or sense of time or place . . . as if she were in a nightmare she had dreamed before.

She pressed the back of her hand against her mouth and tasted the salty, metallic taste of her own blood. And then, from out of the long, swinging shadows that laced her memory, a low moan between the soft, terrible sound of blows . . . For God's love, Miguel . . .

The Conde de Vega—had he lived to be a hundred years old (which, it was rumored in Castile, all of his line did)—could never have understood what happened next. He stood for a moment fascinated by the strange play of emotion on the lovely face before his eyes. It was something fresh and novel in his long and rather jaded experience of love; and he paused, even in his excitement, as if to savor this new and unexpected glimpse into the unpredictable nature of women.

"For God's love, señor!" he heard Josefina whisper.

But such was the enormity of his arrogance that he could not find in the words any meaning save passion. And so, as he turned again with a new zest to the attack, he was totally unprepared for the fury that broke over him.

It was the stinging, lashing, striking, clawing physical fury of a strong and well-conditioned body; and it overwhelmed the stunned Conde like a boiling wave. He buried his face in his arms and backed away from its incredible violence until he encountered a great wardrobe chest against the wall. On this he sat down abruptly, with his head half-buried in a rack of hanging clothes. After a while, since all was suddenly quiet, he uncovered his face and peered from between the costumes of *La Estrella de Sevilla* and the *Cid* at Josefina.

She was standing pale and rigid, her eyes staring almost as if in a trance at something beyond the Conde, and everything was strangely silent in the room. Then the silence was broken by a laugh—by the best-known laugh in Spain and one that Don Lorenzo, if he lived the hundred allotted years of the Vegas, would never be able to forget.

For nobody laughed quite like the Maya.

27

Often, during the days of her wretched flight over Spain, and in the long time afterward under the hard fierce skies of New Mexico, Josefina wondered why the Maya had not killed her then, where she stood, with the little dagger she wore always in her garter.

She would not have resisted. She would have closed her eyes and waited for the small blade to pierce her breast; and it would have been a welcome thing. But the Maya did not do her that favor.

She had left, without a word, to take her part in the second act of

The Girl from Ronda; and never, it was said, did she perform a role so brilliantly. The Conde also had left, but when or how Josefina did not know; indeed, it was only with the greatest difficulty that she recalled, the following day, how she and Tichi had made their way home from the theater. There was the darkness of a dream about everything.

Before the heat of the next morning, a little maid of the Maya's appeared and announced, with the arrogance of those who serve the great, that her mistress wished to see Josefina. "Pronto!" she said darkly. "At once!"

"I advise you not to go, señora," Tichi said. "She will end up by killing you."

Josefina, in her own mind, acknowledged that possibility. She went, nevertheless, a little defiantly, faintly hopeful of the Maya's forgiveness (who could predict her caprices?).

The Maya was having chocolate in bed when she arrived. There was a faint scent of amber about her; but she had stripped herself of all cosmetics and adornments, and her skin had a polished, metallic tautness in the morning light. Her black eyes looked almost brittle without make-up.

"You sent for me, Doña Manuela," Josefina said. "I would have come to you anyway."

"Why?" the Maya asked. "You have nothing to tell me, my dear. Nothing that I don't already know."

She finished her chocolate and settled herself against the pillows. Even in bed, she sat with dignity, her back straight, her breasts—of which the Maya, like all Spanish women, was proud—firm and high. Under the big cross on the whitewashed wall behind her, she looked like a painting—like a representation of every Spanish woman of her somber century, with all the passionate passivity of the Spanish character in her expressionless face and burning eyes.

"Well, little fool," the Maya said, "now that you have made yourself famous and destroyed yourself, all in one night, let us talk about what to do."

She isn't angry with me! Josefina said to herself, incredulous. She doesn't hate me!

A storm of sudden emotion overwhelmed her. She threw herself to her knees and buried her face in the silken covering of the Maya's bed, weeping convulsively. The Maya let her weep until the tears were followed by sobs, like a child's. Then she thrust her away gently, and said:

"Compose yourself, estúpida. We have to talk now. There isn't too much time."

"It was nothing I could help," Josefina said miserably. "I owe everything to you, Doña Manuela. You are my dearest friend. There is nothing, even with my life, that I would not——"

"Yes, yes!" the Maya said impatiently. "Mother of Christ! That you sit there now and listen to me."

Josefina took the French chair beside the bed and dried her eyes.

"I am glad you have not asked forgiveness," the Maya said, "because I have nothing to forgive you. *Do you understand that, little fool?*"

There was a strange, fierce insistence in the question that Josefina did not comprehend, but she said, "I understand, Doña Manuela."

"As for Señor Don Lorenzo," the Maya continued with theatrical irony, "it is not the first time he has played the fool. He will be around today, you can be sure, very grave and penitent . . . and, I hope, with the emerald earrings he knows I want.

"As for your success at the Príncipe, that is something that could make me very happy and, at the same time could make me want to poison you, no? To see one's protégée make so great a triumph—that is a natural satisfaction. Ah, yes! But for Manuela Maya it is even more than that.

"Mira!" she demanded suddenly, with a kind of savage intensity. "Why do you think I gave you so much as a glance in Ávila?"

"I do not know, Doña Manuela."

"Well, I'll tell you . . . La Sola," the Maya went on, with a faintly wry smile. "It was because you were so thin and ugly and danced so awkwardly. It broke my heart to see how frightened you were. It made me cry to see how clumsily you executed the salerito. . . . I could feel what it was to be thin and ugly, and to dance awkwardly . . . and to be frightened."

The Maya's eyes softened, with the look that comes into eyes that gaze into a long distance, not in space but in time.

"I was clumsy in the salerito also," she said.

"I am perfect in it now, Doña Manuela," Josefina said, with the slightest edge of pique in her words.

The Maya laughed. "I also," she said. "One can overcome most things, no? It is possible for one to be thin and ugly and yet become beautiful. It is possible for one to be as awkward as a two-day colt and yet become the greatest dancer in all Spain." Her face became grave and pensive. "But it is not so easy for one to overcome fear . . . and the memory of hunger, eh?"

They sat for a little time in silence, the mistress and the pupil, as if sharing not only a remembrance but some deep and bitter truth; which indeed, they were.

"And it is very difficult," the Maya said, "to grow old."

"Señora?"

"You made me old last night, my daughter. You gave the Maya the first push downwards. And for that I should want to kill you—even though I love you like my child . . . like my very self."

"I meant only to please you!" Josefina cried. "To make you proud of me. . . ."

"I am sure of that!" the Maya said dryly. "But let us drop that. The fact remains. There would be a new primera dama at the Príncipe tonight if—" she made a long pause, looking steadily at Josefina—"if it were possible for La Sola to remain in Madrid."

"But Doña Manuela——!" Josefina got to her feet, knocking the light French chair over in her astonishment.

"So, my child," the Maya said, smiling, "I have nothing to forgive you, really. But Don Lorenzo has. And Don Lorenzo does not forgive."

"I must run away?"

"At once—today."

"Ay, Dios mío!"

The Maya said, *"Listen closely to what I have to tell you."*

What the Maya had to tell her was what Josefina, if she had thought about it at all, must herself have realized. Her affront to the Conde de Vega's pride was the most grievous a Spanish nobleman could be dealt: she had not only rejected him as a lover, she had made him look ridiculous as a man. She could expect her punishment to be complete . . . but perhaps not swift.

For Don Lorenzo, the Maya explained, would not be likely to deny himself the full pleasure of retribution. It was possible that Josefina, at first, might even believe that the Conde had forgotten, or at least forgiven—so slowly would the screws be turned in the beginning. But she must not be deceived. The Conde de Vega would hardly relinquish the subtleties and refinements of revenge which were his right as a Spaniard and an Old Christian. . . . Or the final joy, perhaps, of contemplating her naked on the rack or at the stake.

"But I have done nothing!" Josefina cried, shuddering.

"It is not necessary," the Maya said, with gentle patience.

She enumerated some of the ways in which the outraged nobleman could easily arrange for the persecution, or even the ultimate punishment, of a dancer so recently famous and still without powerful friends. Rumors . . . hints . . . denouncements. She adhered to the Austrian party, for instance—spied for the Coalition. Criminal conversations had been overheard—plotting against the regime. Suspicion and fear were spreading like a loathsome epidemic in Spain, and every man was an informer against his brother. And always, of course, there was the Holy Office. . . .

"Stop!" Josefina cried at last. "You have me on the rack already, Doña Manuela! Why do you torture me?"

"Because you must understand how bad things are with you," the Maya said. "How little time you have."

It would be necessary, she explained, to leave the Capital at once—to disappear so completely that the Conde could only with the greatest difficulty discover her whereabouts. She dwelt on this necessity for utter effacement, not only in the Capital but, if possible, in the Peninsula itself.

"It would be best of all," she said, "if you could leave Spain. If you could go to the Indies."

But that, she conceded, was hardly practicable—for a time, at least—and so she had made arrangements to carry out the next-best plan. She had engaged a man with a calash to take her, that very night, as far south as Toledo—a dependable man whom she could trust with her life. From Toledo she could take the postchaise to Córdoba; and near Ronda, in the wildest mountains of Andalusia, she had an uncle. . . .

"You can trust him also," the Maya said. "I'll give you a letter to him. It will be best if you remain with him for a couple of weeks, well hidden. After that, Don Lorenzo will have cooled off a little, and you can venture out. But discreetly, my child, and do not leave the South."

"But how shall I live, Doña Manuela?"

"That," the Maya said, "is something that you must decide for yourself. . . . There are many ways. Perhaps you can dance a little—in the South. Perhaps you will find a rich amigo."

"It will grieve me most to leave you, Doña Manuela."

The Maya looked at her closely for a while. "I had thought," she said, "that you might suspect my zeal in getting you out of Madrid—an easy way to remove a rival, no? But now I see that you trust me. You are very sweet, Josefina mía. You are like a daughter . . . like my own daughter, eh?"

As the Maya said this, tears came to her eyes—the first that Josefina had ever seen there. She made no motion to brush them away, but sat motionless against the pillows, staring at a patch of sunlight on the whitewashed wall.

And Josefina, as if reminded by an inner voice, remembered the time she had seen the Maya after her bath and had noticed that her breasts were the breasts of a woman who had borne a child. Tears rushed to her own eyes again, and she wept despondently in the Maya's arms.

"Courage, my child," the Maya soothed her. "Until death, remember, all is life."

28

When Josefina returned to her own apartment, carrying in the folds of her manta a small purse containing a hundred gold reales the Maya had forced her to accept, she found Tichi gone.

Already? she thought sadly but without resentment. She might have stayed to say good-by, at least!

But the Gallega appeared shortly—as Josefina in her heart knew she would—fresh-faced and cheerful.

"Where have you been?" Josefina asked.

"To the Church of Buen Suceso, señora. I went to the prostitutes' Mass, and prayed for our intention."

"And what is our intention, Tichi?"

"That we get safely out of this lousy town and clear of Don Lorenzo's clutches. We have no time to lose, Doña Josefina. He will denounce us to the Inquisition for certain."

It was Tichi's way of announcing her loyalty; and Josefina made no more than a perfunctory protest.

"But you have done nothing, Tichi. There's no need for you to run away."

"I'm not so sure of that, señora. I saw Don Lorenzo sitting on that chest—and he saw me looking at him."

"He won't denounce you for that, Tichi!"

"But I was laughing, señora."

She went about the preparation of chocolate, which they took hastily. They then began to pack in a large traveling wallet and a couple of hampers the few things they could take with them. While they were engaged in this task, there was a knock on the door.

Tichi's face paled; she crossed herself. "Shall I open it, señora?" she asked in a whisper.

"Of course," Josefina said, with more composure in her voice than she felt in her heart.

It was Guzmán. He looked sad and apologetic and slightly bewildered—possibly by the unaccustomed experience of being abroad so early in the day—and he seemed at a loss for words.

"Never mind, Chico," Josefina said. "I know what you are thinking. You are thinking: 'Here is the little slut who has soured the milk for the great Guzmán, no? Ungrateful wench!' Save your breath, Chico. You are right—I am thankless. I am——"

Tears—which were so near the surface today—filled her eyes, and she choked up. Guzmán came and took her in his fat arms. He made little comforting sounds, as one might to a distressed child.

"Do you forgive me, then?" she asked.

"Sweetheart," he said, "you are an even greater fool than I thought. But a greater artist also. And great art forgives all, no? Guzmán forgives you, my dear. Guzmán loves you. Where are you going?"

"Away from Madrid," she said. She trusted Guzmán—as much as anyone could be trusted in Spain at that distrustful time—but she thought it better not to tell him too much.

"Then you can use this," he said, handing her, with a casual, almost negligent air, a heavy little purse.

She refused the money. He insisted that it was back pay, due her from the Príncipe. In the end, influenced somewhat by Tichi's energetic gestures behind his back, she took the coins. Guzmán sighed.

"Perhaps, some day——" he said ambiguously.

They talked for a little while in an odd, constrained way. Then Guzmán felt in his pockets for his watches, first one then the other, but produced nothing. He arose, nevertheless, as if he had noted the time, and made as if to take his leave. Like all voluble and emotional men, Guzmán sometimes fell strangely silent. He kissed Josefina and gave her a wordless farewell, save for a hurried "Go with God!"

"How much is in the purse, señora?" Tichi asked as soon as the producer had left.

"Count it and see," Josefina said indifferently. The Gallega's question suddenly recalled that little gesture of Guzmán's reaching for his watches, first one then the other.

"A hundred and twenty one reales, señora!" Tichi exclaimed, full of excitement.

"Ah, Chico!" Josefina said softly, to Tichi's wonder. "What a great liar you are!"

They had finished their packing by the siesta hour. Everything they owned between them—except the furniture they must leave behind— was neatly stowed in the big leather wallet and the two hampers. The doll Yolanda lay wrapped in a woolen manta. And in a small hand-basket were provisions for the journey—bread, anchovies, cheese, hard-boiled eggs, and two bottles of wine. It was, Tichi observed wryly, as if they were about to make a pilgrimage to the shrine of San Isidro!

Then followed the long, anxious hours of waiting for the Maya's man with the calash. They sat behind the closed shutters and locked doors, trying not to show their fears to each other. They said their rosaries. They nibbled at some biscuits and grapes. They counted their money and discovered that they had more than three hundred reales in all—a huge sum, it seemed, until they reflected on the uncertainties of their future.

"I have sworn to the Virgin of Atocha," Tichi said, "to light fifty candles if she will see us safely to Ronda."

"You have made more vows already than you can ever keep," Josefina observed.

As darkness came, and they sat in the stripped, unlighted room, their spirits dropped to a very low level indeed, and their anxiety grew. When, at last, there was a knock on the door, they were almost afraid to go to the window and peer through the shutter. But what they saw, in the gloom of the street, was the man with the calash.

While Tichi unbolted the door, Josefina picked up the doll Yolanda. She drew aside the manta and glanced at the little face with its pink porcelain cheeks, and blue porcelain eyes, and hair of heavenly blondness that still shone like dull gold in the semidarkness. She held her for a moment to her breast, tightly; and something in the performance of this small act seemed to reassure her and give her courage. The daughter of Eva Helena whispered:

"That God help us through this time also, my heart!"

29

But now, almost a year later, sitting in her wretched "dressing room" next to the stable of the inn at Roa, Josefina smoothed on some shadow beneath her eyes, contemplated the rather startling results in the broken mirror, and reflected that God, alas, had not been so very helpful after all.

Every kind of misery had followed them: the misery of hunger, and of sleeping on the vermin-running floors of filthy inns, and of shivering in the icy rains of the Sierra Nevada; and the never-ending threat of Don Lorenzo's malice.

When they at last reached Ronda, the Maya's uncle, a half-gypsy smuggler known locally as Largos Pasos, or Long Steps, immediately claimed thirty reales for lodgings in his miserable hide-away in the Sierra de Ronda. It was an outrageous demand; yet, so fearful were they of the Conde's revenge that they gladly gave the money for what they believed to be security for a time. Largos Pasos, although he was a sinister-looking fellow who spent most of his time flipping his knife at an olive tree, proved to be a harmless, even kindly host. When they left he did an incredible thing—he gave them back ten of their gold reales, and saw them safely into Ronda, and promised to pray for their good fortune.

"It's because he's in love with you," Tichi said briefly.

Then, until well into November, they wandered in a kind of aimless despair about the flowery land of Andalusia, enduring not only hardship and hunger, but all the kinds of insult and indignity that were the lot of unescorted women in the mean inns, the town squares, and even the churches of that smiling corner of Spain. And they were never free, actually, from want and depression and fear of Don Lorenzo.

They were haunted by dread of the day when their little store of money would be gone; for there were few ways, they knew, in which they could earn more. All strangers were suspect in these uneasy times, and a careful and complete record of everyone's movements was kept by innkeepers and town officials. Employers were especially mistrustful, and the law surrounded even the hiring of domestics with innumerable rules and regulations. Since engagements for less than a month were illegal, they could not even seek employment as servants. They dared not, they told themselves, risk remaining in one locality for so long a time.

Occasionally they managed to earn a few cuartos—or perhaps only a meal—by odd jobs that it was permitted an unsponsored woman to do. There was sometimes work for a few days at the fairs which all the towns in the South were holding now; they fried fritters, hawked trinkets, made milk omelets, and tended refreshment stands. But what they could gain in these uncertain and precarious ways was never enough. Their pitiful store of money continued to melt away so rapidly that finally, gaining courage from desperation, Josefina began to sing tonadillas and to dance in obscure cafés for whatever copper coins might be flung to her.

"Like any gypsy slut," she said ruefully to Tichi. "The only difference is, the gypsies do better than I, no?"

Then the last maravedi was eventually spent, and they knew that strange feeling of unbelief with which one faces, for the first time, actual and absolute pennilessness. So they sold the few pieces of jewelry they possessed, and whatever other small articles of value they could dispose of: combs, rosaries, fans, a jet perfume bottle, a small gold hair ornament. Josefina saved out only her castanets, which had gotten their tone from the heat and dampness of her own hands and had become a kind of part of herself; and the doll, Yolanda.

When the money received from the pawnshops was exhausted, they sold their clothes, until they had left only the cloaks and white woolen mantas they wore. It was at this time that Josefina was sick near Ojan—an interlude she afterwards could recall only vaguely, remembering little about it except Tichi's unexplained disappearances each night and her returns, sometimes not until morning, with a few coins to pay the sullen peasant for their lodgings.

At last came the two days in Málaga when they were without food at all, save for the snails they picked from the wall beside the sparkling sea. Then, Josefina was sure, they had reached the limits of endurance; and she would not let herself think what might have happened if Tichi had not—by means she would not reveal—obtained the materials for a good hot puchera, which revived not only their strength but also their spirits.

"Bread is the cure for every grief," Tichi observed, for some reason a little grimly. "But a good stew is even better."

And so that day was saved: but there was tomorrow. . . .

30

And then, proving once more the wisdom of the folk, who have maintained in all tongues that the darkest hour is just before the dawn, Uncle Pepe's primera dama ran off with a perfumed young officer on leave from Cádiz.

Uncle Pepe, owner and manager of Pepe Velasco's Famous Players, had contracted for a presentation of Alcarón's comedy, *The Walls Have Ears*, in the courtyard of the Inn of the Pomegranates. The elopement of his leading lady took place only two hours before the performance was to begin. But Uncle Pepe accepted this awkward development philosophically.

"Very well," he said, puffing slightly, not because of emotion, but due to his heaviness. "Let the little slut have her violet soldier. We'll do *The Gardener's Dog* instead. What do you say, my children?"

His "children"—a dozen or so performers affecting the French mode but smelling strongly of garlic and onions—agreed with bored good nature; but the innkeeper proved less compliant. He became quite red with choler, in fact, and waggled his finger under Uncle Pepe's nose.

"Imposters!" he shouted. "You have advertised a performance of *The Walls*, no? And now you propose something that has to do with a dog! Mother of God! He proposes an animal show!"

"It grieves me to hear you say this, señor," Pepe said. "As any ignoramus knows, *The Gardener's Dog* is one of the master's finest comedies, and you insult the memory, señor——"

"I insult no one," said the innkeeper. "But I must remind you, Don

Pepe, my inn is full of people who have come to see something called *The Walls Have Ears*. And they will be very disappointed to find that they are now going to see an animal show."

"I perceive that it is useless to contend with your ignorance," Pepe said sadly. "I myself shall explain the situation and ask their indulgence."

"You will understand why I am a little nervous, señor," the innkeeper continued, "when I tell you that the last company of players to perform here fared rather badly. Unfortunately, the horse trough is very handy, as you can see, and——"

"No threats, please," Uncle Pepe said, with more equanimity than he felt. "I think everybody will understand when I explain that my *primera dama*—the one who plays the part of *Diana*—has gone off with one of your respected guests. An unfortunate but unpredictable circumstance."

"That should be easy to take care of," the innkeeper said. "Let another take her place."

"She had no understudy for the part. There is no one else who can play *Diana*, señor."

He gazed uncomfortably at the innkeeper, fully expecting to hear him say, "Then put on the play without her." His glance wandered to the horse trough. And then he heard someone say:

"I can, señor."

Uncle Pepe turned slowly and looked at the two women who stood in the gateway of the courtyard, one brown-armed and brown-faced and smiling, the other gazing at him with eyes so arresting that he was conscious of nothing but their depth and gravity and odd beauty . . . and of something vaguely familiar.

"What do you want, wenches?" the innkeeper asked. "There's no work here. If you've got other ideas, you'd better be off."

"One moment, señor," Uncle Pepe begged. "Señoras, I am at your feet."

He addressed them both, but his bow was to Josefina. He regarded her with a curious intentness.

"Thank you, señor director," Josefina said. "If you will pardon us, we heard you say that you have no one to play the part of *Diana*, no?"

"That is true, señora."

"I can play it, señor . . . I can play it very well."

Uncle Pepe studied her for a long moment in silence. He was a large man then—almost as big and as fat as Guzmán—with a fleshy face in which his eyes seemed to grow small with thought. It was not an unkindly face, Josefina decided; but she was puzzled by a hint of some anxiety, some tragedy perhaps, behind its jollity.

"Give me some lines," he said. The speech in which Diana asks

123

Marcella, 'Do you love Teodoro?' and she answers, 'I cannot live without him,' and so on, and so on."

So she went through that scene, standing in the blinding sun and surrounded by gaping porters, muleteers, and Uncle Pepe's players. She grew weak and was afraid she might faint; but she completed the scene and even forced a smile when the players burst into applause.

"More, señor?" she asked.

"It is not necessary," Uncle Pepe said. "You know the rest, eh?"

"Perfectly, señor."

"Who are you, señora?" Uncle Pepe asked abruptly.

A sudden silence followed his question. This, and the dazzling sunshine, and the feeling of a score of eyes looking at her, gave Josefina a giddy sensation of floating in space. She heard herself say:

"I am called La de los Ojos Verdes."

"Good, little Green Eyes," Uncle Pepe said. "If that is what you wish to be called, that is your name with us."

He put his arm around her then and helped Tichi to take her to a shady place where he gave her a drink of cool water, then had food brought to her; and she wept a little from weakness and gratitude.

Ah, yes, Josefina, she said to herself now, you should not forget that he took you in when nobody else would: and if he expected a little payment, well that was natural . . . and he did not get it after all. And he did give you the bread and sausage. And he is sick now, and frightened. . . .

The evidence of Uncle Pepe's sickness had grown plainer and plainer as they drifted about the South, bringing Lope and Alcarón and Tirso de Molina and Calderón to the Andalusians. He lost weight rapidly, so that his skin became loose and gave his face a sad, sagging look, particularly under the eyes, which had grown dull and anxious. Yet he did his best to be jolly and to keep up their spirits.

"The main thing, my children," Pepe often said, "is to keep the company together. All will be well, if only we keep the company together!"

They needed everything that Uncle Pepe could give them in the way of courage and a little hope. For they were often hungry, and almost more weary than they could bear, and very dispirited; and they were able to endure their hardships and indignities only, perhaps, because they shared them with one another, and because they pitied Uncle Pepe more than themselves.

But as they moved slowly northward in the spring, avoiding the larger towns, Uncle Pepe became still thinner and his jokes grew to be fewer. In the Montaña, that rough, dour country north of the Capital, their case became increasingly desperate until, in the town of

Valoria la Buena it seemed, at last, that there was nothing more of shame and suffering for them to experience. For there they were stoned and driven from the town by a mob of peasants urged on by an irate priest.

But there, also, Uncle Pepe managed to make still another jest at misfortune, although not a very good one. "Even the peasants of Palencia understand," he said wryly, "that those who perform the plays of Moreto deserve brickbats. Let us admire their perspicacity, my children, and forgive them the bruises."

Fleeing from these perspicacious peasants, they had blindly taken a wild mountain road that had brought them at last to floodbound Roa. And here, for the moment at least—which was the most they had grown accustomed to ask—they were safe in the Inn of the Moor.

Josefina, sitting in the wretched hole the innkeeper had provided as a dressing room, could hear the guests gathering in the courtyard for the entertainment the landlord had promised them. The babble of their voices disquieted her oddly. She had made a brave speech to Uncle Pepe, but her heart was uneasy.

"That they like me!" she murmured, as she traced the half-moon arches of her eyebrows. "That they throw nothing this time!"

But her concern was mostly for Uncle Pepe. It was for his sake really that she must be successful, that she must get applause from the audience—and a smile from the piggish innkeeper. "Otherwise," Uncle Pepe had said, "it is doubtful how we shall eat or sleep after tonight." She smiled and thought sadly, Alas, Uncle Pepe! That God help you to keep the company together!

She went over in her mind the routine that she and the guitarrista Jacinto had worked out.

First, Uncle Pepe had decided, the company would perform one of those short, spicy sketches that all Spaniards loved so much. Then she, Josefina, would dance the seguidillas to Jacinto's guitar. But she had changed her mind. She had promised Uncle Pepe something sensational—something for these yokels and bumpkins of Palencia to remember her by forever.

The seguidillas, she decided, would not do. Even as she danced it, the seguidillas could not lash the nerves and squeeze the heart. It could not bring hoarse cries from the throat. And she must have those cries, she reflected wryly, if they were to eat and sleep after tonight.

"Jacinto," she said suddenly, "let us get to work. That you give me a few chords for the fandango."

It was the smouldering memory of the gypsies dancing their wonderful dances in their littered camps outside the walls of Ávila, and the ancient instincts of her Spanish blood, that had decided her to perform

125

the fandango now for those who were gathered in the courtyard of the Inn of the Moor. But not the fandango as it was given on the stages of Spain, but as it was danced four thousand years ago by the dancing girls of Cádiz. For she felt strangely excited and exhilarated by the very thought of dancing again; and wantonly reckless even of Don Lorenzo's malice . . . and besides, there was the matter of keeping the company together, and of how they should eat and sleep after tonight.

Through the door that gave onto the courtyard she could hear the voices of the players who were already giving a short play entitled *The Gypsy and the Innkeeper's Wife,* which Uncle Pepe, perhaps not very wisely, had considered appropriate for the occasion.

"It will be over in the space of a Credo," Tichi said.

Josefina pulled on her castanets. She bowed her head, said, "Jesús, María, José!" and crossed herself. As she stepped into the short passage-way leading to the improvised state, the performance ended. There was a little applause—and a burst of the ugly, familiar sounds of derision.

Poor Uncle Pepe! she thought. Suddenly a great, sickening wave of despondency rushed through her. She faltered and almost turned back. Then, steadying herself, she breathed deeply, put the famous La Sola smile on her face, and walked toward the entrance doorway.

That you dance, now, Josefina, she said to herself. That you dance as a . . . as a beggar must!

31

The Inn of the Moor at Roa was no worse, and perhaps a little better, than the usual Spanish posada. It consisted of a large hall paved with round stones and open to the street, at one end of which was a great hearth around which the guests sat and watched their food being pre-pared. At night the floor was covered with sleeping muleteers reclin-ing on their pack-saddles and wrapped in the blankets of their animals. The walls were black with smoke and festooned with strings of sausages and slabs of bacon.

Next door were the stables from which the flies and fleas swarmed up to the bedrooms above; and adjoining these, the courtyard, a spa-cious square surrounded by a high wall into which had been built various sheds and shelters for gear, milch cows, and goats, and on occasion surplus guests.

Ordinarily, the guests at the Inn of the Moor were travelers—gentlemen with their own servants who often prepared food for their masters, pack-sellers, peasants, wandering players, and the like. The Moor was also a meeting place for neighboring peasants and villagers, and its most profitable business, actually, was in the sale of wine and brandy to the wealthy farmers, the mayor, village doctor, schoolteacher, apothecary, sacristan, and other town dignitaries who gathered there every evening to play malella and drink the posadero's excellent wine.

On this late June afternoon, however, both the size and the character of the crowd jammed into the courtyard of the Inn of the Moor was unusual. The spring floods had snared many an incautious traveler in the innkeeper's net, so to speak; and word that a company of strolling players had been engaged to provide entertainment for his restive guests had brought in a good many unaccustomed faces from the village and countryside. To Don Antonio Valverde these people were a more diverting spectacle than the performance they had come here to watch.

Before I return to New Mexico, Don Antonio said to himself, I must get me an embroidered waistcoat like the one that caballero is wearing. I don't care much for the looks of that caballero, but one has to admit he is wearing a very handsome waistcoat.

His eyes wandered from the caballero, who was indeed a rather distasteful personality, with coarse, dark features and a loutish manner, and none the better for the wine of the Mancha. Don Antonio passed over the peasants and townspeople in their rustic holiday dress. They did not interest him: in truth he was a little embarrassed by the fact that he himself had grown to manhood among such crude fellows.

He was amused for a little time by a young abbé in priestly black with a white powdered wig and a ruffled shirt, who dropped phrases in French and Italian and picked his teeth with a gold toothpick. A group of peasants were discussing him in some bewilderment.

"He is some kind of priest, no doubt."

"But he has long curly hair."

"He is a soldier then."

"But he has no sword or gun."

Nothing since his return to Spain had fascinated Captain Valverde so much as the variety of types, the infinite diversity of humanity, to be found in his homeland. In New Mexico there were the Indians, the mestizos, and the Spaniards—and sometimes it was hard to tell them apart! Here every province, every village almost, had something new to show in the way of dress, customs, language—and women.

To Don Antonio the women were of a special interest. And at this moment—while his eyes drifted about the crowd, resting for a moment on a French officer, a magistrate in a huge cardboard collar, some students in long cloaks and cassocks, and for a little longer on the bouncing daughter of a well-to-do farmer—his mind was occupied by the image of a particular woman about whom he knew nothing save that she was, he had been told, called La de los Ojos Verdes.

It was a curiously tantalizing image because, in the first place, of its incompleteness, which is the essence of mystery: the memory, merely, of a slender young figure walking—like an angel . . . or a king's concubine—with a peculiar grace and dignity across a sun-soaked square.

"She walks well," he had said to the innkeeper. "I haven't seen her face."

He still hadn't seen her face. And if this, first of all, was the reason for the special fascination her memory held for him, the second cause was the odd circumstance that he, out of boredom or some other foolhardy urge, had resolved on, and even arranged for, the seduction of this stray incognita—who, for all he knew, might well be as ugly as an adobe wall.

Careful, Antonio! he warned himself jocularly. Men have been known to fall in love with a woman's walk—and even to marry it!

But now a certain amusement with which he had contemplated his own middle-aged preoccupation with the conquest of a wench whose walk happened to enchant him had given way to a nervous irritability. He was conscious of a certain reluctance to continue to the end with this improbable adventure: the illusions of middle age, he had found, were more often foolish than beautiful.

"Salvador," he said to his lackey, "let me know when she appears."

"Señor?"

"May you burn in hell," Don Antonio said humorlessly. "You know the one I mean."

"Ah, yes. The one of the green eyes. The one we are preparing the turkey for."

It was infinitely baffling to Don Antonio how much derision his servant could inject into a simple, innocent sentence; he had half an urge to run the brash young Asturian through with his sword.

"Precisely," he said dryly. "Point her out to me. When I have seen her face, we may change our minds about the turkey."

"Let us hope not, señor capitán."

"I'll decide that," Don Antonio growled. "Fetch me some more of that lousy wine."

By the time Salvador returned with a fresh bottle, the curtain had parted on *The Gypsy and the Innkeeper's Wife*. On the stage—an open-faced cowshed provided with a backdrop of red gambroon curtains—three players were reciting the opening lines of the farce: the innkeeper (played by Uncle Pepe), his wife, and daughter. Don Antonio looked closely at the two actresses, then glanced upwards at his servant.

"No, señor," Salvador said in a low voice, and set the bottle on the table.

Don Antonio poured himself a glass of the wine. It was better than the first bottle, he concluded, but still not good. He returned to the play, which he thought dull. The audience appeared to share his lack of enthusiasm; although their silence may have been merely the natural dourness of these mountain people. Only the caballero in the embroidered waistcoat was in the least responsive. He laughed occasionally and sometimes shouted unintelligible phrases to the players.

"He is either drunk or a fool," Don Antonio said to himself. "Or maybe both."

As each new actress made an entrance—until there were five in all—he glanced upwards at Salvador; and each time the Asturian said in the same low, possibly mocking voice, "No, señor."

"By the Blood!" Don Antonio said. "If you are amusing yourself, my fine Asturiano, it will be at the cost of your hide."

"I am very sorry, señor capitán," Salvador said. "The one we are looking for is none of these."

"Let us hope that you are right," Don Antonio said gruffly. "For none of these is worth a turkey. Or even a hen."

He paid little attention to the remainder of the play. When it ended at last—with Uncle Pepe pale and sweating from the exertion of being amusing—he joined in neither the smattering of applause nor the listless demonstration of disapproval. He merely scowled at the spectacle of his own fatuousness.

It must be that Madrid has left you a little soft in the head, Antonio, he said to himself. It is time you were getting back to El Paso!

His mood drifted from one of vague frustration to a fleeting nostalgia. He poured another glass of wine, gazed at its pale gold translucence, and dreamed for a moment of his own vineyards—by all odds the finest in New Mexico—on the Río Grande del Norte. Salvador interrupted his meditation.

"And now, señor," he whispered, "La de los Ojos Verdes!"

Don Antonio became conscious of the music of a single guitar, low, tentative, groping.

"You appear very sure of it. How do you know?"

"The innkeeper told me."

"She sings, eh?"

"She dances, señor."

"Very interesting," Don Antonio said, feigning apathy. "That she can dance better than those lousy players can act!"

"That, señor, is what the innkeeper says!"

The curtain parted again and revealed Jacinto seated on a stool against the red gambroon backdrop. He glanced up, smiled impersonally, and bent his dark head over his guitar. His fingers wandered in aimless melancholy over the strings, drawing from them the dim, disquieting echoes of some ancient tune. A kind of restlessness seemed to flow out from him and into his silent listeners.

"Olé!" a man growled: he was a muleteer from the South, and half-gypsy plainly. "Chico!"

His excitement ran through the crowd as the music's rhythm, faster now, strange and startling, rushed toward a brief, savage climax of strident strings. Don Antonio felt an odd, almost reluctant response of his own nerves and pulse-beat; he sensed the return of piquancy and promise to his little adventure, and decided that possibly he was not so much a fool after all.

Who knows? he said to himself. You are not often wrong, Antonio!

The music sank again to a low, melancholy, diatonic refrain: a relic perhaps of some old Eastern chant: a rhythm as ancient as Carthage or even Egypt. And Don Antonio saw Josefina slip out of a shadowy doorway into the slanting afternoon sunlight.

"Ay, caramba!" he muttered. "She is the one, all right!"

She circled the stage in the paseo de gracia, that slow, deliberate, electrifying walk with the arched back and arrogant shoulders and swinging hips—that walk so Spanish that none but a Spaniard should ever attempt it . . . a walk the Gaditanas knew before they ever learned to dance. And Don Antonio watched her with a smug, almost gloating satisfaction.

You are right again, Antonio! he said to himself, and emptied his glass—as if to reward his perspicacity.

Don Antonio fancied himself an aficionado of sorts. He flattered himself that he could recognize excellence when he saw it: in a pure-bred Barb, a master swordsman, a great mustang breaker, or—although here he allowed himself a reasonable margin for error—a woman. There was always something that set the really great ones apart, something you did not have to look for twice. And now he felt a special thrill of pride in perceiving—even in this most unlikely of places—the air and quality of authentic greatness.

At the same time, Don Antonio was almost uncomfortably conscious of a far stronger and less complicated emotion: the simple, sudden impact of this particular dancer's intense femeninidad—her special and personal order of womanliness, which included her undoubted beauty, the disturbing way she carried herself, the sweet and subtle contours of her arms and shoulders . . . and most powerful of all, the magnetism of her eyes which, sure enough, were green as twin emeralds,

130

and rasgados—wide and a trifle aslant, and extraordinarily large in the shadows of their long, dark lashes.

"Don Jesús Cristo!" he murmured, without knowing exactly what he was trying to express. "This is more than you bargained for, Antonio!"

He watched Josefina saunter to the edge of the little stage. She paused and bent forward, gazing at her audience half-smiling, half-frowning; she reached out her arms and drew them all to her with little motions of her upturned hands, and asked their help.

"Give me some palmadas, some dry handclaps," she said in the ancient formula, "to see if we are beginning to understand each other."

The palmadas and the low gutturals of encouragement were given, but with reserve, almost grudgingly at first. Then, as the music, still low and tentative, searching and melancholy, began to "talk" more directly to the listeners, and as the first provocative movements of the fandango began to suggest themselves, the response built slowly to a tense, expectant act of participation. Suddenly audience and performer were one: Josefina raised her arms in a wide brazeo, and flung down the first resounding carretilla of her castanets.

"Anda! Anda! Salero, chica!" the swarthy muleteers growled. "Jaleo!" A stir of excitement, of anticipation, ran visibly through the crowd. The peasants and villagers moved a little closer; the abbé stopped posturing and was staring hard at Josefina. The caballero in the embroidered waistcoat, Don Antonio observed, was also staring at her; he had got to his feet and was gaping at Josefina in a manner that Don Antonio found both curious and distasteful.

The fandango is wild and violent and infinitely complex. It is inflamed by sensuality and surcharged with an oriental voluptuousness. It is of the passionate South, of hot countries and dark peoples; yet, so elemental and powerful is its effect on the emotions that even the dour peasants of Palencia began now to feel its sensual challenge. Disquieted by an odd and unaccustomed stirring in their cold northern blood, they glanced at one another sheepishly, shifted their weight, and began self-consciously to join in the jaleo of the muleteers. "Olé!" they shouted shyly. "Qué gracia!"

By degrees they grew bolder, and the gathering excitement broke out in cries and low whistles and handclaps. A large farmer in a leather jerkin jostled Don Antonio in his efforts to get a better view of the dancing. "Careful, you oaf!" Don Antonio warned absently; but he was hardly conscious of speaking: he was aware only of a dancer they called Green Eyes.

First he had seen her as a woman—a girl of extraordinary beauty, to be sure, with a quality of strangeness that had intrigued him enormously; yet still a woman. But now an astonishing thing had happened. Suddenly and mysteriously this woman had become a pattern of searching arms and curving shoulders, of honeyed hips and bending, swaying knees. She had become a wild and sensual rhythm, a surge of passion, a flame, a prayer, an incantation. Something older than the skill and art of all the dancers of Spain—older than the race itself perhaps—had possessed her lovely body.

Even Don Antonio, a soldier long used only to the crude simplicities of his New Mexico, felt in his nerves and senses the impact of a profound and mysterious experience. He was fascinated, excited, and vaguely bewildered; and he watched Josefina with a concentration so utter that it took him a little time to realize that something unexpected was happening: a disturbance, an incident of some sort that appeared to center on that unprepossessing figure, the caballero in the embroidered waistcoat.

"Bless your mother!" the caballero was shouting in a loud and drunken voice. "Bless your mother . . . La Sola!"

As the words *La Sola* penetrated the sound of the music and the castanets and the crowd noises, Don Antonio observed a frown pass like a shadow across Josefina's face. But there was no pause in the proud and violent movements of the dance; the castanets missed not a single *tok*. Instead, the spiraling body, the clattering fingers, the strident strings of the guitar, joined suddenly to build toward a wild, triumphant finish, toward a climax of ecstasy and exhaustion that was never to be reached. For, all at once, the caballero in the embroidered waistcoat stood in the circle of everyone's attention: and opposite him, sword drawn and greatly wondering, stood Captain Don Antonio Valverde.

32

The caballero had a large mouth with a very long upper lip, and one would expect his voice to be loud and to carry far. When he called out "La Sola!" the words hurtled at Josefina like the report of an arquebus.

"Madre de Dios!" she thought. "Who is it that knows me in this miserable hole?"

She felt nothing but this faint curiosity. She was too completely possessed by the emotional force of her performance to have room for fear or even astonishment. Her very mind was like that of another asking, "Who can know me here?"

The clatter of her castanets increased in tempo and volume, while her eyes searched for the owner of the voice. They found him quickly enough, for he was directly in front of her and lurching unsteadily toward her.

Ay, caramba! she said to herself, with the first flutterings of panic. It is Don Diego!

She could not be mistaken. Don Diego de la Prada had a face that was not easy to forget. It was a coarse, ugly face—but that of a caballero, nevertheless, and a member of the powerful military order of Santiago, and the friend of many a personage more noble than himself, including His Excellency the Conde de Vega.

In return for what services Don Diego enjoyed the favor and indulgence—if not the actual friendship—of such great men was the subject of much speculation in the Capital, some of it scandalous. But it was true that he enjoyed the patronage of even the grandees; and it was at the country place of Don Lorenzo, indeed, that Josefina had met him. That meeting—like Don Diego's face—was not easy to forget.

Ah, yes, it flashed through her mind. You are the one I had to fight in the garden. I still show the scratches of the box trees. I had to threaten to call Don Lorenzo. . . .

She tossed Jacinto a glance he understood: the music swept suddenly into a faster, wilder tempo; the dance swirled toward its stormy climax. But Josefina, watching Don Diego through half-closed eyes, felt an edge of fear cut through the excitement and exaltation that always, at this moment, possessed her.

Mother of God! she thought bitterly. That I should deserve such luck!

She saw Don Diego become drunkenly entangled with his sword. She saw him collide with a heavy-set man in military garb, whose rather pale face became very red above a neckcloth of a gay mariposa color. He and Don Diego exchanged low, angry words. Then, over the clamor of her castanets, she heard Don Diego shouting again:

"La Sola! So here you are, my beautiful little slut! So here we find you at last! I swear by all hell, La Sola——"

Then he did a drunken but still incredible thing: he suddenly lunged at her, got hold of her bodice, and ripped it from her shoulders. She felt his fingers bite into the flesh of her upper arm; she struck at him blindly and screamed with pain and fright.

After that a great confusion surrounded her for a little while. Tichi was in the confusion, clawing at Don Diego; and Jacinto, clutching a broken guitar; and the innkeeper sputtering and beseeching peace; and many others she could not identify. But the melee ended soon,

133

with the innkeeper and a muleteer holding fast to Tichi, and the man with the mariposa neckcloth restraining Don Diego.

"Whore's son of a whore!" Don Diego was shouting wildly. "Let me go! Let me get at you!"

The man in the gay neckcloth thrust the caballero from him. There was a kind of contempt in the way he did it. He looked at Don Diego with a red-faced, quizzical expression—as if a little incredulous of what he saw.

"Is it the custom here to go about attacking wenches in public?" he asked. "Or is it a specialty of the señor's?"

For answer, Don Diego whipped out his sword and made a few reckless passes that quickly dispersed the crowd.

"Draw!" he shouted. "Draw, or, by God, I'll kill you!"

A moment later Don Antonio found himself, sword in hand, facing the caballero in the embroidered waistcoat. He was filled with a kind of wonder—and some embarrassment—to discover himself thus suddenly in the circle of everyone's attention. Yet, for some reason not plain to him, he felt a certain pleasure, too, in having this particular caballero at his sword's point.

"Come on then," he said, placing himself on guard. "Lay on, you lousy coyote!"

33

Don Diego did not understand this insult, but he needed no spur to his fury. He attacked immediately; and, for one so laced with wine, his assault was at once fierce and remarkably skillful. Don Antonio realized instantly that his opponent was an expert, determined, and suddenly sober swordsman. He gave a little ground and tightened his guard. Careful! he warned himself. Easy, Antonio!

His own fault was a certain rashness in attack, too much reliance perhaps on physical strength; besides, one grew a little rusty on the finer points of swordplay in New Mexico. He had once been very good; he had a fleeting doubt of his fitness now. He beat off Don Diego's first assault successfully, but with little to spare. This caballero was the real thing—the "Royal City," as they said here in Spain.

"How do you like it, my friend?" Don Diego asked, lowering his point. "Do you want more? Do you want me to kill you? Or do you ask my pardon—and the pardon of all here?"

"Come on, coyote," Don Antonio repeated.

He felt the contact of Don Diego's blade against his own at once. The caballero's return to the attack was less impetuous, however, almost cautious now. The taunt, of course, was merely a ruse. Don Diego had no real expectation that his opponent would confess himself beaten—and a poltroon into the bargain; but he did hope to disturb his calm, to infuriate him a little. Don Antonio saw through this easily enough, and with no little satisfaction.

So you begin to wonder! he said to himself. Maybe you were a little hasty, eh?

They settled down to a few cold, deadly moments of measuring each other out. This was all a rather silly business, Don Antonio reflected. But it was, nevertheless, a very serious matter for them both. Unless the authorities arrived quickly, it would certainly end in a bloody finish for one of them. He feinted and noted Don Diego's reaction. He exposed his own flank, inviting the caballero's attack.

A man, Don Antonio had long ago discovered, reveals not only his technique but his innermost nature in the assault. He peered under the crook of his elbow and lowered point, and waited for his adversary to respond to his invitation. He laid himself wide open; but Don Diego hesitated to accept his invitation.

"What's the matter, señor?" Don Antonio taunted. "Have you lost your appetite? Have you filled your breeches?"

The caballero grunted an obscenity and charged. He was fast, clever, and full of tricks—an even smoother swordsman than he had seemed at first. But his play was marred by a certain rashness that appeared genuine, and he was still a little drunk perhaps. Don Antonio felt a certain relief.

If that's your best, señor, he said to himself, we don't worry, eh? But at this instant the caballero's point grazed his flank, and he prudently decided to keep a little ground between them.

His own style, he realized with some misgiving, was almost too elementary; he regretted vaguely that he hadn't given a little more time to the study of swordplay. He had always relied on simple parries for defense, and on a natural strength and quickness in the attack. And these qualities had served him well enough in the Indies. In half a dozen bouts he had never come out the loser.

But this caballero in the fancy waistcoat, with his elaborate coups, thrusts, and Italian passes, was something different. Don Diego's long Spanish sword performed a kind of rhythmic exercise that baffled and bewildered Don Antonio. Again and again it passed uncomfortably close to his throat; and once it grazed his sword arm. Suddenly the insistent repetition of these close calls had an effect on Don Antonio: he realized that he was frightened.

That there were some way to break this off! he thought dimly. He cast a quick glance toward the gate, hopeful of the constables' arrival. He wondered ruefully why he had ever become entangled with this odious caballero and his even more odious sword.

A moment later he knew why. In a little pause—a few seconds' hiatus in the clish-clash of steel—Don Antonio stole a swift glimpse at the spectators banked silently against the wall. He caught sight of Josefina. Her face was a mask of fascinated horror. Her eyes were enormous. Even as he parried another thrust, Don Antonio felt the impact of her terrified stare.

It flickered through his mind that it was those eyes, and that girl, and the fatuous dream his foolish brain had woven around them, that had got him into this troublesome business with Don Diego. So he cursed Josefina in the same breath that he cursed the caballero. But, even while he fought off fear and felt resentment, he was conscious also of deriving a certain romantic glow from acting the bravo on behalf of so beautiful and fascinating a woman.

That you but live to taste her kisses, Antonio! he thought wryly. If only this ugly devil would open up a little!

Don Diego quite suddenly abandoned the impetuous vigor of his attack and now settled down to a careful but energetic line of play. This Don Antonio liked even less than the first reckless rushes. He had beat those off, largely by main strength; he found the caballero's cautious tactics harder to cope with. Time and again the dancing point of Don Diego's sword missed him by only its own breadth. Then it actually grazed his neck; and Don Antonio, passing his hand over the spot where the steel had touched him, felt the sticky wetness of blood between his fingers. It was not a serious cut—hardly more than a careless valet might inflict in shaving—but it gave him a sickening start. He glanced again toward the gate, through which the constables would come—if, by God's kindness, they came.

In Christ's name, Antonio! he said to himself. Pull yourself together, or he will kill you for certain.

All at once Don Antonio was conscious of a thing he should have noticed long before.

Despite his cleverness and spirit, Don Diego had one bad habit. Always after a parry he removed his blade. To make certain of this, Don Antonio feinted a couple of times. In both actions Don Diego reacted by parrying, then disengaging. Don Antonio smiled. He had fought a Creole dandy once—over a tawny girl from Potosí—who had been unfortunate enough to possess the same habit. Don Antonio had found out how to handle him. He resolved to try the same tactic against Don Diego.

He made as if to launch a furious attack. "Hah!" he ejaculated, like a bullfighter taunting a bull. Blocking Don Diego's blade, he made

136

him feint. He lunged and thrust—and felt the caballero's blade withdraw after the parry. Instantly, so swiftly that the action appeared to those watching to be but a single movement, he thrust again at Don Diego's flank. It was a perfectly executed action.

But at this point, in the next fraction of a second, something untoward happened. A moment later, instead of looking down at Don Diego run through by that last lunging thrust, he found himself joined in a furious struggle with the caballero, body to body, swords locked, and he was straining every muscle to free his blade and himself.

For a whole minute, perhaps, they swayed back and forth in this desperate embrace. Don Diego's strength was surprising—but inferior, Don Antonio discovered with relief, to his own. The discovery gave him a wonderful, almost arrogant surge of courage. He wrenched mightily at his weapon. Failure to disengage it infuriated him, and—now that he felt so reassured—he was in a sudden, confident rage to kill Don Diego.

"Louse!" he grunted. "Now I crack you!"

He wrenched again. Don Diego spun once, like a child's top—and sprawled on the ground. His sword flew into the air, so high and far that the gaping crowd scattered to avoid being pierced by it. Don Diego thrust out his arm, palm outward, as if to ward off doom.

"Get up, señor," Don Antonio said coldly. "Get up and let me kill you on your feet."

Actually, he had lost his desire to finish off the caballero—if, indeed, such a thing were thinkable. He could not very well run a defenseless man through—before so many witnesses, at any rate. And he had no urge to give Don Diego back his sword and resume the bout. The caballero also, it appeared, had lost his stomach for combat. He made no attempt to regain his feet or recover his weapon.

"In God's name, señor," he said, with a wry smile, "let us say that honor is satisfied. Frankly, I've had enough."

"Do you want me to kill you?" Don Antonio asked ungraciously, trying hard to remember Don Diego's exact words to himself a little earlier. "Or do you ask my pardon, and the pardon of all here? Particularly the señora's."

"The señora? Do you mean the one they call La Sola?"

"I don't know what they call her," Don Antonio said impatiently. "God's blood! Do I have to know the victims of your insults personally?"

"I meant no insult," Don Diego answered, getting to his feet. "It was merely enthusiasm, señor. It was the wine."

"The wine didn't spoil your swordwork," Don Antonio commented dryly.

"Good wine never does, señor," Don Diego said sadly. "But alas, it sometimes affects my judgment in matters concerning women."

Don Antonio unconsciously placed the palm of his hand against the scratch that Don Diego had dealt him on the neck. The slippery feel of blood, still oozing from the cut, reminded him how close he had come to death at the caballero's hands. His rage surged up again.

"Broil me!" he growled. "You don't amuse me, señor. Do you apologize or do you fight?" He advanced toward Don Diego with the stride of an angry and determined man.

"I ask your forgiveness, señor," Don Diego said hastily. "I acknowledge myself to blame for everything. I also ask the forgiveness of all these good people for interrupting their entertainment. And as for the lovely señora——"

He turned with a courtly gesture toward the spot where Josefina, as motionless as an image of the Virgin in a brocaded gown, had stood watching. His eyes darted about in search of her; he shrugged his shoulders and smiled.

"As for the lovely señora," Don Diego finished, "she is gone. She does not wish to hear my act of contrition. Ah, well."

"Señor?" Don Antonio demanded.

"Yes, yes," Don Diego said. "Perhaps you will convey to her, señor, my profound expressions of regret. I kiss her feet. I ask forgiveness ten thousand times." He smiled a slow, knowing smile. "As for yourself, señor mío—that you have a pleasant evening. . . ."

34

The spring floods had raised the Duero to such a height that the stone bridges in Roa scarcely cleared its rushing crest. By leaning over the low parapet, Josefina could have wet her fingertips. She stared down at the muddy, debris-littered stream and felt the fascination that swift-moving water has always had for the troubled in mind and the sick at heart. She drew her mantón more tightly about her bare shoulders and shivered.

"That would be a poor way to die, Josefina," she said aloud, "in such muddy water!"

She had no real intention of killing herself. That was not why she was standing here, in the early dusk, staring down at the dirty flood of the Duero. She had merely paused here, to catch her breath, in her blind flight from the Inn of the Moor. But, having stopped, something had held her, for the space of a rosary now; and, if her thoughts were not seriously about death, they were, at least, about the futility of living.

She had reached that point at last where one refuses to think in the symbols of reality: where one can experience only a vague, enveloping sense of spiritual malaise.

I am almost always hungry, she said to herself, and at night I sleep in filth and am cold. If I should be sick again, I would shiver in some farmer's cowshed, like any whelping bitch. And now, alas, we are thrown out of the inn because I soured the milk for Uncle Pepe. Where shall I go now? What shall I do? What is going to become of me?

She remembered Jesusita and experienced a pang of nausea in her empty stomach. Yet, even these cruel, sawtoothed thoughts did not hold what Josefina felt as she leaned over the parapet and watched the turgid water of the Duero slip away from her, and listened to the distant sounds of tumult still coming from the courtyard of the inn. And then:

"That I had someone," she said with infinite weariness. "That I had a place to go to. . . ."

Sometimes, when this soledad—this loneliness beyond loneliness—and this great depression possessed her, she thought of Eva Helena and took courage from the memory of her courage.

"You will see, children. This is but a little rain that will blow away —and ay! how lovely the sun will shine for us then!"

She could almost hear the very words in her mother's gentle, husky voice. But they gave her no bravery, no resolution, now. Instead, she was vaguely horrified to hear herself thinking: Alas, Madre mía, how good and strong—but also how innocent, how stupid you really were!

And, having thought this, there was nothing left for her to cling to —unless it were the straw of Uncle Pepe's fatuous optimism. She closed her eyes and thought how easy to throw oneself into the water, if one had even a little courage. One had but to lean out thus, and then a little farther. . . .

"Careful, Doña Josefina!" she heard a voice calling.

She whirled about and, full of anger and shame, faced Tichi. She was ashamed and angry, not because the Gallega had caught her in a disgraceful act, but because she had not the will to perform even that last poor gesture of the utterly defeated.

"Why did you follow me here?" she asked coldly.

"I have good news, señora."

"For me?"

"For all of us."

"Well, what is it then?"

"I cannot tell you, Doña Josefina. Uncle Pepe wishes to—he himself wishes to give it to you."

"And where is Uncle Pepe now?" she asked.

"At his apartment in the Moor."

"Holy Mary! Don't make jokes, Tichi," Josefina said angrily. "Hasn't the landlord turned us all out?"

"Oh, no, señora. We all have lodgings at the inn tonight. And Uncle Pepe has an apartment with a flock bed and a brazier."

Arriving at the inn, they were met by the smiling landlord, who conducted them directly to Uncle Pepe's apartment by means of an outside stairway, thus avoiding the crowded common room.

"It will spare the señora the stares of the carriers," the landlord said delicately.

This I do not believe, Josefina said to herself.

Uncle Pepe, carefully controlling himself in the presence of the innkeeper, bowed them into his apartment with an air of grave importance. It was a large bare room with shuttered windows, a tiled floor, and beamed ceiling, furnished with a bed in an alcove, two chairs, a table, and a brazier: a really luxurious apartment, as one found them in Spanish inns, particularly in country places such as Roa.

"This I do not believe either!" Josefina said.

Uncle Pepe closed the door softly on the innkeeper. He held out his arms and tears filled his tired eyes. "My daughter!" he cried brokenly. "We are saved!"

"Very well, Uncle Pepe," Josefina said, freeing herself. "If you have finished playing this fine scene, perhaps you will tell me what has happened."

Uncle Pepe made them sit down on the chairs. He laughed at the way Josefina's eyes went over all the details of the room.

"Ah yes!" he beamed. "It is my good fortune that the guest who formerly occupied this apartment—a certain Señor Don Diego de la Prada—was in very urgent haste to get on to Madrid. Only half an hour ago he decided that the road is passable at last and departed in his calash. Personally, I think he was very unwise to start out so near to nightfall."

"Por favor, Uncle Pepe," Josefina begged. "I am tired and I have a headache. That you tell me as quickly as you can whatever it is you have to tell."

"I am sorry, daughter," Pepe said. "I guess I am a little drunk. It has been so long since Bitch Fortune has given us one of her sour smiles. A little good news goes to my head, eh?"

He began to walk up and down the room in a brisk, thoughtful manner, as if his mind were filled with important plans and projects.

He is always acting, Josefina thought wearily. Now he is the great director again!

"Let us pass over the unpleasant events of this afternoon," Pepe continued. "And yet—and yet—I think this unfortunate affair may have been God's answer to my prayers."

"It is hard to see how that could be," Josefina said. "But go ahead, Uncle Pepe. Only that you tell it in a few words."

"It has saved us," Uncle Pepe went on, "from a desperate situation. Consider, my dear. Now—now we have lodgings, all of us, at this very fine inn. In a few minutes we will all sit down to a good puchero and a skin of Valdepeñas. There will be no lack of food and wine tonight. We shall eat all we can hold—thanks to you, my child!"

"But I don't understand," Josefina said. "You make me dizzy in the head, Uncle Pepe."

"We have a friend—a patrón."

"Ah, yes?"

"Precisely. The Señor Don Antonio Valverde y Cosio. He is providing everything—everything."

"He must be a very rich man, no?"

"Undoubtedly. He is a representative of His Majesty in New Spain and very wealthy, naturally."

"Where did you find him, Uncle Pepe? Have I seen him?"

"Have you seen him?" Uncle Pepe roared with sudden laughter that ended in a fit of rather alarming coughing. "My dear child, he is the señor who fought and so brilliantly defeated Don Diego de la Prada. In your defense, chica."

"Ah, yes," Josefina said gently. "That was very romantic, no?"

"Exactly!" Uncle Pepe exclaimed. "Romantic. *Very* romantic."

"That you tell me some more about this romantic señor," Josefina said.

"I know only what the landlord has told me, chica. That he is a bachelor from these parts—from Villa Presente, to be exact—of a noble and much-respected family whose motto, 'Ask Valverde,' is a kind of byword in this region."

"What is he doing in Roa?" Josefina asked idly.

"Having come to Spain to settle certain private affairs," Uncle Pepe continued, in his pompous style, "Don Antonio is now returning to the Capital, from which he plans to go to Seville and embark for Vera Cruz. Had it not been for the floods, which have detained him here——"

"We should be sleeping hungry in the fields tonight. Let us thank God, who sent the floods!"

"Ah, yes," Uncle Pepe said. "You see the turning point in our fortunes. From here we go ahead. The company stays together. Our worries are over, thanks to God and Señor Valverde—and to you, my dear child."

Alas, poor Uncle Pepe, Josefina thought. Do you really believe what you say? Then, suddenly curious again, she asked, "But why do you always thank me, Uncle Pepe?"

Pepe gazed at her with a look that was at once tender, anxious, shrewd, and desperate: a look that made her feel vaguely uncomfortable.

"Why not?" he asked, a little too sweetly. "Why do you think our Señor Valverde has performed this magnificent act of generosity? For me, Pepe Velasco? For the company? Because it amuses him to spend great sums of money?" He laughed, made a gesture of dismissal, and looked at her coyly.

"Never mind, Uncle Pepe," she said, suddenly sickened. "You don't have to tell me." Los hombres! she thought. They have but one answer to everything.

"It is natural," Pepe said, "for great beauty to arouse admiration. And you, my child, are one of the most beautiful women in Spain. So is it surprising that Señor Valverde——?"

"You are very tiresome, Uncle Pepe. What are you coming to?" She let her fan drop open and began to fan herself slowly: the air, even in that large room, had become heavy and oppressive.

"I have discovered, indeed," Pepe continued blandly, "that Señor Valverde was captivated by your charms even before he saw your face. Only from watching you walk across the square!"

"How do you learn these things, Uncle Pepe?"

"The señor has a valet," Pepe explained, "a young Asturian who is somewhat talkative and, moreover, has an eye on our Cristina. This young man informed me of all this. The fact is, chica, Don Antonio's heart was lost even before he knew who you were. And now that he has found out—that you are actually the great La Sola herself——"

"Ea! It would be something to tell his comrades in New Mexico, no?" Josefina said dryly. "How, in Spain, my friends, I slept with the famous La Sola!" She fluttered her fan a little faster. She heard Tichi cough a small, embarrassed cough.

Pepe looked at her for a moment reproachfully. "Is it too much," he asked, "that we show Señor Valverde a little gratitude for his great kindness?"

"It is your idea, then, Uncle Pepe," she said wearily, "that I play the whore in order to save the company?"

"Let us put it this way," he said with an odd doggedness. "We are at the mercy of Don Antonio. Only he can keep the company together. With his help, we can go on. Without him—pfft!"

142

"And so, Uncle Pepe?"

He looked at her for a little while mournfully, with an infinite dejection: an old and sick man with but one small hope left in life: and he said, in such a low voice that she could scarcely hear him, "Would it be too much, my daughter?"

For a moment she experienced no emotion, but only a curious blankness of feeling. She regarded Pepe over her fan and, during that long interval, was conscious of a quietly violent and rather frightening sensation of transformation. It was as if she were a vessel from which was being slowly emptied all that the daughter of Eva Helena, all that the girl and then the woman called Josefina María del Carmen Torres had been . . . and into which was being slowly poured all that she was now to be.

It was a sensation so real and so tangible that she found herself waiting, with a kind of patience, for it to complete itself. And when it was over—when the vessel had been refilled—she felt a strong, deep, hard surge of exaltation. For now she knew that nothing could ever hurt her again.

"Señor Valverde has asked me to present his compliments," Pepe said, "and to request the pleasure of your company at dinner in his apartment this evening."

"And you have accepted for me—to save the company."

"I took that liberty, my child."

A strange thing happened then. As Pepe stood looking at her, waiting for her to answer him, tears gathered in his eyes and soon a drop ran down each side of his nose.

"Very well," Josefina said. "I'll have dinner with Señor Valverde, and I'll entertain him very well afterwards. He shall have something to tell his friends in New Mexico, no? But understand this, Uncle Pepe: I do not make a common *puta* of myself to save the company. . . . May the company burn in hell, and you with it, Uncle Pepe! I am interested only to save myself. Do you comprehend, Uncle Pepe? *From now on, everything is for Josefina.*"

He blinked at her with his teary eyes, then smiled horribly and tried to throw his arms around her. She pushed him away. The thinness and boniness of his body, which had once seemed pitiful to her, suddenly was repulsive. She felt no compassion now for Uncle Pepe, no warmth at all; she resisted a violent impulse to strike him with her fan.

"Bless you, my child!" Pepe said, groping behind him for the door.

"Get out, Uncle Pepe, in God's name! That you go away and leave us alone for a little while."

She crossed the room to the window, leaned her forehead against the grillwork, and looked down at the scattered knots of men in the dusky courtyard. She spat at them. After a while the door opened, and Tichi came in.

"Look, Doña Josefina," Tichi said, "I have obtained a needle and some silk. If you will come over to the light, I'll mend your dress."

Josefina looked at her with a kind of curiosity. She had all but forgotten the Gallega. She had become almost oblivious, in fact, to everything around her; and it surprised her a little to see the tall candle on the table, and Tichi standing in its glow, her face serene, her soft eyes incurious. She went and stood before her.

"Tichi," she said. "How would you like to go to the Indies—to New Mexico, maybe, where they have no money and everything is free?"

"I should like that, señora. I am always ready to go anywhere. And I have told you what I heard in Madrid, Doña Josefina: that there are some—especially ladies from Spain—who do not make out so badly in the Indies."

Josefina was silent for a little time; she was thinking about Don Antonio and trying, to recall his appearance. This was difficult, because she had seen him only in combat, really, when his face wore the stern, intent, almost preoccupied expression of a swordsman. But it seemed to her that it was a strong face, not ugly, and not old; and she did not remember it unpleasantly.

"Well, we shall see," she said pensively. "Perhaps in the morning we shall know."

35

Mother of God! she thought. What a long time ago: how far away it was!

It was so far away and long ago indeed that now, as she sat under the high vigas of the palace dining room in the Villa of Santa Fé, and tried to recall that night at the inn at Roa, there was hardly any of it that she could remember.

And that is odd, she said to herself, for I do have a very good memory. I can remember clearly things that happened when I was but a very small child in Ávila. Perhaps it is that I am growing old! Or that I drank too much of the wine that night. . . . Or maybe a woman forgets what she takes no pleasure in remembering. . . .

Yet, strangely enough too, and for reasons equally obscure, there was one brief interval that had not blanked out, that was like one of those moments when a fire on the hearth flares up suddenly and illuminates briefly the darkness of an unlit room. And this fragment of memory flickered up in her mind as she gazed down the long table at the candlelit features of Don Antonio Valverde y Cosio, Governor and Captain-General of the Kingdom of New Mexico.

It had grown cold toward morning, for Roa was a mountain town, and the chill before dawn could be bitter in June. She lay in the great flock bed, listening in the darkness to Don Antonio's heavy breathing, and shivering in the icy draft that swept through the shuttered but unglazed window.

She had never learned to stand cold. Her southern body, her Andalusian blood, suffered from it; and it depressed her spirits, at times profoundly. There was something about cold that, like darkness, too much suggested death. To lie awake in the darkness, and to be cold, was for Josefina more than a physical discomfort; it was—and on this desperate night more than ever—a frightening thing, a kind of horror, that gathered and grew in the blackness surrounding her. She trembled under a scrap of thin blanket at Don Antonio's side.

He groaned in his sleep and turned toward her. His bulk, stretched out beside her, seemed enormous; enormous and massive, solid and unassailable; for in the very inertness of his great insensible form there was a kind of contempt for all such fears and anxieties as lurked in the shadows of her own mind. With a sudden, almost convulsive movement, she fled to the warmth of that body, the security of that untroubled strength. Don Antonio heaved a deep, contented sigh, reached his arm around her and began drowsily to stroke her thigh.

When the sounds of morning began to filter through the shuttered window—the twittering of birds, the shouts of muleteers in the stable, the bells of all the churches in Roa ringing the Angelus—they lay quietly and warmly, watching the room fill slowly with the light of a new day. Don Antonio was thinking of a parry he might have used to evade a certain one of Don Diego's thrusts; of the deal he had made with his uncle in Villa Presente, and whether he might not have squeezed a few more reales out of the old man; of a bay stallion for which he had traded three women slaves to the Apache; of springtime in New Mexico. . . .

Josefina was also thinking of New Mexico, of what Don Antonio had told her about it the evening before—after his astonishingly silent devotion to the baked turkey, that is, and before he had snatched her up suddenly and roughly, and had carried her to the great flock bed: Don Antonio, she reflected wryly, had a quite amazing capacity for concentration on whatever happened to be his pleasure of the moment.

And one of these pleasures, plainly, was talking; particularly, it would seem, about that scarcely believable place beyond the ocean called the Kingdom of New Mexico. But how much could she believe, really, of what he had told her? What of those vast plains where the bulls ran and the earth shook under millions of hooves? Or of the savage city on a great high rock (in the very clouds, he said!) and a church there with room for three thousand souls? Or of the snow on the desert, a vara deep, under which the soldiers and horses slept as under blankets, without ever getting wet?

Such things were not only hard to swallow, but enough to frighten one also, even one who had been about and had seen as much as she had. Yet they were not frightening, but only curious as Don Antonio told them. For he told, besides, of the peaceful green valley of the Río de Santa Fé; and of flowery passes in the hills; and of his fine vineyards at El Paso del Norte; and—with a special gusto—of his favorite sweet made from the tiny nuts of a kind of pine tree and honey, and of how his girl slaves spent weeks cracking the nuts with rolling pins for this confection.

On such details—the details of comfort and even simple pleasures in a rude land—Don Antonio dwelt with a nostalgic enjoyment. He made life in New Mexico sound so simple and uncomplicated and secure that Josefina discovered in herself the unfolding of an intense, almost unbearable desire for escape to that pleasant kingdom, too far away for trouble to follow, where the slave girls served one's household, and there were so many enchanting things to eat. What had been but a vague idea before, now became a sudden determination, hard, solid, and as real as the feel of Don Antonio's strong arm under her shoulders. She stirred and tightened with the intensity of her thoughts.

"What is it, my little hummingbird?" Don Antonio asked lazily. "What are you thinking of now?"

She moved impulsively closer to him and lay her head in the hollow of his shoulder.

"That you take me back with you, amor," she said. "That you take me to your Kingdom of New Mexico."

"Y cómo no?" he asked gruffly. "And why not?"

36

. . . Well, he had kept his word, she reflected now, a little sadly. One might say that for eight years he had kept the bargain he had made with her that morning in the great flock bed in the inn at Roa. And not without some danger, at first, to himself.

For a while they tarried in Seville, detained there by interminable delays in clearing *La Nueva España.* Spain was in her death grapple with the Coalition; and a great wave of suspicion, informations, denouncements, and persecutions of supposed enemies of the regime had swept out of the Capital and over the whole Peninsula. It was an ideal climate for the hatching of any plans for revenge the Conde de Vega might have formed; and Don Antonio, in fact, had received reports that the Conde not only had discovered Josefina's whereabouts, but had actually sent Don Diego de la Prada to carry out his long-delayed coup.

True or not, this rumor was enough to drive Josefina and Tichi into hiding—at Don Antonio's insistence—for almost a month. It was a long month and a dangerous one, not only for Josefina but also for Don Antonio, who had his own enemies in Spain—as, indeed, who did not?—and could ill afford to be suspected of collusion with the King's enemies. It was also a month of terrible heat.

Then, somewhere, late in July the battle of Derain was fought. Marlborough was defeated, the French monarchy was saved, the Coalition fell apart, and Spain was triumphant over her enemies. A carnival of madness took possession of Seville, and for a few days there was such a reign of delirious joy—such a forgetting and forgiving of old scores—that Josefina dared to go unmasked to the victory fiestas. And even when, at one of these, Tichi was sure that she had glimpsed Don Diego, she was not perturbed.

"Don't worry, Tichi," she said with an odd recklessness. "Can't you see that the times have changed? Even the jails are being emptied, no? The Conde de Vega himself cannot harm me now."

"I don't know, Doña Josefina," Tichi said. "I don't trust this mob of gypsies. They kiss you today and kill you tomorrow."

And Tichi, as it turned out, was right. The reaction, when it came a few days later, was violent and terrifying. Where dancing, singing, flower-throwing crowds had only yesterday been celebrating the victory, shouting gangs now roamed the streets and plazas hoarsely demanding revenge. And the whole town was filled with the dread sound of soldiers knocking on doors.

On the first night of this fury, Don Antonio had smuggled Josefina and Tichi across the river and had hid them both in a dark, sinister, evil-smelling cellar on the waterfront for a week. Then, also at night, he had got them aboard *La Nueva España.*

By what means Don Antonio had accomplished this escape—for it was, she learned afterwards, an escape actually enough, with Don Diego's men on the stairway when they left by the roof—Josefina had never learned. But she knew it to be the act of a resolute and resourceful man, and one that Don Antonio must have performed at no small

147

personal risk. And for this—even after what had happened during the eight years since, even while she sat now, opposite Don Antonio in the high-vigaed dining room of the palace and sensed a vague, half-formed hatred for him—she had never ceased to be grateful.

But how, she asked herself, could such a thing as this have happened?

It was not only—or even principally—a matter of physical change. Don Antonio had never, except in the eyes, looked the soldier. He was fatter now, and heavier in his movements, and his pale pear-shaped face had acquired a kind of sad, sagging resignation. But Josefina had known men with such bodies and such faces to be great captains and men of strong will and driving energy: the kind of men that Don Antonio Valverde y Cosio might well be still, if only——

She was about to say, If only he would let me help him again. For he no longer turned to her, as he once had, for counsel in dealing with his friends and enemies at the Viceroy's court; he seemed even to resent the memory of the help she had given him in México.

Yet the fact remained: even though he had been the great Vargas's friend, and even though he might have had, as he claimed, some slight influence at the court of Philip V itself, Don Antonio would never have become, as everyone knew, governor and captain-general of this Kingdom without the aid of Josefina. The fact remained, perhaps, to irk him.

So she wasted no more of her time in wishing; she put all such nostalgic thoughts away; but she could not cease to wonder. In México, where they had tarried for a time after fleeing from Spain, she had heard the story of Coronado, and how that famous man had suddenly changed from a great conquistador to a small, mean, and ineffectual man despised even by his servants. And she wondered if the mysterious thing that had overcome the great Coronado in New Mexico—perhaps some sickness particular to this desolate land—might not also have undone Don Antonio.

In her anxiety to learn if other cases like Don Antonio's were known to the physicians, and if so what cure was recommended, she had even written to Tafora, the Viceroy's powerful advisor and secretary. And Tafora had replied with his usual polite cynicism: "Since the cause of such declines, my dear señora, is generally to be found in a too-faithful devotion to the board and alcove, I take the liberty to suggest that the cure, after all, is most properly in your own beautiful hands."

But Don Antonio had always eaten and wenched more than was good for him. And yet, she decided after a little thought, perhaps Tafora was right after all. Since he had become governor, Don Antonio's table certainly had set forth an astonishing variety of fine foods,

148

wines, and brandies; and the girl captives, claimed by custom by the governors, had for a long time been more numerous and more beautiful than usual. And it could be said by no one that Don Antonio had ever shirked his gubernatorial duties to these comely slaves. To have pleased Don Antonio, indeed, became a distinction that actually doubled the value of a girl captive; for she could then be resold, when his excellency had tired of her, with the recommendation, "Que ya está buena"—"She is but good!"

Josefina smiled wearily and watched Don Antonio's eyes follow the undulating hips of the young Navajo slave as she left the room after refilling his goblet. The girl's name was María, for she had accepted baptism and had been "reduced." She was singularly good-looking, as the women of the Navajo Apache sometimes were, and bold, and very young. Josefina admired and hated her; and her hatred for María was mingled with, and no doubt related to, hatred of a vaguer, less active, and almost irksome sort for Don Antonio.

She had never loved Don Antonio; and so, until lately, his rather flagrant infidelities had never perturbed her overmuch: they were, after all, the custom of this time and this land. But recently, it had seemed to her, Don Antonio had made rather too much of a display— even a flaunt—of his amoríos.

"Tichi," she had demanded of her Gallega one day, "look at me closely. Am I growing old? Have I lost my good looks?"

Tichi gently took away the silver-gilt hand mirror into which Josefina had been looking, and proceeded with her arrangement of her mistress's hair.

"Really, Doña Josefina," she said, "must I tell you again? You grow more beautiful each day. You are only twenty-six years old, no?"

"Twenty-seven, Tichi."

"Well, even twenty-seven. It is remarkable, señora, how you keep your youth. And your figure also. I have grown fat—everybody grows fat here—but look at you, señora! You still have the figure of a girl. Why this dress, as you can see, is just as loose about the waist today as——"

"Sometimes," Josefina said pensively, "I think that Don Antonio does not see me quite as you do."

"If you are thinking of that slut María," Tichi said, "you might just as well save yourself from any worry on her account. She will be worn out in a few months and sold for a couple of horses. Then——"

"Did I say anything about this slave—this María?" Josefina asked icily. "When I wish you to do my thinking for me, Tichi, I shall let you know."

"Well, as you yourself must admit, señora, no servant ever loved and respected her mistress more than I do. But I must say, I can't

149

find any of the same feeling to spare for His Excellency. Do you know, Doña Josefina——"

"Yes, Tichi?"

"We have been together for a long time, and so I shall risk your displeasure again, señora, by speaking frankly."

"Has it ever been your habit to speak otherwise?"

"Señora, we have been through much together. More than I ever want to go through again." She paused reflectively and made a little grimace. "Even more, Doña Josefina," she added, "than you know."

Josefina said nothing. She thought of the time she was sick with the fever in the greedy peasant's hut near Ojan, and of their starvation in Málaga; and she remembered Tichi's mysterious disappearances at night, and her return from them with a few coins or the materials for a puchero. But she could only look at Tichi gravely and say nothing.

"God knows what would have happened to us," Tichi continued, "if Don Antonio had not brought us here in that stinking boat. And for that we owe him thanks. But now señora, I think it is time again for us to consider ourselves."

"Why do you say this, Tichi?"

"A servant, señora, sees and hears a lot of interesting things, no?"

"I don't doubt it," Josefina said. "For example?"

"Well, for example, Doña Josefina, I have got the impression from gossip I have overheard here in the palace that Señor Don Antonio is about finished."

"More softly, Tichi! Be careful how you repeat such preposterous talk!"

"Preposterous or not, señora, it is what everyone is saying. Don Antonio has lost favor with the Viceroy. He is suspected by the Audiencia. His own men call him a coward and thief. He is allowing the affairs of the Kingdom to fall into confusion. Right now an order is on its way from the Viceroy, recalling him to México for an accounting."

"That," Josefina said coldly, "sounds like the talk of Don Antonio's enemies."

"I have made allowance for the spite of his enemies, señora. My impression still is that Señor Don Antonio will be out of the Palace and in jail before fall."

"Tell me, Tichi," Josefina asked gravely, "why do you disturb me with these malicious rumors?"

"Because, señora," Tichi said obdurately, "if these things are going to happen to Don Antonio, where shall we be? What will become of us? If we have our wagon hitched to a sick horse, I say let us look around for a well one. Before it is too late, Doña Josefina."

"Delicacy of expression has never been one of your faults, Tichi," Josefina said after a moment of silence. "But I understand what you feel. And I thank you for telling me of this. And I ask your promise never to repeat it."

"I promise," Tichi said, a little defiantly. "But I have told you this only because I think you should know it, señora. And because I love you as my own child."

But, although Josefina could command Tichi to be silent, she could not silence her own thoughts, nor deny what she should long ago have seen—what her eyes told her now as, looking over the candle-light at Don Antonio, she observed sharply and clearly what a pitiful thing he had become.

"Here is a man, alas, who is all but finished!"

She said it a little sadly—since the threads of their lives had been so long entwined—and with a deep disquiet. She could not, like Tichi, surrender herself to fear; but neither could she shut out the memories of her poverty-haunted childhood. She felt—because she was so much older now—a faint, sudden surge of desperation; but it passed and left her, if not with courage, at least with a certain sense of hardness.

Qué lástima! she had whispered to herself. What a pity that this should happen to us! Then, quickly correcting herself in her thoughts, she said, Let us leave ourselves out of this, Josefina!

She considered what could be done, where she could turn. In the morning, she decided, she would write to Tafora for advice from México. She saw no way to save Don Antonio, but perhaps she could still save herself. She would form a plan. She would think of something. She heard Don Antonio saying through her reverie:

"Don Pedro in my place, eh? That is a very interesting suggestion, my dear. How did you happen to think of it?"

His eyes absently followed María's slender figure down the room, and he raised his silver goblet to his lips. Watching Josefina over the rim, he tipped it toward her in a slightly mocking gesture of a toast.

"I don't know, Antonio," she said, pretending to conceal a yawn. "It is just something that occurred to me. That you excuse me now—I have a headache."

She sat for a moment longer and regarded Don Antonio Valverde y Cosio, the Governor and Captain-General, with pensive eyes.

It is best, Josefina, she said to herself, almost sadly, that whatever must be done should be done quickly. For what was it that Doña Manuela used to say? . . . "Time is never on our side, no?"

Book Two

Ella que espera, desespera.

She who lives by hope dies in despair.

1

OF ALL the trails wandering into the Villa of Santa Fé from the pueblos of the Río Grande valley and the mountains beyond, Josefina delighted most in the one that was glorified by the name of El Camino Real—the Royal Road.

It had become Josefina's habit to take frequent rides into the country surrounding the Capital, sometimes accompanied by a soldier —selected by Don Antonio for his trustworthiness and gray hairs— who followed at a respectful distance as her protector, but sometimes alone.

She rode in a man's clothing, not in the usual fashion, sidewise in the saddle with stirrups removed and a sash looped around the horn to support one foot, but astride like a vaquero. The people of Santa Fé had become accustomed to seeing her thus, mounted on her black mare Negra, and did not consider the sight unusual. Nothing, for that matter that La Dama Josefina might do was any longer thought to be unusual—or, at least, unexpected—by the inhabitants of Santa Fé.

On this day, early in the spring of the year 1720, she was alone. She had ridden a little farther than she had intended, because she had been thinking furiously all the way, and when she thought hard, she rode hard. Negra had taken her up the long hill, far beyond the northern defense wall of the Villa, to the very highest level of the mesa. From here she could follow the road looping over the piñon-dotted hills to the pueblos of Picurís and Taos by way of the green meadows of Tesuque. She turned her back to it and looked southward. Below her, in its snug valley, lay the Royal City of the Holy Faith, capital Villa of the Kingdom of New Mexico.

Compared with other cities she had seen from other mountain heights—Madrid itself, for example, viewed from the road to Ávila— it was not a very impressive sight. It was but a small Spanish colonial town, laid out as all Spanish colonial towns were plotted, in accordance with the king's own directions: a dusty plaza faced on the north by the long, low whitewashed bulk of the Royal Palace, on the east by the big twin-towered church that the Marqués de Peñuela had

155

built; and for the rest, a sprawling pattern of flat adobe houses (some of which had encroached into the plaza), cultivated fields, and patio gardens through which curved the silver, willow-fringed Río de Santa Fé.

Not even its name, which was "The Royal Villa of the Holy Faith of Saint Francis of Assisi," could make a notable city of such a humble settlement. Yet its very isolation and insignificance imparted a certain tinge of greatness to this lonely protector of Spain's outermost frontier. Such was the grandeur of its setting—the vast encircling sweep of the Sierra Nevada and the dark, mysterious tumult of the Jémez peaks in which, it was said, the gods lived—that surely, Josefina thought, no other capital in the world could equal it.

She had grown to love dearly this little city of the good St. Francis. She always paused, as she did now, to contemplate it for a little while from the height of the mesa. Today, under the scoured spring sky, in the vibrating light of early March, it seemed to be enveloped in a special enchantment. How secure and contented and lovely it lay in that peaceful valley of the Río de Santa Fé that Don Antonio had told her about . . . so long ago, so very long ago in Roa.

Ay, Madre de Dios! she said to herself. That only my heart were as serene!

She dismounted, loosened Negra's cinch, and dropped the reins to the ground. There was a chill edge to the wind that blew from the snow-splashed Sierra Nevada. She drew her cloak a little more closely about her and settled her mannish French hat firmly on her head. For a few minutes she stood beside her mount, gazing down at the town, idly trying to make out the meaning of various antlike movements and activities in the streets and fields and patios.

But only her eyes, really, followed this distant stir of life. Her mind was occupied—as it had been all day—with something far closer to herself; yet, oddly, immeasurable miles away. Her thoughts were beyond the mountains to the east, far out into the buffalo plains, and even beyond them. She was thinking of the French.

She was thinking of a thing that filled all minds nowadays—the specter of a French invasion of New Mexico. Not only in Santa Fe, but in the City of México and in Madrid itself, the "French Threat" was discussed with growing apprehension. And now that actual war had broken out between Spain and France in Europe, apprehension had turned into something like panic.

In México, Josefina had learned—among many other things—that whatever brought concern and anxiety and fear into high places could somehow be made to serve a clever woman's ends. That it was easier, also, to make use of great events—such as wars and threats of wars and the difficulties of dynasties—than small ones.

How, she mused, might she make use of the French Threat—which had now become the "French Scare"? How might she advantage herself from it? How might it serve to free her from Don Antonio . . . and provide a little security, a little safety, for Tichi and herself in a hostile world?

She turned her eyes eastward. She thought of the settlements of the French beyond those mountains, far off across the plains where the bulls ran, where beautiful white women (the Apache said) wore their hair tied up on the crowns of their heads. She wondered what was afoot there—and what it might portend for her.

Negra neighed and pawed the sandy earth, impatient to start back. Josefina adjusted the saddle girth, mounted, and began the long descent into the valley. Halfway down, on a level stretch of the trail, she allowed Negra to break into a canter. She had become a superb horsewoman, riding short in her small Moorish saddle, but with stirrups a little longer than in the old jineta style; and she never failed to experience a pleasurable excitement when she felt the sudden release of Negra's tremendous power between her knees.

Her cheeks were flushed and her eyes shining with the exhilaration of her fast ride when she reached the long, high wall enclosing the Casas Reales. She pulled up Negra at the approach of a rider whom she recognized as Don Pedro Villasur.

It was pure chance that at this particular moment a small spotted pig should have scurried across the Camino Real, almost under Negra's legs; but it was not by accident that almost simultaneously the long rowels of Josefina's spurs dug sharply into her horse's flanks.

Negra reacted rather alarmingly with a violent lunge, followed by a series of rearing plunges and curvetings that tossed Josefina about so sharply in the saddle that her tricorn hat flew from her head. She curbed Negra in hard, struck smartly with her quirt, and gradually lashed the excited animal into a state of submission.

"Vaya!" Don Pedro exclaimed. "Done like a Comanche, señora!"

He angled his big roan toward her and reached out for Negra's bridle. His gloved hand seized the reins under the horse's muzzle.

"Por favor, señor," she said, breathing fast. "If you please, I need no help. That you let go."

She loaded her words with scorn. Don Pedro released his hold. She looked at him for a long moment, then down at her hat, which had been made by Colbert in Paris, lying in the dust of the Camino Real.

"Perhaps you will give me my hat, señor," she said coldly, "before your horse tramples it."

Don Pedro smiled. "My horse steps only where I permit him to," he said. "He has never yet trampled a lady's hat, señora."

He dismounted in a smooth, swinging motion, and retrieved the hat. He blew the dust from it, brushed it on his sleeve, and handed it up to her.

"Thank you, Don Pedro," she said. "It grieves me to be the cause of so much trouble."

He looked a little surprised, perhaps at hearing himself called by name. He gazed at her for a time with an odd expression—of uncertainty, or perplexity, or possibly amusement . . . she could not decide which.

"On the contrary, señora," he said, bowing. "It was I who caused you trouble."

"You?" she asked. "In what way, Don Pedro?"

"I frightened the pig," he said with a contrite smile. "And for that I beg a thousand pardons, Doña Josefina."

She looked at him closely. She had never exchanged more than a few polite phrases with Don Pedro. Ever since his arrival from Nueva Vizcaya, he had been almost constantly absent from the Capital on those endless tours of inspection demanded by the pueblo government. They were, in fact, still strangers to each other.

Nobody appeared to know much about Don Pedro—unless it were, perhaps, Don Antonio, who had brought him up from Nueva Vizcaya. But among the women of the Villa, the gossip was that he had a very reserved, even shy nature; that the most beauitful señoras of Chihuahua and Durango had not succeeded in turning him from his well-known devotion to duty; and that, although he was reputed to be recklessly brave in battle, he was never rash or incautious in other affairs— as those beauties of Neuva Vizcaya could wryly attest.

So she was a little surprised—and not at all displeased—at the faintly boyish quality of his smile and the disarming way in which he begged these thousand pardons for frightening the pig.

"Well, I grant them all, señor—" she smiled back at him "—although I think that only the pig himself was to blame."

He laughed, and said, "Well, let us agree to that, then."

She looked again, with a suddenly aroused interest, at Don Pedro's dark, handsome and not altogether forbidding features.

Don Pedro, she judged, was about thirty-five years old. His body had the lean, taut lines and bearing of a man almost constantly in the saddle: his bronzed, smooth-shaven face was one to go with such a body. It was the face of a soldier, a vaquero, a noble of Castile . . . and, she realized with a little shock of surprise, of a scholar—or even a poet!

Ah, yes! she said to herself. This does not quite fit into the legend, Josefina!

Her gaze met his. "The eyes," Tafora had always said, "are the true windows of the soul." And so she sought Don Pedro's eyes with hers.

They met and held for a long searching moment in which she read, as surely as if she had found it in a book, that the legend was *not* true.

I do not find you exactly as you have been described, Don Pedro, she mused. It seems to me that you have eyes for finer things than horses and guns and maps and the other concerns of soldiers. I doubt, Don Pedro, that you have room for nothing behind them but your famous devotion to arms and the King's service. . . . And I think you are very good-looking, Don Pedro—although a little too reserved, perhaps, to charm . . .

She had an odd difficulty in removing her gaze from his. She turned her head (her profile was very pure and pleasing) and looked off toward the Jémez range.

"We have not seen much of you, Don Pedro," she said, as if addressing those mysterious mountains. "You have been much missed in the Villa . . . I have heard."

"The Móqui," he said. "The Móqui and the Zuñi and the Keres. I have been among them the whole winter."

"And now?"

"Now, señora, I shall remain for a while in the Villa. I shall be very busy, no?"

He appeared to take it for granted that she knew all about some activity or other that was to occupy his time in the Villa—something that Don Antonio, as was his habit lately, had neglected to tell her about. She decided not to conceal her ignorance.

"With what, Don Pedro?" she asked.

"Why, with preparations for the Entrada, señora."

"Of course!" she said. "I had forgotten. There is always some entrada to prepare for, no? And now I must go. Con Dios, señor."

"Con Dios, señora!" he said, a little absently, and made her a deep, courtly bow. She reined her horse about and left him standing beside his mount in the Camino Real.

"I wonder if he saw me put the spurs to Negra?" she thought, as she rode away. She rather hoped that he had.

2

At the earliest hint of daylight a little Apache slave girl tiptoed into Josefina's chamber to make a fresh fire, for the high air of Santa Fé could be sharp on a March morning. She moved as gently as her own shadow on the whitewashed walls—quite unaware that the governor's lady was awake and observing her.

Josefina had not slept well. She had lain with open eyes, thinking, far into the darkness, and afterwards had rested so lightly that even so slight a sound as that of Doloritas's movements had been enough to arouse her. Yet now, even at such an early hour, she felt oddly alert and stimulated.

She watched Doloritas kneeling before the fireplace in the corner, blowing on the embers. The kindling burst into flame. Doloritas nursed the infant fire, stacked some logs upright around it, and swept up the hearth. She left softly, impersonally, a slave, without a glance in Josefina's direction. The sweet smell of burning piñonwood crept into the room.

Josefina lay for a time watching the glow of the fire wash over the snowy yesoed walls. At home she had loved the big brass braziers, fragrant of lavender, so dear to every Spaniard's heart; but she loved this little New Mexican fireplace even more. She loved this room of hers, whole and entire . . . more than any she had ever known. She wished never to leave it.

For this chamber was so very much her own that she could—if she wished—deny even Don Antonio entry to it. Don Antonio's chamber was separated from hers by a thick adobe wall, with a little sitting room adjoining both. But hers was the largest sleeping room in the Palace, and by far the finest.

It was a square, high-raftered room with a single window tunneled through the enormously heavy wall. This window, grilled with a spindled wooden reja and glazed with sheets of mica from a nearby quarry, gave onto the portal of the patio which, in summertime, was filled with vines and flowers and mockingbirds in amole cages.

The light of the new, clear day filtered but slowly through the mica panes. It contended with and gradually overcame the fitful illumination of the fire; and little by little, the details of the chamber took shape and color. And Josefina watched with a kind of grateful fascination the rebirth of this little personal world about her.

Her room was white and clean and cool and very simple. Its ceiling was beamed with vigas of red cedar, carved a little but unpainted; and over these were laid, in a herringbone pattern, round willow sticks stained blue and green. The walls that seemed, in the early half-light to slope up to this shadowy ceiling, were unbroken except for the single window and a big carved door of cottonwood.

Josefina yawned, stretched, pulled herself up to a sitting position. She arranged the silken pillows behind her back and smoothed a woolen spread over her knees. She glanced around the room, as she

160

always did on waking up, almost as if to reassure herself that all her things were still in place.

Her eyes went from her beautiful chests—the carved and painted one from México and the leather-covered one from Spain—to her two red-lacquered Andalusian chairs. Then to the plain pine table that held a silver-and-crystal crucifix and two candles. Then to a smaller table, of old dark wood, beneath a gilded mirror, on which her ivory beauty-box rested. And lastly to Yolanda, still blonde and lovely beyond description, gazing with her blue porcelain eyes from a cozy angle of the fireplace.

They were all there, all in place; and they were everything the room contained, save for a Virgin of Atocha in a niche beside the door, and some Navajo rugs on the smooth abode floor. Yet in all New Mexico there was not another room so richly furnished. It was doubtful, Josefina believed, that in all New Spain there was another room so charming. It was a room in which to be happy and serene and at peace—*and she was none of these.* She was sad and troubled and afraid; and, as she looked about this beautiful room, warm and rosy now in the light of the purring fire and the pink dawn, she thought of the House of the Three Acorns. She frowned and wished that Tichi would come with the chocolate. She lay for a little while longer, reflecting, then became restive and slipped out of bed.

By the time Tichi appeared, she had made her toilette, donned a silken robe, and had got back into bed, which was the only place to have one's breakfast. It was a simple enough meal, consisting only of chocolate and some sugar-coated sopapillas—a kind of light, fluffy cakes made of puff-paste; but not even a dinner for the Viceroy himself could have been prepared with more care and vigilance.

This was due to Don Antonio's excessive fondness for chocolate. All Spaniards were rather immoderately partial to this beverage which, in Spain and in New Spain also, was not simply a decoction of the cacao bean, but an esoteric composition of chocolate, sugar, and cinnamon, usually made into cakes and prepared and drunk in a very special manner. Don Antonio's affection for it was extreme.

"It is the mark of a civilized man," he often said, "to recognize a good cup of chocolate; it is the mark of a barbarian to swill coffee."

So much importance, in fact, did Don Antonio attach to the preparation of his chocolate, that a special cook—whose sole duty was to grind, blend, decoct, and whip up to a creamy froth Don Antonio's own personal selection of ingredients—was employed in the Palace kitchen.

"The only good chocolate comes from Bolivia," Don Antonio also said. "It is the most fragrant and the least bitter, and it requires little sugar."

He would admit, however, that the chocolate from Soconusco and Tabasco in México was also of a good grade and could even be substituted for Bolivian Moho in cases of extreme need. There were some who thought privately that Don Antonio rather overplayed this role of aficionado; but since the result was that those who dined at the Palace enjoyed perhaps the finest chocolate in the whole world, nobody made a point of his opinion.

The chocolate that Tichi brought Josefina was of such a rich, dark, purple thickness that it scarcely poured from the thin porcelain cup in which it was served. It was not drunk at once. First, Tichi filled a glass with cool water from a silver pitcher and dropped into it several light pieces of sugar of different colors—a luxury that Don Antonio had brought at great expense all the way from Spain. When she had sipped some of this, Josefina found the chocolate cool enough to drink. She had three cups, dipping her cakes into it, then finished with another glass of water.

When she had completed this, her "first breakfast," she felt relaxed and more content. Often, when she was pondering some problem, she experienced the feeling that her mind had at last got hold of the matter, and if she would but be patient and wait, a solution would come to her without effort—almost as if another were thinking for her. She had that feeling now. And she was quite sure, also, that in some way the French and Captain Don Pedro Villasur would be part of the answer, when it came; although she could not yet see, even vaguely, how this might be.

"Tichi," she said lazily, "since you overhear so much, and learn so many things by means that I cannot imagine, I should like you to find out something for me about Captain Don Pedro Villasur."

"What do you wish to know, señora?"

"Everything, Tichi—even the smallest thing. I should like to know, for example, what Don Pedro likes to eat and drink. How he amuses himself. What he talks about. . . . What he thinks about, no?"

"That might be hard to find out, señora!" Tichi laughed.

"Hard, but not impossible. At any rate, Tichi, you can discover such things as these: Is he friendly with the frailes? What do his soldiers say about him? Has he an amiga? Especially that, Tichi—*does he have an amiga?*"

She already knew the important facts about Don Pedro Villasur. She knew about his noble Castilian birth; his career as a soldier, both in Europe and the New Spains; his experience of war and politics in Santa Bárbara, Chihuahua, Rosario, El Paso del Norte, and the mines of Cosaguriachi; and all the honors he had won.

Now she wished—and greatly—to learn the small private details of his life. Such details, for example, as Tichi might pick up from the chitchat and gossip of servants, slaves, soldiers, farmers' wives, and travelers up and down the valley of the Río Grande.

"I understand, Doña Josefina," Tichi said.

"That you overlook nothing, then."

"I shall find out everything. And I can tell you right now, Doña Josefina, what Don Pedro is doing here, in the Villa."

"Really?" Josefina asked, her eyes widening. "And you haven't told me?"

"I have just found out about it," Tichi said, "from the chocolate cook this morning. She has orders to prepare two arrobas of chocolate for the Entrada."

"The Entrada?"

"Yes, señora. The expedition that Don Antonio has been ordered to make against the French. Don Pedro is making the preparations."

She was surprised that Tichi should know about the expedition: yet, who could expect a secret to remain long a secret in the Villa of Santa Fé?

Don Antonio had told her something of this Entrada, of course—something, although she suspected that he withheld much. It was a thing very close to the Viceroy's heart—a great reconnaissance to the northeast that would decide, once and for all, the questions that preoccupied and tormented not only the Vice-Royalty but the Crown itself:

Where were the French? What were their intentions? What was their strength? How, where, when would they strike at Spain's frontiers in the New World?

The "French Scare" was not new. More than thirty years ago a Frenchman named La Salle had made a daring attempt to occupy the province of Texas, on New Spain's very borders. His venture had failed and La Salle had been assassinated by three of his men, one of whom, Jean L'Archévèque, now lived in Santa Fé.

But even before La Salle's time, the French thrusting westward from their forts on the Río Mississippi and the Río Missouri had scattered consternation among the Spanish settlers of New Mexico. As early as 1687 they had carried their daring to the point of invading the Navajo country and fighting a great battle with the Indians in an attempt to recover children and cattle stolen from one of their posts to the east. Although they had killed almost four hundred Navajos (the Apaches reported), they were not successful in getting back the children and livestock; but the memory of their great intrusion was still an uneasy memory in Sante Fé, in México, and even in Madrid.

With news of a declaration of war between France and Spain, the situation had suddenly taken so serious a turn that everyone—including even the Viceroy—was thrown into a great pother by a rumor—reported by no other than the Governor of Parral—that six thousand Frenchmen were marching on Santa Fé and were, indeed, only seventy leagues from the Capital!

This rumor, of course, had proved to be nothing more than the excited imaginings of a lonely frontier captain; but it had shaken the Spaniards badly, and orders now poured in from Madrid for putting the borders in shape to repel an invasion.

Governor Antonio Valverde was commanded then to make a reconnaissance to the northeast to determine, if possible, the whereabouts and strength of the French in that direction. He was directed, also, to catch and punish the Comanches, who had been harassing the friendly Apaches around Taos.

This expedition Don Antonio had undertaken with much pomp and fanfare, marching out of Taos at the head of more than six hundred men, with almost a thousand animals and huge supplies of pinole, chocolate, tobacco, and presents for friendly Indians. Don Antonio also took along for his own use several casks of wine, a small keg of "very rich spirituous brandy," some glasses, and rich melon preserves for important saints' days.

Don Antonio had sighted not even one Comanche on that great expedition, but he had talked with friendly Indians who told him that the French were allied with the Pawnees, that they had built two towns, "larger than Taos," on the Río Jesús María, and that these new towns were being supplied with firearms and other things from the older settlements on the Río Mississippi.

This information Don Antonio sent by courier to the Viceroy in a report that reflected much credit on himself, but still left unanswered the great questions: Where were the French? What was their strength? How, when, where would they strike?

Whoever could find the answer to those questions would have the gratitude of the Viceroy—of the King himself. He would be an important man in New Spain . . . the rule of this Kingdom of New Mexico, no doubt, would be his for the asking. . . .

Josefina lay for a while after Tichi had carried out the breakfast things, gazing at the fire, and thinking about this . . . and about the new Entrada for which Don Pedro Villasur was making the preparations. And for some reason—she could not yet say what it was—she felt another step nearer now to the answer she was seeking to her own problem.

Tichi returned shortly with a very large silver basin, fluted like a seashell, and Josefina bathed in the clear, fresh water of the Río Chiquita. Afterwards Tichi rubbed her with a large square of linen cloth and smoothed on a little sultana water, which imparted an agreeable fragrance to the skin.

Following this, Josefina sat down, quite nude, at the small table before the gilded mirror and made up her face while Tichi arranged her hair. Long ago the Maya had taught her how to rouge her mouth and apply a little shadow—in the fashion of the Moors—to give the eyes a piquant cast; and even after so long a time, and such a great distance from the streets and salas of Spain, she had never relaxed the care with which she attended to the grooming and adornment of her person.

Her hair she dressed in the fashion of a married woman in New Mexico. She parted it in the middle, drew it back over the ears, then made two thick braids which were crossed and wound around the head, with a little black velvet bow where the ends met. The severity of this arrangement was relieved by bangs over the forehead, and by a pair of earrings hanging pendant below the dark, glossy mass of her hair.

Since she had decided to go out to Mass this morning, she draped a small black mantilla over a high back-comb, and dressed herself in black. When she had finished, she looked at herself critically in the mirror. She saw with satisfaction that she appeared haughty, modest, devout, and discreet, as a Spanish woman should look on her way to Mass. Then she smiled—as any Spanish woman might—to think of all that lay beneath this appearance.

She picked up her prayer book and rosary and set out afoot for the Parróquia, the great church that Peñuela had built on the Plaza.

3

As she stepped out of the passageway leading from the Palace to the Plaza, a soldier saluted smartly. She said, "God give you good morning, Tomás," with a little smile that the soldier, keeping his eyes stiffly front, returned.

On the portal, running the full length of the low, fortresslike Palace, Josefina paused and took several deep breaths of the mountain air. This year spring had come a little earlier than usual to Santa Fé. The fields and meadows in the Realito across the river were already green; and the willows along the Río Santa Fé had taken on a lovely chartreuse color, although the cottonwoods were not yet in leaf. The morning was brisk, but sunny and warm for March; it was a bright, exhilarating beginning of a new day, and Josefina's heart was suddenly and inexplicably light.

All around her she could sense an extraordinary atmosphere of bustle and excitement. For the Villa of Santa Fé was preparing for the most important event of the whole year—the arrival of the great Conducta from the Chihuahua Fair.

Even at so early an hour, the big Plaza in front of the Palace was beginning to fill with people and animals: leather-jacketed soldiers, settlers from the upper valley, Indians from outlying pueblos, blue-robed frailes from remote missions, chattering women and girls, and vendors of wood and all sorts of other wares, all asking one another the same question: "What is the latest word, señor? When does the Conducta arrive?"

Ever since the great wagon train had left El Paso del Norte on its way northward, riders had come into the Villa almost daily with news of the caravan's progress up the Río Grande valley. Now it was at Socorro, now at Alburquerque, now at Bernalillo, and yesterday a courier had reported it near Santo Domingo. In two days, or at the most three, it would surely come into sight on the long slope south of the Villa. Madre de Dios! What a time of waiting!

As Josefina strolled down the long walk of the portal, little knots of men and women stepped aside to let her pass, sometimes with a quiet greeting, often with a smile. Once, when her progress was blocked by a group of disputing Villeños, a rough-looking soldier opened a pathway for her with reproachful shouts: "Señores, señores— make way for La Dama Josefina."

Beyond the Palace she crossed the Camino Real and walked beside the garden wall of Captain Diego Arias de Quiro's corn and wheat fields. Then she passed a number of small houses, each with a passage-way connecting the Plaza with its placita. She crossed the plaza toward La Parróquia.

This great ugly adobe church, built only a short time before by Peñuela to replace the old Parróquia destroyed in the Indian uprising of 1680, dominated the eastern end of the Plaza like a jaundice-eyed old hen watching over her chicks. Because it was the church nearest the Palace, Josefina customarily attended Mass in La Parróquia, al-though its cheerless interior depressed her. She much preferred the charming little Lady Chapel, where La Conquistadora was still kept. So today because she wished to sit and meditate for a while when Mass was over, she had chosen to go to this Chapel of Our Lady of the Conquest. As she passed the convent adjoining the church, she encoun-tered Fray Juan de la Cruz and greeted him with her usual friendly respect.

"God give you a good morning, Padre. You are abroad early, no?"

Fray Juan, a frail man with a pale, sensitive face, raised a thin hand in friendly greeting.

"That God give it good to you, my daughter," he said in a voice surprisingly deep and firm. "In this Kingdom one must rise early to get ahead of the devil. Is it not so?"

"It is so everywhere, Padre."

They laughed and chatted for a few moments about the thing that was on everyone's mind just then—the Conducta from Chihuahua. Fray Juan, like everyone else, was impatient for its arrival: it was bringing a new organ for the mission at Santo Domingo.

"The old one is nearly a hundred years old," he said. "It is being held together only by a miracle."

It passed through Josefina's mind: What an astonishing thing that there should have been even one organ in this remote land a hundred years ago!

She bade Fray Juan de la Cruz good-by and continued on her way. She liked Fray Juan. As Custodio of all the missions in New Mexico, he was burdened with cares and fatigues almost too heavy for his frail constitution to bear. Yet he carried on his labors among the Indians, and the never-ending struggle of the frailes against the governors and the bishops of Durango, with a courage and cheerfulness worthy of his great namesake who had won a martyr's crown among the Tiguex almost two hundred years before. He was a saintly yet very human man—which could not be said for all the Friars Minor. On several occasions he had loaned Josefina the forbidden novels of Cervantes, Quevado, and others, which he had smuggled up from México. She liked Fray Juan de la Cruz very much.

She went into La Parróquia. She hurried through its ugly and depressing interior, and went directly to the Lady Chapel on the Gospel side.

The Lady Chapel was even newer than the church itself. Its immensely thick walls were still spotlessly white, the tempera colors of its decorations fresh and clear. But all was softened and gentled here by the light that filtered through two small windows, high up in the eastern wall, screened by carved wooden grillwork.

The Lady Chapel was gay—alegrita. It was gay with its brightly adorned high altar, its red-and-yellow railings and mouldings, the small Saints in their painted niches, the rich pictures, carvings, and rugs. One does not often find such gaiety and perfect tranquility together. Because she found it here, Josefina loved this small home of La Conquistadora.

She seated herself on one of the painted benches placed near the front of the nave for old people and ricos. Besides herself, only a few women were in the chapel. Most of the Villa's worshipers were in the main church, where Mass had already begun. So it was very quiet and infinitely peaceful here, and all was pervaded by the presence of La Conquistadora.

She stood in her special place—a large niche in the high altar—a little wooden image no taller than a child, stiff and doll-like, with almost arrogantly delicate features; and so nearly alive with a strange *other kind of life* that it seemed odd that she did not move or speak. Vargas had called her Nuestra Señora de los Remedios, "our special protectoress and mediator"; but now she was known as Our Lady of Victory, and by the people simply as La Conquistadora. But she seemed to be aloof and indifferent to all attention and all supplication.

And it was precisely because of this, perhaps, that the people, in the strange manner of all folk, gave her so generously of their love and clothed her in garments stiff with gold, and had placed on her tiny head a small gold crown brought from Spain. She was so young, so girl-like, and yet so old. Who could tell where she had been or what she had seen? It was known only that she had gone with Diego de Vargas, the great Reconquistador, when he set out from México to win back this Kingdom from the rebellious Pueblos; that she had made the terrible Journey of Death with his soldiers; that she had seen the fighting in the Milpas of San Miguel; and that she had been carried triumphantly by the mounted troops into the Plaza of Santa Fé.

She was a woman who had been through much. She had seen peril and suffering and terror. She had known triumph and riches and adoration. And they were all the same to her. One could do worse, Josefina thought, than to emulate La Conquistadora. She was much woman.

The padre who said the Mass was in a hurry—for his breakfast perhaps—and finished the service with astonishing expedition. Josefina listened with but half her mind to the mumbled ritual, and gradually her thoughts coalesced in a firm pattern around the matter that had so much occupied her of late. She sat for a long time in the dim, empty chapel, motionless and erect on the painted bench. And while her fingers crept along the beads of her rosary, a part of her mind went off in search of what she had, somehow, to find . . . and found it.

When Josefina left the chapel she had composed in her head almost exactly the letter she would write to Tafora.

4

Don Antonio struck out at the small Navajo slave who was shaking him timidly by the shoulder. The Indian retreated and ducked to evade a kick from the governor's bare foot.

"Son of a whore!" Don Antonio shouted. "Let me alone! Get out of here, coyote, or I'll have you garroted!"

"The padre is waiting, señor," the Indian said stolidly. "Last night, señor, you gave the order to——"

"Get out!"

The Indian bowed, without expression, and backed out of the door. Don Antonio raised himself on his elbows and glared after him; then, with hardly less choler, he gazed down at María's inert form. Her brown body lay as relaxed as a sleeping infant's; not even Don Antonio's shouting had broken through her childlike slumber. In this—perhaps only because she was so young and could sleep so well—Don Antonio found cause for additional annoyance. He watched the gentle rise and fall of her breasts for a few moments, then fetched her a sharp blow on the thigh with his hand.

María's eyes flew open and she emitted a whimpering, animal-like cry of surprise. She threw herself off the bed and rubbed the place where Don Antonio had struck her. She looked at him with hurt and hatred in her black Indian eyes. Then she went slowly and sleepily over to the fireplace and squatted beside the little flame.

Don Antonio laughed heartily. María had begun to put on airs of late. It amused him to see how easily a good whack on the buttocks could knock the arrogance out of her. Then he remembered that he had no use for a girl without spirit. He considered whether he should sell her.

"María," he said, "how much did I pay for you?"

She looked at him sullenly and made no answer. She could understand him a little, but had no Spanish in which to reply. Nevertheless, Don Antonio had asked a question and demanded an answer. He heaved himself out of bed, stood up and stretched himself, and flexed the muscles of his arms and back.

"Favor, señor!" María whispered in all the Castilian she knew. "Please, señor!"

He answered for her: "Twenty pesos of silver."

Well, he could double that, he reflected. She was a little beauty. If she were worth twenty pesos in Taos, she would fetch forty in the Villa. Maybe more. He could give her a "Que ya está buena."

He recalled a rumor that two French girls, who had been captured by the Navajos, would be offered for sale at the next Taos Fair in July. Perhaps he could get one of them—or even both—in exchange for María and a few blankets.

Nothing—unless it were food—occupied Don Antonio's mind more agreeably than thoughts of women and pecuniary gain. His humor softened perceptibly.

"Get dressed and fetch the chocolate," he said almost amiably.

María slipped on the Spanish dress that Josefina had given her, tucked her feet into a pair of snowy Navajo moccasins, and glided from the room. Don Antonio held the door open a handbreadth and listened.

How droll, he thought, if Josefina should meet her coming out of my chamber!

Don Antonio began to dress himself in the elegant and rather formal "military style" which—although it was ten years behind the mode in Spain—was accepted in New Mexico as the very latest fashion. When he had finished, he knelt down and said his morning prayers.

Don Antonio had a great reputation for piety, and it was his constant concern to live up to it. To that end he had built, at his own expense, a new military chapel—although not a very fine one—called Our Lady of Light; and he had been at pains to give the people, the frailes, and the Viceroy himself, many other proofs of his devotion. At last, indeed, he had come to believe in it himself.

So he said his Pater Nosters and Ave Marias with what was, to himself at least, a genuine fervor. Then he buckled on his sword, kissed the hilt, and made the sign of the cross with it. When María returned with the chocolate, he drank it hurriedly, standing beside a great chest.

It was not Don Antonio's habit to begin the day at such an early hour. He was doing it on this occasion only because he wished to give Fray Juan de la Cruz a taste of the governor's authority—and the sooner the better.

"It is about time," he had said to Miguel de Alba, his secretary of government and war, "that these lousy frailes find out who is running this Kingdom."

His ire began to regenerate itself as he left his chamber, crossed the adjoining anteroom with a glance at Josefina's door, went through the large sala where official receptions were held, and entered his own office. But in New Mexico, as in Spain, everything must be conducted according to the strict rules of etiquette; and so Don Antonio greeted the padre very correctly, even with a kind of official geniality.

"God give you a good morning also," Fray Juan responded, and added pleasantly but with a pointed formality, "I am at your orders, Excellency."

He looked even frailer than usual, standing there in his blue cowled robe, in the center of that great massively barren chamber. Don Antonio marched to his chair behind a big trestle table and motioned Fray Juan to sit down.

Fray Juan accepted the invitation and quietly waited for the governor to begin. His gaze wandered slowly over the simple details of the room and, for a long silent moment, came to rest on the only decoration it boasted—some festoons of Indians' ears above the windows. A shadow of distaste passed over his face. Don Antonio cleared his throat loudly and got down to the business of their meeting.

First he took the fraile to task for a letter Fray Juan had written to the Viceroy concerning the baptism of the Taos Apaches—over his own head, Don Antonio contended hotly. Then he blustered about the management of the missions and the administration of the sacraments. Finally, he launched into a furious tirade against what the Holy Office not very euphemistically called "solicitation in the confessional."

Don Antonio shouted and pounded the table, and his pale face took on an alarming magenta hue. But when the interview was over—with many expressions of esteem, for the rigid forms of Spanish courtesy must be observed at the end, as at the beginning, no matter what happened between—he was not a very happy man. As he walked rapidly back to his apartment he had, in fact, an uncomfortable feeling that Fray Juan had got the better of him. It vexed him to think that the little padre could give him this sense of discomfiture simply, as it were, by sitting quietly and saying almost nothing. And his anger mounted rapidly—as it often did with Don Antonio—so that by the time he entered the little sitting room adjoining his and Josefina's chambers, he was in no mood at all to enjoy his breakfast.

So upset was Don Antonio, in fact, that he blindly pulled open the door of Josefina's room instead of his own. For a moment he was confused by the error. Then he saw Josefina seated at one of her tables. Before her was an inkpot and several sheets of paper; in her hand a large, businesslike quill of the type used by scriveners. Josefina laid down the pen and looked up at Don Antonio with a trace of discomposure.

"Hola!" she said. "You startled me, Antonio."

Don Antonio did not return her greeting. He looked over the materials on the table. The paper, he noted, was clean.

"What are you writing?" he asked brusquely.

He strode over to the table, stood beside her for a moment, then suddenly flipped over the top sheet of paper.

171

"You can see for yourself, my dear," she said lightly. "As yet, nothing."

"This is not a good time to joke with me," he growled. "I don't feel like joking. What are you writing, my heart?"

There were occasions, Josefina had long ago discovered, when an endearment from Don Antonio was the equivalent of a threat. She determined, if possible, to avoid unpleasantness.

"Must you know?" she asked with a reproachful little smile. "I was about to write to Doña Juana de Moya about the spread she is making for me. I have decided to have the Tree of Life design instead of the morning-glory blossoms. What do you think, Antonio?"

"And for this you use our best paper?" he demanded.

"It is all I could find——"

Suddenly she got up and put her arms around Don Antonio. In a kind of habitual reflex action, he spread his hands against her back and pressed her to him.

"Antonio," she said, "why do you worry yourself about my small doings?"

All at once Don Antonio felt better—less frustrated, more sure of himself: a vague sense of power flowed into him, as it always did when he had Josefina in his arms. In the morning especially, how fresh and lovely she was. Don Antonio embraced her tightly and kissed her hard on the mouth. She laughed and struggled free from him.

"Antonio!" she cried in mock scandalization. "You have not even had your breakfast yet!"

The mention of breakfast pulled Don Antonio up. He kissed Josefina once more and let her go. He felt vaguely complimented—and also relieved that there was no necessity for proving himself further, so early in the day—and Fray Juan's victory seemed somehow less galling. In fact, Don Antonio was not sure that after all, perhaps, he himself had not got the better of the miserable little priest.

"You are still the most beautiful woman in the Two Spains, 'Fina mía," he said by way of amends.

"In your eyes, Antonio."

"In the eyes of a good many others also," he said, without smiling. "That your letter about morning glories doesn't go to one of them, my dear!"

A few moments after he had left, Josefina opened the door slowly and peered through the crack. Then she softly turned the great key in the iron lock, and went back to her writing table.

She wondered again, as she dipped her quill into the ink, whether Don Antonio suspected her correspondence with Tafora. . . . She wondered also why she had not received a letter from Tafora for so long a time.

5

Her strength with Don José Francisco Tafora, personal secretary and advisor of Don Baltazar de Zúñiga, Marqués de Valero, Viceroy of México, lay in her faithful disregard for an old and honored rule of Spanish officialdom: "Put it in writing, make three copies, and never tell the truth if you can help it."

Josefina always told the truth to Tafora. This was a hard thing for Tafora, who had come to power by extremely devious routes, to believe at first, and he had set numerous traps to catch her in the usual dissimulations. But having once determined that—to him, at least—Josefina never lied, there was little that he could refuse her.

For Tafora recognized immediately the tremendous advantage of having in his confidence a woman who was young, clever, extraordinarily beautiful, of pure Spanish blood (very important in New Spain) —and whom he could trust. And Josefina, having sized up Tafora very soon after her arrival in México, and having surmised that this was exactly how he would feel, had laid down, and rigorously hewed to, a line of absolute veracity in all her dealings with the Viceroy's gentle, middle-aged, and extremely powerful secretary.

It was an arrangement that had worked greatly to the benefit of them both. In a capital where all offices and even justice were openly for sale, where graft and corruption were the source of all wealth, social standing, and power, there was much that a beautiful woman with talent could do to advance the ends of her friends. Josefina had made herself useful to Tafora in a thousand pleasant ways: and so— although this she had kept from him, and he had always attributed his advancement to his own energy, acumen, and chicanery—useful also to Don Antonio Valverde.

"I do not understand, señora," Tafora once said to her, "why you remain faithful to this stupid fellow. Are you in love with him?"

"I have never been in love with anyone, Don José."

Tafora looked at her long and curiously, and said, "But you will be, my dear. It is the doom of every woman to fall in love."

"Alas, Don José," she said with an expression of mock tragedy, "I am a distant flame and a sword far off."

"I know that one," Tafora laughed. "It is one of Don Miguel's jokes. A great joke told in the speech of angels."

"Perhaps," Josefina said absently. "But if it was a joke, it was a cruel one, Don José!"

"I shall not be pleased when you fall in love." He smiled. "For then you will no longer be of any use to Tafora."

Was he himself in love with her? Sometimes she thought so, sometimes she was quite sure. But he asked nothing of her, not even a small show of affection. Tafora wanted nothing from her but the truth.

So now she glanced at the locked door, dipped the big quill into the ink, and prepared to tell him the truth about the situation in the Villa of Santa Fé—and also about herself. She began:

> Muy señor mío:
>
> I have received no answer to my last letter, which perplexes me. Nevertheless, because you wish me to keep you informed of all that passes in this Capital, I write you again.
>
> I write you, Don José, about a matter of grave concern to this Kingdom—the new Entrada his lordship the Viceroy has ordered to discover the intentions of the French on the Río Jesús María.

She was being very direct, she thought, the least bit doubtfully; but she had no time for subtleties. And besides, it was best to be direct with Tafora. She continued:

> I can well understand the need of this reconnaissance. But why, señor mío, must the command be given once more to Don Antonio?
>
> Is not Don Antonio's great expedition of only last year still fresh in everyone's mind? What did it accomplish? Did it punish the Comanches? Did it quiet the terror of the pueblos? Did it bring back (save for a few scraps of hearsay) any new information about the French?
>
> You and all the Court know, Don José, that the answer to these questions is No. Don Antonio did not so much as sight a single Comanche. *And there are those who say he took care not to.*
>
> By what logic, then, does His Lordship expect more from Don Antonio this time than he has already received? Believe me, Don José, there are many reasons—many more indeed than I can give even to you —why this should not be done.

She flipped open a fan and fanned herself contemplatively for a little while, then dipped her quill into the inkpot and got down to the real business of her letter to Tafora.

> And now, my dear Don José—if you will accept this from me, who has never yet misinformed you—I respectfully submit the following proposal, having in mind the interests of the Crown, the Kingdom of New Mexico, and—as you will see and understand—of myself, Josefina.
>
> Send out the reconnaissance, by all means. However, let it not be such a great cumbrous affair as that which Don Antonio led out onto

the plains last summer. Let it be a light, swift, well-equipped troop of veterans who know the nature of the country and the savage tribes who inhabit it. And, most important of all, Don José, let it be commanded by a leader of energy and courage. . . .

So now, at last, she had come to it! To the answer that had quietly whispered itself to her as she sat in the Chapel of Our Lady staring at La Conquistadora. She must think very carefully how to say it to Tafora.

> To the study of this matter I have given infinite thought and much time, Don José; and what is apparent to all in this Villa also appears right to me. There is really but one choice for the command of this Entrada. And that is Señor Don Pedro Villasur. Do I surprise you, señor mío? I do not think so! Surely, you and all at the Court of México are aware of his gifts as a soldier and an administrator. Who in all New Spain is better fitted to lead this Entrada?
>
> There are, I must admit, two points that might be raised against him. All his experience is of war in the European style; and he is new to this country. But there are many here in this Villa who can supply this experience and skill in Indian warfare, such as the scout José Naranjo. And besides, the purpose of this expedition is not to fight, but to obtain information, no?
>
> Do not listen to any who may oppose Don Pedro on these grounds, Don José. Believe me, there is no other here so well fitted as he!

Next she came to that part of the letter where she wished greatly that she might be face to face with Tafora. For she could think of no subtle or graceful way to say what must next be said. With Tafora, however, she could be direct: she plunged into the next paragraph with a kind of reckless candor.

> Ah, Don José, have you already read my thoughts? I doubt it not! But you are wrong if you think that I have fallen in love at last. I am not in love with Don Pedro—I swear it by the Cross.
>
> So do not, I pray of you, think that my judgment and counsel are affected now by my emotions. But if what I have proposed should work to my advantage, is that bad? I think not. And so—as you have already guessed, my good friend—I shall do that which is necessary to advantage myself. I shall (need I be demure with you?) seduce Don Pedro.
>
> For I am not so obtuse as not to see that whoever leads this reconnaissance, and brings back to the Viceroy a true account of what the French are up to, can ask what he wishes from his lordship: which, in this Kingdom, would naturally be the governorship. So I shall cast my lot with Don Pedro.

She wrote this with a good deal more self-assurance than she actually felt. But it never paid to appear indecisive with Tafora, nor to bore him with details. Tafora was interested only in plans—not in how they might be carried out. He would trust her as—she now proceeded to make clear—she trusted him. She wrote:

This may take a little time—if what one hears of Don Pedro be half-true!—so I shall waste none. I shall venture to go ahead with my plan, señor mío, on the assumption that, not forgetting the many bonds that have united our interests, you will find it to be a reasonable and desirable proposal, and that you will send the necessary orders to Don Antonio. I am sending this letter by Mateo.

Why have you not written to me? Are you well? Does all go rightly in the City of México? I am worried, Don José! That His Divine Majesty guard you. I kiss your hands.

Santa Fé,
March 16, 1720.

She slowly reread all she had written, then added her signature and rubric, the latter an intricate pattern of loops and flourishes that no one but herself could possibly have duplicated. Then, after sitting pensively for a little while, she wrote at the bottom of the page:

Alas, Don José, how deep and cruel is the memory of hunger!

When she had folded the letter and sealed it with a wafer of pink wax, she dressed herself for riding. Within an hour, having crossed the Río de Santa Fé and the mother ditch that watered the fields south of the river, she arrived at Los Álamos, the estancia of Don Ramón de la Rosa on the road to Pecos and the buffalo plains. An old mestizo took charge of Negra. Josefina waited in the patio for Doña Mercedes, the mistress of Don Ramón's great establishment, to welcome her.

6

How safe and peaceful it always seemed in Doña Mercedes's patio! It was the heart and center of Don Ramón's vast holdings—his thousands of acres of wheat and maize and pasture lands, his endless ranges on which uncounted sheep and cattle grazed, his great household of more than twenty families and nobody knew how many Indian slaves and servants; but it was also a little sheltered island of friendliness and gaiety in an immense, hard, essentially hostile land . . . a place where a woman might sit and drink her morning chocolate and listen to the chatter of the birds in the cottonwoods without a fear of anything.

On all four sides of Doña Mercedes's patio ran a white portal from which the ollas hung in the shade, filled with cool water; and back of them were ranged the low adobe buildings—apartments for Don Ramón's ever-expanding family, and beyond these the servants' quarters. A little stream gurgled through the patio stealing a bit of water away from the maize and wheat fields for the flowers and vines and cottonwoods that, a little later, would fill this sunny, sheltered square with the fragrance of blossoms and delicious shade.

In the evening the patio was almost always a place of gaiety, of music and singing, and dancing to the guitar. And here Josefina— who had never danced elsewhere, except in México, since her flight from Spain—sometimes amused Don Ramón's ménage with a seguidillas or, perhaps, a tonadilla composed especially for his family and guests. Such occasions delighted her—although it was delight mixed with a certain nostalgic sadness—but most of all she loved the quiet morning hours when the shadows were long and the adobe walls still cool to the touch.

At this time all of Don Ramón's great household was occupied with the many tasks of the estancia. The young men were away, cultivating the mud-walled fields or tending the flocks and herds in the hills or the farther reaches of the valley. The old men and the women were busy somewhere with the grinding of corn, the baking of bread, the endless replastering of adobe walls, the making of chests and the repair of leather gear, and the pleasant rituals of the kitchen. . . .

Josefina listened with a kind of sadness to a sweet-faced girl singing an old Spanish ballad in the fresh morning peace of Doña Mercedes's garden. And while she listened, the doña came out to welcome her.

"Ah, Josefina mía!" she exclaimed. "How good to see you! As always, my house and all it contains is yours!" She embraced her visitor and kissed her; then holding her off and regarding her with something like wonder, she demanded, "But what, in the name of God, brings you here at such an hour?"

Doña Mercedes was a woman of the country. That is to say, she was a daughter of a reconquistador. Her father, Don Alfonzo Rael de Ayala, had marched with Vargas to reconquer the Kingdom of New Mexico from the Indians who, having killed every Spaniard they could find, had held the towns and presidios of the province for twelve long years.

As a reward for his help in the reconquest, Don Alfonzo received (besides his share of Vargas's captives) one of those vast grants of land that flanked the Río Grande del Norte between the settlements of Alburquerque and Bernadillo; and there he became wealthy in sheep and cattle and raised his family of nine children. When she was fifteen, Mercedes was married to Don Ramón de la Rosa, who went with the Conducta to México and brought her back a red silk dress and two Indian slaves as wedding presents. They settled down on Don Ramón's estancia, almost within sight of Santa Fé, and had lived there ever since.

So Doña Mercedes had never known anything but the life of this remote and isolated land. For all of her thirty-six years she had been out of touch with the world—ignorant alike of the great joys and the great miseries the Motherland had seen. She had no knowledge of books, for she could not read. What she knew of art and music was a hundred years old. For Doña Mercedes—as for nearly all in this forgotten Kingdom—time had long ago stood still.

Even her speech had a strange, archaic flavor that amused and delighted Josefina. She loved to hear Mercedes drop her *ll*'s almost completely, saying for example *cabeo* instead of *caballo,* and *sia* for *silla.* She adored Doña Mercedes's costumes—such as the uncorseted bodice of green silk and the many-ruffled skirt she now wore—that seemed to have, if vaguely, an equally antique quality. For Doña Mercedes wore her odd New Mexican clothes with a *ton,* and spoke her quaint New Mexican Spanish with a spirit that would have made her utterly charming in any land or any century. She was here—as she would have been in Madrid itself—a true Spanish lady.

"What is the matter, Josefina?" she insisted. "Something must be the matter, or you would not have come here so early, and alone."

"Is Don Ramón at home?" Josefina asked.

"Ah, no. He has gone down to Santo Domingo to buy some cotton. What a pity!"

"Well, I wish to send a letter by Mateo," Josefina said.

Doña Mercedes's eyes widened just the tiniest bit. She was a rather plump, serene-faced woman who permitted only those emotions to show that she preferred to show; yet she was not quite successful now in hiding her surprise. She said nothing, however, but clapped her hands once and called to the girl singing at her loom:

"Go fetch Mateo, Crucita. He is at the horse corral."

Crucita trotted off, and Doña Mercedes begged Josefina to come into the house. They went into the spacious sala, a cool massive room with whitewashed walls and a dark-raftered ceiling whose extremely deep doors and windows gave it the feeling of being, as indeed in a sense it was, the inner citadel of a fortress. Yet it was a pleasant room, beautifully proportioned and softly contoured, and made friendly by a few pieces of home-carved furniture and richly colored Navajo rugs . . . and by the gracious presence of Doña Mercedes. How much lovelier, Josefina often thought, were these simple and perfect rooms of New Mexico than the ornate drawing rooms of New Spain. How sternly but warmly they sheltered one!

A servant girl brought chocolate and some little tarts stuffed with honey and piñon nut meats. They talked pleasantly—mostly about the Conducta, of course, but also about the feud between the bishops of México and Durango, and about the best way to stuff a wild turkey, and whether short or three-quarter sleeves looked best with a low-cut bodice—until Mateo appeared and stood in the doorway with folded arms. Then Doña Mercedes excused herself, and Mateo entered the sala and stood in front of Josefina, his face dark and impassive.

He was a rather villainous-looking mestizo, this Mateo, and Josefina did not trust him to quite the same extent that Tafora did. But it was probably true, as Tafora insisted, that there was not a tougher man, nor a more resourceful one, in all New Spain; and certainly not a better horseman.

These qualifications, no doubt, fitted Mateo well for Tafora's purpose —which was simply to be on hand at all times to carry urgent messages between himself and Josefina. Don Ramón knew why Tafora had sent Mateo up from México to serve as a caballerango on his ranch, and so did Doña Mercedes. But no one else knew—least of all Don Antonio. It was, perhaps, the best-kept secret in the Villa of Santa Fé, where not much was held private for long.

"Mateo," Josefina said, "what is the fastest time that has ever been made between this Villa and the City of México?"

"Thirty-six days, señora."

"That is too long. I have a letter that must be delivered to Señor Tafora in thirty days."

"That is impossible, señora."

"Here is the letter," Josefina said, drawing the folded paper out of her bodice. "How soon can you start?"

"At once, señora."

"Very well, Mateo. If you can't make it in thirty days, at least you will do better than thirty-six, no?"

"I'll try, señora."

Mateo flashed an unexpected smile at her and slipped the letter inside his leather jacket. You are right, Don José, she thought, as usual! Aloud she said: "That's all, Mateo. Go you with God."

Even before she had said her adiós to Doña Mercedes, Mateo was off on his fifteen-hundred-mile ride to the City of México. He left on a black stallion with a remount, his saddlebag stuffed with corn and chocolate, his leather bottle full of brandy; and all on Don Ramón's hacienda wondered at his sudden and mysterious departure.

7

Riding back to the Villa of Santa Fé, Josefina reflected how coldly she must—like any courtesan with darkened eyes and moon-shaped brows —carry out the plan she had described to Tafora. She was so absorbed in her thoughts that when she glimpsed a horseman riding furiously toward Santa Fé, it did not occur to her to wonder who he might be—or to note that he came from the direction of Los Álamos.

Having committed herself so unequivocally to Tafora, she experienced that good feeling that comes to one after having made a necessary and decisive step; and back of this a certain tingle of excitement at the approach of challenge and, perhaps, adventure.

But as she neared the Villa, these interesting feelings gave way a little to a sense of uncertainty that merged at last into a mild form of panic. It occurred to her that she had never yet been under the necessity of seducing a man—least of all a man of Don Pedro's formidable reputation—and she was not at all sure of her skill in that unpracticed field.

Who would believe it? she said to herself wryly. María Purísima! I feel like a nun!

Yet it was true that, while she was with the Maya, none of the liaisons she had made so obediently—and indeed so innocently—to her protectoress's wishes had cost her any effort. Chiefly she had been concerned in those days with turning aside the numerous and sometimes troublesome advances evoked by her youth and beauty and the glamour of her name and person: not even Don Lorenzo had required so much as a flutter of a fan to kindle his unfortunate passion.

Considering these curious facts as she rode over the rolling chamiza-covered hills toward Santa Fé, Josefina set them aside as something of no pertinence, really, and began to think of the practical aspects of her problem.

"This may take a little time," she had written Tafora, "so I shall waste none."

Yet how, first of all, was she to manufacture occasions for meeting Don Pedro? She could not depend on improvisations, such as the incident of the frightened pig, for example. That had been a fortunate chance and, she reflected with a certain naïve pride, she had acted very swiftly to make the most of it. But she could not trust too much to luck. She must create opportunities, not merely wait for them.

Unfortunately, it was now the season of Lent; and Don Antonio, always zealous in proving his piety, had wrapped the Palace, so to speak, in the purple of self-denial and mortification. For almost a month—until the joyful arrival of Easter Sunday—there would be no more of the gay dinners, parties, and dances with which the governor loved to spice the official life of his poor capital . . . and at which a really astonishing amount of intrigue could be conducted, even in so small a place as Santa Fé! For a month one would be very quiet and go often to church.

But if this were a problem—this necessity of her finding occasions to see Don Pedro again, and alone if possible—it was one, surely, of no great difficulty. She set it aside, also, as something that would solve itself in the course of a few days.

And now, she said to herself, with a little grimace of distaste, we come to Don Antonio.

Ah, yes, Don Antonio! He must be considered. He must be disposed of. There was the matter of his pride, of course: a certain amount of face-saving would be necessary. But Don Antonio's pride did not go very deep beneath his pale, thin-looking skin. How vast, actually, was the cowardice, slackness, falseness, and vulgarity of Don Antonio!

Vaya! What have you to fear, Josefina, of such a man? she said to herself. Besides, isn't he tired of you? Perhaps he might even welcome a chance to turn you out of the Palace, no? Perhaps he would get pleasure from the idea of setting you free—unprotected, he would think—in this miserable wilderness of New Mexico. So let us not worry too much about Don Antonio for the present. There will be time for that later. . . .

But Don Pedro—there was not much time to do what must be done about Don Pedro. She could have wished to know a little more about him.

She recalled the legend of Don Pedro the soldier: of his iron devotion to duty; and his stern regard for the forms and loyalties of his profession of arms; and of what, it seemed to her, must be a rather excessive sense of honor, even for a Spaniard. These were the things that could not be taken lightly, and she thought about them deeply as she neared La Parróquia.

Be thankful, at any rate, she said to herself, as she rode into the Plaza, that you have no complication of the heart in this matter, Josefina. Be glad that what you wrote Tafora is the truth!

8

Josefina circled the crowded quadrangle and guided Negra through the wide passageway which cut through the massive bulk of the Palace and communicated with the patio in its rear.

Here, inside the encircling portales of the soldiers' barracks, the stables, and the servants' quarters, it was cool and comparatively quiet. Josefina dismounted beside the curbed well, and a mestizo servant poured a bucket of water into a wooden trough for Negra. Josefina dipped a gourdful from the same bucket; she drank it as she watched the pigeons fluttering about the dovecote on the coachhouse. She was conscious of voices, raised in heavy argument, funneling out of the passageway.

"But I have told you," one of the voices, with a strong French accent, was saying, "I'll provide my own animals. And my own servants to look after them."

Glancing over her shoulder, Josefina saw two men, Jean L'Archévèque and José Naranjo. They were coming out of the Palace where, no doubt, they had been to see the Governor.

"What's more," L'Archévèque added vehemently, "I'll arm my men at my own expense. To the last peso!"

He was a heavy-set, almost corpulent man, in a suit of black English cloth with silver buttons. He wore a large beaver hat and a French sword. His eyes were black and darting in his turgid face. He gestured violently, and apparently angrily, with his stodgy hands as he talked.

"Mother of God!" the other man said in a soft, and oddly gentle voice. "Are we to have nobody on this Entrada but priests and traders?"

This man, José Naranjo, the celebrated scout and Indian fighter, was known from Taos to El Paso del Norte, and respected by all who knew him—including the Comanches. He was not an old man, but he had already made four entradas, and had served under Vargas. Although he could neither read nor write, he spoke excellent Spanish and fluent Apache; and the mark of a fine and sensitive intelligence was in every line and contour of his dark face. He was dressed now in his usual nondescript costume of tanned leather, half-Spanish, half-Indian. His hair was banged over his eyes and cut off at the neckline,

Pueblo fashion; he wore a pair of long-shanked iron spurs with points three inches long.

"You will pardon me, Don Juan," he added quietly, "but I think you are crazy."

José Naranjo's feud with the clergy was well understood to be a pose, but his dislike of traders—particularly this one—was real, and Jean L'Archévèque knew it.

"Sacrebleu!" he sputtered. "At least I am not afraid of the Comanches."

"Have you ever met a Comanche on the open plains—with a French gun, on a Spanish horse, señor?"

"No, but I——"

"When you do, señor," Naranjo said smiling, "you will be afraid of the Comanches."

There was just enough jocularity in all this to prevent its leading to something serious. But, Josefina could sense, *just* enough.

"Hola, señores!" she called, dropping the gourd back into the bucket. "What are you disputing about on such a fine day?"

Both men whirled around, Naranjo with an embarrassed look, L'Archévèque with an irritated frown. Naranjo inclined his head and touched his bangs in a kind of salute; L'Archévèque swept off his beaver and made a deep bow.

"Buenos días, Doña Josefina," Naranjo said.

"At your feet, señora," L'Archévèque murmured, and added, "We were only arguing, señora, about the best time ever made by the wagons."

"I shall be glad when the Conducta arrives at last." Josefina laughed. "If only because it will end all the talk about the wagons, the wagons."

"That is a good point, Doña Josefina." Naranjo grinned. "There is too much talk about the wagons . . . and also about other things. Adiós, señora." He touched his forehead again and went away with his great spurs tinkling down the passageway.

"I do not agree with Captain Naranjo," L'Archévèque said tolerantly. "Since all the records of this Kingdom were destroyed in the Uprising, it is our duty to determine the truth about such things and preserve it for posterity. Don't you think so, señora?"

"Perhaps you are right, señor," she said.

"Posterity will want to know such things," L'Archévèque went on. "How long did it take the Conductas to come up from México? . . . *How long did it take a horseman to cover the same distance?*"

He looked at her with his darting eyes and rubbed his jowl with his stodgy fingers. Both the look and the gesture were habitual with him, but this time they gave her a little start.

Holy Mary! she thought. Can it be that he knows?

"These are interesting questions," L'Archévèque added reflectively.

It is impossible! she said to herself.

She not only detested L'Archévèque: she mistrusted him deeply. She suspected him of all sorts of intrigues against Don Antonio, herself, the Kingdom—against all, in fact, that might be sacrificed to advance his evil ends.

Nobody, perhaps, knew the real depths of Jean L'Archévèque's depravity. It was generally understood, for instance, that he had taken a hand in the murder of the noble Robert Cavalier Sieur de la Salle in the province of Texas. After that treacherous act—which, however profitable it may have been to the Spanish, won no love for L'Archévèque in New Spain—the assassin was sent to México. He settled down in Santa Fé and married. Traveling widely on his commercial ventures through New Mexico, Senora, and even to México, he became wealthy and influential. He was Governor Don Antonio de Valverde's friend and crony.

Such facts about Jean L'Archévèque's unsavory history were well known; but who could discover the whole truth about such a devious and crafty scoundrel? What, for example, was his influence—and by what means did he exercise it—over Don Antonio? Nobody was ever sure how much Jean L'Archévèque knew—or how he might use it. And it was this uncomfortable knowledge that caused Josefina to ask herself: Can it be that this French degenerado knows about Mateo and my letter to Tafora? Could he have got word of it already—almost before I myself have returned from Don Ramón's? It is impossible, Josefina! You are nervous. You suspect even this serpent too much.

Yet, she could not help but wonder who, at Los Álamos, might have overheard her conversation in the patio with Doña Mercedes. Who, seeing Mateo's mysterious departure, had guessed its meaning? Who at Los Álamos might have been in L'Archévèque's pay—for the very purpose, perhaps, of keeping an eye on Mateo?

Then, on top of all this, she remembered the horseman she had glimpsed between the hills on her way back to Santa Fé. She had scarcely noticed this rider then—so engrossed had she been in her thoughts—but she remembered him now. He had seemed to be hurrying towards the Villa. . . .

Vaya! Vaya! she chided herself. That you get hold of yourself, Josefina!

She twisted her riding whip almost double in her gloved hands. The Frenchman, gazing at the taut arc of plaited rawhide, smiled.

"Very interesting questions," he repeated. "Don't you think so, señora?"

"To tell you the truth, Don Juan—" she smiled back at him—"nothing could interest me less. Adiós, señor!"

She turned abruptly and with quick steps, as if she were hastening away from something repellent, entered the Palace.

9

After a hearty noon meal—a puchero, perhaps with peppers, onions, and tomatoes, together with some frijoles and well-baked tortillas—it was the custom of the better-to-do ladies of New Mexico to observe the siesta by undressing and going to bed for a couple of hours.

Following the siesta—one felt the need of a pick-up, of course!—came the merienda, a repast of chocolate and cakes flavored with anise seed, or perhaps stuffed with ground meat or dried apricots mixed with piñon nuts. Not unnaturally, all up and down the Río Grande one noted in the big estancias and the more pretentious townhouses an almost uniform and not unpleasing plumpness among the women.

In contrast to these well-rounded New Mexicans, Josefina was remarkable for the slenderness of her figure. This was her reward for a carefully regulated, almost austere mode of life—for remembering what the Maya had taught her. She allowed herself only three meals a day, as opposed to the usual five or six, and ate sparingly at all of them. For physical exercise she took frequent long rides on Negra. Except at the height of the hot season, she abstained from the siesta altogether. She was a little fanatic, the New Mexicans thought, in her ideas of bodily cleanliness.

But to exist otherwise, to become fat and stupid with food and sleep, was for Josefina a vulgarity and a scandal. And so she was probably the only woman over twenty-five in all New Mexico who could ride a horse like a man and look good in the saddle. She was the only one who could wear the clothes of a paisana and look like a duquesa . . . and did.

"Well, she is a Castellana," the New Mexicans said. "Who knows what to expect from a woman of Spain?"

When she appeared about the Palace, and even on the Plaza of Santa Fé, in the chemise and skirt of the New Mexican countrywoman, nobody but a few old dowagers claiming pure Spanish blood, but native-born nevertheless, were shocked. Everybody else was delighted.

"Qué linda!" they exclaimed. "How charmingly La Dama Josefina's skirt swings when she walks!" Even Fray Juan saw nothing scandalous in the shortness of her dress or the freedom of her low-cut blouse. "She pays a compliment," he said, "to our native ways."

For Josefina had transformed the costume of the paisana—which consisted simply of a rather full flannel skirt and a cotton chemise, the top half of the latter serving as a blouse, the lower half as a petticoat—into a colorful, comfortable, and not inelegant mode of dress. And she was especially pleased with the newest addition to her wardrobe which 'Toñita, a comely young mestiza seamstress, had just brought to the Palace for a fitting.

"What do you think, Tichi?" she asked. "Is the skirt too short?"

She turned slowly, her arms outspread, so that the very full skirt of white lawn, flounced with several bands of coral-colored silk, belled out and revealed her white silk stockings halfway to the knees. The two women, Tichi and 'Toñita, stood gravely with arms folded and observed the effect.

"Not unless Doña Josefina thinks so," Tichi said.

"And you, 'Toñita? What do you say?"

"It is lovely," 'Toñita said shyly. "On the señora it is too beautiful."

"I think you are a couple of flatterers." Josefina laughed. "But I agree with you. It is beautiful. Every stitch of it, 'Toñita!"

She fingered the sheer white material of the blouse, embroidered in bright colors. It was cut in the paisana style—very low, so that the twin dimples in her shoulders were revealed, yet full enough to conceal the round firm contours of her breasts in its snowy folds.

"It is too lovely to take off," Josefina said. "Even though I am not going out, I shall wear it today."

'Toñita sighed and smiled. She was a very young girl—perhaps fourteen or fifteen—with a sweet and faintly sad face. Skillful with the needle, she had not only cut and sewn this dress for Josefina, but had embroidered the upper, or blouse, part of the chemise. Her sigh was one of relief.

"I am happy," she said. "I never think that what I have done will be fine enough for la señora."

"Tichi," Josefina said. "Bring us some chocolate and cakes. And a sweet for 'Toñita, no?"

After Tichi had left, she invited the little seamstress to sit down; but instead of taking a chair, 'Toñita sank cross-legged onto one of the Navajo rugs. She smiled up at Josefina and reached out her slender brown fingers toward Yolanda in her cozy angle of the hearth.

"Tell me, child," Josefina said. "How does it go now with you and Rafael?"

"Not well, señora," 'Toñita said, with a little moue. "The difficulties increase every day. I despair. I pray and hope, but I still despair. But Rafael, he thinks there is a way. Is there a way, señora?"

'Toñita's plight was not an uncommon one among young lovers in New Mexico. For even as they struggled together against hunger and the Comanche, the settlers of this rude and hostile land had drawn tight against each other the bitter lines of class and race.

Young Rafael Serna, for instance, came of a family that passed for pure Spanish, although on the side of his mother it had been settled in México for almost a hundred years. His father, Don Salvador Serna, claimed direct descent from a First Conquistador—Don Tomás Serna, who had come to New México with Don Juan de Oñate's great Entrada in 1598. There were many Sernas in New Mexico now; and every Serna's sword was eager to maintain these claims to pure Spanish blood.

As for 'Toñita, she was a mestiza. Her father, Martin Montoya, it is true, was a Reconquistador: he had shared in Vargas's glorious retaking of Santa Fé from the Indians in 1692. But he was a mestizo, nevertheless, and made no bones about it. Even worse, 'Toñita's mother had been born in the pueblo of Tesuque of a Tewa father and a Spanish girl who had been captured by the Indians in the Great Rebellion of 1680.

She was a mestiza: some of Rafael's relatives even went so far as to call her a coyote, so bitter had become their opposition to the marriage of a Spanish-born Serna to this sweet-faced girl with the smooth dark hair and soft eyes . . . and Tewa blood.

"Do you think there is any way, señora?" 'Toñita asked again.

"There is always a way, child," Josefina said. "For a determined woman nothing is impossible."

As she said these words, she seemed to hear again—but very faintly now, for she had almost lost the power to recall the tone of Eva Helena's voice—her mother saying: "Everything is possible, children —if you but wish hard enough."

She smiled a little sadly and reflected how good Eva Helena had been, but how much wiser the Maya; how it was not enough for a woman to hope and wish—that the proverb was right which said that *she who lived thus by hope died in despair*. Nevertheless, she said to 'Toñita:

"There is always a way, child—for a determined woman. That you continue to pray for your intention—to whom do you pray?"

"To my saint, señora, to San Antonio."

"Why don't you try La Conquistadora? She is a paisana, no? And a woman. Perhaps she will understand better."

"I shall pray to her, señora."

"Good. And in the meantime I shall apply myself to the problem also. I promise you, child."

Having thus committed herself, she made a note in her mind to consult Fray Juan de la Cruz about the matter: if there was a way, he would know it. Tichi returned with the chocolate, which they took chatting about small affairs. Then 'Toñita left.

"Now, Tichi," Josefina said, "what have you found out?"

"About Don Pedro, señora?"

"Yes, and before you begin, perhaps it will be just as well to glance out of the window, and also to look outside the door."

"I think so too, señora!"

Having taken these precautions, Tichi seated herself comfortably and took from a small basket her colcha work. She threaded a needle with a length of fine wool dyed bright yellow with the juice of the chamiza plant. On a large square of very fine homespun cotton—called sabanilla by the New Mexicans—she began to make tiny colcha knot stitches in the seeds of a pomegranate design.

"About his amigas?" she asked, looking up from her embroidery frame.

Josefina nodded.

"Well, he hasn't any," Tichi said. "Not here in the Villa, anyhow. Don Pedro lives alone with his servants, a cook and a maid he brought with him from Nueva Vizcaya. It is the cook, whose name is Rosita, that told me about the amigas."

"Is that all she told you?" Josefina asked dryly.

"Oh, no, señora. There have been various amigas from time to time. Rosita could not remember all of them. But there was one named Viqui in Durango, and also in Chihuahua—she was Don Pedro's amiga for a long, long time, señora—who possessed a pair of jeweled spectacles and six pairs of red shoes."

"Was she beautiful, this Viqui?"

"She must have been, señora."

"Where is she now?"

"The smallpox, señora."

Josefina made a note to have her fawn-colored slippers dyed red, and nodded for Tichi to go on.

"Except for Viqui, who was with him for so long, there were none who deserve much mention, señora."

"Well, tell me about them anyhow," Josefina said, affecting an air of unconcern.

"Let me think, señora. There was one named Chanela, no? She had a mania for ices—made with snow from the mountains. And another, whose name I forget, that had a lion cub for a pet—a very destructive animal that chewed up Rosita's shoes. And another—this one's name was Francisca and she read novels—who tried to poison Don Pedro in Santa Bárbara. But the others, señora——"

Tichi shrugged to indicate nothing worth mentioning, and re-threaded her needle with another length of yellow wool.

"What about the last one," Josefina asked, "before he left Nueva Vizcaya?"

"Ah, yes!" Tichi said, brightening. "María del Carmen Córdoba. She wished to come to New Mexico with Don Pedro. There was a very difficult time, señora. She made it very difficult for Don Pedro, even threatening to kill him. She is a hellcat, Rosita says, and Don Pedro is well rid of her."

"It appears to me," Josefina observed pensively, "that our Don Pedro has not lacked for amigas, and some of a certain picturesqueness, no?"

"He is a soldier, Doña Josefina. He has moved about a great deal."

"He is not quite as I have heard him described."

"Señora?"

"With the women."

"Well, he is very discreet. He does not become involved. He has never found himself in a state of embarrassment on account of somebody's wife—or mistress."

"Perhaps that is only because he is more astute in his amours than some."

"I correct myself, señora. There was one case."

"Ah, yes?"

"Yes. There was the case of the wife of the President of the Audiencia—Doña Micaela Ribera y Tapia."

"I remember her. A slut."

"No doubt, señora, but a powerful one in México. Because Don Pedro rejected her attentions—which were very public, it seems, a scandal really—Doña Micaela brought false accusations against him to her own husband."

"How droll!"

"It was not very amusing to Don Pedro. Doña Micaela's friends at the court were not helpful to him. And when he had cleared himself at last, he was sent to supervise the mines at Cosaguriachi. Since then, Rosita says, he has been even more careful about his friendships."

"All this is very interesting, Tichi."

Tichi drew a colcha knot tight and made a quick inspection of her mistress's unsmiling features.

"Does what I have learned disappoint you, Doña Josefina?" she asked gravely.

Josefina laughed. She got up, stretched her arms above her head, and walked over to the window.

"On the contrary, Tichi," she said, gazing into the patio. "But it does suggest certain difficulties. What else did you learn about Don Pedro—that does not concern women?"

"The small things, no? Well, let me try to remember, señora. What was it you asked me to find out—I have forgotten."

"You have a short memory for anything but gossip and scandal, Tichi. How, for instance, does he stand with the frailes?"

"I think well, señora. Don Pedro and Fray Juan Minguéz are very good friends. They often play cuarenta and drink a little wine together. They are both from Santander—for which they share a great longing."

"Of what dishes is he fond?"

"He is the despair of Rosita, señora. He likes very much all the fine things she cooks for him—but he would be just as content, she thinks, with a few beans and tortillas and a little atole."

"How does he amuse himself?"

"In the usual ways, señora, although he appears to take very seriously the affairs of his command. He is very strict, for instance, with his soldiers, although he is well liked by the troops. He is so conscientious about his duties, señora, that he appears to have but little time left for pleasure—unless one should count the reading of books a pleasure."

"What kind of books, Tichi?"

"Rosita can't read, señora, so she can't tell. But there is one from which Don Pedro reads to Rosita sometimes, and to Fray Juan, and anybody else who will listen. It is about a crazy hidalgo called Don Qui-somebody."

"Ah, yes," Josefina said pensively. "The Knight of the Mournful Figure. . . ."

"Well, perhaps, but it doesn't sound right, señora."

"You have done very well, Tichi," Josefina said. "You have answered your catechism very well. And now——"

"There is one thing I have forgotten, Doña Josefina. It is thought unlucky in Don Pedro's family if a hare should cross one's path."

"And little pigs also?"

"Pardon, señora?"

"Nothing, my dear."

"And one thing more, señora——"

But one thing suggested still another to Tichi, each item more trivial and gossipy than the one before. And Josefina listened to this flow of intimate detail so attentively, even so eagerly, that she felt it necessary after a while to remind herself: This bores you, Josefina. But listen closely, nevertheless; for one never knows what small thing will be useful, no?

At last, however, she was forced to silence the voluble Gallega.

"That will be enough for today, Tichi." She laughed. "Now I think I begin to know our Don Pedro a little better."

"He is a man of noble character," Tichi said.

190

"So it would appear!" Josefina agreed, a little dryly.

For a while it was quiet in the room, except for the rhythmic sound of Tichi's thread passing back and forth through her embroidery. Josefina leaned her head against the deep recess of the window and looked through the spindled reja at the patterns of light and shadow on the mica glazing.

She began then to consider, a little dreamily, in what ways she might make good use of what Tichi had told her; and back of these reflections was the simple and very practical problem—always in the shadows of her mind—of how to meet with Don Pedro again . . . under favorable and, if possible, seemingly fortuitous circumstances.

But fate—or possibly La Conquistadora, to whom she had prayed so earnestly for help—may already have arranged this small matter: it was permissible to hope.

She was musing on this possibility when she became conscious of a rising surge of sound from the direction of the Plaza—a hubbub of shouts that faintly penetrated the thick adobe walls, then the clangor of a bell ringing, and finally the reports of some arquebuses, all mixed with the braying of asses and other ordinary sounds of the Plaza at midday. She went over to the door and pulled it open. The excited shouts from the Plaza echoed down the long hallway and into the room.

"Los carros! Los carros! La Entrada de la Conducta!"

10

The roof of the Royal Palace was a fine vantage point from which to view the arrival of the Conducta. From here Josefina and Tichi could see everything without the discomfort of mingling with the excited crowd that had gathered to welcome the wagons. They could see, not only down into the teeming Plaza, but also across the hills to the south where the great caravan was approaching the Capital under a moving column of dust. It had been within sight since morning, and it was now preparing to cross the river. Soon the first wagons would be in the outskirts of the Villa itself, although the tail of the long, serpentine convoy still lay beyond the purple horizon ridges.

"How much longer do you think, señora?" Tichi asked. "In another fifty Credos it should be here, don't you think?"

"I hope so," Josefina said. "My eyes are weary with watching."

191

To rest them, she let her gaze drop to the scene below. Seen thus, from this height, the Villa always had a new, fresh look; and she examined it with a kind of childlike curiosity.

"It is hardly like a city," she mused. "It is more like a corral. No, Tichi?"

"In more ways than one, señora!" Tichi said dryly.

The Villa of Santa Fé was, in fact, little more than an enclosure, a hollow square, a citadel defended by the walls of its homes and buildings. It was a great rectangle, twice as long as it was wide—that shape "best fitted for processions and for fiestas in which horses are used"— entirely surrounded by massive adobe walls and dominated by the twin symbols of Spanish power: the Royal Palace on the north and the vast Church of San Francisco, called La Parróquia, on the eastern end.

Today the Great Plaza, the center of this squat, fortresslike collection of adobe structures, crawled with half the population, it would seem, of the Kingdom of New Mexico. For a little while Josefina watched the crazy, illogical movement of the great mob of settlers, soldiers, Indians, and slaves from across the river.

They are excited, like the children on Noche Buena, she said to herself. They run about, filled with excitement because soon, for a moment, the world will touch them.

She always felt sad at the time of the Conducta's arrival. Ah, how far away was the world! she thought. And not for them alone. She raised her eyes to the Calle de San Francisco, that street on the opposite side of the Plaza that became the Camino Real at its western end and led to the settlements of the Lower River, and to the other Spanish provinces in the south . . . and even to Spain itself by way of Vera Cruz.

Beyond the Plaza, there was nothing to be seen except the small earth-colored houses strewn over the milpas; then the Chapel of San Miguel on the other side of the river, and the beautiful green meadows bordering the Río de Santa Fé; then the pale gold chamiza-covered loma, with the worn Cerrillos hills beyond; and over all, the curving New Mexican sky into which rose the great dust column of the Conducta. Its first wagons had now crossed the Río de Santa Fé; its tremendous journey was all but over.

"Los carros! Los carros! La Entrada de la Conducta!" Nothing in the whole long frontier year could equal the excitement of this moment. Nothing so made the heart leap as this cry: "The wagons! The wagons! The Conducta is coming!"

Each year in November the Conducta left Santa Fé for the great fair held in January at Chihuahua. For a whole month, the Kingdom of New Mexico was in a ferment of excitement as it prepared to join the immense, southward-flowing stream of people, animals, and wagons.

Traders and settlers from the Upper River began to trickle into Santa Fé, their carts and pack-animals laden with the crude, raw products of their impoverished land: with furs and hides and buffalo skins, with blankets, rugs, leather tents, and dressed deerskins, with salt and piñon nuts. They brought with them also Indian captives—Navajos, Apaches, and Comanches—to be sold as slaves. And their own women and children, safer with the great caravan than if left behind in the lonely, unprotected settlements and estancias.

Day after day, down the rocky canyon trails and along the shaded river roads, they converged from every corner of the Río Arriba—the creaking ox-carts, the loaded mules, the mounted men and their chattering families, the silent captives. They flowed into, and filled, and overflowed the Great Plaza. Impatient, restless, intoxicated by the unaccustomed excitement, they created a problem for the officials of the Cabildo with their squabbles and love-quarrels and occasional outbursts of drunken hilarity. (There were many in Santa Fé who came to long for the day when they would be on their way!)

At last, with cheers and the ringing of bells and the firing of guns and the explosive shouts of muleteers and cargadores—*Arré! Arré! Caramba! Nombre de Dios! Anda! Anda!*—the Conducta and its military cordon departed on its seven-hundred-mile journey to Chihuahua. The next rendezvous would be at La Joya de Sevillita, below Alburquerque, where the wagons and pack-mules from the Río Abajo would join those of the Río Arriba, and the long train of vehicles and pack-animals would be broken up into sections.

For by this time the Conducta, having snowballed steadily during its southward progress, was far too big and unwieldy to travel as a single unit. Some Conductas had as many as three hundred wagons, twice as many pack-mules, three thousand oxen, and four hundred horses. And it was a small one indeed that could not boast at least five hundred men and almost three times that many women and children.

Yet, even so great a multitude as this would be swallowed up in the vastly greater throng at the Chihuahua Fair. How many from Chihuahua, Coahuila, New Mexico, Sonora, and even Texas for this immense gathering? How many traders, settlers, friars, soldiers, officials of the Crown, adventurers, crooks, and camp followers in all those brightly striped tents scattered over the plain? Forty thousand souls, perhaps? Fifty thousand? Maybe even more!

Nobody knew for sure. But who from La Cañada or Santa Clara or any other New Mexican village had ever seen so great a number of people as this? Or so many wagons, oxen, and horses? Or so many campfires on the prairie at night? Or such dazzling display of merchandise from so many corners of the earth?

For, besides the Chihuahua merchants with goods from all the provinces of México, one found here the merchants of Jalapa with European goods, and those of Acapulco with products of China and the Philippines. Here you could buy a lace mantón from Manila, a silver-mounted saddle from the City of México, a high comb from Seville, a Toledo blade or a French pistol. You could obtain a hot-blooded Spanish horse or a pair of Atacapaze slaves. There was little, indeed, that could not be found in the booths and display tents here. And all, of course, was not business and trading at the great Chihuahua Fair.

"Caramba! The things that can happen to a man there, señor!"

"Let us not speak of them."

"That is a good idea."

"Let us agree that it is a good thing the Chihuahua Fair does not last more than two weeks."

"It would be better if it did not exist at all."

"You have right there, señor."

"I am a living proof of it. Consider this, señor. I came from Santa Cruz with a wagonload of cleaned wool, two Apache girls worth thirty silver pesos apiece, and half a dozen fine leather shirts. And with what do I return? With this lousy pair of iron spurs, no más. And I am lucky to possess even that, eh? There was a whore there from Parral——"

"Let us not speak of it, señor."

"Her name was La Paquita."

"I know, señor. Let us not speak of her either."

But for most of the New Mexicans who made the great five-hundred-league journey over the Camino Real, the adventure was both profitable and pleasant. The return trip was easier, for the wagons were lighter. Now they were loaded with sweetmeats and candied fruits, spices, chocolate, and honey; with hats, gloves, silk stockings, and fine garments of cotton, silk, and velvet cloth; with jewelry, silverwork, stationery, perfumes; with saddles, bridles, horseshoes, tools, hardware, and household articles; with arms and ammunition; with trinkets to trade to the Indians—and gifts, of course, for stay-at-home sweethearts and relatives.

Hearts were lighter, too, refreshed and filled with memories by the wondrous sights and experiences of Chihuahua. Neither bitter cold and snow, nor even the terrible Journey of Death—that eighty-mile stretch of absolutely waterless desert below Socorro—could dismay these returning pilgrims. They sang the old ballads; they danced to the music of guitar and tombé; they gambled at banca and sacanete; they told stories, and acted out the folk plays of Old Spain and New Mexico; they quarreled a little, made love, gave birth to babies, and

194

buried a few dead along the wintery trail. But even the stone-heaped graves were soon forgotten—by all but one or two, perhaps—in the high spirits and gaiety of the return home. . . .

Suddenly the Plaza exploded. Josefina saw a squad of horsemen and two blue-robed priests ride through the Calle de San Francisco gate. The late sun glinted on the soldiers' helmets and lancetips as they pranced their mounts through the surging crowd. Smiling, the padres extended their hands in a kind of combination greeting and benediction. Close behind rumbled the first ox-wagon, filled mostly with women and screaming children and excited pets. *Viva! Viva España! Hola, Panchita! Pablo! Bienvenido!*

So another Conducta had arrived home safely. Kisses. Abrazos. Tears of joy: a few of sorrow. Prayers and candles of thanksgiving in La Parróquia. A little fiesta before the sad Week of Passion. A little tasting of the great world's sweets . . . but first the parading of the wagons.

Josefina scarcely looked at the traditional procession of the Conducta down the long Calle de San Francisco. Her eyes, restless and indifferent, darted about. She had seen four Conductas come back to Santa Fé: this was not unlike the others. Her thoughts were also restless.

She said to Tichi, "This kind of thing makes me want to fly. You also, Tichi?"

"Not me, señora. I like it."

"I wonder if Fray Juan's organ arrived safely at Santo Domingo."

"I wonder." Tichi leaned out over the parapet to get a better view of the scene below.

"How many varas of green velvet did we order, Tichi?"

"Four, señora."

"And how many pairs of stockings?"

"Six, señora."

"Tichi."

"Yes, Doña Josefina?"

"Do you remember the Guadarramas . . . how they appeared from Ávila . . . at this time of the day?"

"I have almost forgotten."

"Much like that, no?"

She made a little gesture toward the Sierra Nevada. Directly behind La Parróquia the great mountain range seemed to rise out of a pool of deep purple shadow; its snowy peaks blazed in the saffron light of the late afternoon sun.

"Very much, señora," Tichi agreed.

She cast a quick, faintly curious glance over her shoulder at her mistress, then returned her attention to the procession of the Conducta.

She wonders what is the matter with me, Josefina reflected. I wonder myself!

All afternoon her mind had jumped about in a kind of nervous unrest; but always, at last, it came back to one thing—to the reception that Don Antonio was giving this evening in celebration of the Conducta's safe return.

Don Antonio was a very religious man, but even though the sober season of Lent was in midcourse, it did not appear to him that a quiet affair—a small reception—would be inappropriate on such an extremely important occasion as the arrival of the Conducta.

"God does not wish us to act like Huguenots," he observed, "even during the holy season of Lent." And the frailes, if not inclined to agree with him, at least offered no opposition to his plan. So the Governor's reception had become an annual affair.

That it would be the usual bore, Josefina had no doubt. But Don Antonio would enjoy it. It would give him a chance to dress up and flaunt his rank—and show off herself, Josefina.

He takes pride in me, she thought bitterly, as he does in his black Andalusian mare!

Once she had actually heard him whisper to a stranger at a ball, "She is a Castellana, señor." It meant much to him, her pure Spanish blood. It gave a certain cachet to his official functions; it flattered his ego, also, to possess a true Castellana. He was fond of repeating a quotation that someone has passed on to him from Cervantes, often as a toast: "To the Spanish woman—an angel in church, a lady in the streets, and a devil incarnate in bed."

Sometimes, if she were present, he would even cast a quick, sly glance in her direction when he held up his glass.

She found herself becoming overwrought, and she made a conscious, almost impatient, effort to put such reflections aside.

It is foolish, she told herself, to let these things agitate you so. They are over and done with—or almost. That you look ahead now, not backwards, Josefina!

She sought for something pleasant to occupy her mind, and she recalled—she had almost forgotten!—Don Antonio's promise to give her a necklace like the one her mother, Eva Helena, used to wear. She had seen just such a necklace in the City of México once . . . once when she had no money to buy it . . . and she had longed for it ever since.

"Perhaps it is still there, who knows?" she had said to Don Antonio. "It was exactly like my mother's—a string of silver beads, with an amulet of jet representing Santiago the Moor Killer. Look!"

She had gotten a piece of paper and drawn a picture of the necklace for Don Antonio.

"I saw it in a shop on the Street of the Silversmiths," she said. "Do you think it could be there still, Antonio?"

"We shall see, my darling," Don Antonio, who happened to be in a genial mood that day, had said. "If we can't find it, we shall have one made, no? Exactly as you have drawn it."

"Exactly as my mother wore hers."

"I shall arrange to have it brought up with the Conducta in March. You shall have it when the Conducta comes."

She felt almost fond of Don Antonio as she recalled this. Then she closed her eyes and saw her mother again—very vaguely now, however—and how the necklace with the amulet of Santiago the Moor Killer looked around her slender neck. And she had a pleasant warm feeling when she reminded herself that now, this very moment, this necklace was perhaps in Santa Fé, in one of the strong, ironbound chests of the Conducta that would be opened tomorrow. . . .

She turned her thoughts to the Governor's reception that evening, and wondered a little about the odd sensation of excitement that this gave her. It could only be because Don Pedro, of course, would be there; and she would be very dull indeed if she could not create an opportunity during the evening to be alone with him.

"Tichi," she said suddenly, "which dress should I wear tonight? The green taffeta or the red silk?"

Tichi straightened up from the parapet and looked at her mistress with an air of knowing exactly what was in her mind.

"The red is more daring," she said judiciously, "the green more demure. I think, señora——"

"I think I shall wear the green," Josefina said.

11

The Royal Palace in Santa Fé had none of the flamboyant elegance of those great government structures which, in the rich southern provinces of New Spain, reflected the cultural propensities—if not always an unerring taste—of the Viceroys. It had no sculptured doorways, or beautiful balconies, or gardens with walks and fountains.

This was but a poor Kingdom, almost completely encircled by the vast territories of the fierce Apaches and Comanches, in which life was unbelievably hard and dangerous; and the Royal Palace was a grim acceptance of that harsh fact. It was a fortress, actually, from which went out the authority of the Spanish Crown, as far as the Río Missouri, the Californias, and the unknown limits of the Northern Mystery. Only incidentally it was the residence of the Governors of New Mexico.

Before that great uprising of the Pueblos, in which every Spaniard who did not escape to El Paso del Norte was murdered, the Royal Palace had possessed two imposing towers, one of which had served as a dungeon and power magazine, the other as a military chapel called La Hermita. But these were torn down after the glorious re-taking of Santa Fé by Vargas. Now there remained only a low, massive, hollow block of adobe, with narrow windows sliced through white-washed walls four feet thick. Its single entrance was wide enough to admit a troop of cavalry to the interior patios.

Due largely, perhaps, to the great height of the ceilings, even the smallest chamber of the Palace had an atmosphere of disciplined repose, an air of tranquility and spaciousness. The larger salas, finely proportioned, had a kind of virile and positive dignity that fitted them well for the social and military functions of this austere outpost of Spanish authority.

For as soon as the season of Lent was over, there would be resumed here an almost nightly round of receptions, balls, dinners, and parties. Like every other capital of New Spain, the Villa of Santa Fé would do its brave best to imitate the pomp and pageantry of the court of Philip V itself . . . to evoke, even in this far and forgotten corner of the Indies, an echo of Spanish etiquette and ceremony.

The reception that Don Antonio gave each year to celebrate the Conducta's arrival was large or small, gay or restrained, depending on whether or not it took place during Lent. In the year 1720 Easter came late—not until the seventeenth of April—and so the date of the reception fell in the middle of the holy season. It would, accordingly, be only a quiet reminder of those elaborate affairs at which, in other years, His Excellency loved to play the cordial—but always exacting—host.

For whatever might be his neglect of the Kingdom of New Mexico, it could not be said of Don Antonio that he ever scrimped a party. He had planned this one with his usual care; and now, with Josefina at his side in her green taffeta dress, he welcomed his guests with the ease and assurance of one who knew he had provided well for their enjoyment.

"Ah, my good Captain García! You have come all the way from Alburquerque! And you also, Doña Cruz? I am at your feet! My house is yours!"

198

"Don Alfonso, welcome! You do my eyes good, old friend. What passes in Pecos?"

"You are more beautiful, Doña Carla, each time I see you. The air at Laguna agrees with you, no?"

"I kiss your lovely hand, señora."

It was Don Antonio's privilege (he thought) to be as informal and even as familiar as he liked. But from his guests he exacted a deference—it might almost be said an obeisance—that was hardly a viceroy's due. They must bow and curtsy and address him as Excellency or even Excelentismo; and he received all this with the smug affability that is the highest form of arrogance.

"He makes a ceremony of his offensiveness," the pert young wife of Captain Padilla had once observed; and there were few in Santa Fé who did not understand her meaning.

Yet, to Josefina they paid their respects with a true Spanish love for etiquette and graceful usages. As she stood at Don Antonio's side, smiling and gently fluttering her half-opened fan (everywhere in Spanish lands the subtle sign of friendly greeting), they kissed her hand and saluted her with a warmth and pleasure that even Don Antonio must have noticed.

They called her Doña Josefina when they addressed her; and among themselves they spoke of her as La Dama Josefina. Like the mistress of the great Vargas—who had once lived with the famous Reconquistador in this very Palace—she was never, even in their thoughts, an amancebado, but simply Don Antonio's lady; and the Villeños of Santa Fé could not have shown a greater respect for a condesa.

She pleased and delighted them in endless ways. They loved her exquisite Castilian speech, pure and precise and rich in graceful diminutives. They admired her daring and colorful, yet modest, style of dressing. They found in everything she did or said a freshness and novelty, so that even a pair of Moorish earrings, worn by Josefina, became something more than adornment—a kind of expression, they sensed, of every Spanish woman's ancient and elemental and mystic satisfaction in the wearing of jewels.

She was the only Castellana among them. To the men and women of New Mexico alike, she both awakened and, at least a little, satisfied a homesickness that had lingered for a hundred years in their immutable Spanish blood. But to the women of this starved and all-but-forgotten land she brought something of a special preciousness: a reminder, it might be said, of the dignity and strength and gentle resolve to possess one's own soul that, despite centuries of oriental suppression, still burned in the eyes of every daughter of Spain.

Only the Bacas and Bustamantes, with their fanatical pride in their pure blood, held themselves a little aloof from Josefina and indulged in mild speculation about her past. Over the edge of her fan, she observed several members of these First Families of New Mexico at the end of the long sala where they had naturally gravitated toward one another. Soon they were joined by a few Roybals and Ortizes, almost equally exclusive and condescending toward such comparatively recent arrivals—and of mixed blood, to boot!—as, for example, the popular Armijos.

"It is hard to tell when the Bustamantes leave off and the Roybals begin!" Josefina thought, watching the swarthy men and stout women in their old-fashioned finery sampling Don Antonio's wine.

Much more interesting to her were the two young couples who had just arrived: two animated, warm-eyed girls and their dark, soft-spoken, smiling escorts. The girls were the daughters of Don Sebastian Martín, who for more than thirty years had served the king in the conquest and pacification of New Mexico. The men were their husbands, the celebrated Indian fighters, Captains Juan de Padilla and Don Carlos Fernández.

Don Juan and Don Carlos had made themselves famous by a great slaughter of the Comanches only three years before. The story of their exploit was much repeated in Santa Fé and had even been made into a long and particularly bloody poem by a bard of the new Villa of Santa Cruz.

It was a little difficult for Josefina to associate that tale of death and horror with the gentle-mannered young men and their gay brides whom she was now welcoming to the sala. But what man in the room, for that matter, had not plied fire and sword in the subjugation of the Gentiles—or in their conversion to the Holy Catholic faith? And who would not do it again? For such was life in this remarkable Kingdom of New Mexico!

Why have I not seen Don Pedro? she asked herself suddenly. Can it be that he is not coming?

Her eyes traveled methodically around the sala. In the back of her mind she had thought of little except Don Pedro all evening. She had been so occupied with greeting Don Antonio's guests that there had been no time, really, to wonder actively about his absence; but it was a thing that was never quite out of her consciousness—just as she had never ceased to ask herself, with a kind of vague curiosity: Has the necklace come, I wonder? But no! That would be a miracle—a greater miracle even than finding Yolanda. But if it has come, will he give it to me tonight? Here? Ay, Dios! That you get the necklace, Josefina, but not here!

For she dreaded the scene that Don Antonio would be sure to make —the courtly, loving speech that he would deliver as he fastened the silver beads around her neck—knowing well that every soul there would perceive the falseness of his words. That was the sort of thing that Don Antonio enjoyed, as a kind of joke, perhaps. She had become almost used to it. She did not mind it too much any more. Yet, badly as she wanted the necklace, she would rather not have it than to suffer this humiliation before the whole Villa of Santa Fé. She would rather . . .

She began to move casually among the guests. She stopped to exchange a few words with Captain Roque Madrid, that silent old soldier who said so little and killed so many Navajos. She complimented Captain José Naranjo on a new suit of black buckskin with silver buttons: "You make it difficult for the women of this Villa, Captain!"

For a little time she endured the oily persiflage of Don Miguel Tenorio de Alba, alcalde of Taos, and Don Antonio's secretary. She had little love for this fawning official who, she was sure, informed against her falsely to Don Antonio; nor for his stout, gimlet-eyed wife who stood perspiring at his side in a tightly laced bodice.

Extricating herself from Don Miguel's verbose flattery, she passed slowly among the guests who now almost filled the long, candlelit sala. "The flower of Santa Fé"—as Don Miguel had grandiosely expressed it—was present tonight. All the officers of the garrison were there in military uniform; the members of the Cabildo, most of them in uniform also, for this was a land where politicians were soldiers and soldiers politicians; some alcaldes mayores from nearby pueblos; and a number of ranchers who had ridden in—some for a hundred miles or more—from their big estates up and down the river.

Almost all of the men were accompanied by their wives and daughters, many of them handsome women in fiesta dress, their hair in ringlets and kiss-curls, their shoulders made decorous with lace mantillas or exquisite silk rebosos. They fluttered their fans, and smiled, and chattered in their quaint sixteenth-century Spanish.

Josefina greeted Don Juan Páez Hurtado, who was hated by Don Antonio because, among all of the great Vargas's friends, he alone had remained faithful, while Don Antonio himself had proved the most treacherous.

"You are looking very well, Don Juan," Josefina said to him. Then, to his pretty young Mexican wife, "And you, Teodora, you are always more lovely! You make me despair! I adore your new eardrops. How are the children—how are Antonio and Gertrudis and Juan?"

"They thrive wonderfully," Teodora said. "Like weeds, no?"

"And more like Indians every day," Don Juan added. "You must come to see them, Doña Josefina. It has been too long since you honored our house."

"The children," Teodora said, "often ask about their Tía 'Fina."

"Well, tell them their Aunt 'Fina will see them soon. I wouldn't be surprised if some small gifts arrived for them with the Conducta, no? As soon as the packets are opened, I shall bring them to the children."

"But really, Josefina mía——"

"That you kiss them for me," Josefina said, with a suddenly abstracted air. "It has been so pleasant, my dear friends . . ."

She saw, then, that Don Pedro had arrived at last. He was making his way toward her, pausing at intervals to greet friends. She watched his erratic progress and felt a curious interest in her own reaction to his appearance.

I am thinking nothing, she said to herself, absolutely nothing. And yet, my heart appears to be thumping and it is a little difficult for me to breathe. This is very odd, Josefina!

She had, in fact, an abrupt and almost irresistible impulse to go to her apartment and loosen her bodice. Then this impulse turned into a simpler one, an urge merely to fly: she was, in fact, on the verge of a kind of absurd panic.

Yet, when Don Pedro finally reached her, she turned to him a serenely smiling face. She gave him her hand and, as he bowed to kiss it, smiled at him with lowered lids and fluttered her fan—as the Maya had taught her long ago to do it—so expertly and delightfully that many in the room interrupted their conversations merely for the pleasure of watching her.

"And now, Don Pedro," she said with mock severity, "one must have a very good excuse for arriving so late."

"I have, Doña Josefina," he replied with all his Castilian gravity. "I was detained, unfortunately, by His Excellency's hams."

"Perdón, señor?"

"The hams from Spain, señora, that were expected with the Conducta."

"Ah, yes! Don Antonio has talked of little else."

Two years ago Don Antonio had been seized with an intense longing for a certain kind of ham made only in the mountains of Granada, a ham cured in snow and sugar, with little or no salt, and smoked in a special way. These Granada mountain hams, Don Antonio maintained, were comparable, in another order of excellence, to the cheeses of Peñafiel. Compared to other hams, they were as Frontiñán wines to those made from the sour wild grapes of Laguna. And so strong was Don Antonio's yearning for them that he had actually ordered three sent to him all the way from Spain.

"Did they arrive?" Josefina asked.

"In the very last wagon, señora. Don Antonio himself waited as long as possible. Then he asked me to take his place. I could not refuse, señora."

"Of course not. Those hams, I know, are very precious to Don Antonio."

"As for myself," Don Pedro said, "I would not have all the hams in Spain for the hour my eyes have been deprived of you, Doña Josefina."

"Really, Don Pedro! One should be able to think of a prettier figure than that!"

"Well, all the silver of Potosí, then . . . or the gold of the Indies. Is that better, señora?"

"Much better," Josefina said, laughing. "But less original, no? I think I prefer the hams after all, Don Pedro."

Her laughter died abruptly. Across the room, through an opening in the crowd, she glimpsed Don Antonio watching them. His eyes and mouth—his pale eyes and his small pink mouth—were sad. It was a peculiarity of Don Antonio's that when his face took on this melancholy and reflective look, something unpleasant was to be expected of him. Josefina had long ago learned the meaning of that expression, and she said to Don Pedro from behind her agitated fan:

"That you excuse me now, Don Pedro. I must go and see why the refreshments haven't been served. You are hungry, no? I am."

She wondered, as she went away, what Don Antonio might have read in her own face while she was talking with Don Pedro. She had striven to make it show nothing. And yet Don Antonio had very sharp eyes. Could he have seen the strange and improbable agitation that— for no reason at all, despite her stern efforts to control herself—had seized her at the very first sight of Don Pedro? Could he, perhaps, have noticed it and learned from it something that . . . that she herself did not understand?

As she approached the anteroom where the tables had been laid and the candles lit for Don Antonio's refresco, she saw several girls coming from the kitchen with trays of food: confections just arrived with the Conducta from México—cakes, fine bread, olives, anchovies and other imported delicacies, together with such New Mexican treats as piñonate, sopapillas and little tarts stuffed with honey and piñon nuts. Behind them came other servants bringing silver pitchers of cool water, Talavera jugs of frothy chocolate, and jars of Don Antonio's own wine from El Paso del Norte.

They were dressed in their best skirts and whitest chemises, their hair glossy from washing with yucca suds, their dark eyes bright with the excitement of taking even a slave's part in this great fiesta of their masters. Josefina paused to admire the innocent, fresh beauty that seemed to shine in the faces of the plainest of them. Then——

"Dear Mother of God!" she whispered.

It required a very great effort of her will to refrain from crying out . . . to keep her face coldly impassive . . . and to gaze disdainfully into the dark, arrogant eyes of the Navajo slave girl María, who was wearing a necklace of silver beads from which was suspended a jet amulet representing Santiago the Moor Killer.

12

It was cold in the patio, with a thin, clear coldness that seemed to come from the new, pre-Easter moon riding high in the metallic sky. Josefina shivered and looked about her with a curious sensation of slowly clearing vision.

The patio was a tangle of shadows: the dense masses of darkness cast by the heavy walls of the Palace; the wavering strips of black laid across the portal floors by the columns supporting the vigas; the sharp-edged pattern—like splatters and rivulets of ink—traced on walks and whitewashed walls by the old lilac tree, the three or four cottonwoods, the leafless vines and shrubs.

Except for Josefina and the shadows imperceptibly moving with the slow progression of the moon, nothing was alive or stirring. It was almost quiet in this secluded place: even the sounds of fiesta came but faintly through the thick adobe walls. Yet, as if to hide from some unseen presence in that deserted spot, Josefina shrank back into the deepest shadows of the portal and pressed herself, shivering, against the dampish wall.

She was oppressed with an intense, almost unbearable feeling of shame. She was ashamed for Don Antonio, who could have thought of such a thing as he had done . . . and for herself, that she should have played a part—if only the victim's—in Don Antonio's dreadful little conceit . . . and for yet someone else.

Staring at the weird jumble of moonlight and shadow and seeing nothing, she said aloud, slowly and distinctly, without hearing herself say it:

"Ay, Madre! That you forgive your daughter!"

For had not Don Antonio contrived to outrage not alone her own decency and dignity, but also that of her mother? Was not that, perhaps, the cream of his jest? It was like Don Antonio—it was so very like him!—to have thought of that. How he must have laughed when the idea occurred to him! She remembered now how he had watched her, smiling, when it happened, when his joke bore its sickening fruit. . . .

She had done nothing, she thought, that she need regret. She had not flown at María and torn the necklace from her and scratched her eyes out. She had said nothing whatever, she was sure. It was difficult to remember, but she recalled that she had controlled herself very well. She had glanced over the table, and had asked one of the servants to trim a candle, and then—because she had felt a sudden faintness—she had rested for a moment or two on a bench.

It was while she was seated on that bench, fanning herself with deliberate slowness, and wondering if she were very pale, and keeping a small smile on her lips, that she had observed Don Antonio watching her from the far side of the room.

He had been talking with Jean L'Archévèque, and while he talked with the Frenchman he kept his eyes on her, never for a moment diverting his gaze and never for a moment ceasing to smile in his sad, thoughtful way; much as the devil, she thought, might smile at the sight of the poor suffering souls in hell. Then there was a space of time she could not recall; and now she was here, in the patio of the Palace, shivering against the wall and wondering vaguely how she had got there. She must have intended to go to her apartment, she supposed, and had taken the wrong door. . . .

"Ah, señora!" a voice said. "So here you are."

"Don Pedro?"

"At your orders, Doña Josefina."

He stood before her in a mottled patch of moonlight, holding something in both hands.

"Your mantón," he said. "It slipped from your shoulders when you left the sala. It is cold out here, no? I thought you would need it."

"Thank you, Don Pedro."

She turned her back a little toward him and he placed the light wool shawl over her bare shoulders. She drew it tightly about her, enjoying the immediate sensation of cozy warmth.

"Are you perfectly well, señora?" he asked, after a long interval.

Did he see? she wondered. Does he know? For who could tell about Don Antonio, how widely he might have shared his joke. She said, "Why do you ask me that, Don Pedro?"

"You are a little pale, perhaps," he said. "One is naturally concerned . . ."

"It was warm in there," she said hastily. "The air was bad, so many people, such strong scents. . . ."

Her voice trailed off. He took her lightly by the arm, and said, "That you sit down here, Doña Josefina. I shall bring you something. A glass of water—a little brandy, no?"

205

He guided her to a long pine bench and she seated herself in the shadows of the portal. She leaned her head back against the wall. Her weakness had almost passed; it was being followed by a feeling of indifference—to everything—even to Don Pedro. She was vaguely annoyed by his attentions, and not sorry for an excuse to send him away for a little while.

"A glass of water, please," she said. "And Don Pedro . . ."

"Yes, señora."

"I am still cold. I wonder if you would lend me your cloak?"

"Of course, señora. If you will excuse me, in just a moment."

He bowed and strode rapidly away, leaving her with a little time in which to get hold of herself, and arrange her thoughts and consider her situation.

Ah, Josefina, she thought listlessly, now you have what you have wished for, no? Soon you will be sitting with him in the moonlight . . . wrapped in his cloak. . . .

She smiled meditatively, slowly opening and closing her fan. Qué romántico!

She tilted her head back and gazed pensively at the sliver of the moon. It passed behind a tiny cloud, edged it with cold light, and swam out, bright and lucent, into the curving sky. It filled her with a feeling of remoteness . . . of la soledad. . . .

Then, quite suddenly, there rushed into this sense of emptiness a cold and bitter flood of anger. Her mind churned with a confusion of maddening images . . . a jet amulet of Santiago the Moor Killer between María's tawny breasts . . . Maria's mocking eyes . . . Don Antonio's sad and thoughtful smile . . . Don Pedro's handsome, solicitous face.

For even Don Pedro—for some reason deeper, perhaps, than she could ever understand—was swept into the torrent of her resentment. This perplexed, then frightened her. Alarmed by the very violence of her emotions, she sat clutching her fan, fighting quietly against the destructive passion that threatened to possess her.

Of all times, Josefina! she reproached herself. Of all times, you choose this one to lose your senses . . . to be stupid and crazy!

Little by little she calmed herself, with an effort. By the time Don Pedro returned, she was outwardly serene; inside she was heavy with the burden of spent emotion. She felt strangely apathetic, insensitive . . . charged with a kind of coldness that she once might have called majota.

Don Pedro shook out his blue military cloak and settled it about her shoulders. She snuggled into its heavy, masculine folds, sipped the water he had brought her, and smiled her thanks at him.

"I could wish to have a cloak like this," she said. "It warms like a fire."

"It is made from warm wool," he said, sitting beside her. "It was woven from the wool of those sheep they raise around Ávila. If you have ever been to Ávila, señora, you will know why those sheep have to possess wool of a special warmness——"

Even in the darkness, he must have seen the sudden, startled movement of her head and hands.

"What is it, señora?" he asked. "Is there something——?"

"Nothing, Don Pedro," she said, and managed a little laugh. "Tell me some more about this fine cloak."

It was strange, she thought, how at certain times a single word could pierce into one's mind, and explode there . . . such a word, for instance, as Ávila. . . .

"I have had this cloak for a long time," Don Pedro was saying. "I brought it from Spain with me. I have worn it on more campaigns than I can remember. A cloak such as this becomes a part of a man —like his sword or saddle."

"I should like to have one like it," Josefina said. "But a little smaller, of course."

"I'll tell you something, señora," Don Pedro said. "When I wear that cloak I have a feeling that I have wrapped something of Old Spain about me. Do you miss Old Spain, señora?"

Her eyes widened a little: one did not expect poetry from a soldier! She was impressed also by the earnestness, one might say the intensity, with which he asked his sudden question.

"Always," she said. "And you, Don Pedro?"

"Every day, señora."

He said this so seriously, with such a nostalgic echo in his words, that she threw him a quick, instinctive glance of understanding. His reaction was an odd, impulsive movement toward her, immediately checked, which caused Josefina to say to herself: But perhaps this is enough of Spain—for now! Maybe we can squeeze a little more conversation out of the cloak. At any rate, let us try.

She caressed the dark broadcloth with her fingertips. It was, in truth, a little threadbare from so much wear. She said: "I have often wished for a bullfighter's cloak, to wear when I ride. But such a one as this would be even better. It turns the rain, no?"

"Not as well as it used to," Don Pedro said, a little absently. "Do you ride often, señora?"

"In good weather, almost every day."

"But not alone, señora."

"Usually," she said. "But sometimes old Sergeant García goes with me."

"It is just as well."

"Don Antonio," she said with a wry smile, "insists on it."

Don Pedro remained thoughtfully silent for a while. She waited, without much feeling, except a kind of faint indifference, for him to ask the next questions: "When do you ride next, señora?" and then, "Where?"

She was a little piqued when he asked nothing else at all. He looked up at the moon with a sudden interest, observing the great halo of polished sky that surrounded it, and said: "We are going to have some fine weather, I think. It should be fair tomorrow."

"Quién sabe?" She shrugged. "Who knows?"

"That is true," Don Pedro said. "The weather in this country is unpredictable. One never knows what to expect of it."

"But at least," she said dryly, "in a place where the weather is so uncertain, one is never at a loss for something to talk about."

"That also is true."

"Yes."

They both sat in a long silence, neither glancing at the other. At last Don Pedro turned and looked at Josefina, whose eyes were even larger, if possible, than he had remembered them, and of an indescribably deep and emeraldlike pellucidity in the moonlight; and he asked with an odd abruptness, "Do you feel better, señora?"

"Much better, Don Pedro. I am quite all right now."

"Then, señora," he said, with a certain formal stiffness, "I think that perhaps we should return to the sala."

He arose with a rather surprising alacrity and held out his hand to help her up: she sat for a few moments in his big cloak, looking up at him without answering.

Ah, Don Pedro! she thought. It is true, after all, what they say about you!

She took his hand and stood up, allowing her fingers to rest in his for just the merest moment longer than necessary. Then they both turned at the sound of footsteps on the pavement of the portal.

That is Don Antonio, of course, Josefina said to herself. That is what you were afraid of, Don Pedro, no? She watched his face. His features remained utterly without change of expression. At least he reveals nothing. When he wishes, he can indeed have the face of a bulto!

They saw Don Antonio approaching now, with the dignified step of one who can hold his wine very well but has taken a little too much. He came to a stop a short distance away and regarded them owlishly.

"I have been looking everywhere for you, my dear," he reproached her. "I have been asking everyone, 'Have you seen my Josefina?' and 'Where is my Josefina?'"

"Well, you have found me," she said.

Don Antonio came closer, peering at them both in turn with that peculiarly melancholy expression of his eyes and mouth. He smiled sadly.

"I should have asked, 'Where is Don Pedro?'" he said. "That is the way to find Josefina, no? The way to find my Josefina is to ask, 'Where is Don Pedro?'"

He burst into a hearty laugh and slapped Don Pedro on the back.

Josefina said: "I am sorry, Don Antonio, if I have caused you any concern. I became a little ill in the sala. . . . I came out here for a breath of fresh air, and Don Pedro brought me his cloak. . . ."

She stopped suddenly, aware that this long explanation was a mistake. She had made it only for Don Pedro's sake—she herself was past caring what Don Antonio might feel or think. But even for Don Pedro it would have been better if she had merely pretended to laugh at Don Antonio's little joke. Or even if she had kept silent and done nothing at all.

Really, Josefina! she thought. How stupid you are!

"Do you feel better now, my dear?" Don Antonio asked, with a rather elaborate show of solicitude. "Has it passed away, this—this illness?"

"Completely, Antonio," she said. "Except that I have a headache. I think I shall not return to the sala. I should like to go straight to my room now. If you will excuse me, Antonio . . . Don Pedro."

She gave Don Antonio her arm and, glancing swiftly at Don Pedro from behind her fan, added casually:

"I must feel fit tomorrow, Antonio . . . I have a long ride to make over the Pecos trail in the morning . . . I have promised Doña Mercedes a visit. . . ."

13

Except for the gentle glow of the dying piñon fire on the white-washed walls, it was dark in her apartment. She did not bother to light a candle, but kicked off her slippers, got out of her gown, rolled down her long silk stockings and, in the fashion of her time, slipped into bed quite unclothed.

She lay quietly for a little while, watching the rosy reflections of the fire on the ceiling, her mind a curious blank. Then she began to think lightly of trivial and commonplace things. She had neglected to brush her hair. A whalebone in the bodice of her black velvet must be replaced. She yawned. She was chilly and drew up the coverlet. Then she sighed and said softly in the darkness: "Ay, Tafora. Have I lied to you after all?"

For, quite suddenly it seemed, and as surely as she had ever known anything in her uncertain world, Josefina knew that she was in love with Don Pedro Villasur.

She felt at first an inclination to drift pleasantly in a kind of dreamy contemplation of this interesting—and indeed rather astonishing—conclusion. But it was never the habit of her mind to neglect the practical aspects of a new situation. And now, snuggling down beneath the colcha and interlacing her fingers behind her head, she asked herself with pitiless realism: Ah, yes, Josefina—but does Don Pedro love you?

She considered this stark question for a little while; she shrugged her bare shoulders and smiled. It is really of no consequence, she said to herself. I should feel myself very stupid indeed if I could not bring that about! Besides, it is not my hope to become Don Pedro's wife, but only his amiga. It is much simpler for a man to fall in love with an amiga than with a wife. And besides, I think—I think that Don Pedro may already be a little in love with me!

This thought gave her a warm, pleasant feeling, not unlike the glow one received from a glass of Málaga or from a good fire on a raw day. She went over in her mind all that had taken place in the patio of the Palace, recalling everything that Don Pedro had said, the tone of his voice and the expression on his grave, handsome face as he said it. She sought with a kind of idle eagerness for nuances she might have missed, hidden meanings that had perhaps escaped her. And one little scrap of their conversation recurred with an odd persistence—as if insisting on its own importance:

"I'll tell you something, señora. When I wear that cloak I have a feeling that I have wrapped something of Old Spain about me. Do you miss Old Spain, señora?"

"Always . . . And you, Don Pedro?"

"Every day, señora."

All her instincts told her to remember these small fragments of speech. For in them, she sensed, was her key to a certain power over Don Pedro, and to a measure of control over herself . . . even though she had become a woman in love, and so bereft of strength and cunning!

Her meditation became a drowsiness and the thoughts drifting through her mind were hard to follow, the images vague and shifting; and everything gave way finally to a simple longing to have Don Pedro near her . . . with her . . . *at once*. It was a feeling new and strange to her, at first oddly pleasurable, then as it grew and unfolded with the quiet inevitability of a flower unfolding to the sun, it became an aching disquiet.

The fire died out; the apartment was now completely dark. Josefina lay very still in the darkness and felt the cool tingling of her skin, the rapid beating of her pulses, the gentle stirring of her breasts against the coverlet. Suddenly she sat up, almost like one startled out of a deep sleep, and ran her fingers through the dark, loose mass of her hair.

"Mother of God!" she said in a kind of frightened whisper. "That you give me a little help in this!"

As she remained sitting up in bed, staring through the darkness at a dull point of light in the fireplace, she became conscious of someone knocking at her door. Her senses sharpened, and she recognized the knock as Don Antonio's.

So the fiesta is over, she said to herself.

She lay down again and pulled the coverlet up over her shoulders. She turned on her side and nestled her face in the silken pillow. The knocking on the door continued, louder, more insistent, more impatient. Josefina stirred and smiled sleepily. After a little while the knocking ceased.

14

"God give you a good morning, my dear," Don Antonio said pleasantly. "You must have slept very well last night."

Josefina glanced up, a little surprised that he should have joined her at second breakfast in the dining room. She had hardly expected it this morning—even of Don Antonio.

"God give it to you," she said, without expression.

"I called last night to present my compliments before retiring," Don Antonio remarked, "but you were already fast asleep." He broke off a morsel of bizcocho and popped it into his mouth. "The night air, no doubt," he added casually. "True?"

She sipped her chocolate in silence. A slave girl named Pilarcita— at least she was spared María this morning!—brought some chocolate also for Don Antonio, mixed with milk and eggs. Josefina watched him drink this mixture while he tossed fragments of the hard biscuit into his small, pink mouth. Pretty soon he would say, "A soldier's breakfast, my dear. One gets accustomed to it on the march. It is all that one requires, really." Then, a little later, he would send Pilarcita for a dish of atole, an egg or two, a bit of ham perhaps, and some soft bread with melon preserves. . . . At one time it had amused her.

"True," she agreed. "And you, Antonio? Did you have a good night also?"

She asked it ever so politely, with downcast eyes. Don Antonio looked at her sharply.

"On the contrary," he sighed. "A very poor one. I slept hardly at all."

"Too much fiesta, perhaps?" she said dryly. "You must be careful, Antonio."

"Ah, my dear," he said in a hurt tone, "that you knew your Antonio better! It is nothing so simple that keeps him awake at night. It is his worries, no? His concern for the affairs of his poor Kingdom. The burden of his responsibilities."

What, she asked herself wearily, can this be leading to?

She listened idly while he interrupted himself to send Pilarcita for more chocolate, and a bit of fried ham—the mountain ham from Granada that had just arrived with the Conducta—and various other delicacies, including, of course, the melon preserves. Don Antonio's fondness for preserves of all sorts was really inordinate. Once he had even experimented with a dulce made of the fruit of the prickly pear, a delicious confiture prized highly by the Indians but, it was said, deadly poisonous to white men. A taste of it had made Don Antonio wretchedly ill, at any rate. . . . Josefina recalled her horror at a vague but irrepressible feeling of regret that he had not eaten more of it!

"Now," Don Antonio resumed, "it is the Huguenots who rob me of sleep."

By the Huguenots he meant, of course, the French. It was his whim to torture an ordinary struggle for power and territory between two Catholic countries into a religious war.

"What are the Huguenots up to now?" she asked curiously. "You have kept me very badly informed about these matters of late, Antonio."

"Only to spare you worry, my dear."

"I worry only about what is concealed from me—what I cannot face. I should like dearly to know what is happening beyond the plains—what the French are doing out there. Is it true, as some claim, that they are preparing to march on us?"

Don Antonio laughed and waved a pudgy hand. He began, with a great air of professional profundity, to move various objects about the table.

"No, no, my dear," he protested. "Nothing at all like that. Only in México, at the Viceroy's court, do they have such ideas. They are frightened old women, eh? Here we know better. Look, I shall explain everything. Let us suppose that this porringer is the Río Mississippi. This roll, let us say, is La Luisiana and Texas. This cup——"

He began to recount in tedious detail all that was common knowledge about the French threat to Spanish power in the New World. It was true, he admitted, that the French had strong forts in the valley of the Mississippi. In Texas they had posts very near the Río Grande —their ambitions had not died there with La Salle. They were on the Missouri, too, and even among the Pawnees, where they had built two pueblos as large as Taos.

"It appears to me," Josefina commented, "that it is not alone the Apache who encircle us!"

Don Antonio waved away her implied concern. "It is impossible for the French to invade New Mexico," he declared. "Do you know why, my dear?"

"Why?" she asked.

"The distance is too great without horses."

She stared at him, speechless, shocked no less by the magnitude of this inanity than by the triumphant air with which he announced it.

Can it be possible, she asked herself, that he believes this? Does he not know that the prairies are an open road to New Mexico, lacking nothing an army needs—meat, game, grass, abundant water? Can he in fact be ignorant of this? Or is he making excuses for something he has done—his ridiculous Entrada of last year, for instance? . . . *Or is he preparing an excuse for something he is about to do?*

She was pondering the last of these questions, when Pilarcita brought in the rest of Don Antonio's breakfast. His eyes lighted up and a glisten of saliva appeared at the corners of his mouth as he inspected the slice of ham, flanked by two fried eggs, on a silver salver. It was indeed a beautiful sight, Josefina had to admit; and she felt a certain sympathy for Don Antonio in his silent dedication to its enjoyment.

After all, she thought, he has waited two years for this moment!

She sat silently, sipping her chocolate and nibbling a bizcocho, while he finished his breakfast. He cleaned up the salver with a bit of bread, wiped his mouth on his handkerchief, and delivered a short lecture on the superiority of Granada mountain ham over all others, including the Italian.

"And now, my dear," he said genially, "I shall bring you up to

213

date on our plans with respect to the French." He gazed at her with his shrewd, melancholy look. "It is something that interests you greatly, no?"

"It interests all in this Kingdom, I should think," she said briefly, sensing danger.

"Right. Well, here is our design."

Most of what he told her she already knew: that the Viceroy, greatly (and, he thought, needlessly) concerned, had ordered another reconnaissance to the north as quickly as possible; that an expedition was being formed at that moment under the direction of Captain Villasur; that this expedition would, in effect, be a light, fast scouting force consisting of no more than fifty soldiers and militia, plus whatever Apache allies might be picked up; that it would leave early in June, penetrate the Northern Mystery as far as possible, and return before snowfall in the passes.

"Who will be in command?" she asked.

It was an indiscreet question, and she knew it to be indiscreet; but she wished to see what effect it would have on Don Antonio. It could tell him nothing, really, nothing for certain; but his reaction might reveal much to her.

"I lead this Entrada myself," he said.

He spoke these words in a curiously flat and inexpressive voice, spacing each syllable with heavy pauses, and looking at her intently as he placed one word after another. She smiled a gently deprecating smile and murmured:

"Ay, Antonio! When will you ever learn to spare yourself?"

This also was indiscreet, perhaps; but unavoidable. Having taken one step, she must take the next. But Don Antonio registered nothing.

"Ah, my dear," he said heavily, "you have said that so often! But who is there except myself?"

She decided to go no further—she had possibly told him too much already. She shrugged and sat silent, waiting. Don Antonio thrust out his hands in a suddenly demanding gesture.

"Who?" he almost shouted.

Ah, well, she thought, he knows! He suspects, anyhow. He has put two and two together. Or L'Archévèque has done it for him. How much, I wonder, does L'Archévèque really know?

She gazed back at Don Antonio with steady, meditative eyes, and said nothing.

"The answer, my dear," he said more quietly, "is: *there is no one.* I am the Governor and Captain-General of this Kingdom, no? I lead my troops in person, no? Where there is danger and hardship, it can never be said the Great Captain, Don Antonio Valverde y Cosio, hangs back."

The Great Captain! He often described himself in his reports and journals by that title—or had Don Miguel de Alba do it for him—but she had never before heard it from his own lips. She smiled and watched his face turn from red back to its customary pallid color. After an interval he added, with a sheepishness his nature would not permit him to conceal:

"Besides, the Viceroy's bando stipulates that I lead this Entrada in person."

So that was it, at last! Don Antonio, then, had no choice. Even if he wished to stay at home and let another lead this so-easy Entrada —almost an outing, to hear him tell of it!—he could not. He had received his orders from México—from His Excellency the Marqués de Valero himself. Not even the king's word could be more final.

"God guard you then, Antonio," she said, in the formula, "and success to your arms."

"It shall never be said," Don Antonio asserted solemnly, "that Don Antonio Valverde y Cosio failed to defend the plazas and presidios of this Kingdom."

She gazed at him, wondering a little at the depth of his fatuity; and wondering also what she had learned from this unexpected conversation with Don Antonio. She had got some facts: she must study them. She had gathered a great many hints and implications: they must be examined carefully. She felt an impatience to be alone, to go some place where she could think. But Don Antonio had not yet finished. He dipped a piece of sponge cake in his chocolate, carried it dripping to his mouth, and added:

"But you are right, my dear. Even I cannot do everything. It is time that I delegated some of my duties to younger men. To Don Pedro, for example. I believe that was your suggestion, wasn't it, my dear?"

"It was, Antonio," she said, waiting.

"Well, it was good advice—excellent. I have decided to take it. I had planned to go this morning to Taos. But I've changed my mind. I've decided to—as you say—to spare myself."

"That is sensible, Antonio."

"Yes. I am sending Don Pedro in my place. He has already left for Taos—he left this morning."

"I am glad you have begun to think a little of yourself," she said evenly.

"I knew it would make you happy, Negra."

Negra was a term of endearment used by the illiterate settlers of New Mexico. She disliked it, and Don Antonio knew she disliked it. He sometimes used it, she knew, only to irritate her.

"I should be even happier if you could call me something else, please," she said coldly.

Don Antonio laughed. "No offense, my darling. But I must not keep you any longer. I see you are dressed for riding. To see Doña Mercedes, no? Please present my compliments to her, and to Don Ramón."

A mixture of hatred and bitterness and contempt blurred her judgment, and for the third time that morning she was indiscreet.

"I have changed my mind," she said deliberately. "I have decided not to ride this morning."

15

She had not forgotten 'Toñita. She had promised the little seamstress that she would help her, if she could, to break down the cruel barriers of class that were keeping her from Rafael . . . or, at least, to slip through them.

"I must find a way to get those poor innocents in bed together," she said to Tichi. "I have given my word, no?"

"Why don't you see Fray Juan about it, señora?"

"I've thought of that."

She decided to call on the Father Custodio that very morning. She attended Mass in La Parróquia and afterwards went into the Lady Chapel to meditate and collect her thoughts.

But all her thoughts, she soon discovered, were about Don Pedro; and some of them, if not wanton, were not at least the kind that one should have in church. Don Pedro had been away for eight days, and during all that time—during every moment of it, in a certain sense— he had been in her mind. For his presence, it seemed—the sense and feel of his actual physical being—remained in the background of everything she did or said or thought; and at night she often dreamed of him.

It was a form of disquiet that played strange tricks with her heart and spirit, sometimes filling her with an odd content, then with a vast and restless sadness; and occasionally with sudden, exhausting storms of desire.

Now, in the dim stillness of the Lady Chapel, one of these unpredictable and resistless waves of emotion engulfed her. It was not a simple longing for Don Pedro's embrace—it had nothing to do, really, with mere physical desire. It was an aching need that filled her heart and soul to be at one with Don Pedro Villasur, to take and absorb him into herself: it was a torment of possession and surrender, of opposites that were affinities—of sweet pain and gentle violence.

She was perplexed and a little frightened by these passions that seized on her so suddenly and roughly; and she struggled in the quieter depths of her being not to be lost in them utterly. There were many reasons why she must defend herself against them—some of them hard, smooth reasons, such as Tafora might almost turn over in his thin hidalgo's hands, some of them beyond even Tafora's understanding, and some that were hidden even from herself. . . .

Josefina gazed at the painted, doll-like, yet strangely alive features of La Conquistadora, and the little image seemed, as always, to be listening.

"Ay, Señora," she whispered. "That you help me to be hard—majota . . . like Doña Manuela, no? . . . at least when I wish to be!"

Then, for good measure, she said a brief prayer to San José who, as everyone knew, was particularly helpful to girls in affairs of the heart; and after that she sought Fray Juan de la Cruz at the convento adjoining La Parróquia.

"Be seated, my child," Fray Juan said. "I shall be only a moment."

Josefina took the only other chair, except Fray Juan's, and sat quietly, looking around the small whitewashed room, while the priest scribbled something on a sheet of paper at a rough deal table. The room was bare, but cool and restful, deriving all its character from its own simplicity and the gentle serenity of Fray Juan's presence.

"And now, my daughter," Fray Juan asked at last, "what has brought you here?"

"The misfortunes of love, padre."

"Ah, yes?" the fraile murmured. "Are you sure, señora, that you have come to the right place for advice?"

"I am not sure. But perhaps—— It is not my own misfortune, padre."

"Well, tell me about it, my child," Fray Juan said seriously.

"It is about 'Toñita Montoya and Rafael Serna," Josefina began. "Perhaps you know, padre——"

"Ah, yes!" Fray Juan interrupted her. "I do know. A great pity! It is sad that even here we must have our Romeo and Juliet."

"Perdón, padre?"

"Have you ever read the plays of Don William Shakespeare, señora?"

"No, padre."

"They are very good—better, even, than our own Lope's. But now, these children——"

"Can nothing be done for them, padre?"

Fray Juan thought that something could be done. Young Rafael, as a man, could simply marry—no matter how strenuously his family might object. With 'Toñita things were a little more complicated. But there was a way to get around all the difficulties.

"It is only necessary," he explained, "for 'Toñita to take up residence in a neutral home for a time. Let her think things over, undisturbed by either family. Then, if she is still determined to marry her Rafael—there is no one who can stop her."

"But her relatives. Will they let her alone, padre? You cannot imagine the feeling over this! Why, 'Toñita's father threatens to run her through with his own sword if——"

"They will forget such threats, once the two are married," Fray Juan said. "As for interfering with 'Toñita while she is trying to make up her mind, that is against both the civil and church law. It is punishable with excommunication."

There was a long silence.

"I think 'Toñita would do this," Josefina said.

"I shall be glad to instruct Rafael as to the legal steps that must be taken. But after that . . . there is still the problem of finding a neutral home, no?"

"I have been thinking about that also, padre," Josefina said. "Why not the Palace?"

"Why not? If you wish to accept the responsibility, señora."

"Gladly, padre. How could I do otherwise!"

"Good!" Fray Juan said, scratching some words on a scrap of paper. "I am making a note, señora, to bring you the play of *Romeo and Juliet* the next time I come up from Santo Domingo."

She left the priest with a small and vicarious, but quite pleasant, feeling of triumph in her heart; and this mild exaltation must have shown in her face. For when, coming out of the convento, she met Fray Juan Minguéz, that bluff and weathered padre whose eyes were as blue as his blue Franciscan robes, he returned her greeting with:

"God give you a good morning also, Doña Josefina—and it looks as if He already has! It is a pleasure to see such a happy face as yours among all the sour fachadas of this Villa."

"On such a fine day, padre, who could feel unhappy?"

"That is my viewpoint, señora. But there are some who lock their hearts, even in springtime."

"How poetic you have become, padre!"

"It is the time of year, my child."

She liked Fray Juan Minguéz: everyone did—even the Zuñis. The Zuñis were not fond of the priests of the Conquerors, but they liked Fray Juan. He was a man toughened and somewhat battered by sun, wind, and the frosts of high passes; but his voice was gentle, and there was humor, understanding, and deep masculine piety in his blue eyes. How old was Fray Juan? Nobody could tell for sure. But when he tucked up his skirts and set out with the troops, there wasn't a soldier who could outsoldier him. He could walk, ride, starve, and, if need be, fight with the best of them.

"Ah, yes. It is a wonderful time of year!" she said, with another smile for Fray Juan. "Go with God, padre."

"Con Dios, señora."

It was such a beautiful day that she decided to take a little stroll before returning to the Palace. She turned into the winding street that led from La Parróquia to the river. In the convent garden the apricot trees had burst suddenly into blossom. There were not enough of them to perfume the air, but they were lovely to look at in the manzanilla-pale April sunshine; and the famous air of Santa Fé needed no embellishment. One took a pleasure in the mere act of breathing it, as Josefina did now while she followed the wandering little street past the high convento wall toward the Río de Santa Fé.

Occasionally she met a countrywoman hurrying with a jar or basket on her head to the market; or a woodcutter beside a burro piled high with piñon logs; or a farmer, in leather breeches and a broad-brimmed hat, from one of the irrigated fields beyond the river. They all greeted her cheerfully, whether or not she knew them; and she smiled at them all and gave them back their "Buenos días!" with a light heart.

She looked up at the huge range the Villeños were beginning to call the Sangre de Cristo mountains, because at sunset, particularly in winter, they became in fact as crimson as the blood of God that one saw flowing from the Cristos in all the churches. It was so near, this range, that it seemed to be a great wave suddenly frozen into immobility just as it was about to break over the town, a wave crested with white and splashed with green of all shades from brilliant emerald to almost black in the canyons. From it trickled down the silvery Río de Santa Fé that brought the water of life to the little settlement at its feet.

Once she had loved these mountains because they reminded her of Spain. Because they evoked memories . . . or something deeper than memories, perhaps—the forgotten *experience* of home and childhood. But now, of a sudden they were dear to her for their own sake. She had become a daughter of this country—a Villeña—at last. She felt at home here, in the sheltering curve of the Sangre de Cristo . . . and oddly safe. She did not want to leave this pleasant little valley.

That I might remain here forever, she whispered to herself. That I might remain here with you . . . Don Pedro.

On her way back to the Palace her mind was occupied with

219

thoughts and images of what this would be like. They were quiet thoughts, for the most part, little idyls of domestic tranquility and wifely happiness; but sometimes—like those whirling dust-devils that raced across the plains on a still day—a gust of sudden desire swept through her and brought to her face and shoulders a tingling flush that, she was sure, all who passed her must notice.

Arriving home, she took off the black dress she had worn to Mass and put on the silken Chinese robe that the Conde de Vega had once given to the Maya, who in turn had given it to her—worn now, but still beautiful and very comfortable—and sent for second breakfast in her apartment.

Tichi herself brought it, poured the chocolate, and hovered about humming a little song:

> Chula la mañana
> Chula la mañana
> Chula la mañana
> Cuando me salgo a pasear
> Con mi chuparasita

The sense of this ditty was, in general, "How lovely the morning when I go to walk with my hummingbird," and Josefina had long ago recognized it as a signal that the Gallega had something on her mind that ill stood keeping.

"And what is the gossip at the market this morning, Tichi?" she asked casually.

"It is being said that Trinidad Flores has been putting powders in her husband's atole to make him lose interest in his mistress, Miguelita Baca."

"Have they had any effect?" Josefina asked, with a straight face.

"Apparently not, señora. Pablo seems to be as hot after Miguelita as ever. It is suggested by some that Trinidad rub him with a certain paste when they are in bed together. But the only trouble with that, señora, is that Pablo no longer sleeps with Trinidad."

Josefina laughed. "The rumors don't vary much," she said. "They are always about women!"

"Naturally, señora!"

Tichi became silent for a little while, and Josefina waited for the information—whatever it might be—that the Gallega was burning to impart. In due course it came out.

"Rosita was at the market this morning," she remarked. "She said that Don Pedro has returned from Taos."

16

"Love is usually born suddenly and violently," she had read some-where, perhaps in one of the works of Don Miguel Cervantes. "And when it takes possession of a heart, the first thing it does is to banish all fear and all shame. . . ."

Josefina watched a small green lizard skitter across a sunny patch of red earth and vanish beneath a chamiza bush. She tossed a pebble toward the bush, and reflected pensively on Don Miguel's words.

Everybody tries to tell what love is, she said to herself, and some succeed a little. But only a very little.

She glanced back at Negra, who was grazing nearby with loose reins trailing on the ground. Then she looked across the level plain, covered with piñon and juniper, sage and chamiza, and all gold and silver and splashes of deep green in the mid-April sunshine, to where the distant Villa of Santa Fé sprawled in the haze among its cotton-woods. There was nothing but a few stray cattle on the rolling hills between her and the greening fields at the edge of the Villa. A faint expression of disappointment, or perhaps merely impatience, flickered across her face.

Well, it was a hard thing to understand—even though it was so much a very part of oneself: even though it seized one so roughly and cruelly at times that one wanted to cry out in pain. . . . But of one thing she was certain. Don Miguel was right when he said that love banishes shame. For she had brought herself at last to do a thing that the daughter of Eva Helena could never have dreamed of doing. . . .

How many days since Don Pedro went away to Taos? How many since his return? It seemed a small eternity, surely; yet it could not have been so very long. Not more than ten days, really.

Time enough! she said to herself bitterly. You could have managed it, Don Pedro, *had you wished*.

She began to make excuses for him—old excuses now—and to find reasons why it had been quite impossible, after all, for Don Pedro to arrange a rendezvous, to find even a little time with her alone. These excuses and these reasons were necessary for her, for her pride. *For surely he knew*.

She sat up abruptly and searched the rolling hills with eyes that had suddenly become angry. She made a vicious cut with her riding quirt at a sun spider.

"Then where have you been?" she demanded aloud.

Certainly, during the ten days since his return he could have found a time and place to see her—even despite Don Antonio's obvious watchfulness. She had not, she thought with a measure of self-reproach, made that too difficult for him! But the ten days—exactly ten, as precisely counted as a decade of her rosary—had passed like any other days . . . except for what had happened inside her.

'Tonita had come—after tears and threats and cajoleries from both the Sernas and Montoyas—to live at the Palace. She was a sweet, brave child, but there are limits to one's resistance; and the necessity for quieting her fears and bolstering her determination served to divert Josefina's thoughts and energies for a time.

Then Holy Week, the Semana Santa, had arrived; and she strove like a good daughter of the Church to put all thoughts of the world and the flesh out of her mind, and to dedicate herself to meditation on the Lord's passion, and to forget even Don Pedro. She mourned the Saviour's agony before the shrouded altar on Good Friday; and rejoiced in her gayest dress and richest mantilla at His resurrection on Easter Sunday.

La Semana Santa had been for her a week of saving preoccupation with unworldly things; but it had also been a week of peculiar disquiet and difficulty. For strange and sometimes frightening things could take place in depths stirred by the gales of religious fervor . . . and during the Semana Santa one was not quite responsible, perhaps, for all one felt and thought and did.

This was a time when the dirgelike chants of the Penitentes could be heard in the dark canyons of the Sangre de Cristo hills, and the thud of heavy whips on bloody backs. Fainting men crawled and staggered under the load of heavy crosses toward the Calvary where one of them, like Christ Himself, became a living crucifix . . . and like Christ Himself sometimes died.

This was a time when prayer and fasting, and the contemplation of great mysteries and great agonies and great joys, surcharged one's soul with almost unbearable tensions; and religious ecstasies sent out echoes in a thousand different—and sometimes most singular—forms. And it was during this week of vast emotional turmoil all around her, that Josefina's love for Don Pedro became this unremitting, overwhelming passion that left her no instant of peace or calm by day or night.

She was helpless in the grip of her torment. She had for so long accustomed herself to the acceptance of love as simply a condition, no more, of living, a thing to comply with as one complied with the passage of years or the minor whims of fortune, that she could not become used to the astonishing fierceness of her feeling for Don Pedro.

She admonished herself: What of your plan, Josefina—yours and Tafora's? Have you forgotten Tafora completely—what you wrote him?

She smiled wryly at the recollection of what she had written him. How little she had known herself! She threw herself into every sort of activity—those of the Church and the Palace and her own personal life—with an energy that astonished everyone. She ordered a great spring cleaning of the Palace, and became the terror of the servants. She invaded the kitchen, littered her apartment with the paraphernalia of seamstresses, wrote innumerable letters, visited Doña Mercedes, took Negra on long hard rides across the monte.

She who had always been so discreet, began to feel an odd disregard for everything but the drives of her emotions. She had become a little reckless in the fever of her passion for Don Pedro; and, although her face remained a mask of reserve and dignity, her mind and heart were constantly agitated in the most irrational and unpredictable ways. For the first time in her life, she knew the tortures of jealousy.

Who knows what girls he has languishing for him in the pueblos and settlements of the Río Arriba? she thought. Perhaps in this very Villa itself!

She went over in her mind the mestiza girls, and a few of pure Indian blood, who might qualify as his amiga; but she could think of none worthy of him. How, then, about the other settlements he had visited so often—Bernalillo, El Paso, Santa Cruz, Galisteo, Taos . . . ?

"Are you certain," she demanded of Tichi, "that there is no one?"

"There is no one at all, señora," Tichi answered, looking at her thoughtfully, even a little anxiously. "No one, at any rate, who could properly be called a real amiga. I don't know, of course, what small diversions Don Pedro permits himself on his trips about the——"

"Holy Virgin! Have I asked you about that? Get out, Tichi! Leave me!"

She was even jealous of the mistresses Don Pedro had possessed long ago in far-off Durango and Chihuahua and Nueva Vizcaya. When she thought of these women—of Viqui and Chanela and Francisca and María del Carmen Córdoba—she was depressed and miserable; and sometimes when she imagined them in his arms, she was seized with a dark, frightening fury.

So, since Don Pedro's departure for Taos, had passed almost two weeks of storm and torment during which she had often thought of Tafora's aphorism, "It is the doom of every woman to fall in love," and of how well he had, as usual, found words for his wisdom.

At last, without strength or will to prolong the struggle—even, she thought, without shame—she had written a note to Don Pedro, asking him to meet her on the Pecos trail a half hour's fast ride from the Villa. Tichi had delivered the note to Rosita the previous evening; and now, scanning the tawny hills with impatient eyes, Josefina searched for the small moving cloud of dust that would signal his approach.

Surely, she said to herself, he would have sent me word, had he found it impossible to come. . . .

She had been waiting, she judged, for a little more than half an hour—it had been that long since she had heard, very faintly, the church bells announce the end of siesta. The sun had crossed over and beyond the Cerrillos hills where the sacred turquoise mines were, and was spattering gold over the snowy peaks of the Sangre de Cristo range. It was growing late; and she became very restive and even, at last, a little angry. But all these troublesome feelings were swept away in a sudden rush of pleasurable excitement when she saw the looked-for dust cloud moving toward her on the Pecos road.

Ay, caramba! she said to herself, almost exultantly. He is riding very fast, no? That it is a good sign, Josefina!

She was acutely conscious of the accelerated beating of her heart as she produced a hand mirror and a tortoise-shell comb from a saddle-bag and, after removing her French hat, began very carefully to examine the condition of her face and hair.

17

Don Pedro did not dismount.

"At your orders, señora," he said, looking down at her from the back of his big roan stallion. "If you will follow me, por favor."

"But Don Pedro——"

"That you follow me, Doña Josefina. I shall explain afterwards."

He wheeled his mount about and set off at a slow trot in an easterly direction. Vaguely resentful of his peremptory manner, Josefina watched him until he had disappeared over the nearest hill; then, with a bit of mild profanity for Negra, who had become skittish in the presence of Don Pedro's stallion, she swung into the saddle and followed him.

This does not begin exactly as I had planned it! she said to herself wryly.

Don Pedro's course was taking him toward the big canyon called Piedras Negras, or Black Rocks; but just before reaching it he swung sharply northward between two small peaks, the last elevations of any note on the south end of the Sangre de Cristo range. Beyond them, Josefina knew, opened up the wide high valley where, under shelter of the Atalaya Mountain, Don Ramón's ranch lay. She wondered if he were leading her to it.

But suddenly, with a quick backward glance, he disappeared behind a thicket of junipers; and Josefina, touching spurs to Negra, cantered after him into a small box-canyon or, more properly, a kind of pocket under the sheer eastern side of the hill. The junipers and piñons grew thickly here and, with the chamiza bushes, formed a kind of protecting screen; it was a perfect place of concealment. She marveled that he should have known of it.

"A soldier must be familiar with his terrain," he remarked, apparently reading her thoughts. "This is the kind of ambuscade one could never forget."

He helped her to dismount; they loosened saddle girths and secured their horses to a gnarled piñon. Josefina looked about at the steep, rocky sides of their hiding place.

"Whom are we planning to attack from our so-fine ambuscade?" she asked dryly.

Don Pedro ignored her gentle sarcasm.

"I received your note, of course, señora," he said, "but it explained nothing."

Under his outward calm he appeared to be concealing a certain annoyance. Josefina, for her part, experienced a return of the faint resentment she had felt at Don Pedro's very first words, his brusque order to follow him to this hide-away. Between them had sprung up a vague but appreciable barrier of hostility.

Vaya! What passes here? she said to herself. What a fine start! She flashed a sudden smile at Don Pedro. It had the desired effect. He returned her smile—but, she thought, with a certain reserve.

When she had written her note to Don Pedro, she had been unable to think of anything to say but:

> That you do me the favor, señor mío, of meeting me tomorrow afternoon at the end of the siesta on the road to Pecos where it passes El Canyon de las Piedras Negras.
>
> J.

That was all; but it had seemed to her enough. One cannot beg for love, she thought, like asking alms! She had seen women do just that —hidalgas and even marquésas—in shameless little notes. But she had always despised such women. And now, having herself approached very near to their abandon, she was almost morbidly anxious to conceal the nakedness of her passion.

Yet, here was Don Pedro saying, "I have received your note . . . it explained nothing."

No, Don Pedro? she said to herself. I should have thought that it explained everything!

She had hoped that Don Pedro would come to her as a lover—as frankly as, it seemed to her, she had asked him to. But, since he had failed——

Very well, señor! she said to herself. If you are not in the mood to make love to me, we shall go on to other things. She sat down on the sandy banks of a little arroyo and said, almost absently: "If it had been possible for me to tell you more in writing, Don Pedro, I should not have asked you to meet me here in secret. . . . Believe me, it is on a matter of great importance that I wish to talk with you." It made her glad to hear herself say this. These words were an escape for her Spanish pride. They saved her from shamelessness. "It is only for this reason," she added, "that I have asked the favor."

Don Pedro was looking at her with sober and reflective eyes. "Doña Josefina," he said suddenly, "that you permit me, before you go on, to tell you why I have hidden you away in this—this so-fine ambuscade."

"Willingly," she said, wondering.

"I am suspected by Don Antonio."

"But why?" she asked, as if she did not know.

"I think," he said, with a slow smile, "I think His Excellency suspects his lieutenant-general's personal loyalty."

"In what respect, Don Pedro?"

She asked the question with the very slightest exaggeration of innocence. Don Pedro gazed at her with an expression in his dark eyes that she found difficult to analyze. It might have been one of thoughtfulness, or questioning, or even quiet amusement.

"Let us say, Doña Josefina, that His Excellency suspects both of us, and has taken certain measures. As a matter of fact, I have been under surveillance ever since I returned from Taos . . . and I doubt not that you have been watched also."

"He thinks I am unfaithful to him—that you are my lover. And so he is having us watched. How droll, no? And so, Don Pedro——?"

"So I was late in coming here," Don Pedro said, rather lamely. "I had a little trouble in evading my watchers. That also is why I have brought you into this ambuscade."

"Is that also why you have so carefully avoided me all these ten days in the Villa?"

"Yes "

He said this so simply and directly that her heart gave a great thump. She examined with infinite care a tiny snag in her white silk

226

stocking. She asked him, almost gently: "And besides this supposed interest in me, Don Pedro, do you know of any other reason why Don Antonio should have you watched?"

"None, señora."

"Then," Josefina said slowly, "I think I must tell you of the matter . . . of the matter we have come here to talk about."

She sat for a while in silence, arranging her thoughts, studying how best to begin. She was not at all sure what Don Pedro's reaction would be. Now that the time had come to tell him, she was almost frightened: he might be little pleased, indeed, to hear what she and Tafora had undertaken without his permission, even without his knowledge.

How much, she asked herself, dare I tell him of the truth? How much must I lie to him?

This would be a much easier thing to do, she thought, if all had gone as she had planned . . . if it were possible, for example, to talk to him as a woman might to her lover. It would have been much better if——

He broke into her thoughts with a sharp whisper. "Quiet!" he warned. "Take care! Be very quiet, señora!"

18

She heard the faint sound of approaching horsemen. It came from the Pecos Road, the broken, unrhythmic beat of hooves that would be made by a party of searching riders. It came closer—she could hear the tinkle of spurs, a muffled exchange of words, and then the actual creak of saddle leather. Don Pedro glanced apprehensively at their own horses, which had pricked up their ears with curiosity; but they made no sound. The hoofbeats became fainter and disappeared altogether at last in the direction of the big valley to the north. A little dust drifted through the junipers in their wake.

Don Pedro relaxed his grip on his sword and smiled wryly. They both crossed themselves.

"Perhaps they were only Don Ramón's riders," Josefina said.

"Perhaps," Don Pedro shrugged. "But more likely Don Antonio's. . . . This is a *very* fine hiding place, no?"

They both laughed. The tension, so perceptible up to now between them, suddenly eased—as if this brief sharing of danger had broken down some barrier.

"Don Pedro," Josefina said. "Little takes place in México concerning this Kingdom of which I am not well informed . . . even before it happens."

"Everyone is aware of that, Doña Josefina."

"If you will permit me, I should like to ask a question, Don Pedro."

"I am entirely at your orders, señora."

"Would it please you, Don Pedro, to command the Entrada?"

He was plainly surprised, unready for an answer. To gain time, he asked, "The reconnaissance to the Río Jesús María—against the French?"

"Yes, Don Pedro. Would you care to lead it?"

She asked her questions with abrupt directness. She had hoped to discover, not so much by his answers as by his expression, what his secret reactions were. She watched his face closely, but it revealed nothing except a kind of bewilderment.

"I do not understand these questions, señora," he said. "Why do you ask them?"

"I shall tell you afterwards, Don Pedro. But first—would you care to command the Entrada?"

"I am a soldier, Doña Josefina," Don Pedro said, a little stiffly. "I take commands. I obey orders. I have received no order to lead this Entrada."

"But in the event——"

"As a matter of fact," Don Pedro broke in, "Don Antonio has received explicit orders from México to lead this expedition himself."

"Yes, I know."

"Then why do you ask, señora——?"

She smiled, to reassure him, and asked, "What if Don Antonio decides not to lead it?"

"I cannot imagine that," Don Pedro said slowly. "Don Antonio would hardly give up the command. If this Entrada is successful— who knows? Who knows what plum may fall into Don Antonio's lap? New Spain is laden with prizes—Havana, Quito, Popayan, Caracas, Veracruz, Potosí. . . . No, señora, I do not think that Don Antonio will give up the command."

"Don Pedro!" She laughed. "Why do you try to make Don Antonio into something that he is not? The prizes are there, yes. But not for Don Antonio. He is through, done for, finished, no?"

"Who should know better than yourself, Doña Josefina?"

She disregarded an odd tinge of bitterness in this question and pressed him: "What, for example, if the Viceroy should countermand his own order? What if he should relieve Don Antonio of his command and appoint another in his place?"

"But señora, why do we discuss impossibilities?"

She looked at him for a long, steady time, so that her words would carry all their meaning to him unencumbered. She asked:

"Don Pedro, what if he should appoint you?"

"In that unlikely event, señora," he said slowly, "I should, of course, obey the order of his lordship, the Viceroy."

"Against all opposition?"

"Naturally," Don Pedro said. "But no one opposes the Viceroy."

"But Don Antonio might refuse to accept such an order."

"Refuse to accept an order of the Viceroy's?" he asked incredulously.

"Well, evade it, then. I have no doubt that Don Antonio could find some way to do it."

Don Pedro gazed at her in deep and silent contemplation: she could almost feel the press of puzzled thoughts surging through his mind. "That would be a little awkward, señora," he said, almost gently. "But I should find the means to obey His Lordship's commands."

"Ay, Don Pedro!" she sighed. "You have no idea how good your words sound to my ears!"

She leaned back on her stiffened arms, her legs outthrust, and smiled up at him happily. She could imagine that Don Pedro, looking down at her thus, must find her rather tempting. She felt a warm tingle of excitement—almost expectation—spread over her whole body. She watched his eyes change. She dug her fingers into the soft sand on the arroyo bank and whispered to herself: Ay, Josefina mía! That you keep a tight hold on yourself for a little while . . . that you finish first what has to be done, no?

But her face remained a mask. Don Pedro, looking down into her eyes—in which, at this particular time of day, the emerald shadows were deepest and most mysterious—could not have guessed what storm had gathered and broken there while he watched.

"Why have you asked me these questions, Doña Josefina?" he said abruptly.

"You would not understand, Don Pedro," she answered him. "But you *will* understand—no?—that I am not repeating gossip when I tell you this: *You will be given command of the Entrada.*"

She looked at him very closely, to catch some expression of surprise in his face. But he revealed nothing, neither astonishment, nor disbelief, nor exasperation. She could catch not even a flicker of discomposure in his dark eyes. Ah, Pedro mío! she thought. You conceal too much!

"Does Don Antonio know of this?" Don Pedro asked, almost casually.

"No, he does not know. Only one person in this Kingdom knows."

229

"La Dama Josefina?"

"Yes."

"I see," Don Pedro said, and remained silent for a while. "Is it a certainty?"

"Nothing, as you know, Don Pedro, is ever certain in matters of this kind. But it has been . . . it has been arranged. . . ."

"I see," Don Pedro said again.

She drew in her breath sharply. For perhaps the length of an Ave Maria, Don Pedro gazed at her so intently that she squirmed inside herself and thought, Now it comes! Perhaps he will kill me! Then she was on her feet—he had pulled her to her feet—he was grasping her arms—his face was close to hers and he was demanding:

"Tell me, why did you do this?"

"Did I say it was I who did it?"

"Do not lie to me, señora."

"You take a great deal for granted, no?"

"Tell me the truth."

They faced each other silently, belligerently amid the long shadows of the canyon. He shook her gently, but as one might shake a recalcitrant child.

"Tell me," he repeated.

But it was not a threat, as he said it, nor even a demand. It was simply the voice of a soldier and a caballero asking for the truth in a matter that concerned greatly his pride and honor. And all of a sudden Josefina knew that she must give him the answer he had to have.

"All right, Don Pedro," she said softly. "I shall not lie to you. By the Cross! I shall tell you the truth."

She told him everything—all the details of her letter to Tafora, of its dispatch to México, of Don Ramón's and Doña Mercedes's parts in the scheme, even of her anxiety about what Jean L'Archévèque and Don Antonio himself might have discovered. She told him with what dismay she had watched Don Antonio's degeneration into a dismal mass of fatuity, stupidity, lechery, and cruelty. . . .

"I do not think I have done wrong," she finished, almost pensively.

Don Pedro looked at her with what might have been a kind of curiosity—with a puzzlement behind which she could sense the pressure of some stronger, yet tightly reined emotion.

"Did I do so wrong?" she demanded. "Do you condemn me altogether, Don Pedro?"

"I do not condemn you at all, señora," he answered slowly. "But I do not understand you, either. I do not comprehend your reason for doing this—how it could advantage you."

Could he himself be telling the truth now? she wondered. Surely he was only forcing her to say, with her own lips, what she must have already made plain enough—what he already must know. She answered him in a surge of defiant anger.

"Really, Don Pedro? Then I shall tell you! I had planned to gain this command of the Entrada for you. But first I had planned to become your mistress. Now that Don Antonio is finished . . . I had planned to make myself the mistress of the new Governor and Captain-General of New Mexico—Captain Don Pedro Villasur! For my own advantage, no?"

She closed her eyes, having no wish to see his face as she told him this.

"Are you shocked to hear this?" she asked. "Is your pride hurt, Don Pedro—your famous Castilian pride? Do you hate me? Would you like to garrote me with your hands? That you do it then—I do not care."

It was very still in that little canyon. There was no sound except the distant notes of some quail calling to each other in the chamiza bushes. She could hear Don Pedro's breathing; his grasp on her arms tightened.

"But if it will make you feel any better, Don Pedro . . ." she added bitterly.

"Yes, señora," he said after a long time.

"Since I have hidden nothing else from you," she said, opening her eyes and forcing a mirthless little smile. "I shall tell you this also:

"I did not love you then, Don Pedro, but now I love you with all my soul . . . I cannot endure my torment any longer . . . I cannot live without at least a memory of your love, Don Pedro. . . . That you take me, if only for an hour. . . ."

There is no language in the world that has so many love-words as the Spanish. But Josefina heard none of them from Don Pedro. She felt, instead, the sudden, fierce encirclement of his arms, and his mouth on hers; she felt all her senses rushing away from her; she was weak and deliciously empty—and all at once, it seemed to her pounding heart, drained sweet and clean of all the dark and frightful memories of her years. . . .

The moon was rising over the sierra, a thin waning moon of a peculiar blueness that shed hardly any light over the monte, when Don Pedro readied the horses for the ride back to the Villa. Josefina sat with her arms about her knees, watching his tall, shadowy figure adjusting the saddle girths. His movements were sure and workmanlike, and performed with a sort of military precision. She followed them with her eyes and she was vaguely aware of a kind of languid feeling of hostility toward Don Pedro—a half-wish that he would ride away and leave her there alone.

231

When they heard horsemen pass the mouth of the little canyon—Don Antonio's men returning, no doubt—she felt secure and indifferent; but when the hoofbeats had died away and all was quiet again, she said to Don Pedro, "It is impossible for us to return to the Villa together at this hour, no? That you take me to Los Álamos, amor. I can pass the night with Doña Mercedes."

"As you wish, querida. Your horse is ready."

How matter-of-fact his voice sounded, she thought, just as if nothing had happened! But when she came over to mount Negra he took her suddenly, roughly, in his arms; and Josefina, crushed and struggling for breath, discovered that she was weeping violently, almost convulsively against his breast.

"What is the matter?" he asked anxiously. "Why are you weeping, querida?"

"I don't know, amor," she said, smiling wanly. "But when I do, I weep good, no?"

He dried her face with his handkerchief and kissed her damp eyes.

"It is not good to weep too often," she said, "but when you do, weep hard!"

"Who said that, mi vida?"

"The Maya."

He looked down at her with inquiring eyes, but she did not bother to explain to him who the Maya was. She asked him—as if all at once this had become the most important question ever asked—something that she had not dared to ask directly, yet must be answered directly . . . something she could not live without knowing.

"I suppose," she said, "I weep because I love you, Pedro mío . . . Do you love me also?"

"More than my life, querida."

"Say it."

"I love you, Josefina mía . . . more than my own life."

The moon had risen very high above the sierra, almost to the zenith of the cloud-flecked sky, when they started, riding slowly side by side, up the broad valley that led to Los Álamos.

19

"La luna de miel," they called it in Old Spain, and also here in New Mexico: the moon of honey, the month of sweetness. But for Josefina, her "luna de miel," the enchanting month of May, promised to be

only a time of difficulties and frustrations, and those maddening periods of separation and longing that are the special cross of secret lovers.

Where and how to meet Don Pedro were two questions that filled
her mind all day long and haunted her fitful sleep at night. A week
passed, an endless stretch of days during which she caught only occasional glimpses of Don Pedro and exchanged no more than a few
words with him—polite, smiling words, always in the presence of
others, that drove her frantic while she spoke them.

For Don Antonio, to whom the art of spying was not unfamiliar,
marked every move of his mistress and his lieutenant-general with the
thoroughness of a Torquemada. He was, in fact, too thorough: he left
no doubt of his suspicions. Don Pedro warned Josefina of this in
notes he managed to pass to her through the hands of Tichi and
Rosita.

"It is plain that he suspects everything," he wrote her, "but as yet
he knows nothing. We must give him no proof, my darling. Until the
proper time arrives we must be discreet, even though discretion is
torture. You understand this, my soul, do you not?"

"Ah, so! You lecture me! You do not love me!" she cried, tearing
that particular note into little shreds. "I think you even welcome Don
Antonio's watchfulness. You are so brave in war, they say: then why
are you not brave in love also? Why don't you risk a little for me,
brave Captain Villasur?"

For an instant she hated Don Pedro. She hated him for his devotion
to duty. For his sense of honor. For his pride in his profession of
arms. . . . Were these of more weight with him than their love?
Which did he love best: Josefina or glory? Madre de Dios! Why did
she rack herself with such thoughts? He was right, surely . . . she
was more than a little mad. But she replied:

> Much desired:
> For me, alas, there is neither discretion nor rashness any more. There
> is only my love for you, beloved. Yet I would not have you harmed
> by any imprudence of my heart. I shall do all that you charge me to do,
> my life, my soul: I am what you will. I shall strive to endure yet another
> day without you. But God grant us soon to enjoy our love. Adiós, my
> all.

Then Don Antonio decided to inject a certain note of refinement
into the torture he was inflicting—and quite successfully, he suspected
—on Josefina. He gave a dinner, intimate, but very formal, to which he
invited only Jean L'Archévèque and his young wife, Manuela, Fray
Juan Tagle, and Captain Villasur.

"For our closest friends, eh?" he said, smiling owlishly at Josefina.
"Only our very closest."

For this little dinner Don Antonio had set forth the best of every-

233

thing—he could not have honored a Viceroy more. His choicest silver, massive and beautiful, bearing the Mexican mark and his own coat of arms, gleamed in the candlelight. The rarest delicacies of the Palace larder and Panchita's art filled the long, narrow table: a great turkey stuffed with piñon nuts, a roast of mutton, little meat balls seasoned with herbs and saffron, fine white Spanish bread, dried pumpkin, apple rings, frijoles, a dulce of brandy and fruit syrups, stirred constantly for three days over the coals. And Don Antonio's own red wine of El Paso glowed like half a dozen great rubies in crystal glasses. At such a board one could forget, for a little while at least, the poverty and misery of the lonely and always fearful Kingdom of New Mexico!

"His Majesty," Don Antonio proposed. "May God keep him!"

Don Antonio was behaving very well tonight. He was affable and gracious and, sitting solidly at the head of his table in heavy-jowled complacence, he looked almost benign—except perhaps for the quick glances that his pale eyes darted occasionally at Josefina and at Don Pedro who was seated at her right.

After the appearance of the meats, the conversation of the guests settled down to serious matters—particularly the dire state of affairs in Spain—reported in letters and newspapers by the latest mail from México. The ruinous inflation still raged there; poverty was profound; there were no morals any more. The palace was full of Frenchmen, and French philosophy had followed on the high heels of French fashions. The queen still ruled Philip—who, it was rumored, was a little "bewitched"—with an iron bit, and was dragging Spain into a whole series of costly adventures in order to obtain Italian dominions for her sons.

All murmured at the Motherland's sad plight. Even the arts and all intellectual life, it appeared, were dead. There were no painters in Spain any more. The only writers were plagiarists. The theater was like a wilted flower, or a bright fire burned to ashes.

"But there appears to be one bright spot," Fray Juan Tagal said. "The actress they call La Portuguesita."

They all knew of her. She was talked of wherever Spanish was spoken.

"She earns twenty thousand gold reales a year!"

"It is said that she bathes every day—and in cow's milk laced with frangipani."

"I have heard she is very beautiful, takes snuff, and swears like a trooper."

"She is the king's mistress."

"Nonsense. If she were the king's mistress she would have to enter

234

a convent when he was through with her. Portuguesita is too clever to let *that* happen!"

"At any rate, everybody seems to agree that she is a great actress," Fray Juan said. "The finest to appear on the Spanish stage since the one they called the Maya."

"The Maya . . . !"

Hearing the Maya's name spoken thus suddenly and casually, a thousand memories rushed at Josefina out of the dead and secret years. She paled slightly—so slightly none could have guessed the fleeting tumult behind her serene and thoughtful eyes.

"Did you ever see the Maya?" Manuela L'Archévèque asked her.

"Many times, my child."

"Is it true—what they say of her?"

"Much is true, much is lies. But it was all the same to Manuela Maya. She was too great to care."

"One often wonders what becomes of such a one as the Maya at last."

Fray Juan shrugged. "They very commonly wind up in the hospicio."

"On the contrary," Don Pedro said, speaking for the first time. "In the case of the Maya, at least, there is no question of the poorhouse."

"No, señor?" Josefina asked quietly, her heart thumping.

"No, Doña Josefina. My friend Captain Luis Valdez, whom I saw at Nueva Vizcaya and who had just returned from Old Spain, told me that the Maya is now Her Excellency the Condesa de Vega and mistress of a palace with seventeen patios in Madrid. The whole Capital was talking about it."

"The Capital was ever talking about the Maya," Josefina said absently. "But how good!"

"What did you say, my dear?" Don Antonio asked loudly from the opposite end of the table. "What was that?"

Josefina was suddenly aware of the scrutiny of his pale, sharp eyes. She doubted that he had missed much with those eyes, or with his ears either, during his apparent preoccupation with the roasts.

"I only said," she answered quietly, "how good that God has granted such happiness at last to Doña Manuela Maya."

"Yes, yes." Don Antonio nodded, waving a morsel of mutton on the point of his knife. "The Maya is lucky. Her kind usually ends up in the poorhouse . . . or first the streets and then the poorhouse, no?"

Josefina, sitting very erect and gazing at Don Antonio with suddenly enormous eyes, smiled ever so faintly and said nothing.

"Well, my dear," Don Antonio insisted genially, "what do you say? You are a Castellana. Who should be better able to inform us poor

235

provincials about these things? Is it true, what our good Fray Juan has observed about these fine sluts of the theater?"

"Why do we discuss such depressing matters at your so-pleasant dinner, Antonio?" she asked evenly. "Let us talk about something gayer."

"Very well," Don Antonio said doggedly. "But let us continue to talk about the theater—about actresses and dancers. What subject could be gayer?"

"I agree!" Manuela L'Archévèque exclaimed innocently. "Tell us some more, Captain Villasur. What other news did your friend bring from Spain?"

"Did he," Don Antonio asked carelessly, "did he mention, by any chance, one called La Sola?"

"She was a dancer, no?" Don Pedro asked after a little reflection. "And a tonadilla singer?"

"A long time ago," Don Antonio said.

"Yes," Don Pedro said. "Captain Valdez spoke of La Sola also. As you say, Don Antonio, it was a long time ago that she created a sensation in Madrid. But she is still remembered in the Capital. She must have been much woman!"

Such a sudden and immoderate outburst of laughter exploded from Don Antonio's food-crammed mouth that all regarded him with amazement and distaste.

"What happened to her, Captain?" he pressed. "Did La Sola also marry a count?"

"She disappeared," Don Pedro said. "She vanished at the height of her triumph. They still talk of it in Madrid. Some say she was an enemy of the regime—a spy for the Coalition. She is thought to have fled from Spain with a price on her head."

"How sad!" Manuela L'Archévèque sighed. "What a pity!"

"Not at all, my child," Don Antonio remonstrated mildly. "If she was guilty of treason, she should be punished, no? The garrote for traitors to the Crown!"

"This was a long time ago, Excellency," Don Pedro suggested gently.

"That is true," Don Antonio agreed. "But in Spain they do not forget. Neither do they forgive. One day—if she is still alive—La Sola will be taken. And when that day comes . . ."

Don Antonio grasped his throat with his left hand and with the right made a vigorous twisting motion, at the same time uttering an odd strangling sound. This was followed by a heavy silence, which was broken at last by Don Antonio's voice asking just a little thickly, "But what does Doña Josefina think? What do you say, my dear?"

Josefina, who had never taken her eyes from Don Antonio during all this talk about La Sola, smiled faintly and in a low, clear voice that seemed devoid of any emotion except perhaps a little boredom, said, "You are right, of course, Antonio. I doubt not that . . . even after this long time . . . the Crown would be happy to give La Sola to the garrote."

"Eh? What, my dear?" Don Antonio exclaimed.

"And, also," Josefina added softly, "and also, Antonio mío, *those who helped her to flee from Spain. . . .*"

"Yes, yes, of course," Don Antonio said hurriedly, draining his goblet at a gulp. "Death to conspirators! Damnation to all enemies of the Spains!"

"Precisely," Josefina said quietly. "And, if what I have heard of La Sola is true, she can be depended on to take care of herself . . . against any who might think to betray her, no?"

A strange, uncomfortable quiet settled down on Don Antonio's table. None there knew exactly the source of a certain feeling of embarrassment, but all experienced it. Don Antonio fell suddenly silent, gazing at his guests with melancholy eyes. Josefina laughed and made a little grimace of reproach at Manuela L'Archévêque.

"Do you see, Manuelita?" she said. "We begin with talking about the theater and end up with the garrote. Let us avoid this subject and talk about something else—about the weather, for instance."

"You are quite right, my dear," Don Antonio said. His gaze shifted to Josefina and Don Pedro, and his face took on the meditative, melancholy look that Josefina had learned to hate and fear.

What is going on behind those eyes? she thought. It is not very hard to guess! How he must be enjoying himself!

Here she was, so close to Don Pedro that she could press his knee with hers beneath the table. So close that a turn of her body could have carried her into his arms. Yet there was this wall between them —this wall of empty words and polite smiles that Don Antonio had so cunningly erected. . . . And how he watched them!

Don Antonio's gaze dissolved suddenly into a baleful glare. The pale eyes became as hard and cold as moonstones beneath half-lowered lids.

"You are quite right, Josefina mía," he repeated. "Let us talk about the weather, then. About the beautiful season of spring. The season of hope and youth . . . and of love, eh?"

He raised his glass; and all at the table, as if impelled by the intensity of his gaze, turned their eyes toward Josefina and Don Pedro.

"And let us drink," Don Antonio said suddenly in a kind of savage growl, *"to lovers in the springtime."*

A long silence followed Don Antonio's toast, and after that the conversation lagged dismally. As soon as the guests had left, Josefina returned to her apartment, closed the door, and turned the key in the great lock.

She walked restlessly about the room as she removed her jewelry, undid her hair, and began to take off her clothes. The doll Yolanda, she noticed, was not in exactly her accustomed place beside the hearth; whoever had cleaned the apartment that day had been careless.

Josefina picked Yolanda up. She kissed her china cheek and straightened her dress. A long time ago—although she did not remember it now—a child standing before a tiny shop in Ávila had kissed this doll and straightened its dress exactly so. She replaced Yolanda in her niche and paced about the room as she unfastened her bodice.

"Well, at any rate, Josefina," she said aloud, "now you know how matters stand! . . . That only some word would come from Tafora!"

The next morning she fled to Los Álamos for a long visit with Doña Mercedes, whose cheerful company she had so often before sought in times of disquiet and depression.

20

At Los Álamos she had little to occupy her time except long conversations with her hostess and an occasional ride over Don Ramón's ranch. In a great chest with an iron lock there were a few books—including some forbidden novels Don Ramón had smuggled in from México—but Josefina was little inclined to read.

Her mind was restless and preoccupied, for the most part, with only two subjects: Don Pedro, who was never wholly out of her thoughts, and Mateo, who had taken the letter to Tafora. And more and more Mateo pushed even Don Pedro out of her meditations.

She had seen him only once, and then for but a few minutes. He was still to her a kind of figure in a dream. Tafora had picked him for all the qualities he would require in such a man—courage, toughness in the saddle, sobriety, loyalty—and Tafora's judgment was never wrong. But it was not easy to dismiss from her mind all the dangers that threatened a man traveling alone on every league of that endless journey to the City of México. Even Tafora could do nothing about the Comanches and the other savage tribes that infested the provinces to the south; or that dread Journey of Death below Socorro; or the unpredictable disasters of fate and weather. She sought to reassure herself on each of them. Then, losing patience with herself, she said angrily: "Vaya, vaya, Josefina! Why do you wear yourself out with such useless fretting? That you pray for Mateo—and let him take care of himself!"

So, by a considerable effort of the will, she did succeed in shaking off this near-obsession, praying every day in Doña Mercedes's chapel to San Cristóbal, the patron saint of travelers, for Mateo's protection. But, as the days at Los Álamos passed, she could not prevent her mind from speculating, with an ever-growing anxiety, on the date of Mateo's return.

There was so little time, really! It frightened her to think how little. Fifty-five days had passed since Mateo left—she had counted every one of them! He should be back in the first week of June. . . . Just in time . . . or too late, maybe! The Entrada was scheduled to leave the Capital at the beginning of the second week. But Don Antonio was always tardy in his departures: she could almost depend on some hitch in this one, carefully as Don Pedro had prepared it. And she had allowed an over-generous time for Mateo, perhaps, to make the journey.

Madre de Dios! she thought miserably. What a fool I was to wait so long!

The week she had planned to spend with Doña Mercedes lengthened quickly into a visit of ten days. Except for such anxious thoughts as these about Mateo, she found it a time of delightful quiet and rest . . . and then of such happiness as she had never dared to imagine for herself, with Don Pedro.

For Don Pedro, once he had learned their identity, had found it somewhat less than difficult to seduce Don Antonio's spies from their duty. Now he rode out to Los Álamos whenever he pleased without danger of compromising either himself or Josefina. And he was an enormously welcome guest at Don Ramón's big estancia.

Don Ramón himself was a Spaniard, a native of New Castile; but he had been brought to México at such an early age that he could remember little of his boyhood—only enough to whet an almost insatiable interest in all that pertained to Old Spain. And it was his delight to sit at table in his sala, or before a quiet fire, and silently listen to Don Pedro and Josefina talk about the strange and wonderful and sometimes shocking modes of Spanish life, particularly in Madrid.

"Do you suppose, Doña Josefina, there is a woman of fashion in the Capital who doesn't have at least one cortejo?"

"I doubt it, Don Pedro! Even while I was in Madrid, it was a kind of scandal for a woman to love her own husband—or, at least, to acknowledge it publicly. I have heard that things are even worse now."

239

"Things must have changed greatly since my father's time," Don Ramón said sadly. "It was not a husband's habit in his day to allow his wife to be courted."

"They have changed, Don Ramón," Josefina agreed. "And, I think, not for the better!"

"Has no one any respect for the old ways?"

"A few, Don Ramón. In Madrid there are some women the Madrileños call beatas. They are so good and pious that they are afraid to be seen with their own husband—for fear he might be thought a lover!"

"As for me," Doña Mercedes said dryly, "I should prefer the courte-jada to the beata!"

And so they might talk, as did all colonials remembering Spain of the Great Days, about the dismaying breakdown of morals and the old Spanish virtues in the Motherland: the shocking disrespect which, it was reported, many people were showing for the holy images and even the Blessed Sacrament carried in the processions; the scandalous trade in billets of confession from which even common courtesans were enriching themselves; the ignorance of scholars, the lechery of churchmen, the foppishness of the king's officers, the depravity, even, of modern mothers who refused to nurse their own babies but sent them instead to wet-nurses from the Pas. . . .

But more often their talk recalled pleasant scenes and events: the simple everyday remembrances of life in Spain, so dear to their exiles' hearts.

"You remember the Prado, Doña Josefina—when all Madrid would be promenading on a hot night?"

"But of course, Don Pedro. Green hazelnuts! Fresh water from the Recoletos! Fresh chick-peas—just in the best style!"

She imitated with startling and vastly amusing accuracy the cries of the vendors, the pleas of the beggars for alms, the argot of the courtesans. And Don Ramón, sitting beside his fire of fragrant piñon logs, could almost feel himself in the soft darkness of that great park of the Prado, where veiled women darted glances from behind their fans at caballeros in long black cloaks, where Madreliñas met their cortejos, and a passing girl might borrow a guitar from a blind musician and play a seguidillas.

"God give us to see it before we die!" he said.

But he said it without hope. There were few in that lonely Kingdom of grudging land and cruel skies who really hoped. Many dreamed, and some even made vague plans; but almost no one ever returned to Spain.

Nor shall I, Josefina thought. I cannot.

21

Josefina looked up at the rosy lights and shadows the fire was throwing on the gessoed ceiling. What a pleasant room, she thought, and how wonderful to be sharing it in love and tenderness with Don Pedro . . . in love and tenderness and the security of Los Álamos's shielding walls.

Through the little grilled window high above the great bed—surely the most luxurious in the whole Kingdom of New Mexico, where beds of any sort were rare—there drifted the faint strumming of a guitar, and a low voice singing in the soft spring night the old ballad of unfaithful Elena.

> "Pero qué tienes, Fernando? Tú nunca
> vienes así;
> Tienes amores en Francia y quieres otra
> más que a mí."

Eyes closed, she smiled to hear the ancient words voicing the ancient doubts. . . . *But what is the matter, Fernando? You were never like this. You have a sweetheart in France. You love another more than me!* . . . Suddenly, opening her eyes wide, she demanded: "Was she beautiful, this Viqui?"

"Who, querida?" Don Pedro asked vaguely.

"Viqui. The one with the spectacles and six pairs of red shoes."

"Ah, yes . . . Viqui . . . Viqui . . ."

"Viqui . . . Viqui . . . !" she mocked him. "As if you have forgotten her, Pedro!"

As often as she had thought of Don Pedro's former amigas: Chanela, who loved sherbets; and Francisca, who read novels and tried to poison Don Pedro; and María del Carmen Córdoba, the hellcat; and this Viqui, who had been with him for so long in Durango and Chihuahua . . . she had never before asked Don Pedro about them; and now, when she did, she was angry, and ashamed of her anger, but could not help it.

"No, I haven't forgotten her," Don Pedro said slowly.

"Was she beautiful?"

"Yes, querida."

"More beautiful—than I?"

"Nobody is more beautiful than you, querida—nor half as beautiful."

"But this Viqui——" she insisted.

"She is no longer beautiful at all," Don Pedro said. "And when she ceased to be beautiful, she went away . . . I have never learned where."

"Ay, Dios!" she cried, suddenly remembering what Tichi had told her about Viqui and the smallpox. "I am sorry, amor!"

She asked Don Pedro no more about his mistresses after that. But she inquired subtly into many other matters pertaining to his childhood and his early manhood in Spain, and she learned much—more, perhaps, than Don Pedro actually wished to divulge.

She learned that he was a second son of a Castilian nobleman, a knight of the order of Santiago, whose estate included grain fields, olive orchards, and pasture lands in the vicinity of Salas de los Infantes worth sixty thousand reales a year. But from all this wealth, young Pedro de Villasur could hope for nothing. He was a segundón, a second son, and his only hope lay between an ecclesiastical career and the profession of arms. So he had chosen, without much hesitation, the latter. And after an honorable career in Europe, it had brought him at last to New Spain . . . to New Mexico . . . to her.

As an officer of the regular army he had a good and honorable record. This much, with a professional soldier's honest pride, Don Pedro was willing to claim for himself. The rest Josefina gathered from many sources. He was more able than his own word made him out to be. In 1718 he was already a lieutenant-colonel of the king's forces in New Mexico. He was, all said, a thorough-going soldier, a capable if not a brilliant officer, and a brave fighter at close quarters. European-trained, he was perhaps well in advance of most of the military men in New Spain. But some asked the question: "What, after all, does Captain Villasur know about Indian warfare?"

Sometimes, with the very slightest of misgivings, and thinking of what she had written to Tafora, Josefina asked herself this same question. Then she would remember those famous Indian fighters, Captains Naranjo and Olguín, who would accompany the Entrada, and her anxieties would vanish.

Besides, she would reassure herself, it is not a campaign, this Entrada. It is only a reconnaissance, no? There will surely be no fighting. . . .

So, sitting beside the fire and having wine and cakes at bedtime, or lying quietly at each other's side, they talked—but always with a curious reserve—about that distant time before either of them had come to the Kingdom of New Mexico. Don Pedro, with a natural reticence, told little; Josefina, for other reasons, revealed even less about herself.

"Tell me, querida," Don Pedro said to her abruptly one evening. "When you were in Madrid——"

"Yes, amor?"

"How did you happen to know this one they called the Maya so well?"

"I was her protégée."

"You were in the theater?"

"Yes, amor."

"What were you called?"

"I was called," she lied, "La de los Ojos Verdes."

She offered no more about her life in Madrid; and he did not press her for more. They asked very little about each other in the form of direct questions; and when they were asked, the answers were likely to be terse and almost impersonal.

"Why have you never married, Pedro?" she asked him once.

"There are several reasons, perhaps," he said slowly. "When I was young, it was not fashionable for a segundón to marry, particularly a soldier, no? How, for example, could a young lieutenant of cavalry hope to support a wife who paid six reales a day to her hairdresser and ten pesos for a pair of shoes that might last only three days?"

"Was there such a one?"

Don Pedro shrugged his shoulders very slightly and did not answer. "It was a long time ago," his silence seemed to say. "She is forgotten."

"And afterwards—after you came to México?"

"I don't know, querida," he said. "Perhaps it is that marriage is a kind of habit: one that, for certain reasons I have mentioned, I had never fallen into. Or possibly . . ."

"Yes, amor?"

"Possibly I take this business of marriage too seriously."

"Yes, you have the old Spanish ideas of everything. They are difficult enough to live by, even in Spain nowadays. In this part of the world—it is hopeless, I think."

"In this part of the world," Don Pedro said slowly, "a Spaniard can still remember that he is a Spaniard. He may even try to live as one."

"And to marry as one?"

"Perhaps."

Ah, so there it is, Pedro mío! she thought. That is the real reason, at last, why you have not married! You must have a Spaniard bride, no less. A Castellana, no? . . . like the one of the ten pesos shoes. And they are not so easy to find in New Spain, alas . . . At least you have not found yours, poor Pedro!

She mused for a little while on this new and intriguing sidelight on

Don Pedro's character—on what she could only think of as his Hispanidad: his intense and implacable Spanishness. But she never returned to this particular subject, nor did he.

22

So ten days passed at Los Álamos, days made heavy by an ever-growing anxiety about Mateo, yet quite the happiest Josefina had ever known. She loved Don Pedro Villasur tenderly and joyfully; and sometimes she loved him wantonly and asked him, teasingly, in that phrase the Governor had made so famous throughout his Kingdom: "Ya estoy buena?"

The eleventh day brought shattering news to Los Álamos.

Don Ramón returned in the evening from Bernalillo, where he had been to get some apricot trees for his orchard, tired and grave. After a glass of brandy, he asked Josefina into the little room he used as a kind of office, closing the door even on Doña Mercedes. She waited a long and agonizing time, it seemed to her, for him to speak; for she had no doubt that what he had to tell her would not be good.

"My child," Don Ramón said at last, "I don't know why you sent Mateo to México. My obligation to Don José Tafora consists only in providing a means of sending to him whatever messages you may wish to send. It is not my business to know—or even to wonder about—what the messages contain."

"Nombre de Dios!" she cried. "What has happened?"

"But it was impossible for me not to surmise," Don Ramón continued with maddening deliberation, "that his last errand was one of some importance. Now, alas, my surmise is confirmed."

"He is lost!"

Don Ramón, who was all a Spaniard in his inability to come directly to the point, to make a simple declarative statement, suddenly abandoned this circumlocution. He said, in a manner brutally frank for him:

"It is my sad office, my child, to tell you that Mateo never got beyond Bernalillo on his journey south. He was discovered only a few days ago, on the Camino Real . . . or all, it must be said, that remained of him. . . ."

She heard only dimly the rest of what Don Ramón was saying. She sat quietly erect and listened with a composure that Don Ramón marvelled at; but she heard him oddly as a voice far away and in-

244

distinct. Then one sentence came out of the confusion of words, clear and sharp.

"He had been struck from behind—perhaps as he slept—and his skull was crushed: but he had not been scalped."

"I see, Don Ramón," she said, remembering with sudden and astonishing clarity the horseman she had glimpsed that day of Mateo's departure, that mysterious rider hurrying ahead of her between the hills toward the Villa. "That you had been spared, Don Ramón, the burden of bringing me this sad news. . . ."

23

She did not return alone to the Villa. Don Ramón insisted on sending one of his vaqueros with her. But she was unmindful of his presence, even though he remained close beside her; she had no room in her mind or senses for anything but the matter of Mateo's loss . . . of Mateo's murder.

Spring had come at last in real earnest to the valley of the Río Grande. The whole world vibrated with the fresh, clear colors of spring: the crystal turquoise of the sky, the virgin white of the gleaming sierra, the incredibly fresh, young green of the cottonwoods. The peach and apple trees were all in bloom on the verdant milpas. The Río de Santa Fé and every small arroyo and all the ditches, mother and daughter, were running gaily with the clear cold water of melted snows. Birds sang and the vaquero riding beside Josefina sang also:

"Graceful swallow, do me this favor:
Carry this letter to the lady I love."

But Josefina heard neither the vaquero's song nor that of the birds. Everything that Don Ramón had told her—all that had seemed so indistinct and far away as he spoke—was coming back to her now, curiously sharp and clear. And she sickened a little as she recalled it.

That Mateo had been murdered—and not by Indians—could not be doubted. One might have suspected the Comanches, whose entrada from the plains to the Río Grande settlements was near Bernalillo and who had been troublesome of late, except that he had not been scalped.

Nor was there much doubt why he had been killed—while he slept, Don Ramón said. All his gear was missing; but his bones still were clothed. And beside his body, opened and empty, lay the buckskin case in which the letter to Tafora had been carried.

Madre de Dios, she said to herself, with a certain bitterness. How unkindly you have answered my prayers!

But she wasted little thought on the destruction of her plans. What could it profit her to brood over a scheme so completely wrecked? Yet one could—one must—think ahead. What of herself—what now was in store for La Dama Josefina?

She used this term, ironically, for herself: it had carried, for everyone in the Kingdom, such a fine connotation of status and dignity . . . and security. What would it signify now? Even Don Ramón, it was quite clear, was anxious for her now: else why this armed vaquero at her side? From whom was he protecting her? Could it indeed be possible——?

Nombre de Dios! she said to herself incredulously. He would not dare!

Certainly, she had too many friends in México—too many powerful patrons—to make that risk likely. Yet, how far away from México was the Villa of Santa Fé! And what unlikely things could happen there! Had not even the great Vargas, the Reconquistador himself, been thrown into the Palace dungeon for three whole years by that infamous scoundrel, the Governor Cubero? There was little limit, indeed, to the power of a governor and captain-general . . . and was it not always possible for an accident to happen?

Josefina shrugged and rode at an easy trot toward the Villa. She was possessed by a curious indifference to what her fate might be at Don Antonio's hands. She crossed the milpas, passed the chapel of San Miguel, and rode over the bridge into the Villa. Don Ramón's vaquero saluted and silently left her. She touched Negra with her quirt and put on a defiant little display of horsemanship as her mount pranced and curvetted onto the Plaza.

It was the hour of siesta. The long parade was almost deserted, the Palace darkened and devoid of any sign of life. In her own apartment—how cool and quiet and peaceful it was!—almost no light penetrated the shuttered window. She crossed over to undo the shutters: to give herself the somewhat ironical pleasure of seeing again the familiar forms and colors of this room that had come to mean so much to her . . . that she had wished never to leave. . . .

Then, her eyes growing accustomed to the near-darkness, she was aware that something . . . that someone was occupying her bed. She wrenched open the shutters and whirled about to find María, her tawny body dark against the disheveled bedclothes, sitting up and blinking at her in sleepy perplexity.

246

"Perra! Perra muerte!" Josefina said in a low, chilling voice. "Bitch! Dead dog!"

All of a sudden the slave girl appeared to come to a terrified realization of her situation. Without a sound, she scrambled from the bed and dashed toward the door. Josefina thrust herself into the intervening space. She raised her rawhide riding quirt and lashed downward. She flailed the cowering girl's naked back. Again and again, with all her force, she struck in silent, icy earnest.

"Pido Dios!" María moaned in her barbaric Spanish. "In God's name, señora!"

She crowded herself into a corner, covering her head with her arms. But neither her moans nor the sight of her blood had any effect on Josefina's blinding fury. Only the weariness of her arm, at last, brought an end to the blows.

"Get out!" she said, breathing hard. "Get out! And show the streaming of your filthy blood to Don Antonio!"

With amazing alacrity, María snatched up her clothes, scurried through the door and slammed it behind her. Josefina hurled her quirt against the wall. Only slowly a sense of reality, of familiarity with things around her, returned. She raised her arm to the wall and leaned her head against it. Then, for the first time since she was a very little girl, and this same thing had happened to her in the cold, empty church of San Segundo in Ávila, she was wretchedly and desperately ill.

A little later Tichi came into the room. "Ah, Doña Josefina!" she cried. "You are really back. I heard your horse come into the patio——"

Then she saw her mistress clearly, sitting on one of the red-lacquered Andalusian chairs, her face very pale, her eyes frightening.

"Holy Virgin!" Tichi whispered. "What is the matter, Doña Josefina? You are sick. That you lie on the bed, señora mía . . ."

A little shudder seemed to disturb the strange rigidity of Josefina's body. She closed her eyes and said, "No, Tichi."

"Please, señora!" Tichi begged, taking her arm. "That you lie down for a little while."

Josefina wrenched herself away. She directed a swift, horrified glance at the rumpled bed. She said, almost sharply, "I do not *wish* to lie down, Tichi. . . . Bring me some water."

After she had bathed her face in the cool water Tichi brought in a silver basin, they went into the patio and sat on one of the benches beneath the portal. It was very pleasant and peaceful there. The great lilac bush was a fountain of fresh spring green; the tamarisk tree had already decked itself with delicate heliotrope fronds; gilded pigeons fluttered about the dovecote. Josefina breathed deeply of the fragrant, delicious air and let the tranquility of the lovely little square seep into her agitated soul. She reached out and placed her hand over Tichi's.

"Do you remember Málaga?" she asked abruptly. "When we ate the snails off the walls?"

"Very well, Doña Josefina. I have never cared much for snails since."

"Well, let us hope that we shall never see anything like that again. But we must prepare ourselves for difficult days, Tichi."

Tichi showed no curiosity, expressed no surprise. She merely laughed and said, "You do not have to tell me, señora!"

Her laugh gave Josefina sudden new courage. She knew there was little she would have to explain to Tichi.

"Where is Don Pedro?" she asked.

"He has gone to Taos. Something to do with the Entrada."

"And Don Antonio?"

"He has gone to Taos also, with Don Pedro."

Josefina fell silent. It frightened her to think that Don Pedro, still utterly ignorant of all that had happened, unaware of what Don Antonio must have found out, had gone on that lonely journey to Taos with Valverde and his henchmen.

"Who else went with them?" she asked.

"Only Captain Naranjo, señora."

Her apprehension lessened. If the doughty captain—her friend, surely, and Don Pedro's—were along, she really had nothing to fear. Yet . . . who could know what might happen at Taos—what accident might befall there? She would feel much easier in her mind when Don Pedro was safe again at—she almost said "at home."

But her uneasiness grew as the days passed and the Month of Mary drew toward its close. It would have been even greater had there not been so many other things to occupy her time and thoughts.

Among these was a shocking new concern about 'Toñita.

Several weeks before, Tichi had pointed out how strangely the lovelorn little mestiza had been acting—almost as if afraid of something she dare not mention to anyone—and then had hinted all else she wished to say in two words: "Don Antonio."

Josefina had reproached herself often for not having spoken with 'Toñita about this. But something, perhaps her preoccupation with so many other problems, perhaps the very distastefulness of the subject, had caused her to put it off. Now, with Don Antonio away, she put it off again.

'Toñita herself appeared more cheerful, even hopeful. Neither her family nor Rafael's had proved troublesome. Her time of meditation would be over at last—soon she could leave her "neutral home" and marry Rafael. It would not be long, no? The prospect cheered and inspirited her. She sewed beautiful china poblana dresses for Josefina, and embroidered lovely colchas, and smiled with her soft brown eyes . . . and seemed to have forgotten about Don Antonio.

So Josefina, taking the easy course in the maze of her own heavy problems, had put the matter of 'Toñita aside: yet it was never quite out of her mind, and it never quite ceased to perturb her. She had come to feel more than a mere sense of responsibility for 'Toñita. The gentle mestiza's marriage—the absolute necessity of that marriage— had acquired a kind of mystical significance for herself, Josefina. What hidden yearnings of her own heart might have been behind this strange and powerful compulsion, she did not know. She only knew that something inside her would forever remain unsatisfied if Antonia Montoya should fail, after all, to become the proper bride of Rafael Serna.

24

On the last day of May, only a week before the date set for the departure of the Entrada, Don Antonio returned from Taos.

Don Pedro did not return with him. Even before she was told this, Josefina knew it. She had seen the Governor and Captain Naranjo ride into the Plaza without Don Pedro, and she had been seized with a sudden weakness that made her grasp and hold on to the rejas of the window through which she was watching.

"Madre de Dios!" she whispered aloud. "What a state you are in, Josefina! What a frightened hare you have become! He is safe . . . surely."

But of this she could not be certain until, later that day, Captain Naranjo gave her a note from Don Pedro. He slipped it into her hand as they greeted each other under the portal, without a word, with only a faint quizzical smile in his deep Indian-fighter's eyes. She hurried to her apartment, locked the door and read:

QUERIDA MÍA—
I must remain in Taos for several days longer. The mustering of the Entrada, the enlistment of the Apaches, and—who knows?—perhaps the private designs of my commander require it. Every moment away from you is intolerable. But I am a soldier, and my arm is the King's even while my heart is yours. That you guard yourself well, my life.
VILLASUR

249

As she watched the flames curl and blacken the paper, her fears went with his words; but not the heavy uncertainty of her future —of what her star had ordained.

This remained, and Don Antonio did nothing on his return to enlighten her. He greeted her affably, but almost impersonally, embracing her in the customary manner before several members of the Cabildo. Did Jean L'Archévèque observe this little ceremony with a faintly sardonic smirk on his sleek Gallic features? She could not be sure. She only knew that she must return Don Antonio's embrace, and make a little show of being pleased, and reveal nothing.

Don Antonio, quite obviously, had decided to hide whatever he knew or felt—or planned—behind a mask of detached amiability. He smiled and looked a little sad and treated Josefina with a kind of formal deference before his friends. He also spared her those public displays of affection, almost harder to bear than his private brutalities; and he made no attempt at all to come to her in her apartment.

For all this Josefina was somewhat doubtfully grateful. She sensed a quality of patient waiting in the way Don Antonio was acting, a hint of hidden claws. She took the precaution, actually, of writing to Tafora, giving him certain information that might later on be interesting to him . . . in the event that such-and-such should happen. And she sent this letter off secretly with a trusted man of Don Ramón's.

Then the couriers from México arrived with His Majesty's mail, and Don Antonio's extraordinary affability vanished utterly in a great cloud of gloom.

What was the bad news from below? What was in the dispatches from the Capital that so unnerved the governor? All in the Villa asked these questions, but nobody could answer them.

"His Excellency has seen a ghost," the Villeños said to one another. "Don Antonio is trying to drown some ghost or other in the bottle."

For almost immediately after the arrival of the mail, Don Antonio had shut himself up in his apartment with a generous bottle of his own Bernalillo brandy and had been seen only occasionally since, sometimes wandering aimlessly about the Palace, sometimes crossing the Plaza under his big parasol (for the sun had already begun to grow hot).

He emerged at last from his semi-immurement, looking a little seedy and even paler than usual, but quite sober in all his behavior. It was generally agreed that His Excellency had recovered from his juerga; and the Villa of Santa Fé gradually ceased to wonder what had been in the dispatches so to disturb and depress him. For everyone's thoughts were now on the Entrada.

The day for its departure—the second of June—arrived and passed like any other spring day in the quiet, sun-warmed Villa of Santa Fé.

In the Presidio, forty of the Kingdom's finest soldiers—veterans all of the famous campaigns of Vargas, Hurtado, and Ulibarri—had been ready and waiting to march for more than a week. A dozen of the Villa's best citizens, old campaigners also, were armed and equipped to leave at a moment's notice. From Taos, where he was still detained, Captain Villasur had sent word that the Apache allies, mustering there, were ready.

"What is holding us up?" the soldiers asked. "Why in the name of Don Jesús Christ don't we get going?"

Their impatience was due to something more than a soldier's natural restlessness. The march to the Río Jesús María was a long one, maybe five hundred miles, or even more. Five hundred up and another five hundred back—a thousand miles to cover before snow piled up in the passes. And time for that much marching was running out.

"Why does Don Antonio proscrastinate?"

This was the question—phrased somewhat less delicately, it is true, by the troops—that everyone was asking. For nobody but Don Antonio, as far as the perplexed people of Santa Fé could see, stood in the way of the Entrada's leaving. Never before, perhaps, had an expedition been so thoroughly trained, fitted out, provisioned, and armed as this one. Every detail—down to a button over the left shoulder of every soldier to hang his hat on during Mass—had been looked after by Captain Villasur. And yet: "He leaves us here with one foot in the stirrup," the soldiers fumed. "What passes with Don Antonio?"

Josefina, turning this same question over in her mind, tried to relate it to certain other questions that, secret to herself, had plagued her thoughts for weeks. And chief among them was the query: *What has Don Antonio in his evil mind for me?*

He might have her thrown into the Palace dungeon. He might denounce her to the Holy Office. He might even have her killed. . . . Or, he might simply turn her out, brand her as a castoff mistress—a common harlot, strip her of everything she could not carry away in her kerchief.

That would be his most likely course, she told herself. Yet I don't think Don Antonio will take it. He suspects that I am unfaithful to him—he must even know it. But that is nothing to him really . . . so long as others don't know it too . . . so long as his pride doesn't suffer.

If he turns me out, it is himself that will be the real object of scorn in this Kingdom—and he knows that too well. Besides, he needs me to do the honors of the Palace. I am a Castellana. Where could he ever find another like me to sit at his table and stand at his side when he gives his stupid receptions? Besides . . . Besides, this also would be too simple for Don Antonio!

I think he would like to keep me near him for a while longer, she thought, with a little shiver. He has something very special in mind for me, no? I can see that in his eyes. There is no need for haste, really. I am his mouse . . . or so he thinks.

It occurred to her that this had become something like a play—one of Lope's or Calderón's. And this strange delay of Don Antonio's in starting with the Entrada—it also was a thread of the plot. But at last it all became too wearisome even to think about.

Why don't you just leave Don Antonio, Josefina? Why don't you leave this Villa of Santa Fé?

How strange that this, the simplest possibility of all, had hardly occurred to her! And now that she had asked the question, she was a little dismayed at the answer she must give herself.

She was afraid.

She was afraid, simply, of what Don Antonio might do, not only to herself but also to Don Pedro, if she left him openly, before the eyes of the whole Kingdom. He was a man of inordinate vanity: she could imagine nothing he would stop at to revenge a blow to his pride. He was the Great Captain, no? He was also the crony of traitors and assassins . . . and there was Mateo.

As long as she remained in the Palace with Don Antonio, she was probably safe. She was safe for a while, at least—until it was Don Antonio's pleasure to spring whatever trap was set behind those pale, watchful eyes. But if she left . . . she did not like to think about what might happen. . . .

And back of this special and immediate fear, she sensed vaguely, was another one that sank deeper and reached back further. One that had always been with her. And perhaps it was this old fear, really, that confused her thoughts and paralyzed her will, and had brought her to this shameful decision to remain for a while with Don Antonio.

She made excuses.

If this were a degrading thing to do, it was neither more nor less degrading than the life she had accepted during all the years since she had fled from Spain with Don Antonio . . . although her love for Don Pedro now made it seem a greater and different sin.

Besides, Don Antonio would leave soon with the Entrada—he could hardly delay much longer. Then she and Tichi would have the Palace to themselves for a while. There would be time—before the Entrada returned—to think about these things . . . to consider what to do with the broken pieces of her plans.

252

But even as she made these excuses, she felt a growing discontent with herself. Ever since she had returned from Los Álamos, she had made her bed on the floor and had known nothing but hatred for the pleasant apartment she once had loved so greatly. She hated it all—the soft gessoed walls, the carved vigas, the painted chests and lacquered Andalusian chairs and the little fireplace purring with the gentle fires of piñon logs. She entered it as seldom as possible, and always with a sense of guilt. Whenever she was in that room she felt an odd distaste for her very self.

Ay, Josefina! she reproached herself in sadness and bewilderment. You have known shame often enough. But you have never *chosen* to live with it!

She was depressed by Don Pedro's continuing absence. She was filled with longing for him, and all kinds of fears and jealousies and uncertainties, and with an aching contempt for her own weakness. And not even Tichi could lift her out of the despondency that burdened the long days . . . the long hateful days of waiting.

"We have had it much worse, Doña Josefina," the stout Gallega said. "That you trust your star. It will not betray you."

"Ah, Tichi—perhaps our stars do not shine on this side of the world. We are far from where we were born, no? I think our stars have forgotten us."

"They follow you everywhere. I have a feeling in my bones, Doña Josefina, that they have ordained . . . that something is about to happen."

But what happened—although no conjunction of the stars could have borne upon their lives more decisively—was far from anything that Josefina or Tichi could have wished for.

Josefina learned about it the next morning from Tichi's horror-filled eyes as the Gallega stood speechless in the doorway of her apartment. She followed the trembling servant across the patio to the small room occupied by 'Toñita on the opposite side of the little court.

"Who did it?" she asked, looking about the disheveled room, then down again at the sobbing, half-naked, badly bruised form on the low pallet.

"She won't tell, señora," Tichi said. "I think she is afraid to tell."

Josefina knelt beside 'Toñita and put her arms around the girl's quivering shoulders. She made soft little sounds, mixed with a few words—"pobrecita!" "hija mía!"—such as a mother might make in comforting a heartbroken child.

Something glinting on the beaten adobe floor caught her eye and she reached out for it. By the feel, even before she had looked at it, she knew what it was: it was one of the silver-coin buttons that Don Antonio wore with so much childish pride on his purple nankeen jacket. . . .

25

That same afternoon, all uncertainty and all doubt and all indecision having suddenly been swept away, and Don Antonio having conveniently absented himself on a trip to Santa Cruz de la Cañada, the three women left the Palace in the governor's coach.

'Toñita, unhurt except for the bruises hidden by her manta, sat quietly on the seat opposite Josefina. All at once, it seemed, she had become more Indian and less Spanish; and she gazed at Josefina with an almost defiant composure, through impassive Tewa eyes. Beside her, Tichi, dressed as if for a fiesta in her finest dress and rebozo, clutched a large leather wallet containing her personal treasures. The coach screeched and lurched over the Pecos road. The Villa of Santa Fé fell out of sight beyond the rolling, chamiza-covered hills. Nobody spoke.

"There is a certain sadness about this," Tichi said at last, almost as if speaking to herself. "But it is nothing to frighten one. It is but another adventure, no? As for me, Doña Josefina, I like this Villa now no better than I liked Ávila . . . or Arzua. I am content to put it also behind us."

"Ah, Tichi," Josefina said. "Your heart never changes!"

Tichi's words called up a faint, far-away echo in her mind. Her thoughts drifted back . . . to the very edge of remembrance . . . and then beyond. She seemed to hear another brave woman—a very great saint but yet a simple peasant girl of Ávila, as all in that city felt and understood Teresa de Jesús to be—saying: "There is only one thing to fear and that is fear. . . ."

She stretched out her hand and gave the Gallega's knee a little pat.

26

During the next few days they lived in a state of vague suspense at Los Álamos, enjoying Don Ramón's and Doña Mercedes's hospitality uneasily. And Tichi, oddly enough, was the most restive.

"You can't be sure what Don Antonio might take it into his head to do," she said. "I think we should get on our way to México, señora."

"You are not afraid, Tichi!" Josefina chided her.

"The señora knows that I fear neither Don Antonio nor the devil," Tichi said, suddenly very withdrawn. "But I don't trust them either."

"Well, we are safer here than on the Camino Real," Josefina reminded her. "Besides, I don't think that Don Antonio would dare to harm us."

Of this she was less certain than she feigned, of course; but there was nothing to do, really, but put on a brave face and wait for something to happen . . . until Don Antonio made a move perhaps . . . or the Entrada went off to the Río Jesús María . . . or Don Pedro returned from Taos at last. . . .

Don Ramón thought it discreet that they stay away from the Villa for a little time; but plenty of information reached them in one way or another. The Capital, of course, was buzzing with gossip and speculation.

Don Antonio, it was reported at first, had flown into a tremendous rage when he learned of Josefina's flight from the Palace and had smashed everything in her apartment.

But this was untrue, another account said, or at least greatly exaggerated. Whatever may have been his immediate reaction, Don Antonio had later shown only regret and resignation, and a really noble concern about his former mistress's welfare. He had even brushed a tear from his eye, witnesses affirmed, and had said, "Pobrecita! That she find another as affectionate and indulgent as I!"

Of these two versions of Don Antonio's conduct, Josefina preferred the first: the second gave her a more than faint uneasiness.

She also suspected that the first was the true one. Don Antonio, however, had apparently decided to exhibit himself to the Villeños as the aggrieved victim of a light and ungrateful woman. It was his aim, no doubt, to win the sympathy of the people . . . and possibly their indifference to any unfortunate thing that might happen to befall La Dama Josefina in the near future.

"Well, at any rate," she said with forced lightness to Doña Mercedes, "there isn't any doubt in the Villa about what has happened!"

"That is very good, no?" the comely and candid wife of Don Ramón asked. "Now you are free. Now you can do exactly as you wish."

"You mean, amiga, that I can go now to Don Pedro?"

"How can Don Antonio object—after all he has said?"

Josefina sipped her chocolate and watched a small green lizard

255

slither up the patio wall and disappear into the budding roses of Castile.

"If Don Pedro wants me," she said absently.

"Do you doubt it, 'Fina?" Doña Mercedes asked softly, incredulously. "If you do, you are the only one! You have his heart entire, my dear—as anyone with eyes can see. . . . As Don Antonio, I doubt not, has seen for himself."

"God grant that you are right," Josefina said. "As for Don Antonio . . . what do you make of his injured air, Mercedes? It frightens me!"

Doña Mercedes was silent for the space of an Ave Maria. "I think," she said, "that Don Antonio is concerned mostly with saving his face, no? With the troops, the Cabildo, the Villeños, the Viceroy himself, that is always Don Antonio's chief concern—to save his face."

"I will admit that, but——"

"And now he saves his face again. Until you left him, Josefina, how could he go with the Entrada? How could he leave Don Pedro behind, to take you from him, and make him the laughingstock of the Kingdom? But now—now he has escaped that danger, no? You have left him, and he has wished you well—he has even expressed the hope that you will find another protector as admirable as himself! I doubt not that, before he leaves, he will even hint that Don Pedro Villasur is such a one. . . ."

"Ah, Mercedes," Josefina whispered in a kind of awe. "You never cease to amaze me!"

"Don't laugh at me, 'Fina," Doña Mercedes said, a little piqued. "One must have known Don Antonio's mind for a long time in order to understand it."

"I have known it long enough," Josefina said wryly. "Alas, I think there is something there that neither of us has guessed!"

"Perhaps you are right!" Doña Mercedes laughed. "Why do we worry ourselves about it? What about 'Toñita?"

"I am going to Galisteo tomorrow, to talk with Fray Juan Minguéz about her."

Fray Juan de la Cruz, she had learned, was somewhere in the West—at Laguna, perhaps, or Acoma, or even at Zuñi. It would be a long time before he returned from making the rounds of his missions. In the meantime she must consult someone among the padres about 'Toñita and Rafael. Since she had now, so suddenly and rudely, lost her "neutral home," would not 'Toñita again be at the mercy of their warring families? Rumors, in fact, had already reached Los Álamos that her brothers were planning to snatch her away. The little mestiza herself was in a pitiful state of anxiety.

"Never fear, chiquita," Josefina reassured her. "You shall have your Rafael. We shall have you married before long. You trust me, no?"

It was while she was saying this—without knowing, actually, what she could do—that she remembered Fray Juan Minguéz. Early the next morning she set out on Negra to visit him at Galisteo.

27

The small pueblo of Galisteo, around which a few Spanish settlers had clustered, was half a day's ride from Los Álamos. The road was the same as that to Pecos for most of the way; then, where the Pecos trail turned north, it abruptly entered the rugged Apache Cañon and followed it to the Río Galisteo.

The river and all the ditches were full of rushing mountain water on this fine morning. The little fields, spread like blankets over the bright red earth, were incredibly green. The orchards behind the long mud walls were all in bloom. The brilliant sky was flecked with snowy tufts of wool.

Qué linda! Josefina thought. How beautiful! I do not remember that it was ever so beautiful in Old Spain.

Her spirits were high: she hummed the ballad of La Pastorcita as she rode along.

> Estaba una pastora,
> larán, larán, larito . . .

She found Fray Juan working in his little kitchen garden. His blue robe was tucked up above his knees and he had on a broad-brimmed hat and shoes, which the friars of New Mexico were allowed to wear because of the heat and roughness of the country. He greeted her with a slight air of wonder.

"Imagine, señora, to see you here! But on such a lovely morning anything may happen, no?"

He invited her into his small, whitewashed study and an old Pueblo woman brought them chocolate. Fray Juan needed little, wanted little, had little. Unlike some of the clergy, he did not load the Indians with excessive work and payments for Masses, marriages, and burials. Fray Juan had never charged a poor Pueblo a turkey, or three or four hens, for a Mass and a sermon. On the other hand, he had never slipped into those lax habits—those "customs of the country"—that had reduced many a friar to a state of moral and physical inertia. He was a man of faith and conscience. He took the knot for poverty in his girdle seriously; and the room in which he and his guest now sipped chocolate was poor and bare. Its only adornment,

Josefina noted, was a small wooden statue of Santiago, the warrior saint; it was carved and painted to represent a vaquero riding in a New Mexican saddle!

How proper, Josefina thought, that you should be over Fray Juan's hearth!

For Fray Juan Minguéz, as his lean frame and weathered face attested, was himself a man much accustomed to the saddle. His posts were mainly remote settlements and Indian pueblos, and obscure visitas that had no priest of their own. For such work one must have great energy and endurance and courage, and it was well if one possessed a sense of humor. Fray Juan lacked in none of these qualities; he was also a man of direct speech.

"But tell me, my daughter," he said, "why have you come here? It is a long ride from Los Álamos—and, by the way, I am surprised that you should have taken it alone."

He listened attentively while she related the whole story of 'Toñita and Rafael. When she had finished, he said: "Why is it, Doña Josefina, that you have so greatly interested yourself in this love affair of two paisanos?"

She was a little surprised to find that she had no ready answer to this question.

"I don't know, padre," she said at last. "I have no reason . . . except that I desire in my heart to see these children married, as they wish."

The fraile glanced at her swiftly, then turned his gaze through the open door to the sunny, flowering banks of the Galisteo.

"How little we know," he said, as if to himself. "How little we know of the roots from which our longings grow. How little we can tell of the reasons for what we do. . . . Perhaps it is just as well, no?"

"Perhaps, padre," Josefina said, mystified, impatient. "But what of 'Toñita and Rafael? Can nothing at all be done for them?"

Fray Juan, almost reluctantly, it seemed, dropped his air of philosophical detachment. He became the quiet but energetic man of action, which was his more accustomed self.

"Of course something can be done, my child," he said. "I am well acquainted with this case—it is one to try the patience of God! I'm quite certain of what the Father Custodio would do, if he were at hand. What is to prevent me from doing the same?"

"What is that, padre?"

"Marry them!"

"But padre——"

"It can be done, my child. There are ways. Without the ring, coins, and candle, perhaps—but that can come later. If only . . ."

"Yes, padre?"

"This little 'Toñita," Fray Juan asked hopefully, "she is not pregnant, is she?"

"I don't think so, padre."

"Well, no matter. We can still make it a marriage 'to avoid greater convenience,' no?"

"But when, Fray Juan?"

The fraile smiled at her eagerness—and perhaps at the look of disbelief that still lingered on her face.

"You go fast, my daughter," he said, "but no faster than I. It will have to be soon—at once, in fact. I am leaving in three days . . . to join the Entrada."

Josefina was not quite sure that she had heard Fray Juan correctly. "What did you say, padre?" she asked. "Did you say that the Entrada is going to leave in three days? And you are going with it, no?"

"The Entrada has already left," Fray Juan said. "It left this morning."

"Cómo?" she gasped. "What?"

"The Entrada left Santa Fé this morning," the fraile repeated. "I am to join it as chaplain at Taos. As soon as my replacement arrives, that is—he is slower than a Tewa mule."

"I see," Josefina said numbly.

She sat for a while in silence, thinking about the news she had just heard. She experienced the bitter, abrupt finality of defeat—the wretchedness of the utterly vanquished. How completely Don Antonio had won—and now had marched away—leaving her in the wreckage of her ill-starred plans . . . with the memory only of his mocking laugh.

At the same time she was filled with an odd sensation of relief, of deliverance. So Don Antonio had gone away at last. He had left Santa Fé—her world was free of him—there would be no more to fear, at least, from Don Antonio!

And strongest of all, surging through all the confused response of her heart and mind, was the delicious certainty that now Don Pedro Villasur would soon return to Santa Fé and to her longing arms. . . .

But one moment, Josefina, she warned herself. This is too simple, no? It would not be like Don Antonio to arrange such a simple ending to his little comedia. What is there that our good friend Fray Juan has neglected to tell me? What is there that he does not know? *What more is there to this that I should be aware of. . . ?*

She judged it best not to press Fray Juan for further details that afternoon. The next morning, having spent the night at the house of the alcalde, she started back to Los Álamos, still pondering the questions that Fray Juan's news had raised, like the ghosts of uneasy souls, in her restless mind.

28

The purple mists were beginning to gather in the Sangre de Cristo valleys, and the junipers and piñons stood out solid and round in the late afternoon sunlight, when Josefina arrived back at Los Álamos.

Even before Doña Mercedes greeted her at the door of the sala, Josefina knew that Don Ramón's estancia held some secret. An air of mysterious excitement enveloped it. She could sense it in the glances the servants gave her . . . could sense also that, in some special way, she was linked to it. Even Doña Mercedes imparted a certain strangeness to the simple act of sending for food and chocolate. Josefina was puzzled, amused, irritated: why did they all make so much of a thing she knew as well as they?

"Has Don Ramón returned from the Villa?" she asked Doña Mercedes casually.

"Only an hour ago."

"Then you have heard?"

"About the Entrada? Of course. And you—you also, Josefina?"

"Yes, I have heard about it," Josefina said, carelessly. "From Fray Juan."

"Ah, I see!" Doña Mercedes said slowly. "What did he tell you, Josefina mía?"

"Why, only that the Entrada left the Villa this morning," Josefina said, a little weary and a little irked. "What else, pray?"

Doña Mercedes withdrew the cup of chocolate she was about to hand Josefina, and set it down carefully on the small table between them.

"That you prepare yourself, Josefina," she said gently, "to hear what I am going to tell you."

"Nombre de Dios! What is all this mystery? What haven't I heard?"

"Ah, Josefina, there appears to be a great deal you haven't heard."

"For example, then?"

"It is true," Doña Mercedes said, "that the Entrada left the Villa this morning. There was a Mass in La Parróquia, and a blessing, and Don Antonio reviewed the soldiers in the Plaza. Then the Entrada marched away on the Camino Real . . . *But not with Don Antonio.*"

"No?"

"No—it marched without him to Taos . . . where Don Pedro Villasur will take command."

"And Don Antonio?" Josefina asked dully, after some time.

"He remains here," Doña Mercedes said. "At the very last moment, it seems, the 'Great Captain' decided to give Don Pedro the honor of leading the expedition, while he himself stays at home. Everyone is astonished, of course. No one can understand it."

"That is not unusual," Josefina said, with a small, tight smile. "As you yourself have said, Mercedes, one must have known Don Antonio's mind for a very long time in order to understand it."

She sat for a little while, looking down at the smooth, dark adobe floor. Doña Mercedes was surprised to hear a small, odd, quite mirthless laugh.

"And now," Josefina said, looking up quickly, "my chocolate, Mercedes, por favor."

29

The most maddening thing of all was her utter helplessness.

There was nothing she could do: she was unable even to think. There was nothing, indeed, that her mind could pull out of this whole fantastic business except a question: Why did Don Antonio, contrary to explicit orders from the Viceroy, suddenly relinquish on the very hour of its departure his command of the Entrada to the Río Jesús María?

She was weary of speculation: she had surely learned how futile it could be in any matter pertaining to Don Antonio Valverde. And so, partly to occupy her mind with something else and partly because it was a thing that must be attended to at once, she turned all her energies to the business of getting 'Toñita and Rafael married.

The fierceness of her exertion in behalf of these somewhat bewildered young lovers left Los Álamos breathless and a little dazed. But on the very next afternoon a small cavalcade—including an armed escort provided by Don Ramón—left the estancia for Galisteo. On the following morning 'Toñita knelt at the altar of the little pueblo church with Rafael at her side, and Fray Juan Minguéz performed the ceremony of their marriage.

Afterwards there was a little wedding feast at Fray Juan's house to which some of the guests brought presents. And Josefina slipped into the thin lobes of 'Toñita's ears the fine golden wires of a pair of silver-gilt earrings that an old man named Uncle Pepe had given her a weary time ago in a little Spanish town called Roa. . . .

How strange, she thought, as she kissed the pretty bride, that this marriage should give you such a sweet contentment, Josefina . . . almost as if it were your own!

A certain air of apprehension enveloped the wedding party as it rode back to Los Álamos; and as they neared the estancia Don Ramón even sent ahead a scout to make certain that nothing untoward awaited them there. But just as Fray Juan de la Cruz had predicted, neither 'Toñita's family nor Rafael's caused any trouble. Faced with an accomplished fact, both the Sernas and the Montoyas seemed disposed to accept Fray Juan's coup equably. At any rate, during the whole of the day following the wedding—news of which had traveled quickly to the Villa—not a knife was drawn in Santa Fé.

At Los Álamos, too, all was outwardly quiet. Josefina gave no sign to anyone—not even to Doña Mercedes—of the fears, doubts, and frustrations—and the passionate, almost insupportable longing to be with Don Pedro—that were tearing at her heart and mind. She wore, with a kind of insouciance, the mask of impassivity that a Castellana knew how to put on; and not even when a rider, dusty and sweatstreaked, appeared with a message for her from Taos did she betray the sudden racing of her blood.

Josefina took the message to her apartment and tore it open. It was from Don Pedro Villasur, a brief note obviously written in haste:

Querida mía—

Within an hour I shall leave this pueblo in command of the Entrada to the Río Jesús María.

Think of me while I am gone. Pray for the success of the reconnaissance. Remind yourself now and every day that this will be but a short and easy Entrada (God grant it!) and I shall return to you soon.

That I might hold you in my arms but once before I go! Guard yourself well, my heart. I love you with all my soul. Adiós!

Villasur

Her heart sank as it occurred to her, all at once, that Don Pedro knew nothing of what had happened in Santa Fé during his absence. Nothing of Mateo and the undoubted interception of her letter to Tafora. Nothing of her leaving Don Antonio. Nothing of the strange suddenness with which Don Antonio had decided to give up his leadership of the Entrada. Of all this Don Pedro was wholly unaware. . . .

"María Purísima!" she whispered. "Don Pedro thinks the orders have come from México. He assumes that he has been made commander of the Entrada by the Viceroy. He thinks that Tafora——"

Why, she wondered, did this sudden realization so upset her? Had not the very thing that she had planned and plotted come to pass?

262

Had she not got her wish at last? Was not Don Pedro leading the Entrada—as she had so ardently desired?

Ah, yes, she said to herself, Don Pedro has the command. Don Antonio has given it to him. But why? Cannot an act be either good or evil—depending on why it is done?

Here she sensed evil with an intensity that amounted almost to certainty. Yet how could she know? She had not one single fact—nothing at all but suspicion, speculation, and her own knowledge of Don Antonio—to go on. Nothing but instinct, really. . . . But all at once she felt afraid for Don Pedro Villasur . . . and for herself.

30

She was lying awake in her apartment when, in the middle of the siesta, another messenger arrived at Los Álamos. She heard him roll into the patio with a clatter and screeching of wheels that could have been made only by Don Antonio's coach. Wondering greatly, she followed the little servant girl, who had come up to summon her, down. The messenger was Captain José Naranjo.

"Hola!" Josefina said, with an astonishment that was not altogether feigned. "Since when has Captain Naranjo taken to riding about the country with a coach and four mules?"

The scout grinned and touched his broad-brimmed hat.

"That you never let my Apaches know about this, señora," he said. "His Excellency's orders."

"So?"

She studied the famous Indian fighter's face with curiosity and some amusement. Captain José Naranjo had already become somewhat of a legend among frontiersmen. Nobody, it was well understood, could ride, cast a lance, throw a reata, or roll a cigarillo at a gallop as well as José Naranjo. Innumerable exploits—attacks, defenses, rescues of captives, and so on (all of them colorful and most of them true)— were attached to his name. And back of all the tales was a record of extraordinary work in the king's service that no one quite knew how to recognize officially.

There were no titles, really, to fit a man like José Naranjo; and so one was invented for him: "Captain of the Indians of the Pueblos." He was also "Captain-Major of War," this title bestowed by the former Viceroy, the Duke of Linares, himself.

But if José Naranjo had ever been asked to repeat these honors, it is doubtful that he could have remembered them. He was a simple man who took a dim view of the titular trappings that meant so much to the other colonists.

Captain Naranjo, Josefina knew, was in charge of the Indian allies who were to accompany the Entrada to the Jesús María. It surprised her to find him here at Los Álamos; and even more to see the celebrated scout—whose inseparability from his horse was proverbial—arrive in Don Antonio's lumbering coach.

The frontiersman appeared to share her wonder at so strange a circumstance. His dark aquiline face wore an expression bordering on embarrassment as he explained, in three words, that he was acting in such an odd manner only at the governor's command.

"So?" Josefina asked. "Don Antonio has sent you here? And why, por favor?"

"He wishes to see you, señora. He sends you his compliments and requests that you return with me to the Palace. It is some matter of great importance, no?"

"It must be, indeed!" Josefina said pensively.

It required a little effort of her will to keep her composure in the wake of such a startling request; she wished also to gain a few moments for reflection. She said: "But I thought you were at Taos, Captain, with the Entrada."

"I have been there, señora. I am returning in the morning."

"Captain Naranjo," she said suddenly. "You are my friend, no?"

"To the death, señora," the scout said, smiling.

"Well then, if you know, tell me: why does Don Antonio want to see me?"

"I am sorry, Doña Josefina. I do not know."

She lapsed into silence, her head filled with a thousand swirling thoughts—among them a vague but insistent concern for her own personal safety if she should yield to Don Antonio's request . . . which, despite all José Naranjo could do to make it appear otherwise, was actually a command.

"Captain Naranjo," she said after a while, "if I go with you now, will you return with me to Los Álamos . . . after I have seen Don Antonio?"

The scout gave her a swift, understanding glance of his dark eyes.

"I shall conduct you home," he said, using a military term with precisely the meaning he wished it to have, "myself, señora."

"Good!" She held out her hand and clasped his. "In one moment, then, I shall be ready."

31

Several hours later Don Antonio received her at the Palace. She was ushered into his bedchamber by no other than Don Miguel Tenorio de Alba, the governor's Secretary of Government and War, who softly closed the door and left her alone in the high, bare room with Don Antonio.

He was propped up, in nightcap and robe, against a huge pillow in his massive flock bed. Josefina looked at him closely to see if he were really ill or merely feigning illness; but he appeared neither more nor less pale than usual.

He motioned toward a chair with his eyes and said, "It was kind of you to come. . . . That you sit down, my dear."

She glanced at the chair and remained standing. "What is it that you want, Don Antonio?" she asked coldly.

"Only your forgiveness, my dear."

"You called me here from Los Álamos for that?" she asked, incredulously. "Adiós!"

He allowed her to go to the door, and watched her, smiling almost benignly, as she struggled to open it.

"I'm afraid it's no use, Josefina mía," he said. "Don Miguel must have turned the key . . . I have explained to him that we wish to be alone for a little while."

"I did not expect this," she said, "although I might have! Well, what is it you have to say, Don Antonio? That you but say it quickly. That you let me get out of here!"

She made up her mind to hear him without a word until he had finished; and she did this, allowing nothing to show in her face while Don Antonio went back—in quite astonishing detail—over their lives together, recounting all the ways in which he had been her protector and benefactor . . . without ever mentioning, however, his own great debt to her.

Ay, Antonio! she thought. I believe you do really think it was that way!

But she held her tongue—although with some difficulty—waiting for him to come to the point of this long, bewildering discourse.

"So now you leave me," he finished sadly.

"Really!" she said, casting a rueful glance at the great lock on the door. "It seems otherwise to me, Don Antonio!"

"And," he continued imperturbably, "you take your leave in a manner that, to one less generous than myself, might seem ungrateful. Yet, I forgive you everything. I do even more than forgive you—I understand you. I read your heart, Josefina mía, and I surrender to the superior forces of Eros."

"You mean, Don Antonio——?"

"I mean, if Don Pedro Villasur wants you, he can have you!"

He said this with a sudden vehemence that he immediately, it appeared, regretted. For he put on a rather fatuous smile and waved his hand, as if to dismiss what he had just said.

"I tell you this privately, my dear," he continued, "just as I have let it be known abroad. I have found no reason for concealing the fact that you have fallen in love with my friend, Don Pedro. All in the Villa know what has happened; and all know that Don Antonio Valverde wishes you and his friend, Don Pedro Villasur, nothing but the happiness of true lovers."

"That is very kind of you, Don Antonio," she said disdainfully.

Don Antonio gazed at her for a little while in an oddly abstracted and melancholy way. "You have never loved me," he asked at last, "have you, Josefina?"

"No," she said, "never."

"Ah, well," he said, "that is sad, but it does not matter, really. Perhaps you can remember your Antonio as a man who at least could deserve your forgiveness. . . ."

Ay, Dios! she said to herself. What can this mean?

Suddenly she knew—or was all but certain that she knew. Once again, Don Antonio was preparing for something . . . for something, she suspected, that would hold no good for Josefina. He was showing himself to all Santa Fé as a forgiving, beneficent man . . . a man who would be above suspicion . . . *should anything untoward happen, for example, to herself.* . . .

"I am glad that the whole history of this affair is so well known to everyone," she said, looking steadily into his pale eyes. "I have taken the liberty of informing Señor Tafora about it also. . . . *There is nothing, Don Antonio, that is not known, in México.*"

"You would have made a great captain, Josefina. You never overlook details!"

"May I go now?" she asked coldly.

"Not yet," he said. "In a moment, but not just yet. There is something else—I think you will be pleased to hear it."

She waited, quite sure now that what he had really called her to hear was about to come.

"It is about the Entrada. . . ." he said.

"I have heard about it, Don Antonio. It has left—at last. Don Pedro

266

is commanding it. You are to remain here in the Villa, no? What else?"

"Ah, yes," Don Antonio repeated softly. "You would have made a great captain, Josefina. You place a proper value on intelligence."

"I find out as much as I can."

"Then there is something else you should hear—just in case, my dear, you should have occasion to write more letters to México, to Tafora, eh? I should like them to know *from you,* Josefina mía, the real reason why I am not leading the Entrada."

"And what is that, Antonio?"

"As you can see—I am ill."

"It is the old complaint, no doubt—the one that seized you the time you were ordered to México with Don Felix Martínez!"

Don Antonio gazed at her reprovingly. He sighed and said, "You are cruel, my dear."

"That also was a very sudden sickness."

"Señora!" he said sharply. "I think it will be well if we accept the fact that this illness is genuine . . . and the other one also, no?"

She was almost frightened by the baleful light in his pale eyes. You have gone far enough, Josefina—she warned herself. Take care!

She said, with a show of contrition: "Your pardon, Antonio. I . . . I understand."

"Good!" he exclaimed, smiling again. "I had no doubt you would. And so you can understand also my bitter, my almost unbearable disappointment." He paused, and Josefina noted with amazement that tears actually glistened in his pale and vacuous eyes.

"It must indeed have been hard for you to give up the command," she said dryly.

"But what else could I do?" he asked plaintively. "I know this sickness. It must run its course. The Entrada could be delayed no longer—not a day. I fear we may have waited too long already. You can imagine, my dear, what I must have felt!"

"Ah, yes. It is sad!"

"But then," he continued more brightly, "His Divine Majesty came to my help. . . . Or perhaps I should even say that *you,* Josefina, rescued me. . . ."

"I?" she gasped.

"Who else, my dear?" he asked, almost beaming at her. "Didn't you suggest long ago that I spare myself these arduous marches? That I learn to lean a little on my Lieutenant-General, Don Pedro Villasur?"

"Often," she said. "But I never thought you paid much heed to me, Antonio."

"Ah, you were mistaken, my dear! I have never valued anyone's counsel more highly than La Dama Josefina's. And so, when this

267

illness struck me, I thought of your advice: *Let Don Pedro go in your place.* 'Of course!' I said to myself. 'When has Josefina ever been wrong?' "

Josefina turned her head to hide the distaste that, she knew, must be very plain on her face.

"And so," Don Antonio went on in the same gentle tone, "you may feel, my dear, that you, more than anyone else, have been responsible for the solution of this most distressing problem. I thank you, in the name of the Kingdom. And Don Pedro Villasur, I think, can thank you for his own good fortune. . . ."

"I am sure Don Pedro thinks only of his duty as a soldier."

"Of course," Don Antonio agreed amiably. "And it is a great comfort to me to know that complete confidence is reposed in him also in México, no?"

"I think that is so, Antonio."

"I have been told," Don Antonio said with an odd deliberateness, and watching her closely as he spoke, "I have been told that Tafora and others close to the Viceroy have been kept very fully informed about Don Pedro Villasur's excellent qualities."

"That is possible," Josefina admitted. "There is little they don't know about in México."

"It is also quite possible that a successful reconnaissance against the French on the Río Jesús María would redound greatly to the credit of Don Pedro—would advantage him greatly at the Court, no?"

"It is even probable," she said, with a sudden recklessness.

"And also those near to him . . . ?"

She had no further capacity for wonder, or even perturbation, at Don Antonio's apparently limitless knowledge of everything that had happened. She could not even feel an uneasy interest in the meaning of all these obviously sinister questions. She was only bored, and vaguely curious about the only question that Don Antonio had not yet answered: Why, in actual fact, had he so suddenly, and against the Viceroy's explicit orders, given up his command of the Entrada to Don Pedro?

"I am sure, Don Antonio," she said, "that you have not brought me here to speculate about these matters. With your permission now, I should like to leave."

"Yes, yes, my dear," he said genially. "You are quite right, as usual. I wished to see you, once again, merely to thank you . . . and to let you see, also, that I bear no ill-will toward either Don Pedro or yourself . . . and to assure you of my never-ending regard and affection, my dear. . . ."

Then, all of a sudden, she knew—although she could not tell how she knew—that Don Antonio had come to the single question he had left unanswered.

"But before you go," he added, "here is something that came in the mail. From México. It is about the Entrada. You have been very interested in the Entrada, no? You will want to hear this."

Now it comes! she thought. Be careful, Josefina!

"It is a very long communication from His Excellency, the Viceroy," Don Antonio explained. "Mostly about matters that wouldn't interest you. I won't bore you with them. But this part, now—this is something new. Perhaps I should just read it to you. . . ."

He slipped a sheet of stamped paper out of the sheaf on the table, glanced down it, pursed his thin lips, and began to read:

"The Señor Governor will see that the latest news from our spies in La Luisiana must affect very seriously his plans for a reconnaissance against the French on the Río Jesús María. Let him take special notice of these recently discovered facts:

"*1*. The French are now established on the Río Jesús María in walled settlements, to the number of more than two hundred men. They are well armed with arquebuses and long guns.

"*2*. The Pawnees, whom we had supposed to be friendly, are actually joined with the French in an alliance hostile to the Spaniards. Their number is endless; they also are armed with guns.

"Thus, the Señor Governor will readily see that the Entrada he is about to command will be something more than a reconnaissance into peaceful country for the purpose of meeting friendly Indians who can give news of the French.

"It becomes, in fact, an invasion of enemy territory occupied by a numerous and well-armed force. And it will be plain to the Señor Governor that such a dangerous expedition is to be undertaken only with a much stronger force than was contemplated originally for a peaceful reconnaissance. . . ."

Don Antonio looked up from the paper, smiled complacently, and said:

"And now we come, Josefina mía, to the part I like best: 'The Señor Governor,' " His Excellency writes, " 'shall act according to his extensive experiences, and his love and zeal for the royal service. So be it, etc. etc. . . .' "

He laid the paper on the table with a careless air—as if it were a gossipy letter from a friend—and looked at Josefina with mild and melancholy eyes. "If you will knock three times, my dear," he said, "Don Miguel will open the door for you."

32

But Josefina made no move to leave. She stood looking at Don Antonio in somewhat the same way that one might regard an unfamiliar form of life found under an old adobe or in some abandoned rodent's den.

"Does Don Pedro know about this?" she asked.

"Ah, you are not leaving after all!" Don Antonio smiled. "Well, to answer your question, no."

"How large is his force?"

"About sixty Spaniards and some Apaches—I don't know how many."

"And you are allowing him, Don Antonio, to take this small force against two hundred well-armed French and who-knows-how-many Pawnees?"

"What else can I do?" Don Antonio shrugged. "His Excellency has ordered a reconnaissance, no?"

"But even His Excellency points out——"

"That sixty soldiers is not enough, eh?"

"That to send so small a force is to invite disaster—the destruction of them all."

"Well, it is all I have," Don Antonio said, with an air of patient finality. "The defense of this Kingdom must also be considered. I can't spare any more."

"But you could muster six hundred," she said bitterly, "when you led your own Entrada against the Comanches, no?"

"That included the Indians," Don Antonio said wearily. "But why do you keep at me in this way, my dear? You can see that I am ill——"

"Ah, yes, Antonio," she said. "The letter from México made you ill. First it made you drunk for a week. Then it made you ill. Then it gave you the fine idea of sending Don Pedro on this hopeless venture——"

"Is it not what you wished, my dear?" Don Antonio asked gently.

"It was—I make no secret of it. But in God's name, Antonio, how can you pretend that nothing is different now? How can you send these men out to die on the prairies?"

"You are becoming worked up, my dear," Don Antonio said. "It is not as bad as that. Don Pedro, after all, is an experienced soldier."

"But he knows nothing of this. Why haven't you sent word to him? Why don't you still send word?"

"It is too late. He has already left Taos."

"But——"

"Besides," Don Antonio continued smoothly, "Don Pedro will naturally be on the alert: that is a commander's business, to be always on the alert. If there is any danger he will see it. It is better, therefore, not to sow panic among his lieutenants and men with such frightening information as—as this."

He waved toward the paper he had tossed on the table.

How can one hope to follow such a mind? Josefina thought. His blacks are white, his whites black. Surely he is having sport with me! Surely he cannot deny Don Pedro at least a warning!

Through the confusion and bewilderment she heard Don Antonio saying casually:

"Of course, if Don Pedro should ever find himself in a position where he cannot decide what to do, he will have the benefit of Don Juan L'Archévèque's advice. Don Juan, as you know, has a very wide experience in Indian warfare. . . . I have ordered Don Juan to remain very close to Don Pedro at all times. . . ."

He watched her with a curious intentness as he said this, and placed a singular emphasis on the last sentence—a meaningless emphasis, it seemed to her—until, suddenly:

Juan L'Archévèque! she cried out to herself, almost as if in warning. *That assassin!*

She felt herself go all over cold, and her mind swam. Then, all at once, her vision cleared, and she saw very plainly what she must do.

She must not goad Don Antonio any further. She must not question him. Above all, she must not show her scorn, or disgust . . . or the panic that had so suddenly seized her. She must appear stupid—insensible to the dreadful implications of all he had so readily told her. . . . She must be crafty and cunning and try to match his own deceit. . . .

"It is a hard thing to accept," she said slowly, gravely. "But I cannot believe, Don Antonio, that you would do this thing except by necessity."

He looked at her quickly, in obvious surprise.

"It is indeed," he sighed, "a heavy responsibility. But I cannot escape it. His Excellency has entrusted everything to me—alone."

There was a long silence between them.

"May I leave now?" she asked.

"Now? But it will be night, my dear, before you return to Los Álamos."

"I am not afraid of the night, Don Antonio."

"Very well. The carriage will be ready for you. I shall send along Corporal Garzía to see you safely home."

The name of Corporal Garzía gave her a little start. A well-known blackguard and a toady of Don Antonio's, he was not exactly the escort she would have selected for a night ride over the lonely mesa. Something, however, told her to conceal her doubts.

"Adiós, Don Antonio," she said.

In spite of all her hatred and loathing and fear of Don Antonio Valverde, there was almost a sadness in the words as she spoke them. One does not draw a line through eight years of one's life—even though the record of all those years led only to an utterness of disillusionment and despair—without a certain regret. There are many kinds of sadness; and of all of them, the cruelest is that for happiness not lost, but never won.

"Not adiós, my dear," Don Anonio said, with a fatuous smile, "but hasta la vista . . . until we meet again."

Suddenly everything but the hatred and loathing and the fear vanished. She closed her eyes on the image of Don Antonio Valverde—propped up in his great flock bed with an inanely triumphant smile on his pale, sagging features—that was to remain with her to the end of her days, and knocked three times on the door.

It was opened immediately by Don Miguel, who, if he actually had not had his ear against the door, at least had a good idea of what had gone on behind it: his smirking glance said as much.

"Good afternoon, Doña Josefina," he said. "You look very well . . . your usual charming self. . . ."

"Save your flattery for Don Antonio. He pays you for it."

She was relieved to see José Naranjo in the hallway, leaning carelessly against the wall. He had been there, she knew, during the whole of the interview with Don Antonio.

"Let us get out of here pronto," she said to him. "Don Antonio has some idea of sending me back in the coach with Corporal Garzía."

"Don't worry, señora." Naranjo grinned. "I've got a couple of horses saddled and waiting. By the time Garzía gets the mules harnessed to that invention of the devil they call a coach, we'll be halfway to Los Álamos!"

The Sangre de Cristo range floated against the rising moon when they galloped over the Río Santa Fé bridge and out upon the level milpas. The moon was above the snowy peaks and had silvered the whole rolling plain by the time they had flanked the Cerrillos hills. Their mounts were fresh and eager; they tugged at the reins and tossed flecks of foam on the rapidly cooling air.

José Naranjo, sometimes riding beside Josefina, sometimes close behind her where the trail narrowed, said little. The jingle of his steel spurs was about all that came to Josefina through the tumult of her thoughts.

She was thinking furiously, with the almost total concentration of which she was sometimes capable, especially when riding. She was going over in her mind that clear and mortal danger to which Don Antonio had so barbarously delivered Don Pedro and his men. The reasons he had given for his incredible decision were no reasons at all, she saw now, even as Don Antonio conceived reason, but merely a kind of mocking jest. All that he had told her was lies—and the greatest lie of all was his statement that the Entrada had already left Taos . . . and so (another lie!) it was too late to send warning to Don Pedro of his peril. . . .

"Where are you joining the Entrada, Captain Naranjo?" she asked the scout suddenly.

"At Taos, señora."

"Will it still be there when you arrive?"

"Of course, señora. If not, I'll overtake it somewhere soon."

She rode beside the silent Indian fighter, thinking that of all men in the Kingdom of New Mexico, here was the one who could best be entrusted with a message to Don Pedro . . . thinking also of another equally resolute and resourceful man whose message had never been delivered . . . deciding, finally, that what Don Pedro must know could not be hazarded to writing, or explained even to such a one as Captain José Naranjo . . .

"When are you leaving, Captain?" she asked.

"In the morning, señora."

"Captain . . . I'm going with you."

Captain José Naranjo happened to be in the act of rolling a cigarrito. He finished without a pause or a glance in her direction, struck a light, and exhaled a little drift of smoke.

"Very well, señora," he said. "We'll leave at dawn."

Book Three

Los muertos no hablan.

The dead have nothing to say.

1

ƆN A LOVELY VALLEY where the rivers Chama and Río Grande joined was a settlement called San Pedro de Chama. Oñate had founded it in the year 1598, giving it the name of San Gabriel, and had made it his capital, for a time.

Here, a week after leaving Los Álamos, and only one-third of the way to Taos, Captain Naranjo had been stricken by an obscure but violent sickness. Now, three days later, Josefina stood in a darkened room beside his bed and sought desperately to make a decision. Half-frantic with frustration and impatience, she was tempted cruelly to accept the counsel of Fray Juan de Minguéz, whom they had overtaken here.

"Come with me, señora," the fraile had said. "Otherwise it is a certainty that you shall not catch Don Pedro before he leaves Taos."

"But how can I leave him, padre? Look how sick he is!"

"Nonsense, daughter! He has been sick, I grant. But he is over the hump, no? You have said so yourself. In a couple of days he will be as good as new and will overtake us even before we reach Taos."

Josefina gazed doubtfully at the sleeping man. He was lying quietly, at last, his breathing deep and regular. And yet——

"I think I'll stay with him, padre," she said. "For one thing, he's sure of the road at this season."

"Good." Fray Juan laughed. "I'm off then. Until I see you in Taos, señora . . . unless I lose myself on the way."

Josefina watched him ride away with such a feeling of frustration that she was almost tempted to call after him to wait for her. Yet she could not bring herself to leave Captain Naranjo. He was still so weak—and there was always the possibility of a relapse. Besides . . .

If Fray Juan tells Don Pedro I am coming, he will surely wait for me, she thought. Why didn't I send him a note? But Fray Juan will make him see how urgent . . . he will do it even better than a note could. Compose yourself, Josefina!

But she was spared many hours of anxiety. Almost as soon as he could sit up and take a little broth, Captain Naranjo began to fret over remaining in bed. They were on their way before the sun was a lance high the next morning. Captain Naranjo, grumbling and protesting, had to be helped into the saddle, but once up, he sat it firmly enough, and seemed to grow stronger with each league of the journey northward.

That night they reached the pueblo of San Lorenzo. By the next day he was so refreshed they could ride briskly down the long slopes that led from San Lorenzo into the valley of Taos—"the most fertile and beautiful in New Mexico." Thus they covered the eight leagues quickly and arrived at the pueblo and mission of San Gerónimo de los Taos by noon.

Even before they entered the gate—for Taos alone, of all the pueblos of the Río Grande, was walled—they knew that the Entrada had left.

The great central plaza, cut by a deep-bedded stream and surrounded by a towering huddle of adobe buildings, some of them five and six stories high, was strangely empty. On the high terraces of the huge house blocks—all new, for Taos had burned and been rebuilt only twenty-odd years before—a few women were at work mudding the walls, grinding corn, baking bread in the beehive ovens: some old men wrapped in blankets, some children and many dogs, were all that occupied the vast, dusty plaza. All the rest of the pueblo was busy in the fields of corn and beans and squash encircling the town and spreading up and down the valley. Not a leather jacket, not a Spaniard, was in sight.

"We are too late, señora," Captain Naranjo said.

They cut westward through the towering house blocks to where the church and convent rose high above the defense wall. A young Indian semanero trotted out of the convent to take their horses and remove their spurs. He grinned shyly as he unbuckled Josefina's; he had never seen a Castellana wearing spurs before.

"Ave María!" a voice from a doorway greeted them: it was Fray Juan Minguéz's. "Come in señora, compadre, and learn the bad news."

It was very quickly told. Fray Juan, for all his haste, had arrived at Taos a full two days after the Entrada's departure. And Don Pedro, unaware of Josefina's attempt to reach him, had gone off at the head of it.

"I accompany you in your disappointment, señora," Fray Juan said, with deep sincerity. "It is God's will, however, and no doubt for the best."

"I myself question God's interest in this affair," Captain Naranjo said. "We missed Don Pedro because, like a woman or a priest, I got sick; and the señora, may God bless her, thought it her duty to take care of me."

"Stop blaming yourself, Captain," Josefina said, "for what had to be. Perhaps Fray Juan is right. Perhaps it was God's plan after all."

"Quién sabe?" Naranjo shrugged. "I won't make an argument out of what can't be proved anyhow. The question, señora, is what do you do now? You can't remain here."

"When do you leave, señores?"

"Today, señora—as soon as possible."

They were standing under the long, narrow portal of the convent, talking in low, serious tones; and at this point both men looked with a certain concern, even anxiety, at the face of this dauntless woman. She was a little pale under the dusty French hat; but her chin tilted upwards from the silken scarf about her throat, and her eyes were deep and dark with the intensity of some feeling that neither man could trust himself to name.

She is dead tired, Naranjo thought. She has been through too much!

She is soul-sick, Fray Juan thought. Her heart has been bruised. May God help her!

They were both relieved when, after a long brooding silence, she suddenly smiled and gazed at them with eyes that sparkled again, that seemed all at once to have recaptured their calm audacity.

"Good, señores," she said quietly. "I am going with you."

2

There were two ways one could reach the Great Plains and the route northward to the Río Jesús María.

The shorter was to swing around the southern end of the Sangre de Cristo range and then head north, keeping the mountains always on your left. The other was to strike straight up the Río Grande del Norte and cut eastward through Taos.

In either case one had to cross some high mountains in the end; and, although the southern way may have been a little easier, it was also longer. The Spaniards, to whom difficulties had become a kind of habit and a matter of indifference in New Mexico, always took the shorter route. It was the route that had been chosen by Don Antonio for the Entrada; and so the one by which Josefina, Captain Naranjo, Fray Juan, and a Tewa Indian left the pueblo of Taos on this June morning of the year 1720.

The start had not been made without trouble. Captain Naranjo had flatly rejected the idea of a woman accompanying the Entrada. Josefina pleaded with him, stormed at him, wept.

"It is impossible," Naranjo said stubbornly.

"Very well, mi capitán," she said coldly. "Then I shall go alone."

Perhaps he actually believed her, or possibly he only wanted a reasonable excuse to capitulate. At any rate, he suddenly smiled broadly and said:

"But I couldn't allow that, señora. That you are ready then, to leave in the morning."

"Not today?"

"I'll need a little time," Captain Naranjo said, "to find someone who can see you back."

The escort he selected was an Indian named Gerónimo Bartolomé Niño Gonzales, but called La Bolsa, that is The Pouch, because of his generous belly. His appearance was not prepossessing; but he had a reputation for reliability, sagacity, and a good knowledge of the country toward the plains.

Josefina accepted him indifferently and busied herself with repacking the cantinas—two large leather saddlebags—that would be carried by her spare horse. On leaving Los Álamos, she had been provided by Tichi with everything she could possibly need on a journey much longer than she had expected to make. Tichi had even sent along Yolanda!

"For good luck, señora," she had said. "There is plenty of room."

Josephina had been too distraught at that time, really, to care what Tichi's whim might be. But now she frowned as she returned Yolanda's round blue stare. She straightened the doll's dress, gave her a sudden odd little hug, and wrapped her in a spare manta.

"Ah, well, Tichi," she sighed, "for your sake we shall take her . . . for good luck, no?"

She thought of Tichi as they rode out of the broad valley of Taos toward the mountains, following a stream flowing through groves of great cottonwoods. She wondered what would become of Tichi if anything should happen to herself, Josefina . . . on this journey, for example. She thought what was a kind of prayer for the good Gallega: That God take care of you in that case—and find you a good husband, maybe. At any rate, you have always a home at Los Álamos.

3

The road climbed steadily into the mountains, following a turbulent stream through little woods of aspen and cottonwood. Pine and fir, dark and gloomy, swept almost down to the trail; and farther up the slopes, the snow glistened in vast, wind-swept depressions of the bare rock. The air grew cold and thin. They made rapid time over the tortuous but easy trail, stopping only once during the day for a quick meal beside a little fire—for what Spaniard would eat cold meat if he could avoid it?

By mid-afternoon they had succeeded in crossing the first mountain barrier and descended into a delightful, flower-perfumed valley called La Cieneguilla. Here, beside a stream of delicious water, was evidence of Don Pedro's first camp. But, inviting as the meadows were for grazing the horses, Captain Naranjo called no halt.

They left this pleasant valley and began to climb again, arriving shortly at another canyon, very rough and strewn with fallen timber. As the gloom began to gather in this canyon, long shadows of depression also began to cast themselves across Josefina's spirits. And for the first time on this extraordinary journey she was a little afraid.

Shame on you, Josefina! she rebuked herself. What is there to fear, really?

They camped that night in a cave, high up in the rocks and to be reached only by a narrow trail up a cliff; La Bolsa remained below with the horses.

"Only the Devil could find us here," Josefina overheard Fray Juan pant, "provided he could make the climb."

"What the Devil himself can't find, the Comanches can," Captain Naranjo replied.

"Have you seen any signs?"

"Nothing. But with the señora along, I'm taking no chances."

She remembered these words as she tried to fall asleep that night, and wondered about them a little; but they did not give rise to fear—only to a feeling of gratitude for Captain Naranjo's protection. She said a few decades of her rosary and tried to fall asleep.

But, despite her great fatigue, sleep would not come. Something—the strangeness of her surroundings, the hardness of the cave floor, the peculiar night sounds that echoed up from the canyon below—something made her restive and wakeful; and her mind became oddly active.

Why, Josefina, she asked herself abruptly, why are you here? Why have you come on this pursuit of the Entrada? Of the Entrada? Do not lie to yourself, Josefina. You mean—do you not?—in pursuit of Don Pedro . . . in pursuit of your lover!

She considered in the darkness if this, in fact, could be the case. Was it to see Don Pedro only, to be with him, to throw herself into his arms again . . . was this the reason, the real reason, why she had come . . . why she had been driven to make this fantastic journey?

Ah, no, Josefina! she remonstrated with herself. That is impossible! It was her pride, no doubt, her immutable, passionate Spanish pride that protested so. But it was her stubborn Spanish logic, her impregnable sense of la realidad, that forced her to demand: Then why are you here, Josefina? Could you not, after all, have written a letter? Could not Captain Naranjo have delivered it? Why, indeed, do you keep up this foolish pretense—do you really hope to deceive yourself, Josefina?

But after a while, as a great drowsiness from her excessive fatigue began to spread through her mind and body, all these questions seemed to her less disquieting; and, curiously at last, the idea that she had come this long way from Santa Fé—that she had started on this incredible journey for no better reason, really, than to be with her lover . . . such a reason seemed not so improbable, after all. . . .

When her eyes dropped suddenly shut, like an infant's, she dreamed all night—troubled, searching, confused, ecstatic dreams—about Don Pedro Villasur.

Next morning, having made a difficult climb in the darkness down the cliffside trail, they continued on their way before daylight through the canyon, which Fray Juan christened La Palotada because of the vexatious tangle of fallen trees.

"This," Captain Naranjo remarked, "is the purgatory through which one must pass before entering heaven."

They understood what he meant by this when, breaking out of the canyon at last, they entered a whole series of delightful sunlit valleys, in the first of which was a large pond full of waterfowl. They ascended a pass called The Flowery Pass, dropped down into another valley, and came to a little pool where there was a small cross painted on a tree. They stopped here and refreshed themselves in a small grove of rustling poplars.

"When, do you think, shall we overtake the Entrada?" Josefina asked Naranjo.

"Soon," the captain said, "but it is hard to say just when. They have two days' start on us. I am counting on a halt of a day or two at La Jicarilla for provisioning and fresh horses. We should find the Entrada there."

"When shall we reach La Jicarilla?"

"Tomorrow, señora—if our padre's prayers are any good."

This news cheered Josefina immensely. It set a definite limit and boundary, at last, to something that had become rather frightening in its vast vagueness as the leagues of wilderness fell behind them.

"This Jicarilla—" she asked—"what do we find there, Captain?"

"Not much, señora," Naranjo said. "Some rancherías of the heathen Apaches. Some mud houses . . . maize fields. . . ."

"Pueblos?"

"You might call them that, señora."

"I didn't know there were pueblos beyond the mountains."

"There are many things beyond the mountains, señora," Naranjo said enigmatically, "that are not commonly known along the Río Grande."

Rested and fortified with a meal of toasted jerky and biscuits, they toiled up to the last summit they would have to cross. The trail was very rough and steep. Suddenly, in a jumble of great red boulders, it burst into the open and dipped downwards.

Below them lay the plains.

They reached away forever, without limits, without horizons . . . the mysterious Unknown Lands . . . the home of strange and barbarous and hostile people. Directly below, one could make out the dim trails of the Apaches leading by ancient routes into a limitless void of earth and sky; for in all that vast space below them there was no sign of life.

It is so empty, Josefina thought, and a little shiver ran up her spine. It is frightening!

They wasted no time in contemplation of this first glimpse of the Northern Mystery. They descended the slope immediately, crossed a small river, and then a larger one pleasantly bordered by several kinds of trees, which was called the Río de San Francisco.

Their route lay now through a broad valley with a sierra of low, eroded mountains on their left, the great plains on their right, the immense prairie sky overhead. Great patches of light and shadow swept across the flat, open earth—black earth, such as Josefina had never seen in all New Mexico—and the short grass ran before the wind.

Captain Naranjo ranged far ahead now, riding at times to the summit of a low butte, occasionally scouting the rim of a deep arroyo. This, as all in the little party understood, was country in which to keep a careful watch—if not enemy territory, it was at least territory into which the Utes and Comanches had frequently made warlike thrusts.

"There is no danger, señora," Captain Naranjo assured Josefina. "But when there is no danger . . . that is the time to keep your eyes open, no?"

They camped that night beside a stream of cold, sweet-tasting water, and Josefina closed her eyes with the pleasant thought that next day she would, no doubt, be with Don Pedro. Lying in the soft prairie darkness, she ached for the coming of the next day; but it was a sweet ache, and she fell asleep smiling.

Early the next morning they came to a river, larger than any they had yet encountered, which Captain Naranjo called El Río de Nuestra Señora del Rosario. And up this river, scarcely an arquebus shot from where they stood, they saw the chief ranchería of the Apaches—La Jicarilla.

La Jicarilla did not much resemble the neat and compact pueblos of the Río Grande valley. On one side of the treeless river, a dozen ill-made adobe houses, some of them several stories high, sprawled in a disorder of corrals and refuse heaps. On the other, a score of white leather tepees had been pitched—by the mountain Apaches, no doubt —in a great circle. A patchwork of irrigated fields reached up and down the river; and beyond the houses, lodges, and fields, stretched forever the hazy prairie.

This was the last frontier of the Spanish Borderlands. These were the first of the heathen Indians, and the last on whom the Spaniards could count—even precariously—for a certain friendship. For here the Kingdom of New Mexico ended and the Northern Mystery began. Somewhere—más allá!—were strange tribes, horseless and hostile . . . and the French.

"Quién viva?" a voice shouted at them from the distance.

"España!" Captain Naranjo responded to the challenge. He smiled and added, "All is being conducted very properly on this Entrada!"

A young Tewa horseman, clothed in regulation leather jacket and helmet, dashed around a small butte and pulled up before them. He was one of Captain Naranjo's own scouts. He grinned broadly and saluted.

"Your jacket is open," Captain Naranjo observed coldly. "Where is the camp, Vincente?"

"On the mesa yonder, Captain," the scout said, hastily buttoning up.

They skirted the butte and beyond the river, about a league away on top of a low peñol, they could see the tents of the Entrada.

"The Captain Villasur is expecting you, señor," Vincente said. Then, darting his black eyes once at Josefina, he added with true native courtesy, "—and la señora."

4

Nothing, it appeared to her now, was any longer impossible.

Eva Helena had been right, after all, in her gentle, naïve faith . . . and the Maya in her hard, fierce defiance of the world of men . . . and even Tichi in her simple reliance on her star. . . .

All of them had been right. Nothing was impossible. Strange and improbable things took place . . . and once having taken place, immediately lost their strangeness and improbability. Nothing was even surprising.

Things happened to you . . . or sometimes you arranged to have them happen. You were born poor, but with the green eyes and noble blood of a título de Castilla. You were noticed by the Maya. You were carried by a great passion and, perhaps, an uncommon talent, to the very edge of fame—and then hurled into the abyss. You hid and starved, and seduced a captain of the Indies, and fled with him from Spain. . . . In México you became a secret influence and power at the Court: you schemed and plotted for your captain, and won for him the rule of all New Mexico and its provinces: and then you watched him rot before your eyes. . . . You fell in love with Captain Don Pedro Villasur. . . .

All that had happened since—including this incredible journey across the mountains to La Jicarilla—was still a kind of blur. Impossibilities, too, no doubt—until they had taken place. But now no longer strange, or improbable, or even surprising.

Don Pedro had greeted her very formally, almost coldly, she had thought with sinking heart, when she dismounted at the door of his tent. If he had stared at her, it was only for a moment. He had kissed her hand gravely, and murmured, "At your feet, señora," and all so quietly, with such absolute composure, that it must have seemed to his officers almost an ordinary thing for a woman to ride into camp thus, without warning, forty leagues beyond the mountains from Taos!

She herself was suddenly without words. She glanced at the handful of soldiers behind Don Pedro—and could think of nothing she might say in their curious presence. Captain Naranjo rescued her.

"La señora has brought certain information, señor," he said, after briefly reporting himself, "that she wishes to give you. . . ." He glared significantly at the soldiers. "In private, señor."

There was a kind of veiled dimness and a muffled quiet in Don Pedro's tent. She stood before her lover in a little eternity of muteness, acutely and preposterously aware of all the small, distant sounds of the camp . . . the far-off stir of the horseherd, shouts, the tinkle of mule-bells, the pacing of the guard before the tightly secured tent door. . . . She was in his arms, weak, breathless, bereft of reason and weeping violently.

"Ay, dear Mother of God!" she wailed. "I try so to be strong—but look at me! Are you very angry with me, amor? Do you detest me? Do you hate me, really?"

He reassured her with kisses and endearments, and dried her eyes on his handkerchief.

"You are over-weary, querida," he said. "You are exhausted."

"It hits you all at once, no?" she asked, with a rueful little smile.

He became suddenly grave, almost gruff. There was more of the soldier than the lover in his voice as he asked: "But tell me, now, why you are here. Why have you done this?"

They sat down facing each other on rolls of bedding which served as seats; and she told him, with remarkable dispassionateness and in careful detail, all that she had come to tell.

His face remained expressionless, a little grim perhaps, as he listened. He smiled faintly when she told him of Don Antonio's generous relinquishment of his mistress, with so many protestations of good will, to his friend Captain Villasur. When she had finished, he was thoughtful for a little while; then he began to ask questions.

He flung questions at her rapidly, with precision, and sometimes with startling incisiveness. She could almost see the notes being jotted down in a decisive military mind. His voice had a peculiar hardness, even a harshness. Suddenly she had the curious feeling she was talking with quite another Don Pedro Villasur . . . with one who was not Don Pedro at all . . . with a stranger who bewildered and dazzled her—and frightened her a little.

Vaya! she thought drolly. It seems that you have not one lover but two, Josefina!

But when, quite abruptly, the questioning stopped, Don Pedro's manner changed also. He gazed at Josefina for a little while in what, it seemed, was a kind of wonderment. When he spoke, his voice was warm again, almost gentle.

"Querida mía," he said, "let us first thank God and His Most Holy Mother, who must surely have interceded for you, that you have arrived here safely. You do not know what dangers you escaped!"

"Dangers, amor?"

He smiled and nodded, but offered no explanation of his words. He stood up, erect and soldierly, so that his speech took on a kind of formal, salute-like quality.

"As for you, querida—what is there to say? If you were a soldier, I should reprimand you for rash and foolhardy conduct. As it is, I can only thank you—from my deepest heart." He made a little bow. "I thank you for myself . . . for this whole command. The Kingdom owes you thanks. Even His Majesty can be grateful——"

She stood up also and went to his arms.

"That's enough of speechmaking, señor!" She laughed. "I don't want thanks from anyone. Not even from Captain Don Pedro Villasur. All I want is Captain Villasur's kisses."

She had to struggle free from him this time. She looked at him with wide, pleasantly startled eyes while she regained her breath and composed herself.

"Tell me, amor," she asked, as calmly as she could, "will all be well now?"

"Assuredly," he said. "With God's favor and the proper precautions, we have nothing to fear. All will be well now. . . ."

"Ah, good!" she sighed. "I was certain I should come. Although it was not easy to convince Captain Naranjo of it!"

His laugh, in which she sensed a certain forced lightness, was followed by a long silence.

"Amor——" she began abstractedly.

He too appeared to be preoccupied. She marveled at the changeableness of a soldier's moods. She was a little piqued, also, at his distant manner. Nevertheless, she plunged into what she had to say:

"Amor, I must confess something. It was not alone the necessity of bringing you this information that compelled me to make this journey. That is not the only reason why I am here."

"No?" he asked absently.

"There was also another reason. I was not aware of it at first, not until after we had left Taos, really. Then it came to me all at once, at night, in our first camp . . . when I could not sleep for thinking of you. . . . This other reason—it was my longing for you, amor. I could not endure it any longer. There was nothing I could do but come to you. . . ."

Don Pedro said nothing.

She looked at his expressionless face with a kind of wonder. Then she felt the sudden fury that so many women, she knew, had shared with her.

"But that," she said coldly, bitterly, "could be of little interest to Captain Villasur. Forgive me, señor."

"But, querida——"

He seized her wrist so roughly that she winced from pain. He released her.

"It isn't necessary for you to say it," she blazed at him. "This is an army on the march. A small one, it is true, but an army nevertheless. This is the señor commander's tent. It is not the place, nor the time, to be talking of love. No?"

She felt her own astonishment at the wave of anger—of angry frustration—that had so suddenly engulfed her. If Don Pedro was also surprised, he did not show it. His face was deadly serious.

"I do not make the demands of war," he said. "But I must try to meet them."

All at once, as suddenly as it had come, her fit of ill temper passed. She said contritely, "Forgive me, amor. I am jealous."

His eyes questioned her.

"Of that other mistress of yours—the one that all know by the name of Duty. I had forgotten her!"

Don Pedro laughed, a little ruefully. "She is a cold mistress—that other one!"

"I don't mind her . . . so that you love me no less."

She looked about the dim interior of Don Pedro's tent. Beyond the thin walls every sound of the encampment had a startling *nearness*. She listened, in the long pause now, to the steady tread of the guard outside the door. She felt—with an odd sense of having been cheated —no more by herself with her lover than if they had been in the center of the Plaza at Santa Fé.

"And now that I have come this long way to be with you," she said with a little moue, "I can see that we can hardly hope to be alone!"

He smiled, became serious again. "There is something you will have to know—as well now as later."

"What is it, amor?"

"It will be necessary for you to remain here."

"*Here?*"

"In La Jicarilla."

"But why?"

"It won't be safe for you to return to Taos."

"But there is La Bolsa to go with me. Captain Naranjo arranged it——"

"It wouldn't be safe, querida, if a dozen Bolsas went with you. Somewhere between here and Taos there is a war party of Utes. My scouts reported it this morning. Captain Naranjo, I have no doubt, knows it also—or at least suspects it. If he hasn't told you, it is only because he did not want to frighten you."

She considered this for a little while in silence. At last she said: "Then I shall go with you—with the Entrada."

Don Pedro received this pronouncement with equanimity, almost as if he had expected it.

"That would be impossible," he said.

"Why? Why, Pedro?"

"Women," Don Pedro replied, as one might read from a book of military regulations, "women do not go with troops."

"Ah, no?" she asked, with mock surprise.

"Well, not on hazardous expeditions," he amended, "such as this Entrada."

"What is more hazardous," she demanded, "to remain here with these timid Jicarillas, or to go with you? What if the Utes decide to attack La Jicarilla after you leave? Besides, it's not true."

"What isn't true, querida?"

"That women don't accompany troops. There isn't an army in

Europe, as you well know, Pedro mío, that hasn't as many women as soldiers—at the very battle fronts."

"Camp followers," he said contemptuously. "Concubines."

"I'll go as your concubine, Pedro."

He looked at her in grave silence.

"Why not?" Josefina asked, with a sudden tenseness in her voice. "Are you embarrassed perhaps to acknowledge me as your mistress, Don Pedro?"

He had gone over to the door of the tent and was gazing fixedly through a small opening. His back was turned to her. He said nothing.

"I am not ashamed to be known as Don Pedro Villasur's mistress," she said slowly. "To others the name of wife might seem a better thing. But to my heart that of Don Pedro's amiga is sweeter . . . or even, if they wish, that of Don Pedro's concubine. . . ."

"Josefina," he said tonelessly, without turning. "In God's name, querida."

Her eyes were extraordinarily large and dark, her features taut, with an intensity of emotion to which Don Pedro, even though he faced away from her, was surely not insensible.

"So I go with you, no?"

"It is impossible," he repeated. But there was a certain quality of indecision in his voice that made her heart jump a little.

"Tell me the truth, Pedro," she demanded. "Are there not some women with this very Entrada?"

He turned and gave her a faint smile of acknowledgement. "A few Tewa women, to cook and mend gear for the scouts."

"Well, that settles it."

Captain Don Pedro Villasur had the reputation of being an officer who, once having made up his mind, was inflexible in his purpose. It was quite obvious to Josefina now that he had arrived at some decision.

He came to her and took both her hands in his.

She looked up at his grave, dark face in bewildered expectation. There was something in his eyes that she had never seen there before . . . something that made her heart sing with excitement.

"Josefina, querida," he said with an odd formality. "It will be possible for you to accompany this expedition on one condition . . . that you come as my wife."

At first she thought that she had not heard him rightly. She was conscious, all at once, of the vast weariness of mind and body and heart that had burdened her for so long; and her voice sounded tired and hollow as she heard herself asking: "What did you say, amor?"

His answer was a voice in a dream to her now, fugitive echoes of dimly heard words, as she knelt with him before Fray Juan Minguéz. Of what he had actually said she could not be sure. What she remembered may have been only the memory of her own heart's voice; but it seemed to her that he had said, with a kind of tender solemnity: "That you do me the honor, querida mía, of becoming la Doña Josefina Villasur de Torres."

And she, matching his own odd solemnity, had answered: "You know, amor, my heart is yours entire."

And, having said that, she had wept desperately, miserably, happily against his breast. She had burrowed her face into the angle of his neck and shoulder and had refused to look at him. She had clung to him with all her strength—with a vehemence that drew its force from something older, and perhaps even stronger, than her love for Don Pedro Villasur—and waited for the swirling turmoil in her head to cease. . . .

She heard Don Pedro recite after Fray Juan Minguéz the words of Holy Church's marriage service—words mechanically repeated by herself after Fray Juan, after Don Pedro—and she glanced from beneath her veil at the veiled face of the man to whom she was being married on this windy plain, under this vast prairie sky. And once more she asked herself: Por qué, Josefina. . . . Why?

For it could not seem enough to her, somehow, that Don Pedro loved her. She must search for other reasons . . . reasons back of and beyond his love for her . . . something more solid, even, than love to bring reality to this dream.

She had changed from riding clothes to a dress of pale green silk that Tichi—who seemed to have had a kind of clairvoyant foreknowledge of all possibilities—had tucked into one of the cantinas at Los Álamos. And while she was changing and preparing for her wedding with the help of one of the Tewa women, she had asked herself this question over and over, considering many answers—and finding satisfaction in none.

She had not hoped to become the wife of Don Pedro Villasur: she had thought to be no more than his mistress.

He had never spoken of marriage except to say that he had never fallen into the habit of marriage! Of what advantage indeed could it be to him to marry . . . to marry Josefina María del Carmen Torres?

But he loved her, no? She did not doubt this. But this was merely a closing of the circle. This was not answer enough. What could Don Pedro as a husband gain that Don Pedro as a lover did not already have? Could she love him more as wife than she already did as mistress!

I think there is a reason besides love, she said to herself pensively, why Don Pedro wishes to marry me.

She finished dressing and gave up wondering too. Only Don Pedro, she knew, could give her the true answer to this strange question that echoed, even now, through Fray Juan's words and hers and Don Pedro's . . . and, something told her, she would learn it soon. . . .

She felt the cool golden wedding band—much too large: it was one that Don Pedro himself had worn—slip over her finger. . . . Then nothing. . . . Then Fray Juan's voice again:

"The God of Israel join you two together, and He be with you, who took pity on two only children . . ."

And so, on the lonely plain of an alien land, kneeling under the immense sky before the cross that cast the shadow of Holy Faith athwart every Spanish camp, the daughter of Eva Helena became la Doña Josefina Villasur de Torres. . . .

She lifted the veil from her face and cast a quick glance upwards into the illimitable blue of the prairie sky. With what wonder, she thought, must her mother be watching now. With what wonder and innocent joy!

5

The great stars came out. She stood at the door of her tent, a little apart from the officers' quarters, and watched the imperceptible march of the heavens.

Ah, Tichi, she thought, perhaps you were right, after all!

She heard Don Pedro's voice in the darkness bidding someone good night, then his approaching steps. Almost immediately after their marriage—in the very midst of their little wedding feast—he had been called away by the arrival of a scout with alarming news of the Utes. (It had been a lovely feast, with several bottles of Manchan wine, and rich preserves, and white Spanish bread; and it had been served on the silver plate that Don Pedro had brought with him.) But, although the fears of the Utes had proved groundless, it was late when Don Pedro returned from his reconnaissance, and dark before he could come to Josefina. He stopped a few paces away and regarded her quizzically.

"What is this soldier's wife looking for?" he inquired dramatically. "For her absent warrior, no doubt."

"You are wrong, my husband."

"So? For what, then?"

"For a certain star."

"And have you found it?"

"No. But it is there. . . . Come in, amor."

When he took her into his arms, it was with an odd, almost ceremonial kind of gentleness. With tenderness rather than passion. She sensed at once a subtle and vaguely puzzling difference in this lover who had become her husband.

Their lips met then, and for a long frenzied moment the difference vanished.

But it returned again, to perplex and even to trouble her . . . a certain abstracted expression in his dark, serious eyes . . . the way he held her at arm's length, gazing at her exactly as one might savor some lovely—and lifeless—bibelot.

A strange and disturbing image flashed into her mind; the memory of the Conde de Vega appraising a small Roman portrait head with much the same expression of contemplative delight! She suddenly twisted out of Don Pedro's hands and turned her back to him.

"That you unbutton me, señor."

He unfastened her bodice with awkward masculine fingers. When the silk fell away from her shoulders, he kissed each of those twin dimples that some critics, in the old days, had considered one of the minor faults that detracted a little, perhaps, from La Sola's total beauty.

She whirled about, reached up, and laced her arms around his neck.

"Are you sorry?" she demanded.

"For what, querida?" he asked, in genuine perplexity.

"It was a trick, no? I tricked you!"

The bewilderment in his eyes deepened.

"You will never regret it, amor?"

"Soul of my soul! What are you saying?"

She wrenched herself free from the sudden roughness of his embrace, and asked the question to which she herself had not yet been able to find the answer:

"Why did you marry me, Pedro?"

She could feel the pounding of her pulses as she waited for him to answer: she could almost feel her heart leap when—with deeper truth, she knew, than ever he suspected—Don Pedro grinned, and kissed her quickly on the mouth, and said:

"Because I love you. . . . And I will tell you something else, my little heart . . . I have always wanted a Spanish bride!"

6

Sitting her restless horse on a hillock overlooking the parade of the encampment, Josefina observed Captain Don Pedro Villasur's Entrada organize itself for the start of the long march to the Río Jesús María.

What a few, she thought, with a little shiver of apprehension, to go against so many!

Compared to the great expedition of over six hundred men and nearly a thousand animals that Don Antonio Valverde had led the year before, it was indeed a puny force: not more than sixty Spaniards in all, and sixty Indians!

But Captain Villasur had trained and equipped his little command to the last exacting requirement of a notoriously rigorous officer. The soldiers were all veterans of the campaigns of Vargas, Hurtado, and Ulibarri and they were the equal of the best of Spain, which is to say equal to the best in the world. Everything was being done with snap and precision. Discipline was obviously good, morale high.

She watched with what quiet efficiency Don Pedro directed preparations; and she felt a wifely pride not only in Don Pedro but—a thing that proved her to be already a true officer's mate—in his whole tight little command.

Its main body consisted of forty-two presidial troops and three militiamen, all armed and equipped with guns, short swords, lances, munitions, leather helmets, round leather shields, and those leather jackets of several thicknesses which served as a sort of armor and which caused Spanish soldiers to be called "soldados de cuera." Then, separated from the Spaniards by the pack-animals and a flock of sheep, the Indians who served as herdsmen, horse wranglers, camp cooks, and, in a pinch, as fighting men.

On the march, the troops would be preceded by a small vanguard in which would ride Don Pedro, his adjutant Dominguez, Fray Minguéz, the campaign captains Serna and Olguín, and others including Jean L'Archévèque—who had brought with him, to Captain Naranjo's inexpressible disgust, ten pack-horses and three mules laden with trade goods, and a personal armed servant. Another small body would protect the rear; while far ahead and on the flanks, forever searching for the enemy and for water, would range Captain Naranjo and his Apache scouts.

And now the moment of departure had arrived. Don Pedro, his helmet gleaming in the first light of the sun, raised his sword and shouted the order to march. Drums and bugles shattered the momentary stillness, banners and the cross slanted forward, and the Entrada to the Río Jesús María moved ahead in a great cloud of dust and a din of muleteers' profanity.

It was a brave show, put on with true Spanish swagger and arrogance. But to Josefina, looking down from her eminence, this little handful of men suddenly appeared pitifully insignificant, and almost forlorn, against the vast Unknown of the encircling plains. And all she could think of as she spurred Negra down the slope to join the approaching vanguard was:

The French . . . to the number of two hundred, all well armed . . . and the Pawnees, also armed with guns, whose number is endless. . . .

But she forgot her qualms when the presidials raised a cheer as she cantered toward the vanguard. She had always been their favorite. She saluted them, not too gaily, but not too gravely either, and took her place between Fray Juan and Don Pedro at the head of the column.

The route of the Entrada lay due north from La Jicarilla. After a march of two hundred and forty miles, it would arrive at a place called El Cuartelejo, a common resort for roaming bands of friendly —or supposedly friendly—Apaches. There a halt would be made to reprovision, rest the horses, dry some meat, and perhaps recruit a few Indian skirmishers. Then northward again to the Río Jesús María; and eastward along that river to a spot, two hundred miles beyond El Cuartelejo, where it was thought the Pawnees had built their villages.

As she rode along, silently beside her husband, Josefina added up these incredible distances in her head. They had already come more than a hundred miles from Santa Fe. It was another two hundred to El Cuartelejo. And beyond that to the Pawnee country—who knew how far? Another two hundred miles, some said, but others claimed it was even farther.

Ay, caramba! she thought in a kind of awe. This will be no promenade, Josefina!

But as the expedition settled down to its leisurely course of ten or twelve miles a day—it must move slowly because of the sheep—there was something in its steady, methodical progress that reassured her. So many Spaniards had made so many entradas such as this, after all. With them it was a kind of habit!

On each rise of ground she peered hard ahead, as if searching for some clue to the nature of the great Unknown into which they were heading.

"Are there more mountains to cross?" she asked Don Pedro.

"Only the Sierra Blanca," he answered. "About five days march from here."

"And after that?"

"The plains again, as far as El Cuartelejo."

"And then?"

"Quién sabe, querida?" He smiled. "Nobody has ever been farther."

She glanced covertly at the calm, confident face of Captain Don Pedro Villasur riding at the head of his elite little troop, and she put aside the fears that, in spite of her resolution, had mingled with her curiosity.

At Don Pedro's side she felt a quiet assurance of safety—not only from the dangers of this Entrada, but from all others. In his arms she had found more than ecstasy: she had found peace at last, and freedom from those ancient anxieties that had clung to her mind and heart since childhood. It was as if she had arrived safely from a long and often frightening journey. It was as if life were but beginning now. . . .

Even though this Entrada should come to grief, she told herself seriously and dispassionately, even though it should end in disaster for all of us . . . there will be nothing for you to regret, Josefina.

She could make even such reflections without any feeling of sadness now. She was too deeply happy to experience anything, really, except her happiness . . . and her love for Don Pedro. She looked across the rolling hills, swept with great patches of yellow flowers, and up at the scoured sky filled with neat little puffball clouds; and she thought how beautiful and peaceful the whole world was.

They were traveling "by the needle," that is, going ten or twelve degrees east of true north, over a very high mesa of sometimes hilly, sometimes perfectly flat prairie. Their progress was slow but steady and pleasant; for, although the route was less attractive here than it had been below La Jicarilla, they were passing through familiar country and the summer heat had not yet set in.

Camp broke each morning as soon as it was light enough to see. A hasty breakfast was eaten, Mass heard if it were a saint's day—which almost every day was—and the mules loaded.

The sun was usually well up before the march was resumed, and it continued without pause for any respite at noon. After five or six hours of steady advance, camp was pitched, the mules unsaddled and turned loose, supper cooked around a dozen little fires, and perhaps there was evening prayer to Holy Mary of the Rosary before the troops turned in.

All was conducted with the method and order characteristic of a Spanish march. Each morning a man was detailed to count his paces, so that the command could know exactly what distance had been covered. Each evening another noted in the journal of the Entrada all information that might be of interest to the Viceroy: the nature of the country traversed, the Indians encountered, any unusual event. The camp and horseherd of the Indians was meticulously separated from that of the Spaniards. No camp was ever pitched beside a stream until that stream had been crossed.

At night, when officers and men were relaxed for a little while around the fires, there was a democratic mingling of rank and file to be found in no other army of the eighteenth century; for the captains of the Indies ate, dressed, worked, and fought just like their private soldiers. Only Jean L'Archévèque held himself a little apart from both officers and men.

As for Josefina, she appeared to present no problem to the troops. They had for so long been accustomed to expect almost anything of La Dama Josefina that they accepted her presence in the camp without embarrassment, almost without comment. They simply gave her the respect and affection they had always shown her in the Villa; and there was not a muleteer who felt that he must temper the splendor of his profanity because of Josefina's ears.

"She is a Castellana, no?" they said. "Viva la Castellana!" And they let it go at that.

Most of the soldiers were cheerful and carefree men, and Josefina found amusement and entertainment in their endless banter and wrangling.

"Why do the mules follow the mulera?"

"Why do you suppose, tonto? Why do you follow Conchita?"

"Mules are not interested in that."

"Then why do they follow the mare?"

"Because they become accustomed to the bell she wears. They are attached to it."

"Madre de Dios! Pablo, come here! Listen to this about the mules!"

Most of their talk, indeed, when it was not about women or horses or the paucity of their pay—and the difficulty of getting it from Don Antonio—turned to those fruitless and extravagant arguments to which soldiers of all times and nations are addicted.

Was a firelock any better than a bow and arrow?

When was the best time of year to attack an Apache village?

Was a Navajo girl superior in certain ways to one of the Pueblos?

How long could a horse go without water?

But sometimes, particularly around the fires at night, these veterans of so many campaigns against the savage Indians of the plains recounted battles, dawn surprises, ambushes, and exterminations—"by the governor's order, we gave no quarter to any child over the age of

six"—that gave Josefina, even in their telling, cold shivers of revulsion
. . . and apprehension.

On the fourth day after leaving La Jicarilla, having crossed a deep,
wide arroyo called the Río Colorado, they entered a suddenly rough
stretch of country; and ahead of them rose the wall of the Sierra
Blanca.

The climb to the barren, windy pass was so difficult that it was
necessary to divide the cavalry and the horseherds into several groups
in order to get them over the tortuous trail. But when they had accomplished it and stood on the crest of the last mountain barrier
between them and the Río Jesús María, they looked out at the most
tremendous sight of the whole New World: the vast, angry, snow-
covered range of the Sierra de Almagre reaching forever northward
between the Ocean of the West and the Great Plains.

There was a moment when, as they began to descend the slope, the
crest of the Sierra Blanca rose slowly, like a closing gate, behind them.
At that moment Josefina, struggling with all the power of her will not
to look back, kept her eyes resolutely on the broad back of Don
Pedro's leather jacket, and said an old prayer to La Conquistadora
who, she reflected, had never failed her after all:

"That you speak good things for me in the sight of God, O Virgin
mother . . . that you help me now!"

7

Not long after leaving La Jicarilla, Captain Naranjo's scouts began to
bring in vague but disquieting reports. Various suspicious signs and
traces were discovered. The marks of tent poles on the prairie. The
remains of a fire. A loose horse—a pinto and of no value in Spanish
eyes—dragging a neck rope, a bridle thong looped around its lower
jaw—Comanche style.

"There is only one thing I fear more than a mounted Comanche,"
Ignacio Ortega was heard to admit.

"What is that, 'Nacio?"

"Two mounted Comanches!"

To avoid contact with these fierce marauders of the plains, Captain
Villasur marched his troops as close as possible to the mountains on
the left, thus protecting his flank with the least difficulty. The low
foothills of the great sierra were always a few musket shots away now,

and just beyond them the flashing, snow-covered peaks of the Almagre range.

On the right, stretching forever eastward, there was nothing but the empty plains.

The long days and the long miles fell monotonously behind them. Like a worm making its way over the folds and pleats of a doffed mantle, the Entrada undulated over the flowing hills, sometimes skirting a butte, sometimes dipping into an arroyo with sheer red banks and flat, green waterless bottom. The view from the top of each rise was like that from the one before. The mountains were always on their left.

But if the land was unchanging, the sky was never the same. It had not yet faded into that emptiness of color that would come later with the great heats: it was blue as a piece of turquoise from the Cerrillo hills, and Josefina had a strong sense of its nearness, of its envelopment. It seemed to come down to the very ground, and she had the odd feeling of moving not under the sky, but through it.

Sometimes the whole sky was still; and the woolly clouds stood absolutely motionless in the ambient blueness, even though the wind had everything in motion around her. Sometimes it was a vast confusion of movement, with three or four different rain squalls sweeping the horizons at the same moment, and patches of blue spaced between the dark, down-sweeping areas of rain. And at night, when the stars came out, the lonely glory of the prairie sky was almost frightening.

Their progress continued over the thinly veiled hills of hard gray earth at a tedious ten or twelve miles a day. They arrived at a stream named the Río de las Ánimas. The banks of this river were lined with luxuriant growths of poplar and elder; and in one of the cool, clear pools beneath the trees Josefina bathed while her Tewa woman stood guard.

A few days later, a small band of friendly Apaches rode into camp with the news that they had discovered five Comanche warriors and had trailed them as far as they had dared toward their ranchería. Fear of the Comanche flared up again. It erupted into something near to panic when, in the middle of the following night, the whole camp was aroused by the shouts of the sentries:

"To arms! To arms! The Comanches are coming!"

This "Comanche attack" proved to be nothing more than a stampede of the Indian horseherd. But such was the confusion and excitement caused by one untied horse that a presidial named Juan de Dios Padilla was said to have saddled his mount backwards. Whether or not this was literally true, it was a story that undoubtedly would stick to the unfortunate Juan de Dios for the rest of his days.

"How does it happen," Josefina asked Don Pedro, "that these soldiers who have campaigned so often are so nervous?"

"Old soldiers reckon the odds," Don Pedro said. "As you know, querida, they are not in our favor."

"Is there real danger of a Comanche strike?"

"I don't think so," Don Pedro said. "But we are taking no chances. At least there will be no Comanche surprise."

In line with this careful policy, several night marches were made in places where the ground was very dry and dust clouds would have betrayed the position of the Entrada. The route was then laid close to the mountains, and it was necessary to slaughter all the sheep. The camp moved only after darkness, and quartered in wooded depressions in the foothills.

Then, quite suddenly, danger of the Comanches faded.

The Entrada moved out into the flat plains lying south of the Río de Napestle. This was the country of the Carlana Apaches, a strong tribe, implacable enemies of the Comanches and Utes, and powerful enough to keep their vast reserve comparatively clear of intruders. A constant watch was kept now for bands of friendly Carlanas who, it was expected, might join the Entrada and accompany it to El Cuartelejo. But friends, as well as enemies, maintained a kind of invisible presence in the vast emptiness of the prairie; and the Entrada made its way in slow and toilsome isolation.

There were no trails and few landmarks here, and it was not difficult to become lost. To keep a straight course, it was necessary for Indian bowmen to shoot arrows in the direction of march, then from where the first arrow fell to release another in the same line of flight. Sometimes they were helped by hummocks of grass which the Apaches had placed at short intervals to mark their course toward El Cuartelejo. But even these were of no use to the Carlana guides at times; and the Entrada was forced to halt for as much as a whole day while the scouts ranged ahead in search of the trail—and water. For in this arid land the concern of all was forever water.

At last Captain Naranjo, who was then riding with the main body, recognized two little hills on the horizon, exactly alike, sharp and pointed.

"Las Tetas," he said.

Josefina, Don Pedro, and Fray Minguéz all looked at him expectantly.

"The Teats," Captain Naranjo repeated. From here the road was plain to El Cuartelejo.

"God grant it!" Fray Juan murmured devoutly. "If we must depend on our scouts, I doubt that we'll ever reach it."

That same afternoon they came to a great river flowing with deeper, fresher, and more beautiful water than any they had yet encountered. The Indians called it the Río de Napestle. It was more than four times as wide as the Río Grande del Norte and, as Captain Ulibarri had noted in his diary, it bathed the best and broadest valley discovered in New Spain.

It had taken Ulibarri the time of thirty-three Credos recited very slowly to ford this magnificent stream. Now the water was too deep for fording. Captain Villasur was forced to halt here and build rafts on which to make a crossing. There was plenty of driftwood along the banks to supply the material. The rafts were lashed together, the baggage ferried over, the mules and horses swum across; and the whole command landed safely on the other side by the following afternoon.

At this point the Entrada had been on the march two days short of a month. Less than half the distance from Taos to the Pawnee villages on the Río Jesús María had been covered.

8

To Josefina the crossing of the Río de Napestle did not bring the same sense of satisfaction and mild triumph that the rest of the command appeared to feel. It depressed and saddened her. Like the crossing of the Sierra Blanca divide, it was but the closing of another gate behind them.

"I cannot help it, amor," she confessed that night to Don Pedro. "I have no courage. Do I show my fear?"

"On the contrary, querida," he reassured her. "You appear to be the bravest soldier of this command."

"Ah, well," she sighed. "If one cannot be brave, the next best thing, I guess, is to appear brave. That you kiss me again, darling. That is the best cure for fear."

It was true that in Don Pedro's arms she not only lost the apprehension that dogged her, sometimes vaguely, sometimes cruelly, on the long day marches; but a kind of bold and reckless indifference to danger, to the ultimate end of the Entrada, to her very fate indeed, accompanied her passion. And afterward she could lie quietly awake through the whole night beside her husband, without a whisper of anxiety to disturb her drowsy thoughts or, at last, the contentment of her dreams.

She knew that some questioned the usefulness of Don Pedro's European training against savage foes who fought with every ruthless and unorthodox means. And she herself had wondered a little when she discovered that he had brought along, for his own use, several silver platters, cups and spoons, a silver candlestick and a silver-mounted inkhorn, writing paper, quills, and a silver saltcellar.

Ah, Pedro mio! she thought, in spite of herself. That God give you the favor of His help!

But then, as she glanced sideways at the strong, grave face of the man riding beside her, these doubts would vanish. Her husband, she told herself, was a brave, resolute and competent officer. Did not everyone say so? No one, she had noticed—not even Captain Naranjo—had displayed more coolness and soldierly calm when the horse-herd went into the stampede.

As for the experience, she told herself, there are the captains Naranjo, Olguín, and Serna, no? So she reassured herself—but was never quite reassured.

Don Pedro ordered a day's halt beside the Río de Napestle so that the men could refresh themselves, and the horses, many of which were crippled and footsore, could rest.

It was a delightful spot in which to make a break in the long journey. An abundance of cherries, plums, and wild grapes grew in the groves of tall poplars; and many of the men gathered the delicious fruit. Others, however, could think of no greater pleasure than to nap in the leafy coolness of the river bank. Josefina and Don Pedro bathed together in one of the quiet, hidden pools of clear-running water. And in the evening they feasted on delectable tamales made from the meat of deer and fat prairie hens the Indians had hunted during the day.

All left this pleasant resting place with regret and continued, east-ward now, across the completely treeless plains in the direction of the Apaches' great ranchería. The country they were penetrating was so barren that, for the first time, they had to build their fires with buffalo chips. There was little water, and at times the whole command was forced to scatter in search of a small stream or muddy spring.

On the third day after leaving the Río de Napestle they encountered a band of Carlana Apaches who professed great joy at seeing them in their country and gave them buffalo meat and green corn. These Indians, accompanying the Entrada toward El Cuartelejo, were joined by others, until a great escort, far outnumbering the little company of Spaniards, encircled Don Pedro's command.

"I hope they are indeed friendly!" Josefina said apprehensively. "They look very fierce, no?"

"There is nothing to fear from these people, querida," Don Pedro assured her. "They want our help against their enemies, the Pawnees. They fear the Pawnees more than they hate us. So they are our friends."

"Are they against the French also?"

"Yes, because the French are friendly with the Pawnees."

"It is very complicated!"

But not so very different, she reflected, from matters as they stood on the continent of Europe. There it was always the French, the Austrians, the Spaniards and the English. Here it was the French, the Spaniards, the Apaches, and the Pawnees.

She thoughts of the Maya who, much better than any woman in Spain, perhaps, had known what was required of one to survive in the mad, disordered world of war and duplicity and masculine brutality that was the reign of Philip V . . . who understood best la supervivencia.

Ah, Doña Manuela, she said to herself, what would you have done in my place?

"I don't know, chica," she could almost hear the Maya answer. "But I am quite sure that I would not have found myself on this Entrada!"

She glanced at Don Pedro, holding his reins high and gazing with calm interest at the distant tents of El Cuartelejo.

I am sure of that also, Doña Manuela, she replied silently. But I do not regret anything. Perhaps I am as stupid as ever, no? Or maybe I have become even wiser than the Maya!

9

Early the next morning Don Pedro and his whole camp, dressed "in gala" and bearing the cross and the red-and-gold banners of Spain, rode into the central plaza of the great encampment of more than two hundred Apache tents.

Now followed the usual speeches and expressions of joy, the embraces and assurances of good will. Fray Juan Minguéz intoned the *Te Deum Laudemus* and sang three times the hymn in praise of the sacrament. When these ceremonies were over, Don Pedro drew his sword.

"Knights, companions, and friends!" he said in a loud, clear voice. "Let the great settlement of El Cuartelejo be pacified by the arms of us who are the vassals of our monarch, king and natural lord, Don Philip the Fifth—may he live forever!"

"Is there anyone to contradict?" demanded the adjutant José Dominguez.

"No! No!" the whole command shouted.

"Long live the king! Long live the king! Long live the king!" Don Pedro then cried.

He cut the air in all four directions with his sword, the soldiers discharged their guns, and everybody threw his hat into the air. With that the ceremony in the plaza ended.

Afterwards there was much visiting and giving of gifts—bison meat, roasting ears, tamales, plums, and other things to eat from the Indians; pinole, chocolate, biscuits, gaudy clothing, and trinkets from the Spaniards—and much talk about the French, the Pawnees and Comanches, about alliances and confederations and threats of war and counterplans.

But in all of these momentous matters Josefina discovered an odd lack of interest. She wanted only to remain in her tent, shut off from the raucous tumult of the great encampment. She desired nothing but peace and a little quiet.

Perhaps it was exhaustion that had brought on a depression deeper, and in some manner different, from any she had ever experienced before—even in the darkest days of her early adversity and humiliation. Or perhaps it was a kind of shock, a sudden revulsion of the spirit, that she had suffered at El Cuartelejo.

Among the many reports given to the Spaniards by the Cuartelejo chiefs was one relating to the murder of two French people, a man and a woman, by these same Cuartelejo Apaches. It was a story the Indians told with a great deal of pride, and they exhibited as evidence of its truthfulness some things they had taken from the pair: a long gun, a kettle, a red-lined cap, and some fine French powder. They also showed a scalp of long, straw-colored hair.

"The scalp," Captain Naranjo explained, "is not that of the man. He was bald. It is that of the woman." The Indian fighter's dark face was touched by an unaccustomed softness. "La pobrecita!" he said. "She was pregnant."

For several mornings Josefina had experienced a feeling of nausea; and during the day an odd disinterest in food, a sensation of emptiness, even after eating. She was not unaware of the possible meaning of these discomforts. But it did not occur to her that there was any connection between them and Captain Naranjo's story of the pregnant French woman who had been scalped by the Apache, and the depression which seemed to envelop her like a pall.

Vaya! Vaya! she rebuked herself. How is it, Josefina, that you feel so sad? This is something to make you happy, no?

10

On the morning of July 15, 1720, the feast day of St. Henry, Emperor, the reconnaissance to the Río Jesús María heard Mass, bade the Cuartelejos a brave adiós, and marched away with banners tugging against the prairie wind—but hardly stronger in men or armament than when it had left Santa Fé.

"I don't like the looks of these lousy Apaches," Captain Naranjo said gloomily. "I wouldn't miss them if they decided to stay at home."

"Don't you trust them, Captain?" Don Pedro asked.

"No, señor."

"What do you suggest, then?"

"Nothing, señor. To send them back would be to insult the whole Apache nation. Better to have a few bad bets with us than a thousand enemies in our rear."

"Well, watch them closely," Don Pedro said, "and keep me informed."

"Yes, señor."

The sun climbed up on their right flank, for they were marching directly northward now. The country they were penetrating was the real Unknown, the true Northern Mystery, as the Spaniards since Coronado's day had called it. Coronado, farther south, had hoped to find a Golden Man there and cities glittering with jewels. But he had found no El Dorado, no gold, no jewels. All he had found was misery and suffering . . . and death. What, Josefina wondered, would *they* find?

"Sometimes, amor," she said to Don Pedro, "I have a feeling that this is something from which we won't return."

"That is for God to decide, no?" Don Pedro answered. "As for me, I trust He will bring us back safely. There have been few entradas that have come to grief under His protection. So quiet your fears, querida mía."

"Ah, yes," she said. "I will."

She gazed at the face of her husband, sun-darkened and weathered, beneath the gleaming steel of his morion; and she thought how much —and in what a different way now—she loved him.

"There is only one thing more," she said, after a while.

"Yes, Josefina mía?"

"I should not like to die until after I have had your child."

"Por favor, querida! That you rid your mind of these thoughts!"

She had wondered, even had feared a little, how Don Pedro would take the news of her pregnancy. To be burdened with a woman on such an expedition as this was awkward enough; but to have along a woman with child——!

That I should have done this to you, Pedro mío! she thought ruefully.

But to her relief, and rather to her amazement, Don Pedro had received the news with a grave joy. So great, indeed, was his pride that Josefina had been moved by some deep compulsion to ask him: "Have you no other children, amor?"

"None," Don Pedro answered seriously. "None that bear my name."

He gazed at her for a long moment, and then added all that she needed to know about the ultimate source of his pleasure and pride: "None of the limpieza de sangre."

So! she had thought, in a flash of anger. That is all he cares for, no? He has a Spanish wife—now all he wants is a child of pure Spanish blood. Ay, Madre de Dios! Have you never loved me for myself, Don Pedro Villasur?

But she recognized this as a kind of jealousy perhaps, and of all the vices she had always thought that the meanest. So her pique passed quickly; and now it was a kind of simple desire not to disappoint Don Pedro in anything—which the Maya had mentioned once as a true token of love—that caused her to say: "Well, God grant, Pedro, that we bring our child back safely—and that it will be a son."

"But I would welcome a daughter," Don Pedro said. "One that would be as beautiful as her mother, no?"

They rode side by side in silence for a while. Then: "Pedro," Josefina said pensively.

"Yes, querida."

"There is yet another thing."

He waited for her to go on.

"It cannot be denied," she said slowly, "that it *can* happen. No, Pedro?"

"But, querida——"

"If it does, will you promise that you will do it yourself . . . before the Pawnees can touch us?"

He said, "I promise."

As if by an agreed signal they both spurred their horses into a brisk canter and raced ahead of the column. It was the last time that Josefina said anything about this matter to Don Pedro.

11

The Entrada plodded steadily northward. Even though the sheep had been slaughtered during the night marches, it could not manage to average more than a dozen miles a day. Many circumstances leagued against the Entrada to slow its progress to a painful crawl: it was almost as if a hidden enemy were throwing up cunning obstacles in its path.

Sometimes, for example, the whole command was forced to stand still for hours while the scouts and part of the main body searched for water—for a muddy hole filled with a liquid so thick and black and evil-smelling that not even the horses would drink it; or until a well had been dug in the sandy bottom of a dry arroyo, into which a little water presently might seep. For all too often the water hole promised by the Apache guides would turn out to the nothing but a dried-up buffalo wallow, and the well dug in the arroyo bed would yield nothing but a tantalizing dampness.

"Who knows," Jean L'Archévèque said one night, poking at the buffalo chip fire of their dry camp, "who knows but what we are marching into a country of no water at all?" The others heard him say this in silence. He looked about him and added: "Maybe we had better turn back while we can, amigos—before what little water there is behind us has dried up completely."

"Maybe," Captain Naranjo said slowly, "maybe we could do without ten horses and six pack-mules loaded with trade goods. They drink a lot of water, those sixteen animals."

"I have told you, Naranjo," L'Archévèque said boldly, "they are loaded with supplies necessary to this expedition."

"You have never told anyone exactly what, Don Juan."

"What I do, I do by the Governor's permission."

"It is natural," Captain Naranjo said, with astounding frankness, "to wonder who will share the profits when those goods are traded."

"I demand to know what you mean, señor. I demand——" L'Archévèque shouted.

"If they are ever traded," Naranjo added quietly.

"Can you prevent me from trading them?" L'Archévèque screamed.

"No, señor. But perhaps the Pawnees can!"

Don Pedro interposed to end this quarrel, but it flared up again

306

occasionally as the march lengthened and its difficulties increased. Captain Naranjo was not alone in resenting the Frenchman's presence, as a trader, on this long, hard, and—as they now all understood—dangerous expedition. During the early stages of the march, he was tolerated, even joked about a little—but he was less amusing now that water was so scarce and the heat had set in.

For the heat was as bad as the want of water.

It streamed down now out of a white sky without a cloud, a sky empty of everything except the occasional passage of a bird. It blazed at them from a sun that had them helpless in a land without a tree or even a shrub, without a single thing to cast a shadow but themselves.

Through the unremitting torment of this great heat the Entrada moved over the flat, dry, hard earth from one milky horizon to the other, from one fiery day to the next, from hope of a little rain to the dull acceptance of disappointment. Everything that one saw, or felt, or thought of was related to the heat:

The whirling clouds of dust that raced before them across the shimmering plains were part of it.

The occasional herds of buffalo, startlingly black against the tawny roll of the prairie, sending tremendous billows of powdered earth skyward, were part of it.

The horse or mule, swollen by heat, that would buckle at last under its unbearable load and die was part of it.

The "leather-jacket" talking wildly in his sleep, dreaming of the cool, green valley of the Río de Santa Fé—he too was part of the huge and inescapable fact of the heat.

Fray Minguéz said the special Mass for Rain. He prayed before his cross and a little altar set up on the dusty plain:

"Grant us healthful rain we beseech thee, O Lord, and on the parched face of the earth deign to pour forth showers from heaven. Through our Lord."

But God, perhaps, had meant the prairies to be waterless. His days succeeded one another without even a little rain, without even a little relief.

Then—as if all things must happen immoderately in this crude and brutal land—a terrifying thunderstorm accompanied by driving waves of rain broke over them. It sent the men, cursing and laughing, to cover the packs and to clear the drainage ditches. It soaked everyone to the skin with its chill, delicious downpour. It raged across the whole high prairie sky with a vast and awesome violence that Josefina had never before experienced. After each blinding flash of lightning, she pressed her hands over her ears and waited with startled eyes for the thunderclap that followed.

"Madre de Dios!" she gasped. "Help us!"

Even the presidials appeared a little subdued by so convincing a proof of God's power. Josefina observed Captain Naranjo cross himself after an especially violent explosion of the skies. Fray Juan Minguéz observed it also.

"Our Captain of War is a very religious man—at times, no?" he remarked dryly.

"I know when I am outnumbered, padre," the scout grinned.

After that storm the arroyos and springs along the whole route filled with fresh water again; so the heat, while still intense, was easier to bear. The terrible flatness of the prairie gave way, also, to a rolling terrain covered with fair grazing for the horses and magnificent sweeps of sunflowers and purple sage. And occasionally the Entrada dipped down into a broad and pleasant valley threaded by some nameless stream. Josefina took a new delight now in the great vistas that rushed away from one at the top of every rise. She was almost gay again; and this elevation of the heart, she observed, was a thing shared by the whole command.

We are like the Indians of the pueblos, she mused. Nothing brings us such joy as a little water.

Then the Pawnees appeared. And, all at once, the temper of the whole Entrada plunged into a mood of nervous apprehension.

12

It was inevitable, of course, that sooner or later this should happen. The Entrada had now entered a kind of no-man's-land, a vast tract reaching to the Río Jesús María that was nominally dominated by a confederacy of the Apaches, Comanches, and Utes. Actually, however, it was deserted by all except a few bands of Paloma Apache buffalo hunters.

There was nothing to prevent the Pawnees from ranging this unoccupied region as freely as they wished. And it would have been strange indeed if they had not already got news of the Spanish intrusion and had not sent out scouts to observe its progress.

So the eventual appearance of the Pawnees was not unexpected: it was the manner in which it happened, perhaps, that most unnerved the Spaniards.

No evidence of Pawnee spying had yet been discovered by Captain Naranjo's scouts—none of the usual "signs and tracks" to indicate the existence of anyone in that great void of grass and sky except themselves. Then, all at once, directly ahead on the summit of a long, flat-topped range of hills that rose like a wall across the path of the column, a solitary Indian horseman rode up against the sky. He remained motionless on the mesa for the length of a slow Credo, observing them boldly, without any attempt at concealment, as if to flaunt his presence.

"Hola, enemigos!" he seemed to be saying. "Come along, we are waiting for you!"

That night Captain Villasur called a council of war, not to form any plan—for there was nothing that had not already been prepared against such a development—but to quiet the uneasiness that had seized the command.

How had this Pawnee spy managed to elude Captain Naranjo's scouts?

How did it happen that he was mounted? Did all the Pawnees, then, have horses?

How many others were with him?

Did the Pawnees hit and run like the Apaches, or did they stand up and fight like the Comanches? Was an ambush, perhaps, being prepared?

Such questions as these puzzled and perturbed the troops. Don Pedro tried to ease their concern.

"I must tell you," he said quietly, "that the Pawnees are probably allied with the French. In that case, they are hostile to us. But of this we are not certain. Or, if they are allied, we do not know how strong the alliance is. Our mission, señores, is to determine the truth of these matters so that the Viceroy may be informed."

"What happens," Captain Naranjo asked, "if the Pawnees and French decide to fight us? Do we fight back . . . or do we retreat?"

"Who can tell until the time comes?" Don Pedro parried. "But it is likely that we should fight. It would be a long retreat."

"But we are not to fight the Pawnees," Jean L'Archévèque said, in a loud, nervous voice. "Why else, señor, do you think that I have brought, at such great risk, twenty-two packs of trade goods with me?"

There was a long, embarrassed silence that was broken at last by Don Pedro saying: "I have to remind you, Don Juan, that I am commanding this Entrada. The decision in this, as in all other matters, will be made by me."

"That is not entirely the case," L'Archévèque said.

"No, señor?" Don Pedro demanded, his eyes blazing.

"No, señor Captain," L'Archévèque repeated, with an insolence peculiar to himself.

He reached into his jacket and pulled out a folded sheet of paper. All eyes watched his pudgy hands unfold it and shake it out.

"I have here, señor," he said, with exaggerated respectfulness, "a list of instructions that our great Governor and Captain-General, Don Antonio, has prepared and entrusted to my keeping.

"Included in these instructions," he went on, "are certain rules and maxims of war which His Excellency, in his great wisdom of these matters, thought might be useful to the señor commander of this Entrada."

Don Pedro gazed at the Frenchman in glacial silence.

"I shall not read the maxims," L'Archévèque continued. "I doubt that the señor captain has need of them—yet. Nor the other instructions. There is only one, señor, that I feel to be pertinent to the present situation. . . . With your permission?"

"Read it," Don Pedro said impatiently. "That you get this over with. We have a lot to talk about."

"Very well, señores!" L'Archévèque said. "Here it is." He then read, slowly and carefully, with a style and polish he had no doubt acquired in the schools of his native France:

"The reconnaissance having been carried out, the commander will proceed according to what events teach is the most agreeable. His first attention, however, must be to make friendly contact with the barbarians, fulfilling everything in the spirit of the preceding instructions.

"As a general point, the commander will be guided in this part of the orders by the valuable experience of Captain L'Archévèque."

He held up the paper for all to see, exhibiting what was undoubtedly the signature and the particularly flamboyant rubric of Don Antonio Valverde.

The long silence that followed was broken by Captain Naranjo, who stared hard at the assassin of Sieur de la Salle and said sardonically: "Perhaps we can also open trade with the French. I think the French would be very happy to deal with you, Don Juan. What do you say?"

"Señores, the council is ended," Don Pedro intervened. "Captain Naranjo, you will report to me at once any unusual developments. Captain Dominguez, you will double the night watch and pull in the horseherds. Good night, señores."

13

There was an extraordinary lack of conversation in the camp that night. It was not unusual for a governor to issue written orders to his commander in the field. But never before had such orders been entrusted to anyone but the field commander. The enormity of Don Antonio's breach of military etiquette and decency silenced everyone.

Josefina, who had heard clearly enough almost everything that had been said in the council, could only think: Who but Don Antonio would do such a thing!

She wondered, with a kind of awe, at the long reach of Don Antonio's malignancy. What else, she asked herself fearfully, was in the order that Juan L'Archévèque carried in his jacket? What additional authority did they give him over Don Pedro? What difficulties did they impose on Don Pedro in the hard and dangerous days ahead.

She thought back to Don Antonio, propped up in bed in his robe and nightcap, saying: "I have ordered Don Juan to remain very close to Don Pedro at all times." She remembered what a start his words had given her—how she had cried out to herself: Don Juan L'Archévèque—*that assassin!*

She repeated that frightened cry now; and her sudden fear for Don Pedro's safety crowded out all other emotions—the indignation and anger and sadness that so fine an officer as her husband should be forced to suffer the insults of such a foul poltroon as Don Antonio Valverde.

But when Don Pedro came to her later, weary and low in spirits, she was almost gay for him. She had always remained firm to her resolve never to bring up matters pertaining to the Entrada or the conduct of war with Don Pedro; and even now she remained valiantly true to that determination.

She tried only, in her woman's ways, to cheer him up and make him forget for a little time the cares and anxieties—and now this new indignity—that burdened him without respite. Yet, because he was her husband and she his wife, she could not refrain from murmuring, in that drowsy moment between love and sleep:

"Amor . . . if it becomes necessary—that you do not hesitate to kill that French degenerado first. . . ."

14

Ever since the lone Pawnee had appeared on top of the mesa, Don Pedro had taken the greatest precautions against surprise. Captain Naranjo's scouts, ranging three or four miles ahead of the main body, had been augmented—but only at the cost of grave misgivings in the commander's mind. And they were still sadly inadequate.

"With even one more man, señor, or maybe two," Captain Naranjo begged mildly, "I'd feel easier."

"It is impossible, Captain," Don Pedro was forced to tell him. "I can't weaken the command any further."

"Very well, señor," the scout said cheerfully. "Then I'll do my best with what I've got. That you don't worry, General."

But Don Pedro did worry, constantly. He was not only without a proper force of scouts, flankers, and skirmishers. He was also short of horses. Poor grazing and the long marches had crippled and exhausted the horseherd.

"If I did have the men, Captain," he added ruefully to Naranjo, "how would we mount them?"

In a sense, his little command was traveling half-blind through the heart of enemy country, three hundred miles from the nearest source of supplies and almost five hundred from help. It had been marching thus for two weeks, in the almost certain knowledge that Pawnee spies, invisible and omniscient, were observing every step of its progress.

Even veterans of the campaigns of Vargas, Ulibarri, and Hurtado were not wholly proof against the nervous strain. For Captain Naranjo's scouts—whose business it was to find and observe the enemy —now had the maddening awareness that they themselves were under the constant surveillance of unseen eyes.

"They are ghosts, señor," Naranjo reported ruefully. "They make no camps. They leave no fires. Their horses, if they have any, nibble at nothing, leave no tracks or droppings—they must go through the air!"

Fray Juan Minguéz, who stood nearby, listened to this in unaccustomed silence.

"Well, padre," the scout said gloomily, "that you say what you are going to say."

"I have no comment," the fraile smiled wryly. "I am as scared as you are, Captain."

Two other specters of uncertainty had dogged the weary column all the way up from El Cuartelejo.

One was the absolute strangeness of the country through which they were passing. They had nothing but the sun and stars, and an old, uncertain sea compass to help them find the way. No maps, no guides, only rumors to go on.

Only one man in the whole command had the least familiarity with the great curve of the earth over which they were crawling. He was a Pawnee attached to Captain Serna's detachment of scouts, who had been picked up at El Cuartelejo.

This Indian, who bore the oddly half-French name of François Sistaca, claimed that he had been taken from his kinsmen by the Apaches while still quite young. If so, he must have forgotten much, for he, too, appeared to be strangely unsure of the way. Some, however, considered him merely stupid; some were sure that he was, in fact, a Pawnee spy.

The other uncertainty that plagued the minds and chafed the nerves of everyone was the question of the French and Pawnee intentions.

That the Pawnees were numerous, well-armed, and strongly supported by the French of La Luisiana, the Viceroy's letter to Don Antonio had made clear. That they were also hostile was at least a good conjecture.

But how hostile? Were they willing to confer—even to change sides, perhaps? Or would they attack without preliminaries, maybe without even showing themselves? And, of course, without quarter. . . .

All such questions, uncertainties, and anxieties, combined with the great heat and the constant concern about water, had gnawed at the spirit and endurance of the troops every league of the way from El Cuartelejo. Yet, because they were veterans and Spaniards, and perhaps because they had a certain arrogant faith in God's predilection for the Spanish arms, they refused to confess—except, like Fray Minguéz, ironically—the deep disquiet they all must have felt.

"These are things for the general to worry about," they shrugged. "They are Don Pedro's baby, no?"

And so, in good order, and exactly according to plan—if not indeed with the lightest of hearts—Don Pedro's little command proceeded inexorably northward "by the needle."

313

15

With the Entrada, as with the immensely empty land it was traversing, each day was the same as every other.

Each morning Fray Juan Minguéz said a hasty Mass, sometimes adding a prayer for rain, or for the command, or perhaps a quaint supplication half for, half against the enemy: "O God, our protector, defend thy soldiers from the attacks of the heathen and grant our enemies the pardon of their sins. . . ."

All day long the soldier Simón de Córdoba counted his steps. He tolled them off aloud and at each one thousand he dropped a pebble into his pocket. Sometimes, at the end of the day's march, he would have twenty pebbles, sometimes less. A column that cannot see must travel slowly.

All day long, without a break for food at noon, the troops rode in loose but strict formation, their lances erect in their sockets, shields slung from saddles, helmets gleaming in the incessant sun—a somewhat haggard company, now, of dusty bearded men, weary at times to the point of falling from their exhausted horses . . . but never quite, for they were professionals and veterans.

Each evening Fray Juan conducted a devotion to the Rosary. At first only a few presidials attended; but as the Entrada moved farther and farther into the mysterious realms of danger, their number increased. By the time the Río Jesús María had been reached, the whole camp—with the exception of Captain José Naranjo—was on hand.

"It is remarkable, no?" Fray Juan could not refrain from observing. "The farther these bastardos get from home, the more pious they grow!"

In the evening, too, Don Pedro held whatever councils of war he considered necessary. Afterwards, often while the rest of the camp was asleep, he noted in meticulous detail all the events of the day in his journal of the Entrada. Usually he performed this very important task himself; but occasionally he dictated his notes to Josefina.

Sometimes when he suffered from the severe headaches that had begun to plague him now, Josefina would simply write his journal for him. In other ways, too, she did whatever she could to lighten his fatigues and raise his spirits. She made his chocolate with her own hands; mended his clothes and gear; kept his tent in order; caressed away his spells of Castilian moodiness.

Then she fretted because there was not more that she could do. Nothing was of any importance to her any more unless it related in some manner to Don Pedro. She was concerned only with what concerned him. She had arrived at that state of almost complete self-negation—or pure giving—that the Maya had once defined as love ... and had rejected as a thing not altogether good and beautiful, but in a way evil. And Josefina herself did not accept it without a little questioning—perhaps a small but hopeless struggle.

I have become your slave, Don Pedro Villasur, she said to herself. I, who had thought merely to make use of you, have become worse than your concubine. As wife, you own me, Don Pedro, more wholly than any girl you might have bought at Pecos or Taos.

She mused on this for a little while, not without a certain wonder at the strange way of the stars.

But I do not care, Pedro mío, she thought. If only you love me, I am glad to be your slave.

With Don Pedro, she was still the Castellana, the elegant, gay, remote, and slightly terrifying woman of Spain who—she realized more clearly than he himself—was the object of some dream and desire too deep and obscure for understanding.

She did not try to understand. She merely accepted and, in a way, was grateful. And she did everything she could—even to keeping herself astonishingly fresh and lovely on that wearisome march—to preserve the dream and keep alive the desire.

To the troops, also, she showed herself no less the Castellana in camp and on the march than she had in the Palace at Santa Fé. And without relaxing that dignity and pride that had become associated with her name, she won the hearts—as she had before won the admiration and, sometimes, awe—of these rough and lonely men. They came to her, not unlike children, she thought, with every sort of problem and ailment and trouble.

"Por favor, Doña Josefina, if you will just look at this finger?"

"I have dreamed three times that my Miguelita is unfaithful. . . . What is the meaning of this, Doña Josefina?"

She nursed them when they were sick, bandaged their injuries, even learned to bleed them with a skill that Armijo the barber had never possessed. And when the young trooper Tomás Madrid died of a swift, mysterious malady, she held him in her arms because he had asked it.

"If you do not mind, padre," he had said to Fray Minguéz, with unfailing courtesy. "After you have finished, no?"

Sometimes in the evening she sang to them, accompanying herself on a guitar that belonged to the corporal José Griego. The corporal himself was very good at singing the ballads of New Mexico, and at composing couplets about happenings on the march, often making sly sport of his fellow soldiers. But if the troops enjoyed José Griego's ballads, they were completely enchanted by Josefina's sweet, slightly husky voice singing the ancient songs of Old Spain.

One evening, when they had camped in a grove of poplar trees and there was a good fire, and there had been good hunting that day, so that everybody was well-fed and more cheerful than usual, she sang them a tonadilla—a curiously gay-sad song, strange and unaccustomed and therefore fascinating.

"They say that you now love
    another,
They say that you now love
    another,
But none shall ever guess
    my sorrow,
Ay! None shall tell of my
    shame.
See how I smile with my eyes!
See how I laugh with my lips!
See how I dance in my satin
    slippers!
While my heart hides its anguish,
While my heart breaks. Ay!"

And there was none in that circle of spellbound listeners who could know why, after finishing this song, La Dama Josefina had handed the guitar to José Griego with an odd abruptness and had gone to her tent without even a "Buenas noches, señores."

16

That evening was the last one of cheerful fires and singing and stomachs comfortably full of fresh buffalo meat. They were very close to the Río Jesús María now and therefore to the villages of the Pawnees and French.

At night, hereafter, the camp must be silent—even to the quieting of the mule bells—and fireless. During the day, no buffalo must be hunted for fear of detection by the Pawnees who would note the frightened herd, and also because of the telltale buzzards and crows that would hang about the offal-strewn camp.

Some of the men grumbled a little.

"Who does Don Pedro think he is fooling," they asked, "by making us eat cold jerky?"

"Not the Pawnees, certainly. They watch us every day—they must be bored with watching us, no?"

"Well, Don Pedro takes no chances. He goes by the book. You can't find fault with him for that."

"Just the same, I could do with a good hunk of bull meat—well-browned, nice and juicy, eh?"

But such small outbursts of discontent—when they were not simply the natural grumbling of fighting men with no fighting to do—were caused less by Don Pedro's discipline than by the nerve-racking uncertainty that still enveloped the Entrada like a cloud—a cloud that every day grew denser and heavier and blacker.

It enwrapped them still when, on the eve of Santiago's day, they reached the Río Jesús María at last and turned eastward along its bank. It clung to them for a whole week longer, as they stumbled, weary and travelworn, through high grass and thick willow groves, along the river whose very name had become a kind of blasphemy.

Then, on the eve of St. Stephen's day, all doubt and all uncertainty were ended—forever.

Just before sunset on that day, Captain Naranjo, who had been riding well in advance of even his own scouts, galloped into camp. His report to Don Pedro Villasur was succinct and very conclusive.

"A little after noon, señor, I found a lot of branches and leaves of the sand cherry tree. There were few cherries, however. They had all been eaten by a band of savages who had rested there for a meal."

"How many, Captain?"

"It was hard to tell, señor—maybe a dozen only. They were on their way to a great gathering of their kinsmen about two leagues down the river. I followed their trail. In about two leagues' travel I came to their main ranchería. There were about two hundred Pawnees there—unmounted. They were dancing and singing their war songs."

"Is it your opinion, Captain, that they are preparing to attack us?"

"I don't know, señor," the scout said, with something like a look of bewilderment on his dark and weary features. "There is something very strange about these savages. Either they don't know we are here —which I can't believe—or else they are contemptuous of us. They had no sentinels out, señor."

Captain Naranjo looked at Don Pedro for a long, contemplative interval of silence.

"If we could do a march of six leagues tonight, señor," he said, "I think we could attack at dawn and kill every one of those bastards while they are asleep."

17

Within half an hour after Captain Naranjo's return, Don Pedro—in the tradition of Spanish armies—called a council of war to consider what ought to be done. Because of the extreme urgency of the situation, and in order to free all members of the expedition for immediate military activity, if necessary, Josefina was assigned the duty of recording the decisions of the council.

All the war chiefs and the two settlers, Captains Serna and L'Archévèque, attended. To them Captain Naranjo repeated the report he had given Don Pedro, adding a few new details.

"The dance they were doing was a war dance of the Iroquois," he said. "All the Indians of the plains take their dances from the Iroquois nation. I have seen that dance before, done by the Comanches, as some of you have also. You know what it means, no? It means war."

Captain Tomás Olguín leaned forward. He was a stubborn, hot-tempered man with a black beard and piercing eyes, who had an unpleasant way of making all his questions sound like challenges.

"What do you look for, then?" he barked. "An attack? When? Tonight, Captain?"

"Not tonight," Naranjo replied, with an edge of disdain in his quiet voice. "It is not the habit of the Pawnees, any more than of other tribes, to attack at night. The Captain knows this."

"Well," Olguín said, "what do you expect then?"

"I expect nothing, Captain," Naranjo said. "But a dawn attack one of these days wouldn't surprise me."

Don Pedro's aide-de-camp, Captain José Domínguez, made the next inquiry. His face, Josefina thought, looked very weary and a little sad under the rather ridiculous old-fashioned morion he wore over a bright silk kerchief.

"This is your opinion, Captain," he said gravely to Naranjo. "Then what, in your judgment, should be done?"

Naranjo said: "My opinion is that we should attack the Pawnees first."

"When, Captain?"

"I am suggesting, señor, only what has always been the policy of His Majesty's arms in this part of the world. To go out and attack instead of waiting to be attacked, no?"

"Oíga!" the ensign of the expedition, Bernardo Casillas, exclaimed. "That is right, señores!"

Casillas was a first-rate soldier and perhaps the best horseman in the Kingdom of New Mexico—he could pick up a silver peso from the ground at every pass at a full gallop. And he was so expert with the reata that he was reputed to have roped a flying goose. But it was thought that his impetuosity sometimes outweighed his judgment a little. Naranjo gave him a broad grin.

"As for myself," the scout said quietly, "I would attack tonight."

A handful of men, weary and dispirited, six hundred miles from home and almost as far from any help, received this grim proposal in a heavy silence. The silence endured and seemed to spread. It was broken at last by Jean L'Archévèque.

"Señores," he said, almost soothingly, "we seem to have forgotten the purpose of this expedition."

"One moment, please!" Naranjo interrupted him. "Let me say one thing more, and then I am through."

"Certainly, señor," L'Archévèque said, with a kind of condescending patience. "Go ahead."

"Let us consider our situation," the scout continued. "About six miles from this place are two hundred Pawnees. They intend to kill us—and that, you can be sure, señores, is why they have allowed us to come this far without opposing us."

"They often dance and sing," L'Archévèque muttered. "We have no proof of their hostility."

Naranjo pulled his dagger from its sheath and ran his thumb along its edge: it was a habit of his when he was concentrating on something. "Having no horses themselves," he went on, "these savages do not think in terms of cavalry. They consider themselves safe from attack. They are careless. They have not even put out sentinels to watch while they sing and dance. This I know, because I have seen it for myself."

The veterans to whom he was speaking murmured agreement with this. The carelessness of the Indians—even such experienced foes as the Comanches and Utes—was incredible. It had enabled the Spaniards to attack and kill them time after time in surprise dawn assaults.

"I have said there are two hundred Pawnees over there," Naranjo finished. "Let us say there are twice that many. We are sixty, plus our Indians. But we cannot count too much on our Indians. Let us forget about them, then. But what are even four hundred Pawnees, asleep and helpless in their lodges, against sixty well-armed and mounted Spaniards? Does anyone here fear the outcome of an attack? Then, in God's name, señores, let us attack tonight—*while we have time.*"

Captain Naranjo, feeling perhaps that he had let himself be carried away by his earnestness, stopped abruptly. He appeared embarrassed. He even muttered a low, "That you excuse me, señor!" to Don Pedro. Jean L'Archévèque waited until it was quiet in the tent; then he stood up before the council and asked:

"Have you finished now, Captain?"

The question itself, as L'Archévèque asked it, seemed to throw ridicule on Naranjo's proposal. The scout nodded, his eyes dark and cold.

"Very well," L'Archévèque said. "Allow me, then, señores, to remind you of a few facts that our Captain of War has neglected to mention.

"Number one: We cannot decide that these Pawnees are in fact hostile because they dance and sing: they do that often, merely for amusement, no?

"Number two: If they are indeed hostile, we cannot be sure that their apparent carelessness is not merely a ruse—a trick to draw us into a hasty and unwise attack.

"Number three: We have just completed a hard march of six hundred leagues. Our men and horses are exhausted. We are in no condition to march another six leagues tonight, señores, and then attack an enemy of four times our strength."

The Frenchman smiled complacently. He had made three telling points, and now he was about to play his trump card.

"But all this is really beside the point. Let me ask this question now: *What is the object of this expedition?*

"Is it to make war—to attack the Pawnees and the French? No, señores! It is to make a friendly contact with the Pawnees—and to discover from them the facts His Lordship the Viceroy needs to know about the French. It is information the Viceroy wants—not dead Indians."

L'Archévèque looked around the little circle of officers with an air of smug belligerency.

"It is also Don Antonio Valverde's orders," he added, "that we conciliate the Pawnees, and win them over to our side if possible."

Naranjo shot his dagger back into its sheath: it made a sharp, metallic click. He said: "And even do a little trading with them, no?"

L'Archévèque ignored the scout. "Thank you, señores," he ended. "I have said everything I care to say. We are at your orders, Don Pedro."

"Are there any other opinions?" Don Pedro asked. "Luján? Real? Domínguez? Serna?"

Each of those called on made a brief summary of his views, some in favor of Captain Naranjo, some supporting Jean L'Archévèque and his well-worn arguments in favor of caution, conciliation—and trade.

Then Don Pedro stood up to give his opinion and decision. Josefina noted with a start, almost with alarm, how thin and pale he had become. His eyes appeared sunken and his nose very large.

Ever since they left Jicarilla, Don Pedro had suffered recurrences of some tropical malaise he had picked up in New Spain. They were accompanied by chills and a fever, and occasionally by cruel headaches. Don Pedro had said nothing about his illness to anyone; but Josefina knew about it and had watched its slowly debilitating effect.

She had detected another thing that Don Pedro had taken pains to conceal: his extreme concern about the fate of this expedition.

Not a man in the tent, Josefina had seen, but shared that concern. Not one but realized how insufficient was Don Pedro's puny force for offensive operations against a tribe as powerful and warlike as the Pawnees, armed with French guns.

One by one, each had reacted in his own way to this realization. Naranjo by wanting to attack immediately, desperately, in the hope of beating Fate to the scene of battle. L'Archévèque by wanting to close his eyes to the hostility of the Pawnees, to offer them friendship—and perhaps to do a little trading.

Yet, only Captain Don Pedro Villasur must bear alone the worry and responsibility of command. Only he had known so well—and for so long—the utter impossibility of his position. The shadow of what he knew, and of the illness that had dogged him for so long, was in his eyes now as he got up to address the council.

Madre de Dios! Josefina whispered to herself. Here is a man that needs Your help! And she felt a flutter of panic; and a surge of pity for Don Pedro that squeezed her heart until it hurt.

"I propose for your consideration, señores," Don Pedro was saying, "the main question of this council: Do we, as Captain Naranjo and others advise, make a night march and attack the Pawnees in their ranchería at dawn; or do we, as Captain L'Archévèque and others counsel, refrain from hostilities and attempt to make a friendly contact with the Pawnees?

"I shall give you my own opinion. It seems to me that we would be unwise, considering the condition of our troops, to attempt such a difficult and dangerous operation against so strong a foe. There is always the possibility that the savages are employing stratagem. Moreover, it is true, as Captain L'Archévèque has said, that the real purpose of this expedition is reconnaissance, not active war. In this respect I must follow the commands of the Viceroy and . . . those of the Governor and Captain-General, Don Antonio Valverde."

All in that meeting could guess what it must have cost Don Pedro's pride to agree so completely with L'Archévèque's viewpoint; but all must admire the fairness with which he arrived at his decision.

"What," Don Pedro asked, "is the consensus of this council on the matter?"

When the vote was taken, only Captain Naranjo and Ensign Casillas held out for the dawn attack.

"Very well, señores," Don Pedro said. "It is decided, then. The troops will stand inspection in the morning. In the afternoon we shall cross the river and camp. On Wednesday we shall follow the trail of the Pawnees, discovered by Captain Naranjo, and try to find their village. Captain Domínguez, you will please prepare the necessary orders. Thank you, señores. And now, good afternoon."

Josefina felt a wifely pride in what, it seemed to her, was the efficient and soldierly way Don Pedro had handled the council. The officers of the council, too, appeared to be cheered. There were smiles on their tired faces as they got up to leave. One uncertainty, at least, had been ended: the Entrada knew what it was going to do. Only Captain Naranjo seemed to be disappointed.

"I still think, señores," he said, "that we should give those dancing bastards the Santiago!"

18

The birds were chattering in the cottonwoods along the Río Jesús María when the Entrada stood inspection the next morning.

Don Pedro's sixty veterans lined up abreast against a background of rolling hills to the south. The tiny pennons at the tips of their lances fluttered against the pale prairie sky. Saddle leather, still cold and stiff from the chill of the night, creaked in the stillness of the morning; spurs and bits jingled.

The bearded faces of the soldiers were thin and careworn; but each man sat his horse with a certain spirit, a kind of dogged pride in his calling of soldier, that amounted almost to defiance.

Josefina, wrapped in her cloak against the fresh breeze, wondered what thoughts might be slowly turning over behind their indifferent eyes. They were all old soldiers, veterans of many campaigns. And old soldiers, Don Pedro had said, counted the odds. How had these sixty counted them? How, she wondered, did they rate their chances—the chances of all on this Entrada?

It was almost axiomatic in New Mexico that a small party of men invariably ran great risk of extermination, or at least of disgraceful defeat by the Indians, whose reserves seemed always limitless.

It had happened many times. In Sonora, Captain Don Francisco Tovar and thirty men perished at the ford of Las Palominas. At Janos, Captain Don Antonio de Esparza and twenty-eight men suffered the same fate. In Coahuila, a party of fifty men died in the same way.

All such cases—and many more—were well-known to the sixty men sitting their horses so wearily, yet so gallantly, on the banks of the Río Jesús María this morning. But if they felt any concern, it did not show in their faces. Their faces were marked by fatigue, but certainly not by fear. Josefina, glancing down the brief line of horsemen, took courage from what she saw.

This was a small force, to be sure, but one composed of the finest soldiers of the Kingdom, and extraordinarily well-equipped. Each man wore a double-visor helmet of leather, patterned after the steel helmets of an earlier time; a sleeveless leather tunic or jacket made of seven or eight thicknesses of sheepskin, very effective as armor against arrows, but of little protection against bullets; dark-blue breeches covered by leather chaps or defensas; and a long blue cloak rolled up on the saddle apron. Each had iron spurs attached to his shoes with metal chains.

Their arms represented a curious transitional stage between the age of the sword-and-lance and that of gunpowder.

The basic weapons were still the six-foot lance with a ten-inch iron head, and the broadsword, five Flemish spans long, carried in a steel scabbard attached to the saddle. For defense, each man carried a convex oval shield, made of several thicknesses of untanned bullhide, varnished and painted with the Spanish coat of arms, and slung from the saddle when not in use.

These were the offensive and defensive arms of another age—the age, if one wished to view history ironically (as many in the Indies did)—of Spain's true glory. The soldiers of New Mexico still carried them, because they were still very useful in Indian warfare. But some of them were also equipped with the deadlier weapons of the modern age.

Don Pedro had seen to it that his men were armed with long-range flintlock muskets, in place of the outmoded firelocks still used by some of the troops, but considered no better—if not worse—than the arrows of the Indians. These guns, when not being used, were slung in leather sheaths. The paper cartridges for them were carried in wooden boxes attached to the shoulder belts.

The horse was also a weapon of the Spanish soldier. Since the time of the first Conquistadores, it had represented his greatest advantage —greater even than armor, or steel weapons, or gunpowder—over his savage foes. Those on which Don Pedro's men were mounted were quite typical of the horses of Spanish cavalry. They were small, wiry animals—red roans, buckskins with beautiful black manes and tails, cinnamon-colored canelas, palominos—direct descendants of the horses of the Conquest.

If Don Pedro's men were a little apprehensive of the odds against them, one could never have guessed it from the way they sat their high-cantled saddles.

"Muy magnífico!" the ensign Casillas exclaimed exuberantly. "A well-mounted, well-equipped, and—if you will pardon me, señor—well-led force."

"But not very big, eh?" Captain Olguín said gloomily.

"Big enough, Captain," Casillas said. "Big enough for anything in these parts."

"Quién sabe?" Olguín shrugged. "Well, anyhow, we'll soon see."

The inspection went off quickly, with the snap and precision of a parade on the Plaza in Santa Fé. The corporals reported their squads; Captain Naranjo his scouts; the leader of the Apaches—a fat chief calling himself Don Lorenzo—his band of auxiliaries.

Don Pedro made a brief address, commending the troops on their energy, constancy, zeal, and courage in the service of Both Majesties; and, in return, was cheered by the men.

Fray Juan Minguéz gave the arms of the Entrada a fresh blessing and said a prayer for the troops.

Immediately afterwards the men, visibly cheered and enheartened, began the crossing of the Río Jesús María.

The river at this point was a broad, sluggish stream, heavily wooded with giant cottonwoods and willow thickets, and so obstructed by sand bars that it would have been impossible to get a boat across. A fording place having been selected, the command began to move its baggage across on small rafts and the backs of the Apaches. The Indians protested glumly all afternoon about the coldness of the water.

So difficult indeed did the crossing of the Río Jesús María prove to be, and so loudly did the Apache allies complain about the coldness of the water that the Entrada succeeded in getting over only half its impedimentia before nightfall.

That night Don Pedro was forced to take on himself the unpardonable military sin of making a divided camp, in close proximity to the enemy, on two sides of a river.

It was a dark, cold camp, without fires and as still and silent as an army could be in quarters—for everything possible must be done to conceal its predicament from the eyes of the Pawnees. Yet, there was not a man but could feel almost physically the stare of savage eyes from the darkness. The few who slept at all that night slept on their arms, with their horses tethered to their wrists.

"Have you got a prayer for a divided camp, padre?" Captain Naranjo asked gloomily.

"I've got a prayer for God's help," Fray Juan said, without smiling. "He has helped us out of tight places before. I trust He will again."

"Sorry, padre," Naranjo said. "You're right. This is not a joking matter."

God's well-known partiality to the Catholic arms, or perhaps simple good luck, or possibly even the slovenliness of the Pawnees, got them miraculously through that anxious night. The crossing was resumed before it was light enough to see well; and by noon the remainder of the Entrada was safely with the advance party on the north side of the Río Jesús María.

Josefina recorded the whole incident briefly—and, as far as the facts would allow, without discredit to Don Pedro—in the journal of the expedition. She disposed of the whole affair with the laconic entry:

> Wednesday, the seventh of the month of August. At daybreak, the rest of the baggage and our people were brought over from the other side of the Río Jesús María. This was not without a great deal of trouble, but we finally found ourselves together at midday.

"God grant," she said fervently, closing the heavy buckskin-bound book, "that I have not many such stories to put down here!"

The camp spent the rest of that day pulling itself together and awaiting the reports of the scouts, who returned at nightfall without definite information on the whereabouts of the Pawnee village.

"Are we sure, señor," Captain Naranjo asked, "that there actually is such a village?"

"One, perhaps two, have been reported by our spies in La Luisiana," Don Pedro answered him. "They are even shown on some of the maps of the French."

"Have you seen these maps, señor?"

"No, but many in México have," Don Pedro replied, a little impatiently. "The villages are located on this river. They are shown to be as large as the pueblo of Taos."

"Many strange things are shown on maps, no?"

"Are you trying to imply, Captain, that I have brought you here in search of an espejismo—a mirage?"

Captain Naranjo looked at his commander with a puzzled, even anxious expression on his weathered face.

"With your permission, señor," he said, "you have brought us here on orders from México—and Don Antonio. Let us hope that they are both better informed than is usually the case."

Don Pedro gave his subaltern a long, cold stare.

325

"Your job, Captain Naranjo," he said, "is to find the Pawnees . . . not to decry your superiors."

Naranjo returned Don Pedro's stare with a look that was more perplexed and disturbed than resentful.

"Very well, mi general," he said. "We'll find their lousy village . . . if there is one!"

As Don Pedro watched his Captain-Major of War walk away, he passed his hand across his forehead and smiled wearily. He called to his orderly, Corporal Rodríguez, and asked him to bring in Captain Serna.

The captain entered Don Pedro's tent with his servant, the Pawnee, François Sistaca. The Indian was of a rather portly build, as Indians living on Spanish rations were likely to be. He was dressed in an odd combination of Apache and Spanish clothes: leather leggings, an old jacket of red nankeen with frogs sewed onto the back, and a wide-brimmed hat which he wore in a very dashing manner far back on his head. He had a reputation for bragging.

"My servant says he knows where the Pawnee village is, señor," Serna said, with a small gesture toward the savage. "He remembers it from his childhood."

"Well, where is it then?" Don Pedro asked shortly.

"He would like to go out and make sure that his memory is good. Then he will return and lead us to the village."

"He wants to go alone?"

"Yes, señor."

"Captain," Don Pedro asked, "are you sure that this Indian is all right?"

"I don't vouch for him, señor," Serna replied. "He seems honest enough to me. But I am only saying what he tells me."

Don Pedro sat for a little time in silence, studying the complacent and slightly supercilious face of the Pawnee.

"Ask him how far the village is from here," he said to Serna.

"He doesn't know, señor," Serna said, after consultation with Sistaca. "That's what he wants to find out."

"Well, let him go," Don Pedro said presently.

The Pawnee left the camp on a fast stallion. He paused on the horizon, waved his hat, and dashed out of sight; the Entrada plodded methodically along the intricate and often bewildering course of the Río Jesús María. At midday François Sistaca returned.

"Body of Christ!" Naranjo said morosely. "Here comes that fat bastard, back already."

"What did he find?" Don Pedro asked listlessly.

"Nothing, señor," Naranjo reported, after a brief conversation with the Pawnee. "The stupid son-of-a-bitch got lost."

19

Josefina lay awake under the stars, listening to the muffled stir of the camp around her, feeling the chill prairie wind in her loosened hair, watching the slow movement of the heavens, and trying to quiet her thoughts.

She was on the edge of sleep, but she could not sleep. She opened her eyes and lay for a while on her back, looking up directly into the shining bowl of the sky. Her mind, as if under the hypnotic influence of those remote and innumerable points of light, became oddly active. The current of her thoughts drifted backwards—quite independently of her will, it seemed—like the slow succession of scenes in a phantasmagoria of dreams or fever.

Images . . .

First of those things and persons and experiences near in the order of time . . . the soft, purring light of her little fireplace in the Palace . . . the roses of Castile in Doña Mercedes's garden . . . snow on a string of crimson chile in December . . . the beautiful, quiet hands of La Conquistadora. . . .

Simple, uncomplicated, reassuring images, drifting backwards. . . .

A village of México bright with bougainvillea . . . a silver image of the Virgin at Compostela . . . the Capital itself and its four things fair—the women, the apparel, the horses, and the streets . . . Tafora's gentle smile. . . .

And backwards farther still, more slowly, to the sad and wonderful time of *La Sola* and *La de los Ojos Verdes* and she who went before them. . . .

The smooth feel of the castanets against her palms—of the seguidillas' rhythm running like quicksilver through her blood . . . Doña Manuela's slow, approving smile . . . the magnificence of October in Madrid . . . Guzmán's two watches . . . the roar of the mosqueteros. . . .

And backward even farther, to the warm and gentle beginning of everything. . . .

A place of huge, burning flowers and circling balconies and many cats and children playing dancing games around a fountain . . . the sun-warmed doorstep of Santa Teresa's very house . . . a golden lady in a golden coach . . . a blue-eyed doll. . . .

And at last to a world beyond her world and a time before her time, that lived in Eva Helena's voice which, she thought, must have been very like the Virgin's. . . .

That patio where all the orange and lemon trees burst into bloom in a single day . . . those bonbons perfumed with amber water . . . those silken chemises of the Condesa de Mora's, edged in black-blonde lace . . . the Condesa's two hundred fans. . . .

Ah, yes, she thought, but half-awake. And beyond that what? It was like a stream, no? It was like a stream flowing from an unknown source . . . to an unknown end. It was like the Río Jesús María!

She slept fitfully on the hard, unyielding ground, and she awoke at daybreak, chilled and cramped. The bustle and confusion of the breaking camp was all around her. She sat up and blinked at the bleak silhouette of the eroded hills against a dull, russet horizon. It was not an hour when one's spirits are naturally high.

Ay, Dios mío! she sighed to herself. That you knew what today will bring, Josefina. She stretched herself and yawned and said, "Jesús!" She added, with a wry smile: "But perhaps not to know is better!"

20

The next day was Friday, the ninth of August, and the vigil of San Lorenzo, that great Spanish saint and martyr.

Immediately after the bugle had blown assembly, one of the sentries reported a rider approaching the camp. A stir of excitement ran through the Entrada; but the horseman turned out to be only a messenger from Captain Naranjo.

The news he brought was momentous, but not alarming.

"Eight leagues from here, señor general," he said to Don Pedro, "we have found a party of Pawnees in a bottom. It is the same party, Captain Naranjo thinks, that he discovered before."

"Is it a war party?"

"It is impossible to tell, señor. They were dancing and singing, as before. As you know, señor, it is Captain Naranjo's opinion that all the Pawnees are hostile."

"I am not asking for opinions, Corporal," Don Pedro said, with somewhat unnecessary shortness. "I wish only the facts. How near did you approach?"

"Not very near, señor. We were afraid of frightening them in the night."

"I see," Don Pedro said. "You did not find their village, then?"

"No, señor—only this band. Captain Naranjo thinks it is on its way to the village. The village must be nearby."

"Very well, Corporal," Don Pedro said. "Go back and tell Captain Naranjo that we shall follow his trail."

The corporal saluted, remounted, and rode off immediately.

"We'll cross over," Don Pedro said to his aide-de-camp, "at once." The crossing was made quickly and without incident. Although the horses plunged up to their girths in the water, nothing was wetted. In less than an hour the command found itself—all together this time—on the north side of the Río Jesús María.

The troops were in high spirits about having made a good crossing —the memory of the divided camp was still a kind of nightmare to them. They were relieved, too, about having got some definite word, at last, on the whereabouts of the Pawnees. If one had an enemy, it was better to know where he was! Anything was better, in fact, than the uncertainty that had shrouded the whole operation of the Entrada so far.

"But where is their village?" Captain Olguín asked gloomily. "Where is this lousy village we're looking for, señor?"

Don Pedro glanced at the sour, bearded visage of his second in command; he made a visible effort to answer him cheerfully. "I'll make you a wager we'll find it today, Captain. Or if not today, then tomorrow for certain."

"You seem very sure of that, señor," Olguín said. "I don't share your hopes."

Josefina thought she detected a thinly concealed tone of contempt in the subaltern's voice. She thought: This captain seems to go out of his way to disagree with Don Pedro. I don't like him much. I like him less all the time.

They were marching along the broad, level river bottom, with nothing to impede or slow their progress. By the time the sun was a lance high, they had covered three leagues. Then Don Pedro ordered a halt. Camp was pitched and the horseherd turned out to graze.

At noon Captain Serna's Pawnee, François Sistaca, was again dispatched to find his kinsmen, confer with them, and assure them of the friendship and good will of His Majesty, Don Philip V. It was Don Pedro's idea to send two soldiers with him. "For his protection," he said dryly.

"He says he doesn't want any protection, señor," Serna reported. "He claims he doesn't need any."

"Precisely," Don Pedro said. "I'd like it better if he did. I don't trust this fellow, Captain. We'll send the men along with him."

Captain Serna then had a long consultation with Sistaca, during all

329

of which the Indian's face remained impassive—save for his eyes, which darted about with an amazing independence of the rest of his features.

"I'm sorry, señor," Serna said at last. "He doesn't want the soldiers. He won't have them. He's afraid the Pawnees will doubt his word if anyone goes with him. They'll think he comes in bad faith, he says. He wants to go alone."

"He's probably right, señor," Jean L'Archévèque put in. "He ought to know his own people, no?"

"Do you trust him, Captain?" Don Pedro asked brusquely. "Or am I the only one that suspects this embustero?"

"He's our only means of contact with the Pawnees," L'Archévèque said. "How are we to find out anything unless someone talks with them?"

"Does he have to do his talking alone?" Don Pedro asked wearily.

"If that's the only way," L'Archévèque said, with exasperating calm. "I'd let him do it, señor."

Don Pedro looked hard at the Frenchman for a long moment, then pressed the palm of his hand across his forehead and said: "Very well, then. Send him off, Captain Serna. But you might remind him about the punishment for treason."

A little later François Sistaca galloped away, laden with tobacco and presents for the Pawnees. Josefina watched him drop below the hills with a misgiving heart. Nevertheless, after she had written an account of his departure in the journal, she added: "May God and the Holy Virgin His Mother wish that he have success!"

She also noted that Don Pedro had named the stream they had crossed the San Lorenzo, in honor of the day. Then she closed the book on her lap and sat gazing out of the door of her tent. She was thinking: Why, if he thought it unwise, did Don Pedro allow that ugly savage to go alone? . . . Why does he let others impose their wills on him? . . . *To what is Don Pedro leading this Entrada?*

She sat for a long time, holding the journal of Don Pedro's Entrada against her breast, rocking slowly back and forth as the Moors did when they mourned—or prayed—and gazing with empty eyes out of the door of her tent. Then, in the sudden quiet of her heart, she asked herself: But what does it matter?

It was a thing of no importance, really. Nothing was of any importance . . . except that he was dear to her. Nothing else could matter. Nothing that Don Pedro might do—even if he led them all to their destruction—could matter to her heart.

"Ah, Pedro mío," she whispered, "I could not possibly love you more! *What could ever make me love you less?*"

The shadows slowly deepened between the hills across the Río Jesús

María. Fray Juan set up his little altar and the men gathered for evening prayer. Josefina could hear the fraile's voice clearly, and the deep responses of the troopers. She got out her rosary and knelt in her tent and prayed with them to God's mother for Don Pedro's success and the safety of the Entrada.

21

Just before darkness, the whole camp was aroused by the shouts of the sentries posted down-river. A rider was approaching at break-neck speed from that direction. It proved to be François Sistaca, back from his mission to the Pawnees. His horse was spent and covered with lather. The Indian himself appeared to be in a state of extreme exhaustion.

"He was attacked by the Pawnees," Captain Serna announced.

The camp received this disturbing news in uneasy silence. It waited with a gloomy impatience for Sistaca to recover his breath and get out the rest of his story. After following the river for some time, he said, he had not only discovered the band, but——

"*He has found the main village of the Pawnees!*" Captain Serna put in.

"Well, where is it?" Don Pedro demanded impatiently. "What did he observe? Did he see any French?"

"He says the village is about eight leagues from here, señor. Across the river. He is not certain whether he saw any French. The Pawnees often dress in the clothes of the Frenchmen. He saw some red caps. . . ."

"Well, tell him to go on," Don Pedro said. "What happened next?"

"He says he dismounted," Serna interpreted. "Then he called to the people across the river. He made the usual signs of peace and friendship. Some of the Pawnees began to come toward him. They shouted and yelled and waved tomahawks. My servant confesses that he was badly frightened, señor."

At this point, Sistaca removed his big hat and, looking anxiously over his shoulder, began making gestures with it, as if he were summoning help from someone. He ran backwards a few steps, made sweeping motions with the hat, and finally tripped over his spurs and fell down.

"Is all this play-acting necessary?" Don Pedro asked caustically.

"He is trying to show us, General," Serna said, "how he attempted to deceive the Pawnees. He wished to make them think that his people were on the other side of the hill and he was making signs to them to join him. He was badly frightened, no?"

"It would appear so," Don Pedro said dryly. "Pick him up and tell him to get on with his story."

"There is nothing much left to tell, señor," Serna said. "The Pawnees were not deceived. They kept on running toward my servant, brandishing their hatchets and uttering war cries. So, in fear of his life, he leaped on his horse and galloped the whole way back to camp without stopping once."

A heavy silence followed: one could almost feel the anxious thoughts stirring in the minds of everyone. Only the ensign, Captain Bernardo Casillas, appeared to derive any satisfaction from Sistaca's narrative. "Fine! Now we know where the bastards are. And if what this personage says is true, they're spoiling for a fight. Do we give them a taste of our arms, señor?"

Don Pedro smiled faintly, but did not bother to answer. The silence continued until Captain Olguín said: "Maybe we've learned all we need to know, eh? What is your opinion, señor?"

"Exactly what have we learned, Captain?" Jean L'Archévèque demanded truculently.

"That these Indians are hostile," Olguín said. "That's enough for me. We're a long way from home, Captain. There aren't very many of us. There are plenty of Pawnees—and maybe a few Frenchmen. I'm for getting out of this trap—while we can."

"Hostile or not," L'Archévèque said doggedly, "we've got to contact them. We've got to try, at least, to conciliate them."

"It's in the orders," Captain Naranjo said, with heavy irony.

Don Pedro glanced disapprovingly around his little circle of quarreling lieutenants. They became silent and waited—as they should have in the first place—for the commander to express his views. Don Pedro's were caustic.

"When I want a council of war, señores," he said, "I'll call one. I'll think this over and you'll get your orders in the morning."

Josefina went to his tent that evening. A dreadful feeling of onrushing disaster—of dark and evil events preparing themselves in a welter of uncertainty and ignorance—had taken possession of her.

"Amor," she said, "I have no liking for this Captain Olguín. But I can see some reason in what he says."

Don Pedro looked up at her with strangely bright eyes. The fever had seized him suddenly again. He sat on his rolled-up bedding, clutching his blue military cloak about him.

"Do you mean," he asked dully, "that we should withdraw now—retire to Santa Fé, or at least to El Cuartelejo?"

332

"I do, amor—before it is too late."

"But we have learned nothing about the French. We have not talked with the Pawnees . . . or made any attempt to win their friendship. . . ."

"Ah, Pedro mío!" she cried. "What good will it do to learn these things—to do these things—if we never return from this reconnaissance?"

He pulled the cloak more tightly around him and waited for a spasm of shivering to subside.

"It is impossible to turn back now," he said at last. "You will have to understand, my heart, that when I entered the profession of arms I learned, first of all, that orders must be obeyed. Orders are not examined, querida, to find out if they are wise or foolish. One only makes sure that they are clear—that one understands them. Then one goes ahead. In this case I have received an order to reconnoiter this country and find out what the French are up to here. It makes no difference that since this order came to Santa Fé certain things have happened. I am not supposed even to know about these things. I have only my orders. I am a soldier. I must obey them."

Ah, my only heart! she thought. Perhaps your devotion to duty has made you a little blind. . . . Perhaps it is a bit stupid to value one's honor so much!

As she gazed at the dark, grave face of this man, sitting there in his misery of chills and fever—and as she reflected on the duplicity, perfidy, corruption, depravity, and all the other vices that clung like a loathsome fungus to the body of Spanish officialdom—she began to weep for pity and pride and love of this good, and perhaps a little less than brilliant, man who was her husband.

"What is the matter, Josefina?" Don Pedro asked blankly. "Why are you crying?"

"Nothing, amor," she said, making an extraordinarily successful effort to smile and look happy. "We are marching in the morning, then. No?"

"That is my intention, querida."

"Good!" she exclaimed. "And now I shall tell you why I was crying. I was crying, señor, because I am happy to be married to such a fine, brave soldier as the one they call Captain Don Pedro Villasur."

22

At dawn the next morning the Entrada began to march eastward. Don Pedro moved with great care, keeping close to the protective banks of the Río Jesús María, and scouring the low hills to the north with a strong force of flankers. Captain Naranjo and his scouts fanned out well in advance. The Apache allies formed the rear guard.

At this point the Río Jesús María flowed through a perfectly flat valley perhaps three miles wide. On the left, a range of grassy hills rolled up against the sky; on the right, groves of cottonwoods and willows hid the river from view. The floor of the valley was a level, clean carpet of grass and flowers; the bright sky above it was filled with the lazy movement of immaculate little clouds.

And yet, even in this smiling, pleasant world, there was one vaguely disquieting feature. The hills across the river were not, like those to the north, smooth and grassy and gently rolling; they were high, ugly buttes of bare, black rock. In these hills, which concealed like a vast curtain all that lay back of them to the south, Josefina sensed something sinister. And Don Pedro shared her disquiet.

"I'd feel a lot more secure, Captain," she heard him say to Captain Real, "if we had a few flankers over there."

Thereafter, during the whole of that sunny day's march through that pleasant valley, she was never quite free of the uncomfortable impression that eyes were watching her from those stark, black hills across the river.

At midafternoon Captain Naranjo himself rode back with the news that the Pawnee village was less than two leagues away. It was on a very long island, he reported, the tip of which could be seen from where they stood.

Don Pedro immediately ordered a halt to tighten up the column, bring up the horseherd, and draw in the flankers. After a brief inspection, the Entrada then proceeded with extreme caution until the advance guard had reached a point almost opposite the Pawnee settlement. Here, on a slight rise of ground, where the grass was not too high, camp was pitched and the horses turned loose to graze under a strong guard.

And so, on the tenth of August, 1720, having marched for fifty-two days through more than six hundred miles of largely unknown country, the Entrada to the Río Jesús María arrived at its objective.

The event drew no cheers from the troops; Fray Juan Minguéz sang no *Te Deum;* no tall cross was set up. The command went about the business of pitching camp silently and a little morosely. The men were saddle-weary and uneasy in their minds, their nervousness showing itself in a tendency to bicker and quarrel among themselves.

Their apprehension was mixed with a natural curiosity about what was on the island almost directly across the river. Very little could be seen from the Spanish encampment—only the vague outlines of houses or huts through the willows and cottonwoods. Neither Indians nor French showed themselves in the open. There was no sound from the island except that of some dogs barking.

In order to get a better view, therefore—and perhaps arrive at some estimate of the French and Pawnee strength—Don Pedro rode to the top of a small hill about a league distant from the river. He was accompanied by Captain Naranjo, Captain Olguín, and Josefina. There was a moment of silence as the four of them reined up their horses and looked down at what they had come so far to see: at what Spanish eyes were seeing for the first time.

From this high ground they could look down, over the tops of the concealing trees, onto the mud roofs of a Pawnee village of considerable size. It was not "as large as Taos," certainly, as the rumors had made it; but it was adequate, Captain Naranjo estimated, to house at least a thousand souls.

Some of the inhabitants—mostly women and children—were watching the Spaniards from the rooftops. Other figures could be seen moving about on the ground.

"You have the best eyes among us, Captain," Don Pedro said to Naranjo. "What do you make out?"

"Nothing, señor, that we can't all see," the scout replied, after a long look. "A good many houses: maybe a hundred, no? But none like those Don Antonio described to the Viceroy."

"Do you see any French?"

"Quién sabe? It's hard to tell, señor. The French in these villages become more Indian than the Indians themselves. I see no one in French clothes, anyhow."

"Any horses?"

"No, señor. Not one. They have no corrals and no horses—not in this village, at least."

They sat their restless mounts for a while in silence, gazing down at this village which, now that they had at last reached it and were actually looking at it, seemed hardly less unreal and dreamlike than it had before. Uncertainty had only deepened to greater uncertainty. Suddenly it seemed to Josefina that this eerie Entrada had ridden beyond the limits of human experience . . . that it had come at last to the very edge of . . . she could not guess what.

We can only wait, she thought, and see what happens . . . what God decides.

23

The first of a series of obscure and therefore vaguely ominous events took place immediately.

On the opposite bank of the river, a group of Pawnees began to gather in the shadows of the cottonwoods. Finally a score or more of them came down to the edge of the stream, which at this point was less than an arquebus shot wide and too deep to ford. It was difficult to see them distinctly: they were but a pattern of shadows against the darker shadows of the trees. But their voices carried clearly across the water.

"What are they saying?" Don Pedro asked Captain Serna. "What does your Sistaca make of it?"

"They're asking peace, señor."

François Sistaca motioned importantly for silence and listened attentively to the guttural sounds drifting across the river. He said a few words to Captain Serna.

"They want him to come over, señor. He says he's willing to go—alone."

"By the Mass!" Captain Naranjo growled. "Yesterday he was dodging their tomahawks. Now he wants to go over and visit with them."

"He says they promise not to harm him," Serna said.

"I'm sure as all hell they won't!"

"You mistrust him, Captain?" Don Pedro asked.

"I think he lies like a Christian, señor," the scout said. "Either he was lying to us yesterday, or he's doing it now, no?"

The Pawnee had begun to remove his red jacket, his big hat, and the rest of his clothes. He was conversing again with his kinsmen on the island. The Indians pointed repeatedly at the western horizon, where a faint afterglow outlined the dusky hills.

"They say they want to be friends, but it's too late to confer with us today," Serna interpreted. "But they want my servant to come to them at once."

"Why not, señor?" Jean L'Archévèque asked softly. "He's the only one among us who can talk with them."

"What do you say, Captain?" Don Pedro asked Naranjo.

"I'd say no, except that we've got to make talk with them sometime," the scout said. "Maybe this is as good a time as any. So let's do it now, señor—and then get out of here."

"Very well, Captain."

A few minutes later, with some tobacco bound to his head as a present to the Pawnees, the Indian slipped into the water and struck out for the opposite bank. All watched him silently. Fray Juan Minguéz, who did not participate in any of the military councils, decided that he could now express an opinion.

"I doubt," he said, "that we'll ever see that lousy heathen again."

Immediate developments appeared to support his view. The Spaniards could see the Pawnee pull himself out of the water and climb up the bank, where he was surrounded at once by his kinsmen. After a while he came alone to the edge of the river, a shadowy, grotesque figure. He shouted something across in the Apache tongue. This time Captain Naranjo did the interpreting.

"He says they're friendly," the scout reported.

There was a long, uneasy interval of silence. Then the Pawnee shouted again, his words echoing curiously out of the almost complete darkness.

"He says he hasn't found any Frenchmen over there," Naranjo said. "And—for once you're right, padre—they won't let him come back!"

Only half the Entrada slept that night, while the other half maintained guard; and no one slept soundly. Don Pedro took the extra precaution of sending a small, well-armed party under cover of darkness to watch the ford, a short distance down the river. Fires were kept brightly burning well beyond the lines of the encampment. Toward dawn—the usual hour of Indian attack—the whole command was awakened and put under arms.

24

The men were listless and on edge for the rest of the day. Reports kept coming in from the scouts, but none of them added much to what was already known. Some French clothing—red hats and long cloth coats—might have been seen: the scouts were not quite sure. A war party had been observed going toward the hills in the rear—it was thought. Nothing definite, nothing really helpful. The screen of mystery surrounding the Pawnee settlement remained as impenetrable as ever.

That day passed and the next night, without incident. On the following day, August the twelfth, a messenger came from the Pawnees. He carried a piece of cloth on a stick, in lieu of a flag, and a very old and dirty piece of paper covered with illegible scrawls. Jean L'Archévèque studied this writing for a long time. Finally he handed it to Don Pedro.

"I can't make it out, señor," he said. "It isn't French and it isn't Spanish. I don't know what it is."

"I'll tell you what I think it is," Captain Naranjo said. "I think these heathen bastards are having sport with us."

Don Pedro regarded the Pawnee emissary with burning eyes. Possibly he had begun to suspect the same thing. The Pawnee stood with his arms folded, his face impassive—yet insolent. He made no attempt to conceal his disdain.

The paper was given to Fray Juan Minguéz, who examined it to see if it might be in another tongue—Latin possibly. He studied the crude hieroglyphics for a little time, then said, "For once I agree with Captain Naranjo, señor. This isn't writing at all!"

Nobody smiled at the thought of the Pawnees playing a kind of humorous guessing game with them. If this were a joke, it was likely to turn out as a pretty grim one.

At last—because nobody could think of a better course—an answer offering peace and friendship was sent to the Pawnees. Don Pedro's silver writing implements were brought out, and the message was written in Spanish with ink and quill on a sheet of paper torn from the Entrada's journal.

The Pawnee messenger was sent off with scant courtesy—and without presents—to his people. Afterwards Captain Naranjo said: "We've made a lot of mistakes on this campaign, no? Well, I think we have just made another."

"What's that, Captain?" Ensign Casillas asked.

"We should have kept that son-of-a-bitch here as a hostage."

"You realize," L'Archévèque said nervously, "that would be the equivalent of a declaration of war."

"Yes, I realize that," Naranjo said.

25

There was no one in the whole Entrada—even down to the muleteers and horse wranglers—who did not sense that a state of actual, if not declared, hostility now existed between themselves and the Pawnees. But opinion as to what ought to be done varied greatly.

Don Pedro called a council of war that night to crystallize the judgment of the command. Fray Juan Minguéz joined the officers this time, and Josefina again recorded the deliberations of the staff.

Don Pedro astounded the council with his opening proposal. After presenting a brief estimate of their situation, he said:

"My own idea, señores, is that we should cross over to their island and see what we wish to know for ourselves!"

Josefina looked up quickly as he said this. Don Pedro was very pale. His features were strangely taut and his eyes burned with an unnatural fire.

But then she knew that it was not the fever speaking from Don Pedro's tight lips: it was his Spanish pride. He had borne all he could stand, at last, of Pawnee arrogance. He, who had been trained and experienced in the great traditions of Spanish arms—whose school had been the battlefields of Europe—could no longer stomach the insults and ribaldry of a miserable tribe of savages.

"I think these heathen bastards are having sport with us!"

She had seen Don Pedro's eyes flash when Captain Naranjo said that. She had sensed then that the reckless courage for which Don Pedro Villasur was famous had suffered a mortal affront. In his rigid code of honor there was now, quite suddenly, only one course of action open: and he was proposing it to this council.

Don Pedro was, in fact, proposing that the troops of the Entrada cross over and attack the settlement of the Pawnees.

They heard him respectfully—if a little incredulously—to the end. Then, just as the final vote of the chiefs was about to be taken, the council was interrupted by the arrival of a messenger from the guard at the ford. Captain Naranjo went to the door of the tent and spoke with him briefly. When he returned, he said, in a remarkably matter-of-fact voice:

"Two of our Indians, señor, who were bathing in the river near the ford, have been carried off by the Pawnees."

The council received this news in deadly silence. The silence seemed to say: "Well, now we know how things stand; now everything is settled for us." When the vote on Don Pedro's proposal was taken, all except Ensign Casillas opposed it.

"Very well, señores," Don Pedro said, without visible emotion. "I think we all agree that our situation here is anything but secure. We shall begin our withdrawal in the morning. We shall proceed tomorrow as far as possible beyond the forks of the river. You will please see to everything, Captain Domínguez. Thank you."

26

On Tuesday, the thirteenth of August, San Hipolito's day, the Entrada struck camp at daybreak and, marching with a doubled rear guard, began its retreat—for all acknowledged it to be that—westward along the Río Jesús María.

Don Pedro's order to retire was accepted by the troops with a distinct feeling of relief. So strong was the general sense of urgency, and so eager was the Entrada to put distance between itself and the Pawnee village, that by four o'clock in the afternoon it had recrossed the San Lorenzo and had progressed almost as far as it had required two days to march on the way out.

On a broad, level spot close to the river, where the lush grass grew to the height of the horses' girths, Don Pedro ordered the command to halt and quarter.

The camp was made with extra attention to defensive precautions. Like all Spanish expeditionary camps, it was laid out in a square large enough to accommodate not only the men but also the horses of the Entrada. And like all Spanish camps pitched on a river, one side of the square was formed by the water itself.

Immediately after selecting this site, Don Pedro distributed machetes to the troops who occupied themselves for half an hour cutting down the long grass. A breastwork, as a defense against night attack, was then formed in the cleared area with saddles, packs, and baggage. Not until then were tents pitched, fires built, and preparations begun for the evening meal.

In the meantime the horses of the Entrada were being cared for in accordance with strict regulations. As soon as the camp site had been cleared and the breastwork erected, all mounts were turned over to the horse guard, who would graze them in the rich grass outside—but near—the encampment until sunset. With the coming of darkness, all would be brought inside the camp, where a range about thirty feet in diameter had been allowed for each animal, and every soldier would halter and picket his own mounts near at hand. At daybreak the horseherd would again be turned loose to graze, in care of the horse guard, until the Entrada had breakfasted and it was time for saddling.

To Josefina, watching these energetic and methodical preparations, there was something very comforting in the reflection that almost never in the whole history of Spanish conquest had such a camp been surprised and taken.

Captain Olguín, however, appeared not to share this feeling. When, at four o'clock in the afternoon, Don Pedro had ordered a halt, he had objected in strong, almost mutinous terms. Josefina had overheard the angry exchange between the commander and his lieutenant.

"I think we should go on," Olguín had said. "They're still too close to us."

"We've come twelve leagues, Captain. That's a long march. The men and horses are tired."

"I know. But it's not far enough."

"Are you afraid they'll still overtake us, Captain?"

"I'm afraid of nothing, señor," Olguín answered stiffly. "Unless it's of what they might have in those hills across the river."

"I do not understand this, Captain," Don Pedro said slowly. "Only yesterday you were of the opinion that we have nothing to fear from these . . . what you called these miserable savages. Now, it seems to me, you are excessively cautious."

"I've changed my mind about those miserable savages," Olguín said hotly. "But that doesn't make me a coward."

"One never changes his mind, Captain, in matters of courage."

Josefina's horrified eyes watched Captain Olguín's hand make a small, almost imperceptible movement toward the dagger in his belt, then drop suddenly.

"Very good," the subaltern said. "All the responsibility is yours, señor."

"On the contrary, Captain," Don Pedro said. "The responsibility for the security of this camp is yours. I should not have to remind you of that. I expect every precaution to be taken. You understand this thoroughly, no?"

"Perfectly, señor," Olguín said, with heavy sarcasm. He saluted negligently and walked away.

Josefina recalled this scene with a mixture of wonder and dismay. That Don Pedro, in addition to all his other burdens, should have to carry the load of this great boor's insolence! It was not that Olguín disagreed sometimes with Don Pedro: that was the privilege of any

Spanish officer. It was the implacable, sullen opposition that this man—whom Don Antonio had appointed second in command of the Entrada—offered to almost every move that Don Pedro made.

It is easy to see, Josefina mused, who this Captain Olguín thinks should command this Entrada!

She watched him as he directed the preparations for the encampment. It was evident to her that he was smarting from Don Pedro's reprimand. Was Don Pedro unreasonable, she wondered? Had he given way to anger too easily? Why had he lashed out at his lieutenant with such sudden heat?

She knew that Don Pedro was despondent over the retirement—the failure, it seemed to him—of the Entrada. And he was sick. But it was not only the fever and the tremendous headaches that had worn his body and mind and spirit to the point of . . . of what she had just witnessed between him and Captain Olguín.

To these physical sufferings could be added the thousand difficulties, annoyances, and humiliations—all so carefully planned in Don Antonio's diabolic brain—that had dogged Don Pedro every mile of this long and wearisome march.

Ah, Antonio, she thought, you might have broken a less resolute man . . . but not such a one as Don Pedro Villasur!

Yet, as she watched Olguín directing the encampment with an odd air of sullen negligence, she was not easy in her mind about Don Pedro. Her anxiety grew when she noted that, as soon as it was pitched, Don Pedro had retired to his tent. She went to him and found him lying on his pallet with a damp cloth across his eyes. She sat down quietly beside him and, whenever the cloth became warm, she dipped it into a kettle of cold water that Don Pedro's orderly, Melchior Rodríguez, had brought up from the river, and replaced it over his eyes. Neither of them said anything.

After a while—it had begun to grow dark in the tent—Don Pedro sat up, shook his head as if to clear it, and said: "That's enough, querida. It's a little better now. I've got to get out and inspect the camp."

She helped him into his jacket and buckled on his sword. Before she let him go, she kissed him on the lips. They were burning hot with fever, but she said only, "I'll make some tea, amor. It will be ready for you when you return."

In Don Pedro's little store of comestibles, tea was an item carried more as a medicine than as a beverage. Josefina took the metal caddy out of the chest in which it was kept and measured out a little of the black, crinkly powder into one of Don Pedro's silver cups. Then she went outside to ask Rodríguez to have some hot water ready. All these small details of preparing tea for her husband gave her a curiously domestic feeling, at once sad and satisfying.

Ah, Pedro mío! she sighed to herself. That I might be really your wife soon! She smiled a faint, rueful smile and added: Instead of your camp follower, no?

She found Rodríguez at his post before the door of Don Pedro's tent. He was the youngest perhaps of the soldiers and the least experienced in actual war. Usually he was high-spirited and carefree in a rather empty-headed sort of way; but now his broad paisano face appeared darkened with care.

"What passes, Melchior?" Josefina asked him. "You look as if you have just received some very bad news."

"It is true, Doña Josefina," the young presidial said blankly. "The news is not good."

She did not press him further. She gave him instructions about the hot water, and then sought out Fray Juan Minguéz. She discovered the fraile at the far end of the camp, setting up a cross and his small portable altar.

"What is this the men are saying?" she demanded. "What is the news that is so bad . . . that I have not been told?"

"Rumors, my daughter," Fray Juan said, polishing the silver-gilt paten of his altar service with the sleeve of his gown. "Only rumors."

"Then, padre," she said, "I might as well hear them. I have never been frightened by rumors."

"I ask your pardon, señora." He told her of the various reports that had come in from the scouts, and from the horse guard, during the afternoon.

Pawnee warriors—in war paint—had been seen lurking in the tall grass surrounding the encampment: one of them had even allowed himself to be seen and had shouted unintelligible words accompanied by obscene gestures.

It was believed that the Pawnees were gathering in the densely wooded island opposite the camp: vague forms had been detected moving about in the thickets.

Splashings had been heard in the water on the other side of this island and it was conjectured that the Pawnees were crossing over from the mainland.

The Indian horseherd had become restive and nervous, in the manner of Indian horses when approached by savages of a strange tribe.

One soldier, at work on the drainage ditches, swore that he had looked up and seen a Frenchman in a red hat and armed with two pistols observing him.

The fraile looked at her with his frosty blue eyes in a manner

343

that seemed to say: "Well, there you have it, señora: man to man!"

"Padre Juan, you keep on evading me!" she said. *"Do we expect an attack?"*

"We always expect an attack when we are in Indian country, Doña Josefina. We are always prepared for one." He glanced around at the defensive arrangements of the encampment. "That we trust in God, now, and pray for His protection. . . . And don't worry, eh?"

"I won't, padre," she said. "But I shall pray, as you suggest!"

She was not nearly as nonchalant as she tried to appear. It was true that this was, as Fray Juan had said, a nervous camp. The men were worn and moody. The weeks of eerie uncertainty through which they had passed had left them jumpy and excitable.

You can't trust the eyes and ears of men in such a condition, she told herself. They hear and see all sorts of things that don't even exist!

27

She went to her tent and changed into her green satin dress, the dress in which she had been married, as was sometimes her custom at the end of the day: it raised her spirits to do up her hair, and put on this dress and slippers, and fasten earrings to her ears. The sun was setting when she left for Don Pedro's tent.

When Don Pedro returned from his inspection, she did not query him as she had Fray Juan. He appeared drawn and pale; and even the simplest conversation, she could see, was an effort with him. They exchanged only a few words:

"Does your head feel better now, amor?"

"A little, querida."

"Why don't you lie down for a few minutes?"

"Later, my dear—after the scouts report."

"I have made some tea for you. Look!"

She handed him the hot, dark liquid in the silver cup. He smiled his thanks and sipped a little of it.

Pobrecito! she thought. That you should have to bear so many crosses!

She had never thought that she would ever feel pity for Don Pedro Villasur! Some people could never be the objects of certain emotions. Some, by their very nature, could not be hated, or envied, or loved. With Don Pedro, it had once seemed that something—a cool inner strength and self-sufficiency—had placed him forever beyond the need of pity. . . . But now——

Ah, my heart, she thought, that I could take some of this pain away from you! I weep for you, amor, as a . . . as a mother might weep for a little suffering child. *I love you, Pedro mío, with such a love.* . . .

But she revealed none of her sadness—and, above all, none of her disquiet—to her husband. The tea seemed to have a beneficial effect on him. He handed the cup back to her with an almost cheerful smile.

"You are better than a doctor," he said. "And also very beautiful."

She kissed him swiftly, almost surreptitiously on the lips: they were still feverishly hot.

At intervals now Rodríguez announced the arrival of a messenger from Captain Olguín, who was supervising the final arrangements of the encampment for the night. It had grown almost dark. The reports came in, as Don Pedro had ordered, from time to time.

"The horseherd has been turned loose to graze, señor, with a strong guard under Ensign Casillas."

"Sounds are still being heard, señor, like those of people splashing in the water, on the other side of the island."

"Apache sentinels have been posted, señor, around the entire camp."

"Dogs have been heard barking, señor."

"Word has been sent in from the Apache guards, señor, that some Pawnees have been seen swimming in the darkness from the island with bows and arrows strapped to their heads."

Don Pedro listened to all these reports—up to the last one—without comment. Then he sent for Captain Olguín. After a considerable time, the subaltern appeared. He was plainly in a sullen, almost defiant, mood. Don Pedro, ignoring this, reviewed the information he had received.

"What is your evaluation of all this, Captain?" he asked.

"This is not the proper place for an encampment," Olguín answered, with a sour glance at Josefina. "Here you can expect anything."

"I don't consider that an answer, Captain," Don Pedro said quietly.

"Well, if you value my opinion," Olguín said, "I think we're being watched. I think Pawnee stalking parties are out."

"This is your opinion, Captain?"

"It is, señor. But you do not have to be afraid. I have taken all precautions. We are secure . . . even here."

Don Pedro chose, although not without obvious exertion, to disregard the jibe and insult. He inquired patiently: "Why have you posted Apache guards, Captain?"

"Because the men are tired out. They need some sleep. The Apaches will do tonight."

"You trust them that much?"

"If I didn't, señor," Olguín said with what, Josefina thought, was both a stupid and insolent smile, "I wouldn't have posted them."

There was a long interval of silence. Then——

"Things are done differently in this part of the world, señor," Olguín added. "We do our best here with what we've got."

When Don Pedro spoke again there was a certain rasp in his voice. "I'm not satisfied with all this, Captain," he said. "I've asked you for facts, and I've been given opinions. I want you to send out a strong party immediately—a party of Spaniards—to reconnoiter the terrain up and down the river and back of the camp. I want you to find out what's *really* going on around this encampment. That shouldn't be too difficult an assignment. Report to me as soon as you have something to report."

"Very well, señor!"

Olguín, who for a moment appeared to have been taken a little aback, recovered himself and saluted. He turned on his heel and stalked out of the tent.

"There goes a very stupid and deceitful man!" Josefina commented.

Don Pedro shook his head and smiled sadly. "He is reputed to be the Kingdom's best soldier. He has campaigned for many years."

"Perhaps too many, no?"

"I hope, querida," Don Pedro added, after a while, "that nothing Captain Olguín has said will disturb you. There is nothing to be alarmed about."

"Don't worry, amor," she said, "I am not in the least frightened. But you do not look well. Perhaps you should rest a little now?"

She could see that the chills were returning, as they often did in the evening. They would grow worse for a while—perhaps for several hours—then they would subside. She persuaded him to lie down on his blankets, and she placed the damp cloth across his eyes again. He lay for the length of a dozen Credos, very still; and she sat beside him, gazing pensively at his face in the fitful candlelight.

"Querida," Don Pedro said at last.

"Yes, amor?"

"When will the baby be born?"

"In March, I think. I think in Holy Week."

"Do you wish for a boy?"

"To tell you the truth, amor, I do. I did not have a brother. Maybe that is why I would like to have a little boy. And you?"

"It is said that every man wants his first child to be a boy," Don Pedro said. "But with me, it would make no difference. I could love just as much a little girl—with green eyes and a dimple in each shoulder, no?"

346

He could not see her face as she bent it over his: he did not know that she was going to kiss him until he felt her lips on his. It gave her an odd little shock to kiss the immobile face of her husband thus; she withdrew with something like a faint shudder.

Outside, Fray Juan was conducting a devotion to the Rosary by the light of a driftwood fire. She could hear his strong, virile voice and the voices of the soldiers.

Complete darkness, without a moon or any stars, had settled over the camp when Captain Olguín returned. He did not waste much time in reporting to Don Pedro.

"The patrol has returned, señor," he said. "All is secure."

Don Pedro dismissed him without further questioning. It was evident that, even if he had wished to talk with Olguín, he would have had difficulty in doing it. His teeth had begun to chatter and violent, almost grotesque tremblings shook his whole body.

When this happened, Josefina knew, there was only one thing to do—only one thing that would bring him relief. She helped him remove his outer clothes, as one might help a child, and covered him with all his blankets and his military cloak. Then, taking off her dress, she slipped under the blankets and drew him tight and close to her. She strove to press the warmth of her own body into his, to drive out with the living warmth of her own blood the chill that ran like streams of ice through his. . . . She clung to him and prayed: she took herself to the Lady Chapel of La Parróquia and she knelt before the little doll-like image of La Conquistadora: and she prayed:

"Sweet Mother of God—keep him and me and our baby from harm. . . ."

The ague left Don Pedro quite suddenly, as it always did, and he fell into a fretful sleep. Then gently, so as not to disturb him, Josefina drew away from him. She got into her dress and, after tucking the covers comfortably around Don Pedro, she touched his damp hair with her lips and went out into the soft, heavy, frightening night.

28

She was surprised to find that only a few of the men had turned in for the night. Most of them, including the officers and Fray Juan, had gathered around a fire at the far end of the encampment. Music drifted toward her through the darkness.

She thought of an old Spanish saying: *When a door is open and a guitar is playing, it is all right to go in.* She smiled and walked toward the fire.

"What passes here, padre?" she asked Fray Juan. "After such a day as this has been?"

"After such a day, my daughter," the fraile said, "one needs a little music, no?"

"That is true, padre."

"Or a little drink. Since we have nothing to drink, let us be thankful for Griego."

She laughed and stood silently beside the fraile, listening to Corporal Griego's singing. He sang in his low, rough voice the old and terrible and almost demoniacally fascinating ballad of *Delgadina.*

The music was even more blood-chilling than the horrible tale of incest and murder: *it was gay.* It was music that reached back into very ancient time . . . into the dark mists of the occult East . . . into the very depths of the Spanish soul. It ended with a shudder.

"That is an odd song," Josefina mused, "for the raising of one's spirits."

"It does them good," Fray Juan said. "It reminds them that they are Spanish. It reminds their blood."

Another soldier began a song—a soft, romantic ballad this time of love and war. Josefina watched the listening faces across the fire. They were the haggard, large-eyed faces of inexpressibly weary men.

Ah, yes, she thought, they sing because they are weary, as soldiers sometimes do. And also because they are afraid. They would be fools not to be afraid tonight. Yet they cannot admit their fear—even to themselves. So they sing to show their courage, no? To themselves . . . *and to the savages.*

They discovered her presence and opened a way for her to the center of their circle. They made her a fine seat of a blanket roll, and she sat down near the fire.

"Thank you, compañeros," she said. "Does no one here know a song that is a little gay?"

"La Jota?" a leather-jacket asked tentatively.

"Good!" she clapped her hands. "That you sing it, Pancho."

Griego's guitar suddenly came alive with the bright, bouncing rhythms of the jota—which was both a dance and a ballad in New Mexico. And Pancho began to sing:

> "Come out, lovely one, come out;
> Come out to your balcony:
> Come out for a moment, at least,
> Gay mistress of my heart."

They all joined in the chorus, Josefina's voice floating above the strong, rough harmony of the leather-jackets.

> "La jota, jota, jota aragonesa . . .
> Viva Zaragoza! duena de mi amor."

Over and over they shouted the gay, defiant chorus into the limitless night. Josefina shouted with them. *All at once she was one of them.* She was one of them in a way she had never been before in all those weary days, on all those endless leagues, up from the Villa of Santa Fé. She was united with them all in a common weariness, and pride, and defiance . . . and fear.

For she also was afraid . . . and she also could not show her fear . . . not even to herself.

"Olé! Bueno, chico!" she called, clapping her hands softly. "More, Panchito!"

But Pancho shrank back into the shadows with an embarrassed smile. Griego bent his head over his guitar, and his fingers began to wander aimlessly over the strings. At times they picked up a few phrases from some old love song or ballad, dropped them. He raised his eyes to Josefina's.

"Por favor, señora," he said, so softly that she could hardly hear him.

But she understood him. He was speaking for them all, she knew: they were asking her to sing for them. They all watched her silently, expectantly. Griego allowed the strumming of his guitar to die away into a pregnant silence. She stood up.

"Ea! Chico!" she cried in the low, rich, metallic tones that had once so thrilled the Madrileños. "Give me a little music to dance by, por favor."

She glanced around her. Beyond the tiny patch of firelight, the haggard faces, rose a wall of darkness. But it was a wall with ears, a wall with eyes. In the high grass, on the shadowy island in the river, in the black hills on the hidden horizon, the Pawnees—and no doubt the French, too—were listening and watching. And perhaps wondering.

Well, let them listen! Let them watch! Most of all, let them wonder!

She would give them something to remember her by, no? She had something to say to them, for herself, for all these weary men, for all their stubborn Spanish souls. She would tell it to them in the language she could speak best, no? In a language that even those heathen in their savage hills could understand. . . .

"Bueno! Bueno, chico!" she cried with a strange, desperate joy. "Louder, Joselito! *Let them hear it!*"

She held out her hands toward Griego, beating her palms softly together in the rhythms she desired from him. Griego watched her intently, his fingers seeking over the strings, testing the tempo. At last, in a kind of triumphant certainty, the rhythms of his instrument found and merged with those of her body.

"Anda, chica!" he growled. "Olé!"

Abruptly, she whirled about, facing the silent circle of leather-jackets. She reached out her arms to them, beckoning them toward her with little motions of her upturned hands. She asked their help in the ancient petition:

"Give me some palmadas, señores . . . give me some dry handclaps, to see if we are beginning to understand each other."

The palmadas are given with a will. The voice of Corporal Griego's guitar becomes a strident shout. She thrusts up her arms in a wide brazeo and utters a heartraising little cry. The firelight flares on her frowning face, from her half-closed eyes. Her hips move in the first slow, provocative rhythms of the fandango. . . . And so, enwrapped in a thousand miles of prairie darkness, under the remote and alien stars, Josefina dances for the weary and anxious and indomitable men of the Entrada to the Río Jesús María.

She dances for them what she cannot say in words—what they cannot say for themselves. She speaks for them in a pattern of proud movement, and scornful eyes, and gestures of grave and violent beauty . . . in the language of their Spanish hearts, of their deepest Spanish souls.

And they watch her in silence. They gaze at her from moody eyes as the light and graceful movements of the fandango begin to trace themselves in firelight against the night. They make no sound at all as the rhythms of that ancient dance gather momentum, rush deliriously on, and plunge to a wild and sensual climax. And when it is finished—when the frenzy of spiraling body and curving back and undulating arms halts abruptly in that frozen immobility with which the fandango always ends—there is no applause, there are no palmadas. There is only, from that strangely silent ring of darkness, a low exclamation, half a shout, half a sob:

"Viva España!"

She is bewildered, a little frightened. She cannot think what to do. She can only do as her heart urges. So she flashes a smile at them, and holds out her arms, and shakes her shoulders in the old, sweetly wanton manner of the Gaditanas; and she tells them:

"Ay, compañeros—I love you all!"

Then, with sudden, almost frightening violence, the men of the Entrada to the Río Jesús María answer to the ancient urgings of their blood. They stand up and shout what is in their hearts. The

things they understand and the things they do not understand. . . .
"Viva Doña Josefina!" they shout. And, "God bless your mother!"

They cheer and even laugh, and all at once Josefina knows for
certain that she has not danced for nothing. She adds a little shout
to theirs, and laughs with them . . . and hopes the listening hills can
hear. They clamor for more; but she is spent, exhausted, and begs of
them to let her go.

"Another time," she promises them. "Soon, soon, señores. And now,
good night!"

As she left them, returning through the darkness to her tent, she
was conscious of a strong feeling of exhilaration. She was filled with
a strange sense of recklessness—a serene indifference to the odds. It
was not an altogether new sensation. She had always felt it after
dancing, particularly after dancing the fandango. But this time the
feeling was deeper . . . and somehow different. As if it were something *shared*.

Perhaps it is a kind of courage, she said to herself. Perhaps it is
what *they* feel. Then God grant that I keep it!

She stopped at Don Pedro's tent on her way to her own. He was
standing in the doorway, enveloped in his big blue military cloak
. . . the cloak that enwrapped him in something of Old Spain itself.

"Hola, amor!" she said, surprised. "Were you watching too?"

He smiled at her in a strange, almost reproving way and held out
his arms: she went to them.

"Yes, I was watching," he said, with a kind of wondering tenderness
in his voice. "It was magnificent . . . *La Sola.*"

She kissed his feverish lips compulsively and held him tightly to her.

"I am sorry, amor," she whispered. "I had thought it something
best forgotten."

His answer was strangely like an echo of her own tortured thoughts
only a little while ago:

"*Querida—what difference could it make?*"

She kissed him again quickly, freed herself, and ran through the
darkness to her tent: she did not want him to see her weep tonight.

The Tewa woman who shared her quarters was snugly asleep in
her corner. Josefina undressed in the dark, not wishing to disturb her.
She knelt and said her evening prayers and lay down on her pallet
of buffalo robes.

She lay awake for a long time, thinking. She could not get rid of
drowsy but insistent thoughts of death.

Like all Spaniards, she was preoccupied—more than the people of
other races—with the great, inevitable, ultimate fact of death. It was
not a morbid prepossession. She was not afraid of death, although
she did not wish for it. But she was concerned greatly with the

351

manner of its coming to her. Like all Spaniards also, she wished to make a good death.

What might befall her if the Pawnees should attack tonight? She had tried to keep this bothersome conjecture at the back of her mind; but it intruded itself so persistently that she found herself becoming warm and prickly with fright . . . with something close to panic. She felt a sudden urge to flee from her tent—to rush back to Don Pedro. She fought this impulse off, although the effort left her weak and damp with perspiration; then she quieted her fears at last with the remembrance of the promise Don Pedro had made to her not long after they had left El Cuartelejo.

But just before she fell asleep, she heard a sound that sent little chills and tremors through her blood again. It was the sound of a dog barking in the night . . . from the direction of the island opposite the camp.

29

The sun was well up when the Pawnees struck.

As dawn broadened into daylight, the troops of the Entrada had felt a great, though carefully concealed, relief that the customary time of an Indian attack had come and gone without incident. They showed this relief in a rather unnatural exuberance. They made jokes and laughed at them, however poor, with laughter that was perhaps a little loud and a little high. They went at the tasks of breaking camp, preparing breakfast, and making ready for the march with an energy and willingness unusual in soldiers so early in the day.

The horseherd, which had been picketed during the night inside the encampment, was turned over to the horse guard, under Ensign Casillas, and taken a little distance into the high grass to graze. Casillas and the presidials comprising the horse guard were the only mounted men in camp, or near it, at this time. The rest of the Entrada was busy *afoot* inside the improvised breastworks of saddles and packs that had been thrown up the night before.

Thus, between the time the horses were led out to graze and the time when they would be returned for saddling—an interval of not more than half an hour—the Entrada was in its most vulnerable position. Without horses, it was all but defenseless; for a Spanish expeditionary soldier without a horse was almost no soldier at all.

That the Pawnees should have selected this brief period for a surprise attack could mean but two things. First, they had been well informed by the spy François Sistaca about the precise behavior on an Entrada on the march. Second, the Apaches posted by Captain Olguín as sentries had either been caught asleep or had gone over to the enemy.

For the assault came utterly without warning and with blood-chilling violence.

Everything happened simultaneously. From the high grass surrounding the encampment on all but the river side came a tremendous outburst of wild, inhuman and completely horrifying yells. Over this rose the scarcely less terrifying sound of the horseherd going into a stampede. And only an instant later the deafening blast of musketfire pouring in from every quarter.

The soldiers of the Entrada were veterans of many campaigns; but even veterans can be nonplussed by the impossible, and the immediate effect was a simple mental and physical paralysis. Then, in almost the next moment, habit and training—and sheer instinct—took over. The bugler Manuel de Silva unslung his bugle and began blowing the call to arms. He succeeded in getting out only a few alarm-edged notes, however. In the middle of a bar he dropped his instrument, looked about him with a surprised expression, and began to run with a Pawnee arrow protruding from his back.

In the interval of relative quiet following the first pandemonium of shouts, shots, and the sounds of animal panic, the sharp, barking commands of the squad corporals crackled through the encampment; and those who had survived the first assault disposed themselves to defend their camp and their lives.

It could hardly be said that a defense was organized. There was no time for anything but a wild rush for cover behind the wall of saddles and baggage and a blind round of fire into the tall grass from which the rain of sudden death had swept. This, however, had a deterrent effect on the attackers; and the remnant of the Entrada to the Río Jesús María was granted a few minutes in which to look around and check its losses.

They were appalling. At least half of the whole presidial force had been wiped out by the first volley of musketfire, spears, and arrows. Captain Pedro Luján had met his death a lanzado—by being pierced with a Pawnee spear. The spear had entered his chest and the captain clutched it with both hands; he twisted a little on his back, digging his spurs into the earth, then suddenly relaxed and lay still with the shaft of the spear pointing grotesquely skyward. Corporal José Griego—who owned the guitar and composed ribald songs about his comrades—had been shot cleanly and mercifully through the forehead. Presidial José Fernandez had been obscurely wounded: he crawled around the enclosure of the encampment, holding his stomach with one hand and calling out, "Dios! Dios! Dios! Dios!"

Josefina, lying flat behind the barricade, saw as much of this as her unbelieving eyes could take in through a dense haze of dust raised by the stampeding horses and the smoke of their own and the enemy's muskets. The figure of Fray Juan Minguéz darted dimly about, sometimes pausing merely for a glance, sometimes a little longer over a prostrate soldier. Shouts, hoarse cries, and occasional screams came out of this haze that stung the eyes and clutched at the throat. A great wave of nausea rolled toward Josefina. She went under it. She turned her face downwards and clutched at the trampled grass.

From somewhere off to the left there was a crash of musketry, shouts, a thin cry of "Santiago!" and the single scream of a horse. Ensign Casillas was creating a diversion, perhaps making his own private defense, perhaps attacking. . . . A sudden hope stabbed through the numbness of her senses: Maybe they are coming to help us. . . . Maybe they will bring the horses. . . ."

She had begun to think again. The smoke and dust had cleared a little, so she raised herself to look around. A hand pushed her down again. A voice—Don Pedro's—said brusquely: "Don't expose yourself. Stay down."

She obeyed. The sound of Don Pedro's voice—perhaps the matter-of-factness of his tone—brought back her sense of reality. She turned her head so that her cheek pressed against the damp grass. A small blue flower was growing a few inches from her eyes. It was a kind of wild aster, she thought. It had escaped trampling. An ant hurried past it through the jungle of grass. . . . Everything, grass, flower, even the ant appeared enormous. . . .

There was a lull. The noise being made by the horseherd off to the left, somewhere in the tall grass beyond the cleared area of the encampment, had died down. Only the nearby complaints of the wounded but still living came through the minor noises of hasty preparations for another defense. She heard Don Pedro's voice saying: "They will be back soon. Keep your head down, querida."

"Is there any hope?" she asked.

"A little. The horse guard is trying to get through."

"Amor . . . you remember the promise?"

"I haven't forgotten," he said. "But there is one thing to think about." He interrupted himself to shout an order to someone. "I think there are some French here. If that's so, there's a chance——"

"Yes, amor."

"There's a chance they might be able to restrain the Indians. You might be spared . . . you and the chaplain."

Hell broke loose again on the left. It was not another attack, however: it was Ensign Casillas trying to break the ring of Pawnees. He did not succeed. He got near enough to the barricade, however, to be clearly visible astride his horse above the high grass. Five or six of his presidials appeared to be still alive and still mounted. Josefina could see their shadowy figures through the haze of the fight, laying about them with their broadswords and lances. Half of the few remaining soldiers in the camp let loose a round of flanking fire and yelled desperately.

Casillas's gallant effort failed, however. The ensign's little force suddenly wheeled and galloped out of sight. But it was an orderly retirement and gave promise of another attempt. Only one of the horses carried back an empty saddle.

The Entrada—or what remained of it in the encampment—took advantage of the lull following Casillas's attack to strengthen the barricade and shorten the perimeter of defense. Saddles, packs, tent rolls, everything that could stop a bullet or an arrow, was pulled in toward the center of the camp and toward the river. The wounded were cared for by Fray Juan, who bandaged them up as best he could, carried water to them, and for not a few performed the last rites of Holy Church. The dead were kept within the horseshoe of the breastworks.

For the first time now, Josefina became conscious of individual figures around her, and of the actions of these figures, as something distinct and separate from the great confusion of the battle. Don Pedro was close beside her, crouching on one knee behind the barricade. There was little need for him to shout orders to anyone: every man was carrying on his own defense now, fighting his own small, isolated battle for survival—or, at least, for some payment in kind for his life. Not more than a score were still alive.

So Don Pedro contented himself with encouraging his men, urging them to reserve their fire, and to keep covered. Occasionally he disregarded his own orders and stood upright for a better view of the defense arrangements. Once he flung a few angry words at a soldier who was crawling frantically from place to place in search of better shelter: this was his own orderly, the young Corporal Melchior Rodríguez.

All of the war captains, Naranjo, Olguín, and Serna, and the aide-de-camp Dominguez, were still alive. Captain Naranjo, however, had been hit twice by musket balls in the first volley. He sat with his back against the barricade, his carbine across his outstretched legs, and the far-away look in his eyes was that of a man who knows he is finished. The other captains were doing a steady job of organizing the small defense units to which each had attached himself.

"Padre!" Captain Naranjo called in an oddly small but urgent voice. Fray Juan Minguéz turned from giving a soldier the last rites and glanced toward the dying frontiersman.

"When you're through there, padre," Captain Naranjo said with a vaguely chagrined expression. "Por favor."

The fraile crawled over to the scout. He glanced at his wounds, then looked quickly away. He gave Captain Naranjo absolution and touched him with the holy oils. He gave him also a light abrazo and said: "Adiós, amigo mío. Go with God. I'll join you soon."

All at once the drugged-like feeling of unreality that, up to now, had clouded all of Josefina's thoughts and perceptions vanished like a ground mist in a sudden sun. That Captain José Naranjo could be dying was somehow an incredible thing. But the very fact that her own eyes were witnessing this incredible thing—that, in some way, seemed to make everything else possible.

María Santísima! This is a strange place to die, she said to herself. What a very strange place, Josefina!

She looked about her, clearly for the first time, at the soldiers still alive. They numbered fewer than a score. Her mind made a quick, almost hopeful, calculation of their chances against the enemy.

How many French? Who could tell, even now? Don Antonio's letter had said two hundred. That was ridiculous! There could not be two hundred Frenchmen in that grass! Maybe there was none at all. Still, she had seen splashes of red—hat or coats maybe—moving about.

And the Pawnees? Their numbers were endless, Don Antonio's letter had said. How many did that mean? How many was endless? A thousand, perhaps? Two thousand?

Suddenly her heart sank and she left off thinking about numbers. She made herself think of Ensign Casillas and the horse guard. Perhaps they would try again . . . perhaps they would break through . . . but there were only five of them . . . what could they do against . . . ?

"Cuidado!" a soldier shouted. "Here they come!"

Everyone stiffened, peering into the grass, straining to catch the first glimpse of a new assault wave, the first stalking figures of the next attack. Josefina felt a musket and a hard fist jam into her side. The fist was Fray Juan's; it was holding the gun.

"Take it," the fraile said. "It will give you something to do."

"Thank you, padre," she said with an odd, unconscious politeness.

"Who knows?" Fray Juan said, without smiling. "You may hit something!"

She examined the priming—for by this time she was not unacquainted with the use of firearms—and waited. She noticed from the corner of her eye that Jean L'Archévèque was moving uneasily from one spot to another. He would waddle squatting, or crawl on his hands and knees to a place; then he would peer intently into the grass and would go to another locality where he would repeat this performance. His face wore on intent, fixed expression.

Several minutes passed. The presidials maintained an odd silence— as if by being very quiet they could conceal their presence from the Pawnees. Only the wounded made any sound. Everyone peered hard into the grass—which by this time all cursed as their undoing—and reported in whispers any movement they thought they detected. Some began to think that the soldier who had shouted the warning had gone a little loco, perhaps, under the strain of waiting. They cursed him for it, or perhaps made a grim joke, and relaxed a bit.

Then Jean L'Archévèque stood up, in full view of anyone that may have been watching from the tall grass. His turgid face was livid with fear, and a kind of crazed fear was in his black darting eyes. He pointed with his pudgy hands at something in the grass, half-accusingly, half-beseechingly; and he was shouting loudly in French.

"I see you! I see you, Joutel!" Josefina understood him to be crying. "But let me explain, Joutel. Let me say one word—just one little word. Nom de Dieu! You will see how innocent I am!"

All knew that it was just such a place as this, in the far-away province of Texas, that Jean L'Archévèque had helped to murder the great commander Robert Cavalier Sieur de la Salle. In a place of high grass, on a river bank, very oddly like this. . . .

"Joutel!" he screamed. "It was not I. It was Duhaut and D'Ynctot. I am not guilty! In God's name, monsieur, do not——"

He broke down, unable to finish anything, and stood there crying; and it seemed to Josefina, as it must have to others, that a loud, mirthless laugh came from the high grass and could be heard over Jean L'Archévèque's soft blubbering.

From where he sat with his musket across his knees, Captain José Naranjo watched all this with sad and unbelieving eyes. Then he called out, not very loudly, with the last words he ever spoke: "Get down! Get down, you crazy son-of-a-bitch!"

At almost the same moment the Pawnees and French attacked again. But before they raised their yell, and before they loosed their storm of bullets and arrows and lances, a single musket report exploded in the tall impenetrable grass, and Jean L'Archévèque died with an oddly surprised and reproachful look on his face.

357

30

The Pawnees, and whatever French were with them, apparently wanted to get done with this affair. Perhaps, not knowing the true weakness of the Spanish force, they were fearful that those afoot in the camp would effect a juncture with the mounted soldiers of the horse guard. This might be managed either by a sortie of the besieged troops or by an attack from the rear by Casillas's men. The result could be the escape of the Spaniards—or even a disastrous attack by remounted cavalry. Time was thus an element in the enemy strategy.

Not more than ten minutes had passed since the first rush. During this time, Casillas had made his abortive attempt to break the Pawnee ring and bring help to the beseiged presidials. That had required a certain amount of supporting activity on the part of Don Pedro's little force. The remainder of those ten minutes was devoted to a rather pathetic attempt to buttress its defenses.

There was little that Don Pedro could do to help. Like big battles, this little one had now taken over its own direction. Each man had become a little island, an isolated bit of humanity fighting his very solitary—and in all probability his last—battle for life. Don Pedro tried as best he could to improve the disposition of his men and to assure a plentiful supply of ammunition—which fortunately was not lacking—to all points of the defense perimeter. He also gave them, like a good commander, the example of his own coolness and courage.

Josefina saw that Don Pedro's fever, as was often the case in early morning, had left him. He appeared pale but strong. His words and acts were clear-headed and energetic. Josefina felt a strange happiness —strange in these shadows of almost certain death—that he was feeling better.

So, even in this nightmare of death and destruction, her thoughts slipped into the accustomed channels. She watched Don Pedro with a wifely concern for his safety, and a wifely pride in the way he bore himself . . . and a simple, uncomplicated love that suddenly swelled to a feeling of such intensity that it was almost too much to bear. It was as if all the love she might have felt in all the years to come were trying to crowd itself into a few remaining minutes. She called out to her husband in the brief silence: "Amor!"

He looked her way through the haze of smoke and dust: he gave her a faint, curious, almost apologetic smile.

"Is it the time, amor?" she asked.

He shook his head, looking at her blankly. Then he made a sudden motion with his hand and pulled something out of a crevice in the barricade. He handed her his pistol and she closed her fingers around its great, heavy grip.

"Not yet, querida," he said, staring at her strangely. "That you wait until . . . that you wait a little longer, no?"

Ah, Pedro mío! she thought. You are not keeping your promise exactly. But I forgive you, amor. I should not ask such a thing of you!

She looked at the pistol Don Pedro had given her. What she had suspected was so. It was not loaded. She had thought that she had seen Don Pedro fire it: he had forgotten—it was natural in the confusion. She lifted her head and smiled across at him.

"Gracias, amor," she said. "I love you."

He reached out and touched her hand with his and said gravely: "I return all your love, querida. . . . That you forgive me."

She had no time even to wonder at what Don Pedro meant by this. Because at that moment the Pawnees and the French—some of whom were very plain to see in this rush—made their second attack. She raised the gun Fray Juan had given her and fired at a leaping Pawnee and thought she saw him sprawl backwards before she closed her eyes.

When she looked again, it was to see Ensign Casillas and his horse guard charging through the grass from the Pawnees' rear. With an instinct amounting almost to military genius, he had chosen the precise moment of the enemy's attack to launch his own counterassault. It was all that saved the besieged Spaniards from instant destruction.

Two separate battles were now being fought at the same time. On their front the Pawnees were pouring a sharp fire of arrows—from which the Spaniards gathered a little hope that their ammunition was nearly used up—into the barricade. With this fire was mixed, however, a scattering fusilade of musketry. Josefina, crouching low, heard the balls thud into the packs. One of them splintered a wooden saddle cantle an arm's reach from her head. She saw another hit a presidial: his helmet flew off with an almost comic effect and he lay as still across a half-struck tent as if he had never lived.

Some of the Pawnees got across the clearing and attempted to climb over the breastworks. One succeeded. He struck a trooper down with a war ax and, unable to resist the temptation to take the first scalp, drew his knife. Fray Juan shot him. The others were met with musket fire, pistol fire, lance thrusts, sword strokes, and the blows of guns, picket stakes, and whatever else was at hand.

Don Pedro's veterans were tough, cool, skilled men; and they defended themselves silently but well—and with a certain disdain—against the horde of yelling savages. Yet they very quickly would have concluded their last fight—the last of many for most of them—if it had not been for Ensign Casillas's diversion.

The Pawnees of the Río Jesús María, like most of the other Indians of the Great Plains, were not mere amateurs in the art of war. They understood quite thoroughly both the theory and practice of military tactics; and so, like any other trained body of troops, they were at first made uneasy, then acutely disconcerted by an energetic attack on their rear.

That this attack was made by no more than half a dozen men did not matter. They were all mounted—which made each one the equal in striking power, and even more in demoralizing effect, to a score of Indians on foot—and they struck with a fury and abandon that was in itself terrifying. The Pawnees actually broke. Casillas and half of his small command fought through the rim of besiegers to the very edge of the encampment. Then——

Josefina saw the ensign's face as he looked down, from the back of his horse, into the bloody half-circle of the barricade. It was the face of a man gazing into hell.

His eyes swept the breastwork, seeking for Captain Don Pedro Villasur; they found him. Josefina saw Don Pedro raise his hand in a gesture that meant—with a finality that words could never convey—only one thing: *we are finished.* She saw Casillas turn his horse then, and make a motion with his raised arm, and shout something to his men.

It was all done in an instant. It was over with in the time it took to strike two blows. And it told Josefina everything that was to be known. The situation of the Spaniards had become hopeless. So few men were left alive after the second rush of the Pawnees that nothing except an authentic miracle from heaven could now save the survivors. It was useless to ask a few men still on horseback to sacrifice their lives in so completely lost an engagement. It would be well if two or three, at least, could get away and carry the news of defeat—of extermination—back to Santa Fé.

All this had been said in a couple of gestures and a shouted word. All this and more . . . sweet Mother of God, how much more! One's eyes can take in only so much at a glance: one's mind can grasp only so much in the time of a few heartbeats.

Josefina thought she saw the ensign Bernardo Casillas fall from his horse. He appeared to be alone there, in front of the barricade. There had been others with him, but then Casillas was alone, and suddenly he lost his seat in the saddle. He fell off his horse very awkwardly, clinging to the high pommel for a while, then letting go and sliding to the ground. His horse, which was a very large and powerful animal—as horses were found in New Mexico—went mad then, and plunged snorting with the terrifying snort of a wild mustang into the coalescing mass of the Pawnees. And it was edifying—or at least very satisfying to one's sense of drollery—to see those naked savages leaping and skipping in terror of the great beast, and running for cover in the high grass . . . in the high bloody grass . . . in the high, bloody, bloody grass. . . .

But why should Captain Olguín—that stupid and stubborn man— why should he be out there now, so far beyond the barricade? Ah! He is trying to lift up Casillas from the ground, no? But he is having difficulty. He is bleeding himself, Olguín, from the arm. His leather jacket is black and dirty with his blood: his blood is dripping from the fingers of one hand. And so he is having difficulty.

But Don Pedro is helping him now. Don Pedro appears to be unhurt, and so he can probably accomplish what Olguín could not do because of his useless arm. . . . Ah, yes! They have Casillas between them now . . . now they are bringing him up to the barricade. . . . And now——

"Ay, Dios! Pedro!"

She thrust out her hands, as if to help Olguín save Don Pedro from falling. Casillas's lifeless body slid face downward into the trampled grass. Olguín let it lie there: he sprang to Don Pedro, got under him, and staggered toward the encampment, dragging Don Pedro with him. Josefina reached out across the barricade, helped him lift and pull her husband over the low wall of packs and saddles. They got him inside at last. . . . How strangely still he lay. . . .

"Pedro!"

She continued to call him, at first loudly, and then more softly, until she was merely whispering his name. She felt an arm around her shoulders. She looked away from Don Pedro and up at Fray Juan.

She observed with an odd clarity of perception all the details of the fraile's face. Around the mouth it was black from biting off the ends of cartridges. The sweat ran down in streaks through the dirt and smoke and powder stains. The stubble on the lean jaws was gray. The eyes under the sweat-dampened brows were keen and blue—as blue as the robe that Fray Juan wore, which was the Virgin's color. They were not the eyes of a priest, she thought: they were the eyes of an Indian fighter. They were fixed on something in the tall, trampled grass; and they did not shift away for an instant while Fray Juan pressed her gently with his free arm and said:

"Courage, my daughter. In just a little while God will free us."

She got no comfort from the fraile's words. It seemed to her that she had no feeling. She felt no emotion of any kind. She looked at Don Pedro. He was dead, she knew; but the fact of his death had no meaning. Perhaps that was because she herself was as good as dead also. The dead did not mourn the dead. She felt no grief. She felt nothing.

And yet, with this curious absence of feeling, she was aware of an extraordinary alertness of the senses. She took in everything around her with an almost painful grasp of detail—as she had Fray Juan's face. The sensation of unreality that had once possessed her was gone. In its place was this still stranger acuteness of sight and sound, and even smell . . . but without feeling.

Her mind understood as clearly as her eyes saw. She had no trouble in comprehending exactly what had happened . . . and what was about to happen. The horse guard's valiant attempt to break the ring of Pawnees and French had not failed. It had simply proved futile. Casillas and his men—or what remained of them—had only come too late. The men behind the barricade did not need help any more because all of them—or almost all of them—were dead.

The ensign Casillas had seen this at a glance. Don Pedro had only told him what he already knew. And so those who could had escaped, to carry the news to Santa Fé of what had happened to most of them . . . and was about to happen to the rest.

It was quite sensible. But had it been sensible for Captain Olguín and Don Pedro to expose themselves so madly in order to rescue the ensign Casillas, who had already died anyhow? The answer was an easy one: *they did not want to see him scalped before their eyes*. In view of everything, this was not a sensible answer, perhaps, but it was an easy one and it was the right one. Her mind told her this with assurance, and she was glad to know why it had been necessary for Don Pedro to die so suddenly. She was glad also that he had died suddenly.

Captain Olguín was still alive. One arm was useless, but he held his sword with the other, and he appeared impatient to use it—perhaps before his strength went. Fray Juan, of course, was also alive and even unhurt: he had two loaded muskets beside him and another in his hands, and he was waiting. Who else? She glanced around and saw no more than three or four other men who appeared able to fire a gun or strike a blow.

Off to the west—in the direction from which they had all come so long ago—there was a lot of dust and noise: yells, musket reports, horse sounds. The remnant of Casillas's detachment was trying to fight its way free. These noises became fainter and farther away, and at last they died completely. Perhaps some had escaped. Perhaps all were dead.

In the encampment too a sudden silence had fallen. Even the wounded were quiet—except for one man who had dragged himself down to the water's edge and was emitting occasional screams. The screams began to come closer and closer together: they seemed to be building up to some horrible climax. Josefina shuddered and wished vaguely that this soldier would die and cease screaming. . . .

In a little while the Pawnees and the French would come back again. Why didn't they come? Could it be that they were afraid of a few Spaniards with one more round to fire before they admitted death? Or had they all gone off in pursuit of Casillas's men? Or were they merely contemptuous of time?

Josefina gazed with pensive eyes at the corpse of Don Pedro Villasur. The face was strong and calm and a little stern in death, as it had always been in life. The steel morion had fallen off and the kerchief twisted over the dark, crisp hair was soiled and sweat-soaked. There was a small hole in the leather jacket, just below the buckle on the shoulder strap: a trickle of dark liquid oozed from it. Josefina touched it and looked curiously at the stain on her fingertip. She rubbed it off on the leather jacket. Before, she had accepted the fact of Don Pedro's death with her eyes; now, by this little act, she experienced its actuality.

Ah, my heart, she said to herself. It is too bad that the time was so little.

Tichi had believed that when one is about to die, one's entire life passes before one's eyes—a whole lifetime in an instant perhaps. She remembered this and was interested to find that it was not so. One who is waiting for death does not think: one merely waits. This kind of waiting precludes thought, because it demands the concentration of all one's forces on itself. Or, at the most, only lightning flashes of thought break through this terrible concentration.

If you must die now, Josefina, she reflected thus, I wish that it could be in some other place . . . in some other manner.

She picked up Don Pedro's pistol and examined the priming, to make sure that the weapon had actually been fired. She dropped it, hardly conscious of what she had done.

I also wish with all my heart, passed through her mind, that I might have seen our baby. . . .

She leaned quickly over Don Pedro's body and gave it a little abrazo, pressing her cheek briefly against his.

"But I regret nothing, amor," she said aloud to the still face. "How much I loved you, my husband. . . . And now that I have lost you . . . I do not care . . . although I do not wish to die so."

The terrible thought of what the Pawnees would do to her crashed through the numbness of her mind. She searched desperately for some little hope—for one little thing to catch hold of—one little place to hide. She thought of what Don Pedro had said:

"I think there are some French here. If that's so, there's a chance . . . there's a chance you might be spared."

Why did not the Pawnees come? Why did they take so long? Why was it so still? Even the presidial at the river bank had become quiet. She could hear Fray Juan say distinctly: "Cover your eyes, child."

She knelt low behind the barricade, sitting on her heels, and bending over as if to protect something against her breast. She buried her face in her palms and tried to pray. She tried to say an Ave María to La Conquistadora.

But the words that she heard were not in the accustomed voice of her mind, and they were not the words of the beautiful old prayer to the Virgin. They were in the soft, gentle voice of Eva Helena, and this voice seemed to be saying:

"You will see, my children. This is but a little rain that will blow away—and ay! how lovely the sun will . . ."

MADRID JOURNAL *of Don José Francisco Tafora, one-time personal secretary, advisor and criado of Don Baltazar de Zúñiga, Marqués de Valero, Viceroy of México. 1730.*

Letters arrived today from friends in Paris together with some recently published accounts of the destruction of Captain Don Pedro Villasur's expedition to the Río Jesús María.

These writings are from the pens of M. Bossu, Captaine dans les troupes de Marine, and M. Batel-Dumont. They are distinguished by the inaccuracies, exaggerations, and bigotry common to all French accounts of the massacre. They assert, for example, that Don Pedro's pitiful Entrada consisted of a caravan of no fewer than fifteen hundred men, women, and children, with thousands of horses and oxen; and that its real purpose was the extermination of the Missouris!

The authors of these absurdities have evidently forgotten the prudential maxim: It is better not to know so many things than to know so many that are not true!

Yet I find myself reading even such ridiculous histories as those of Messieurs Bossu and Batel-Dumont with the deepest interest. I collect and examine everything written about the Río Jesús María massacre. For it is ever my hope that some day I shall yet find the answer to a question that has long haunted my retirement: What was the actual fate of my faithful collaborator and cherished friend, that beautiful and remarkable woman, Señora Josefina Torres?

A good deal of mystery still surrounds the melancholy affair on the Río Jesús María. It is well established, of course, that all save a few who straggled back to Santa Fé perished with Don Pedro. Yet even here the evidence may be faulty—or at least incomplete. For the writings of other Frenchmen closer to the event than Messieurs Bossu and Batel-Dumont raise some doubts, however faint, that the destruction of the Entrada was quite as thorough as reported to the Viceroy by the survivors Aguilar and Tamariz.

Among the rumors mentioned in these writings, the most persistent is one concerning the chaplain of the expedition, Fray Juan Minguéz, a very popular missionary of the Seraphic Order. According to the story—for it can hardly be referred to in more substantial terms—Fray Juan's life was spared by the French and Pawnees; and the Indians, since they had no horses and did not know how to ride, forced the good fraile to exhibit his horsemanship for their amusement.

This he was required to do every day until, after several months, having secured a supply of food and having selected the best horse as his mount, he suddenly galloped away toward the west and was never again seen by his captives.

This, of course, is contrary to Father Escalante's statement that Fray Juan perished with all the rest: "Que perecieron los más entre ellos el padre Fray Minguéz, misionero de esta custodia." And if the fraile did indeed escape in such a manner, he must have died of starvation on the lonely prairie or at the hands of the Utes or Comanches; for nowhere is there any record of his having returned to Santa Fé.

Much more reliable, if less entertaining than these narratives, is the information to be found in the letters and reports of such Frenchmen as Father Charlevoix and Sieur de Boisbriant.

Father Charlevoix, in his letters written from the French post at Michillimackinac, tells in detail of the spoils which, he says, were scattered over the whole battlefield. Among these he lists Fray Minguéz's prayer book and his shoes (which were worthless), his pistol, a jar of ointment, some rosaries with their crosses, and some printed songs to the Virgin.

In the original letters there is also a strange reference—deleted in the revised edition as, no doubt, too bizarre for credence—to a small image of a child with golden hair and rich clothes having been found on the battlefield!

The letters of M. Boisbriant, commandant of the French province of Illinois, are crowded with interesting details relating to the aftermath of the massacre. It was to M. Boisbriant, then at Kaskaskia, that the news of the catastrophe was brought in October, 1720.

In his letters to M. Bienville, governor of the province of La Luisiana, M. Boisbriant related that the victorious Indians presented to him Fray Minguéz's robes of priestly office, together with the silver altar service. One savage had hung the sacred chalice, as if it were a bell, about his horse's neck, while the chief wore the paten on his breast as a shield and the chasuble on his naked person.

All these articles the commandant purchased from the Indians—together with the best of the captured horses—and sent them to M. Bienville in New Orleans.

M. Boisbriant also sent to the governor a few pages torn from the diary of Captain Don Pedro Villasur, describing the last fateful days of the Entrada. Did not so many mysteries surround Don Pedro's expedition, one might dismiss as fantastic the governor's comment that they appear to have been written *in a firm yet distinctly feminine handwriting.*

Since I have made it my rule to reject nothing concerning the Río Jesús María massacre as too improbable for sober consideration, I must now mention another rumor—almost as persistent as that of Fray Juan's escape—that has come to me from various, and mostly obscure, sources. It relates to the capture of a beautiful white woman at the battle of the Río Jesús María.

I am not unaware that legends of beautiful white women are often connected with the various Indian tribes by our romantic French historians; but in this there seems to be something—from my own viewpoint, at least—of a more solid interest.

The story of *La Belle Espagnole*—as she is referred to in these rumors—is sometimes rich, sometimes exasperatingly vague in detail. Briefly, the main elements of the story, as I have gathered them from various New World sources, are these:

On the night before the battle of the Río Jesús María, French and Pawnee spies watching the Spanish encampment from high ground were astonished to observe a white woman in a long court dress perform a dance of extraordinary fire and beauty for the troops. Although the enemy had kept our column under constant surveillance for many days, he had not before discovered the presence of this woman (the reason being, I assume, that Josefina habitually rode in the attire of a man). Following the incident I have just described, however, the French commander issued strict orders to his own men and to his Pawnee allies that no harm was to be done to *La Belle Espagnole*.

At the battle of the Río Jesús María, accordingly, *La Belle Espagnole* was carefully protected from harm. Fray Juan Minguéz was also spared, together with several Tewa women. No other captives were taken.

The Indian women were kept by the Pawnees as slaves. But *La Belle Espagnole* was taken to Kaskaskia, from whence she was sent to New Orleans where (the romantic French scribblers of history aver) she gave birth to a child.

In New Orleans, it is said, *La Belle Espagnole* received the sympathy of everyone and won all hearts by her charm and brave acceptance of her misfortunes. One heart in particular—that of a young French nobleman then present in New Orleans on a tour of inspection for the Council of the Regency—was most powerfully affected.

Here, unfortunately, the rumors drift away into silence, and *La Belle Espagnole* with them. Nothing more is mentioned in any of the accounts of the French in La Luisiana—in any, at least, that have come to my attention.

But among the letters received from Paris today is one from my friend M. Henri Montesquieu—who is well acquainted with my private interest in everything pertaining to the Río Jesús María massacre —which transmits a rumor that may well be a flickering survival of the legend of *La Belle Espagnole.*

There is now living in Paris, my friend has heard, one Baron Paul de Vuillier, a soldier and functionary of some importance in the Office of Foreign Affairs, whose wife is a beautiful Spanish lady of uncertain background.

Only the vaguest details have reached M. Montesquieu—and these appear to him to consist more of Parisian gossip than actual fact— but they do include some obscure allusions to a great battle fought by the French and Spanish on the Río Missouri: which could very well, of course, be a reference to the Río Jesús María massacre, garbled in the usual manner of the French historians.

In this battle, Madame Vullier is said to have been captured by her husband himself! For her own private reasons, the rumors add, the lovely captive found it inconvenient to return to her country and so took ship for France where she was received with the same respect and sympathy that the citizens of New Orleans had shown her, and where she eventually became the wife of Baron de Vuillier.

My friend M. Montesquieu, having no curiosity himself about this matter, and being little inclined to gossip, expresses the opinion that, whatever the truth may be regarding Madame Vuillier, it might better be left in her own keeping. She appears from all reports, he says, to be living happily with her charming little daughter and her husband —a kindly gentleman of genuine worth and distinction—and it is his judgment that no good can come from prying into her past. He adds, however, that if I wish it, he will pursue any investigation I desire him to make.

But I am inclined to agree with my friend. Greatly as I should like to know the true facts regarding Madame Vuillier, I am myself romanticist enough, I must confess, to wish simply to believe that she is indeed *La Belle Espagnole,* which is to say, of course, La Dama Josefina; and that she has found at last such peace, and perhaps even happiness, as is granted to us in this troubled world.

Gazetteer

Alburquerque: So spelled in colonial New Mexico—a Spanish settlement, now the city of Albuquerque, N.M.

Battlefield: Villasur's force was ambushed on the south bank of the North Platte River, near present North Platte, Neb.

Bernalillo: A Spanish settlement in New Mexico, same place, same name today.

Camino Real: The Royal Road ran for 2000 miles between Taos and Vera Cruz, passing through Santa Fé, El Paso, and Mexico City. In New Mexico it roughly followed the Rio Grande, except for 80 miles between San Marcial and Rincon, the "Journey of Death."

El Cuartelejo: Perhaps in Otero or Kiowa County, Colorado, probably near Las Animas, Colo.

El Paso del Norte: Modern Juarez, across the border from El Paso, Tex.

Jémez Mountains: same as today.

Jicarilla: Near present Cimarron, N.M.

Río Colorado: Canadian River.

Río Grande: today's Rio Grande, but sometimes called Río del Norte, Río Bravo, or Río Grande y Bravo del Norte.

Río Jesús María: The South Platte.

Río Napestle: The Arkansas River.

Río San Lorenzo: The North Platte.

Río de las Ánimas: The Purgatoire.

Route of the Entrada: Roughly, Captain Villasur's route followed today's US 64 from Santa Fe to Taos, although he detoured through Picurís. He continued on present US 64 over the mountains, through Eagle Nest, to what is now Cimarron, N.M. (Jicarilla.)

His route was then NE to present Dillon, N.M. and over Raton Pass to the Purgatoire River, which he crossed near Trinidad.

From this point he traveled nearly due north, skirting Walsenburg on his left and turning suddenly eastward near Pueblo, Colo., after crossing the Arkansas River. He then marched about 40 miles NE to the great Apache camp of Cuartelejo, perhaps near Las Animas, Colo.

From Cuartelejo Villasur resumed his course due north, with the site of modern Denver 40 miles away on his left. He reached the

South Platte River at a point probably near present Dearfield, Colo. He then followed the South Platte eastward to the Pawnee village beyond the Forks. Retracing his steps, he arrived in a day's march at the battlefield near present North Platte, Neb.

Santa Fé: One of the two Royal Villas in New Mexico and capital of the Kingdom; now capital of the state of New Mexico. Part of the Royal Palace still stands and is in use as a museum. The Lady Chapel of La Parroquia is now a wing of the modern cathedral. San Miguel's, the 18th-century church of the slaves, is still in use. Little else of the ancient capital, except its plaza, some streets and acequias—and its indestructible charm—remains.

Sierra Almagre: Vermilion Mountains, the present Front Range in Colorado.

Sierra Nevada: The magnificent mountain range dominating the city of Santa Fé, and known today as the Sangre de Cristo Range.

Taos: The great Tiwa pueblo in northern New Mexico, a little north and east of its present location.